James Thomson

Poetical works of Thomson and Gray

James Thomson

Poetical works of Thomson and Gray

ISBN/EAN: 9783337278069

Printed in Europe, USA, Canada, Australia, Japan

Cover: Foto ©Andreas Hilbeck / pixelio.de

More available books at **www.hansebooks.com**

POETICAL WORKS

OF

THOMSON AND GRAY.

Well may they
On equal terms with ancient wit engage,
Nor mighty Homer fear, nor sacred Virgil's page,
Our English palace opens wide in state,
And without stooping they may pass the gate.

DRYDEN.

LONDON:

T. NELSON AND SONS, PATERNOSTER ROW;
EDINBURGH; AND NEW YORK.

MDCCCLXI.

LIVES

OF

THOMSON AND GRAY.

———◆———

THE remains of Dryden were scarcely cold when Pope rose to eminence, and Pope had not attained to middle age when the fame of the Author of the Seasons was established.

JAMES THOMSON was born at Ednam, near Kelso, on the 7th of September 1700. His father was minister of the parish in which his son was born, but shortly afterwards removed to that of Southdean, a lonely but romantic district in the heart of the Cheviots. Here Thomson spent his boyish years; and here he first gave evidence of that poetic spirit which long afterwards shone forth so brightly in the Seasons.[1]

---

[1] Allan Cunningham was fortunate enough to discover a fragment written by Thomson at the age of fourteen, which shows how early his style was formed. It was first published in 1841, in a memoir prefixed to an illustrated edition of the Seasons.

> " Now I surveyed my native faculties,
> And traced my actions to their teeming source;
> Now I explored the universal frame,
> Gazed Nature through, and, with interior light,
> Conversed with angels and unbodied saints,
> That tread the courts of the Eternal King!
> Gladly I would declare, in lofty strains,
> The power of Godhead to the sons of men,—
> But thought is lost in its immensity,
> Imagination wastes its strength in vain,
> And Fancy tires, and turns within itself,

At school, Thomson, like so many men who have afterwards risen to eminence,—like Goldsmith, for example, in the following generation, and like Scott in the last,—proved himself a dullard. He was constitutionally indolent, and loved better, we do not doubt, to saunter along the pastoral banks of the "sylvan Jed," than pore over the pages of his Cæsar or his Sallust. In his eighteenth year, he removed to Edinburgh to study for the ministry; and at Edinburgh his old reputation still clove to him. "He remained there," says Johnson, "without distinction or expectation." In the meantime his father died. This event made a great change in Thomson's prospects. His mother was poor, and had a large family to support. She removed to Edinburgh; and her son resolved to abandon his profession.

London, still the best, was then the only stage on which a poet could appear with any hopes of success. It was the only stage, as Johnson has remarked, at that time too wide for the operation of petty competition and private malignity, the only stage where merit might soon become conspicuous, and where it would find friends as soon as it became reputable to befriend it. To London, accordingly, Thomson, on the promise of some assistance from an acquaintance of his mother's,—a promise, however, which seems never to have been redeemed,—determined to repair. In 1724 he left Edinburgh, with the poem of *Winter* and some letters of introduction in his pocket.

One of those letters was addressed to Mallet, then tutor to the sons of the Duke of Montrose. Mallet was a Scotchman, the son of an innkeeper at Crieff, and probably the most successful, as he was certainly the most unprincipled, literary adventurer of that age. He praised and courted Pope while living, so long as praise and courtship could advance his interests. He heaped abuse upon Pope's memory when dead, when he found that such abuse would gratify his patron. He earned an ignominious pension by publishing, under the signature of "A Plain Man," a pamphlet in which he imputed cowardice to Byng. He accepted a legacy from the Duchess of Marlborough, and a pension from her grandson, on condition that he should write the life of the hero of Blen-

---

Struck with the amazing depths of Deity:
Ah, my Lord God! in vain a tender youth,
Unskilled in arts of deep philosophy,
Attempts to search the bulky mass of matter,
To trace the rules of motion, and pursue
The phantom Time, too subtle for his grasp:
Yet may I from thy most apparent works,
Form some idea of their wondrous Author "

heim and Malplacquet. On his death, in 1765, it was found that he had not completed a single page of the memoir. Johnson, indeed, seems unintentionally to have pronounced the highest eulogium on the Scotchmen then in London when he said that Mallet was the only Scot whom his countrymen did not commend.

On the recommendation of this man, Thomson was received into the family of Lord Binning as tutor to his sons. He had in the meantime, however, disposed of the copyright of *Winter* for three guineas; and even this low price, we are told, the purchaser, Mr. Miller, had for a time reason to regret. The generous kindness of Aaron Hill and Mr. Whateley, "a man," says Johnson, "not wholly unknown amongst authors," a man whose talents, indeed, were such as to lead many of his contemporaries to impute to him the authorship of those famous letters which drove Grafton from the Treasury in an agony of shame and terror, and carried dismay alike into the palace, the senate, and the courts of law, at length opened the public eyes. The poem was in the end completely successful, and raised the author to a rank amongst living poets second only to that of Pope.

It is impossible for a literary man of our day to look back upon the age which preceded the time of which we write without feelings of deep shame and degradation. It was the age of private patronage; an age in which readers were so few that men of letters were too often obliged to become the parasites and hangers-on of the rich; an age in which Otway died in the agonies of hunger, and in which Dryden was forced to prostitute his genius to pander to the prurient appetite of a ribald king and a ribald court. Until Pope arose, it is not too much to say that no English writer however eminent, not Dryden, not Congreve, not Addison, was able to earn, by his literary labours alone, a sum equal to that which is now annually earned by a penny-a-liner on the London press. The highest offices in Church and State, bishoprics, deaneries, secretaryships, commissionerships, embassies, were open to the lucky few. But to the many, to ninety-nine out of every hundred of those who made literature their profession, there only existed the alternative of abject penury or abject dependence.

It was, therefore, only in accordance with the custom and necessities of the age, that Thomson dedicated his poem to the Earl of Wilmington, a man known in English history chiefly from the part he took in opposition to Walpole on the accession of George II. For a time he seemed to have sued in vain. But the attention of Wilmington having at length been drawn to the young aspirant by a copy of verses addressed to him by Aaron

Hill, the peer condescended to reward the poet for his adulation with a present of twenty guineas.

The fame of Thomson now rose high. "Every day," says Johnson, "brought him new friends." To the Lord Chancellor Talbot he was introduced by Dr. Rundle. The publication of *Summer* secured him the favour of Bubb Dodington. His invectives against the ministry introduced him to the society of the wits and poets who crowded the saloons of Leicester House. The Countess of Hertford invited him to Sudbourn ; Lord Lyttelton entertained him at Hagley. He had reached the highest pinnacle of fame when he was selected by the Chancellor as travelling tutor to his eldest son.

He returned just in time to take part in that great conflict which drove Walpole from the Treasury to his retreat amid the woods and gardens of Houghton. "The Opposition," says Mr. Macaulay, "was in every sense formidable." The elections of 1741 had been unfavourable to the Ministry. "The majority of the landed gentry, the majority of the parochial clergy, one of the universities, and a strong party in the City of London and in the other great towns, were decidedly adverse to the Government. Of the men of letters, some were exasperated by the neglect with which the Minister treated them, a neglect which was the more remarkable because his predecessors, both Whig and Tory, had paid court with emulous munificence to the wits and the poets; others were honestly inflamed by party zeal; almost all lent their aid to the Opposition. In truth, all that was alluring to ardent and imaginative minds was on that side; old associations, new visions of political improvement, high-flown theories of loyalty, high-flown theories of liberty, the enthusiasm of the Cavalier, the enthusiasm of the Roundhead. The Tory gentleman, fed in the common-rooms of Oxford with the doctrines of Filmer and Sacheverell, and proud of the exploits of his grandfathers, who had charged with Rupert at Marston, who had held out the old manor-house against Fairfax, and who had, after the King's return, been set down for a Knight of the Royal Oak, flew to that section of the Opposition which, under pretence of assailing the existing administration, was in truth assailing the reigning dynasty. The young Republican, fresh from his Livy and his Lucan, and glowing with admiration of Hampden, of Russell, and of Sydney, hastened with equal eagerness to those benches from which eloquent voices thundered nightly against the tyranny and perfidy of Courts. . . . . In fact almost every young man of warm temperament and lively imagination, whatever his political bias might be, was drawn into the party adverse to the Government; and some of the most distinguished among them, Pitt, for example, among public men, and Johnson among men of letters, afterwards openly acknowledged their mistake."[1]

By the side of these men, in the foremost rank of the assailants, observers did not fail to note the obese person and the dull and inanimate countenance of Thomson. Thomson brought to the contest a mind of singular endowments, but fitted neither by nature nor by training for political discussion. He attacked the old statesman, notwithstanding, with a vehemence hardly to be expected from a man of habits so lethargic. But the publication of *Liberty*, although it did much for his fortunes, did little for his fame. High as his own opinion of the poem was, it had few readers in his own day and has almost ceased to be read in ours.

The First Minister retired, the Cabinet was partially remodeled, and the nation soon discovered that its liberties were not greater or more secure under the reign of the patriots than they had been under the reign of Walpole. Thomson, in the meantime, was reaping the profits of a place to which he had been appointed by Lord Talbot. The death of Talbot, however, soon obliged him to vacate it. The poet would not deign to solicit his re-appointment, and the new Chancellor would not re-appoint him without solicitation. Thomson was, therefore, at the age of thirty-seven, once more thrown upon the world, a writer for his bread.

He was, however, partially consoled for his loss by a pension of a hundred pounds a-year bestowed upon him by the Prince of Wales. But this partial consolation was more than compensated by the fate which attended the representation of his Agamemnon. Pope emerged from his retirement amid the groves of Twickenham to countenance the performance. Thomson himself sat in the upper gallery, trembling with anxiety and distress. "But the tragedy," says Johnson, "had the fate which most commonly attends mythological stories." It was tolerated for a few nights, but is now as utterly forgotten as the most worthless of the portentous productions of Behn or D'Urfey.

Edward and Eleonora, Alfred, and Tancred and Sigismunda, now followed each other in quick succession. To Edward and Eleonora a licence was refused. Alfred was written in conjunction with Mallet, and failed. Tancred and Sigismunda alone was successful. Yet, in spite of its success, Tancred, we are afraid, must be content to take its place by the side of the Caractacus of

---

[1] Essays. Art. "Horace Walpole."

Mason and the Irene of Johnson. The genius of Mason and
Johnson was essentially undramatic; and Thomson, when he set
about writing tragedy, failed as signally as Bentley did when he
sat down to annotate Milton.

In November 1744, the Carteret Administration was dissolved,
and Lyttelton accepted office under the Pelhams. A few months
later and the Gazette announced that Thomson had been appointed Surveyor-General of the Leeward Islands. The emoluments of the post were considerable. After paying his deputy,
there remained to the new official an annual stipend of nearly
three hundred pounds.

Thomson was now at ease, and he seems to have made diligent
use of his leisure in preparing for the press a poem on which he
had long laboured, and which, with the sole exception of the
Seasons, is undoubtedly the greatest of all his works, the Castle
of Indolence. But his ease was of short continuance. He caught
cold upon the Thames while journeying to Kew. Fever super-
vened; and on the 27th of August 1748, he died. He was buried
at Richmond; but a monument in Westminster Abbey still remains to commemorate the genius of the greatest descriptive poet
that modern ages have produced.

He left behind him the tragedy of Coriolanus. It added, however, nothing to his fame. It was brought upon the stage for
the benefit of his family with all the advantages it could derive
from the then unequalled acting of Quin. Lyttelton prefaced the
performance with a prologue of much elegance and feeling, which
will probably be remembered when all his other writings are
forgotten. The profits of the tragedy, after discharging the
poet's debts, were remitted to his sisters, to whom, from his
published correspondence, he seems to have been tenderly at-
tached.

Ninety years after Thomson's death, Mr. Peter Cunningham
reprinted for the Percy Society, a poem on the death of Congreve
inscribed to the Duchess of Marlborough. This poem Mr. Cunningham ascribes to Thomson on evidence which we confess does
not quite satisfy us. Nevertheless, it has many of the charac-
teristics of his style—his enthusiasm, his exaggeration, the
peculiar turn of his versification. We shall give an extract; and
our extract shall be from that portion of the poem in which the
writer extols the virtues and the purity of Congreve—Congreve,
whose virtues were selfishness and sensuality, and whose purity
was such that to match his heroes we must sweep the hells of the
Quadrant, and whose heroines could alone be mated amid the
purlieus of Covent Garden.

What art thou. Death. by mankind poorly feared,
Yet period of their ills! On thy near shore
Trembling they stand, and see through dreaded mists
The eternal port, irresolute to leave
That various misery, those air-fed dreams
Which men call life and fame. Mistaken minds!
'Tis reason's prime aspiring, greatly just;
'Tis happiness supreme to venture forth
In quest of nobler worlds, to try the depths
Of dark futurity with heaven our guide,
The unerring hand that led us safe through time,
That planted in the soul this powerful hope,
This infinite ambition of new life,
And endless joys, still rising, ever new.
    These Congreve tastes, safe on the etherial coast,
Joined to the numberless immortal quire
Of spirits blest. High-seated among these,
He sees the public fathers of mankind,
The greatly good, those universal minds,
Who drew the sword or planned the holy scheme
For liberty and right, to check the reign
Of blood-stained tyranny and save a world.
    1*   *   .   *   *   *
Hail, men immortal! Social virtues, hail!
First heirs of praise! But I, with weak essay,
Wrong the superior theme, while heavenly choirs,
In strains high-warbled to celestial harps,
Resound your names, and Congreve's added voice
In heaven exalts what he admired below.
With these he mixes, now no more to swerve
From reason's purest law; no more to please,
Borne by the torrent down a sensual age.
Pardon, loved shade, that I with friendly blame
Slight note thy errors, not to wrong thy worth
Or shade thy memory (far from my soul
Be that base aim!) but haply to deter,
From flattering the gross vulgar, future pens,
Powerful like thine in every grace. and skilled
To win the listening soul with virtuous charms.

We cannot, we confess, transcribe these lines without picturing
to ourselves the cloud of indignation which would have darkened
the brow of Collier could he have read such a piece of impudent
adulation.

THOMAS GRAY was thirty-two years old when Thomson died.
Few poets ever attained to such an age with so few vicissitudes.
His father, a man of harsh and violent temper, was, like Mil-
ton's, a scrivener in London. He had married in early life a Miss

---

[1] Here intervenes a panegyric, which we omit, on "highborn Marlbro'"
and "Godolphin's patriot worth."

Antrobus, the sister of one of the masters of Eton. Thomas was their fifth son. He was born in Cornhill on the 26th of December, 1716.

A few years after his birth, Mrs. Gray separated from her husband. Her allowance from him seems to have been small, as it was to her exertions as a milliner that her son was indebted for his education, first at Eton, and afterwards at Cambridge. At Eton he became acquainted with Horace Walpole and Richard West. West was the son of the Irish Chancellor, and grandson of Bishop Burnett. Like Gray, he was destined to the law, and seems to have disliked the profession even more than his friend. When Gray removed to Cambridge, West was already entered of Christ's Church, Oxford. They corresponded closely, and some of Gray's finest letters are those which he addressed to his friend.

In 1734, Gray became a pensioner of Peterhouse. His residence extended over a period of four years, during which, we are afraid, literature much more than divided his attention with the law. About the year 1738, he set out in company with his friend Walpole on a tour through France and Italy.

They had been absent for nearly a year, and, after visiting all that was interesting in Florence, Rome, and Naples, had arrived at Reggio, when they quarrelled. The wonder is that they had not quarrelled long before. Gray was one of the most sensitive of men: Walpole was not only frivolous, but malicious. He delighted, like a schoolboy, in making mischief; and we may be sure that the man who could not spare his own kindred, would have but little regard for the feelings of his ancient schoolfellow.

They parted, and Gray returned to Florence. From Florence he set out, by way of Venice, for England, making only a slight deviation from his route for the purpose of visiting the Grande Chartreuse. His account of this visit is one of the finest pieces of descriptive writing in the language. It is contained in two letters, one addressed to his mother, the other to his friend West. " It is a fortnight," he writes the former. " since we set out hence upon a little excursion to Geneva. We took the longest road, which lies through Savoy, on purpose to see a famous monastery, called the Grande Chartreuse, and had no reason to think our time lost. After having travelled seven days very slow (for we did not change horses, it being impossible for a chaise to go post in these roads), we arrived at a little village among the mountains of Savoy, called Echelles ; from thence we proceeded on horses, who are used to the way, to the mountain of the Chartreuse. It is six miles to the top ; the road runs winding up it, commonly not six feet broad; on one hand is the rock, with woods of pine-trees hanging overhead; on the other a monstrous precipice, almost perpendicular, at the bottom of which rolls a torrent, that, sometimes tumbling among the fragments of stone that have fallen from on high, and sometimes precipitating itself down vast descents with a noise like thunder, which is still made greater by the echo from the mountains on each side, concurs to form one of the most solemn, the most romantic, and the most astonishing scenes I ever beheld. Add to this the strange views made by the crags and cliffs on the other hand, the cascades that in many places throw themselves from the very summit down into the vale and the river below, and many other particulars impossible to describe, you will conclude we had no occasion to repent our pains."

"I do not remember," he writes to West, "to have gone ten paces without an exclamation that there was no restraining. Not a precipice, not a torrent, not a cliff, but is pungent with religion and poetry. There are certain scenes that would awe an atheist into belief, without the help of other argument. One need not have a very fantastic imagination to see spirits there at noonday. You have Death perpetually before your eyes, only so far removed as to compose the mind without frightening it."[1]

---

[1] Gray's noble Alcaick Ode was written on the occasion of this visit. We give it a place here.

" O Tu, severi Religio loci,
    Quocunque gaudes nomine (non leve
    Nativa nam certe fluenta
    Numen habet, veteresque sylvas;

" Præsentiorem et conspicimus Deum
    Per invias rupes, fera per juga,
    Clivosque præruptos, sonantes
    Inter aquas, nemorumque noctem;

" Quam si repostus sub trabe citrea
    Fulgeret auro, et Phidiaca manu)
    Salve vocanti rite fesso et
    Da placidam juveni quietem.

' Quod si invidendis sedibus, et frui
    Fortuna sacra lege silentii
    Vetat volentem, me resorbens
    In medios violenta fluctus

" Saltem remoto des, Pater, angulo
    Horas senectæ ducere liberas;
    Tutumque vulgari tumultu
    Surripias, hominumque curis."

Gray arrived in London on the 1st of September 1741. He had not been in town two months when his father died. This event determined Gray on relinquishing his profession. His wants were few, and his means sufficient to supply them. In 1742, he fixed his residence at Cambridge.

In the same year his friend West died. In the interval between his return to England and his settlement at Cambridge, Gray had been employed on his tragedy of Aggripina, and a didactic poem in Latin, entitled De Principiis Cogitandi. The shock which he experienced from the death of West seems to have entirely deranged his plans. His tragedy was abandoned, and the only addition he afterwards made to his didactic poem was an apostrophe to his friend, than which nothing can more pathetically display the feelings of a wounded heart.

Gray was now living in quiet seclusion at Cambridge. Here he wrote his Ode to Eton College, which was published by Dodsley in 1747. In 1750, his Elegy appeared, and in 1757, his Pindaric Odes. Four years before, his mother had died at Stoke. Gray seems to have felt her loss acutely. In an epitaph inscribed upon her tomb, he commemorates her as "the careful, tender mother of many children, one of whom alone had the misfortune to survive her."

In 1765 he took a journey into Scotland, where he formed an intimacy with Beattie. He thence penetrated into Wales and the west of England, and seems to have been particularly charmed with the scenery of Cumberland and Westmoreland. His descriptions of the lake scenery have never been excelled for beauty and finish. "Passed a reek[1] near Dummailrouse," he says, "and entered Westmoreland a second time. Now begin to see Helmscrag distinguished from its rugged neighbours, not so much by its height, as by the strange broken outline of its top, like some gigantic building demolished, and the stones that composed it flung across each other in wild confusion. Just beyond it opens one of the sweetest landscapes that art ever attempted to imitate. The bosom of the mountains spreading here into a broad basin, discovers in the midst Grasmere Water: its margin is hollowed into small bays, with bold eminences, some of them rocks, some of soft turf, that half conceal and vary the figure of the little lake they command. From the shore a low promontory pushes itself far into the water, and on it stands a white village, with the parish church rising in the

[1] In the vernacular of the district a "reek" signifies what in Scotland is called a "burn."

midst of it; hanging enclosures, corn-fields, and meadows green as an emerald, with their trees, hedges, and cattle, fill up the whole space from the edge of the water. Just opposite you is a large farm-house at the bottom of a steep smooth lawn, embosomed in old woods, which climb half way up the mountain's side, and discover above them a broken line of crags that crown the scene. Not a single red tile, no glaring gentleman's house or garden walls, break in upon the repose of this little unsuspected paradise; but all is peace, rusticity, and happy poverty, in its neatest and most becoming attire."

We make no apology for the length of this and our former quotations from Gray's published correspondence. For ourselves, we own that we prefer his letters to those either of Walpole or of Cowper. But the public generally, we are afraid, are not of our opinion. Gray's letters, we doubt, are but little read. Yet all of them are written with fine taste, and, for the most part, in an admirable spirit. Even in the earliest of them, such, for example, as those addressed to West, we are struck with the justness of the writer's thoughts and the classic beauty of his language. His entire correspondence with Mason is pervaded in addition with a humour for which those who are familiar only with his poetry will scarcely give him credit. The fragments of description with which the letters from Italy and the west of England abound want only the accompaniments of measure and metre to rank with the finest poetry in the language. Gray's prose, in loftiness of sentiment and vividness of expression, is at least equal to his verse.

In 1757, the death of Cibber created a vacancy in the office of poet-laureate. The post of Chamberlain, in whose gift the laurel lay, was then held by the Duke of Devonshire. The Duke would willingly have bestowed it upon Gray; but Gray had unconquerable scruples in accepting a post which profligacy and inability had so shamefully disgraced. He continued, therefore, to reside at Cambridge, busied with his poetry and his books. At length an office fell vacant, which he was peculiarly qualified to fill. It was the Cambridge Professorship of Modern Languages and History. He applied for it. But there had arisen in Egypt a king which knew not Joseph. The administration of Bute had displaced the administration of Pitt and Pelham. For the first time in British history a Scotsman was seen at the head of affairs. Bute, though no statesman, was a munificent patron of literature and art; and it is probable that Gray would have obtained the appointment had he possessed the marketable talents of a Churchill or a Wilkes. But Gray was no polemic. He

could not cringe for place, and he hated jobbing.   Political
influence, therefore, obtained what was denied to merit.   Sir
James Lowther could command more votes in the House of
Commons than any commoner of his time.   These votes could
not but be valuable to the Government, and Sir James's tutor
was gazetted to the vacancy.   Not many years elapsed before the
post again became vacant.   Bute's nominee, Mr. Brockett, died
in 1768, and the Duke of Grafton, then Prime Minister, immediately and without solicitation, bestowed it upon Gray.   The
favour did not pass unrewarded.   Grafton was in 1769 elected
Chancellor of Cambridge, and Gray celebrated his installation in
strains which the world will not willingly let die, and which
must have been peculiarly soothing to the minister when he
had fallen upon evil days, and was writhing under that tremendous invective which has immortalised alike its victims and
its author.

Cambridge had hitherto been Gray's residence from choice.   It
now became so by obligation.   The chair which he filled had been
a sinecure from its foundation; but the new incumbent was too
conscientious a man to draw the emoluments, while he neglected
the duties of his post.   The French and Italian teachers in the
University he rewarded liberally.   The lectures on history he
undertook himself.   But before his preparations for the course
were completed, he was attacked by a severe fit of the gout, to
which he had long been subject, and from which a life of singular
temperance could not protect him.   He removed to London.   His
lodgings were at first in Jermyn Street; but from Jermyn
Street he was induced, for the benefit of purer air, to migrate to
Kensington.   The virulence of the disease abated, and in the beginning of July, he returned to Cambridge; but on the 24th of
the same month, he was again attacked by his old disorder while
at dinner in the College hall.   The disease had now fixed upon
his stomach, and resisted all the powers of medicine.   On the
29th, he was seized with strong convulsions.   They returned on
the 30th with redoubled strength, and in the evening of the
same day, in the year 1771, he breathed his last.   He was in the
fifty-fifth year of his age.

They buried him at Stoke beside his mother, and almost within
sight of those " antique towers " which he has so lovingly com-
memorated.

The genius of the two eminent men whose lives we have
sketched was even more varied than their fortunes.   The genius
of THOMSON we would compare to a mighty river, now rolling

along in placid majesty between banks overhung with groves of hazel, and bright with myriads of wild-flowers, now foaming an impetuous torrent pent in by precipices "smoothed up with snow," and now stealing away through unfrequented glooms, muddy, tortuous, and unfruitful; while the genius of GRAY resembled a mountain torrent, now lost to view amid the whirling mists, and now leaping forth in wild sublimity to gem the bosom of the everlasting hills.

Of the two, Thomson was undoubtedly the greater. Among descriptive poets he stands alone. Virgil, indeed, amongst the ancients, and Cowper amongst the moderns, may be thought to have approached him. But Virgil certainly could never have conceived the glorious Hymn with which the Seasons close. Cowper never could have depicted that solemn autumn evening in which we see the creeping waters ooze, the marshes stagnate, the rivers wind, and the fogs cluster and swim along the dusky lawns. No episode, on the other hand, in the Seasons, can be compared to the episode of Orpheus in the Georgics. No passage in the Seasons can be compared to those didactic passages in the Task to which all other didactic poetry was, in the opinion of Southey, as a formal garden to woodland scenery. The very points in which lay the strength of Virgil and Cowper were those in which lay Thomson's weakness. But we shall search the Georgics and the Task in vain for such poetry as that in which Thomson has described the Alpine winter, the peasant perishing in the snow, the Siberian exile, and the Arab pilgrim sinking beneath the fiery blast that

"From the boundless furnace of the sky
Sweeps the wide glittering waste of burning sand."

It was only by slow degrees that Thomson attained to such a perfect mastery of his art. If we compare, for example, the first edition of the Seasons with the second, and the second with the third, we will see with what persevering assiduity he elaborated his thoughts and refined his language.

This marked improvement in his style is seen more clearly when we come to compare the Seasons with his last production, the Castle of Indolence. For the materials of that exquisite poem Thomson was indebted, as Mr. Campbell well says, to the Faery Queen; "and in meeting with the paternal spirit of Spenser, he seems as if he were admitted more intimately to the home of inspiration." Never before, indeed, had the genius of Thomson burned with so serene a lustre; for whether we have regard to the style or diction of the poem, the Castle of Indolence is absolutely perfect. The first canto especially impresses the mind, as Johnson has truly said, with a sense of lazy luxury not to be described. The art of the poet could no farther go.

The finer portions of Thomson's poetry are characterized by the same simplicity of design and beauty of form and colour which we see in the natural landscape. The felicity of his touch, which is really marvellous, is only equalled by its fidelity. No other poet combined to an equal extent the glow of Claude and the gloom of Salvator. The poorest portions of his poetry, on the other hand, though better than the best pieces of many who rose to eminence during the period which elapsed between the publication of the Traveller and the publication of the Task, are those which treat of trivial and domestic life. In these Thomson's swelling and exuberant diction, which in his higher flights is, as Campbell finely says, like "the flowing vesture of the Druid," "ceases to seem the mantle of inspiration, and only strikes us by its unwieldy difference from the common costume of expression." It was not thus that Cowper dealt with the familiar courtesies of life. No poet ever so entirely adapted his verse to the nature of his subject, and no poet is consequently so entirely the friend to whose companionship we flee after having enjoyed to satiety the fellowship of his more brilliant and attractive associates.

When we turn from Thomson to Gray we are struck at once with the immensity of the barrier which separates their respective intellects. "As to description," writes the latter to Beattie, "I have always thought that it made the most graceful ornament of poetry, but never ought to make the subject." Hence in the Castle of Indolence Gray could only bring himself to acknowledge the existence of a few good verses. Somewhat similar was the feeling with which he regarded Akenside. If there was a poet of that age whom Gray was better qualified to appreciate than any other, that poet was Akenside. He was a scholar, and a ripe one; and his powers, though perhaps better adapted, as a great critic has remarked, for grave and elevated satire, were still calculated to raise high his fame amongst the masters of the lyric art. His Hymn to the Naiads is a masterpiece in its way. Few poets had ever before displayed so much of the true Greek harmony and feeling. It was the firm and often expressed conviction of Lloyd that no translation of Homer or Callimachus could give a better idea of the ancient Ode than this effort of Akenside. Yet of Akenside Gray could only coldly remark that he was often obscure, and even unintelligible.

Still we must do Gray justice. The wild imagery and shadowy magnificence of Ossian had no greater charm for the victor of Lodi than they had for the secluded scholar of Cambridge. He delighted in the wild superstitions of the North. He caught successfully the fire of the ancient Bard, and transmitted it to futurity in the Descent of Odin and the Fatal Sisters. He loved the great masterpieces of Greek and Italian poetry with a love which warmed his imagination and left an indelible impress on all he wrote. More especially may this impress be traced in the Progress of Poesy and the Bard. These pieces absolutely glow with Pindaric fire. Their harmony, in spite of the complicacy of their versification, is perfect. Their diction is brilliant beyond all parallel. Their only fault is an occasional obscurity, the result of an over-elaborate condensity of expression.

In the Ode to Eton College, the impress we have referred to is much more slight; and in the Elegy it almost wholly disappears. Exquisitely harmonious as it is, the Elegy, we confess, scarcely seems to us to deserve the high encomiums bestowed on it by Byron. Its popularity is principally the result of its connection with every-day life and every-day feelings. But poetry of this class is not necessarily of the highest order. It may command more readers. It may be more generally relished than those majestic creations which rear "sublime their starry fronts" amid the poetic host. But we ought to remember with Young that "a fixed star is as much in the bounds of nature as a flower of the field." Gray's classical allusions and mythological lore must always, indeed, be "caviare to the general." But not the less, we think, will his fame ultimately rest on those noble Odes, which few, we should suppose, can read without a feeling of admiration akin to that with which the ancient Greek regarded the lofty strains of Pindar and Corinna.

THE

POETICAL WORKS

OF

JAMES THOMSON.

CONTENTS.

SONGS.

OCCASIONAL PIECES.

SPRING.

The subject proposed.—Inscribed to the Countess of Hertford.—The season is described as it affects the various parts of nature, ascending from the lower to the higher; with digressions arising from the subject.—Its influence on inanimate Matter, on Vegetables, on brute Animals, and, last, on Man; concluding with a dissuasive from the wild and irregular passion of Love, opposed to that of a pure and happy kind.

COME, gentle SPRING! ethereal Mildness, come,
And from the bosom of yon dropping cloud,
While music wakes around, veil'd in a shower
Of shadowing roses, on our plains descend.
O HERTFORD! fitted or to shine in courts
With unaffected grace, or walk the plain
With innocence and meditation join'd
In soft assemblage, listen to my song,
Which thy own season paints; when Nature all
Is blooming and benevolent, like thee.   10
    And see where surly WINTER passes off,
Far to the North, and calls his ruffian blasts:
His blasts obey, and quit the howling hill,
The shatter'd forest, and the ravaged vale;
While softer gales succeed, at whose kind touch,
Dissolving snows in livid torrents lost,
The mountains lift their green heads to the sky.
    As yet the trembling year is unconfirm'd,
And WINTER oft at eve resumes the breeze,
Chills the pale morn, and bids his driving sleets   20
Deform the day delightless; so that scarce
The bittern knows his time, with bill ingulft

To shake the sounding marsh; or from the shore
The plovers when to scatter o'er the heath,
And sing their wild notes to the listening waste.
   At last from *Aries* rolls the bounteous sun,
And the bright *Bull* receives him.   Then no more
Th' expansive atmosphere is cramp'd with cold;
But, full of life and vivifying soul,
Lifts the light clouds sublime, and spreads them thin,   30
Fleecy and white, o'er all-surrounding heaven.
   Forth fly the tepid airs; and unconfined,
Unbinding earth, the moving softness strays.
Joyous, th' impatient husbandman perceives
Relenting Nature, and his lusty steers
Drives from their stalls, to where the well-used plough
Lies in the furrow, loosen'd from the frost.
There, unrefusing, to the harness'd yoke
They lend their shoulder, and begin their toil,
Cheer'd by the simple song and soaring lark.   ·   40
Meanwhile incumbent o'er the shining share
The master leans, removes th' obstructing clay,
Winds the whole work, and sidelong lays the glebe.
   While through the neighb'ring fields the sower stalks
With measured step; and liberal throws the grain
Into the faithful bosom of the ground:
The harrow follows harsh, and shuts the scene.   .
   Be gracious, HEAVEN! for now laborious Man
Has done his part.   Ye fostering breezes! blow;
Ye softening dews! ye tender showers! descend;   50
And temper all, thou world-reviving sun!
Into the perfect year.   Nor ye who live
In luxury and ease, in pomp and pride,
Think these lost themes unworthy of your ear:
Such themes as these the rural MARO sung
To wide-imperial ROME, in the full height
Of elegance and taste, by Greece refined.
   In ancient times, the sacred plough employ'd
The kings, and awful fathers of mankind:
And some, with whom compared your insect-tribes   60

Are but the beings of a summer's day,
Have held the scale of empire, ruled the storm
Of mighty war; then, with unwearied hand,
Disdaining little delicacies, seized
The plough, and greatly independent lived.
    Ye generous BRITONS, venerate the plough;
And o'er your hills, and long withdrawing vales,
Let Autumn spread his treasures to the sun,
Luxuriant and unbounded: as the sea,
Far through his azure turbulent domain,   70
Your empire owns, and, from a thousand shores,
Wafts all the pomp of life into your ports;
So with superior boon may your rich soil,
Exuberant, Nature's better blessings pour
O'er every land; the naked nations clothe;
And be th' exhaustless granary of a world!
    Nor only through the lenient air, this change
Delicious breathes; the penetrative sun,
His force deep-darting to the dark retreat
Of vegetation, sets the steaming Power   80
At large, to wander o'er the vernant earth,
In various hues; but chiefly thee, gay Green!
Thou smiling Nature's universal robe!
United light and shade! where the sight dwells
With growing strength, and ever new delight.
    From the moist meadow to the wither'd hill,
Led by the breeze, the vivid verdure runs,
And swells, and deepens, to the cherish'd eye.
The hawthorn whitens; and the juicy groves
Put forth their buds, unfolding by degrees,   90
Till the whole leafy forest stands display'd,
In full luxuriance, to the sighing gales;
Where the deer rustle through the twining brake,
And the birds sing conceal'd. At once, array'd
In all the colours of the flushing year,
By Nature's swift and secret-working hand,
The garden glows, and fills the liberal air
With lavish fragrance; while the promised fruit

Lies yet a little embryo, unperceived,
Within its crimson folds. Now from the town,   100
Buried in smoke, and sleep, and noisome damps,
Oft let me wander o'er the dewy fields,
Where freshness breathes; and dash the trembling drops
From the bent bush, as through the verdant maze
Of sweet-briar hedges I pursue my walk;
Or taste the smell of dairy, or ascend
Some eminence, Augusta, in thy plains,
And see the country, far diffused around,
One boundless blush, one white-empurpled shower
Of mingled blossoms; where the raptured eye   110
Hurries from joy to joy, and, hid beneath
The fair profusion, yellow Autumn spies;
If, brush'd from Russian wilds, a cutting gale
Rise not, and scatter from his humid wings
The clammy mildew; or, dry-blowing, breathe
Untimely frost; before whose baleful blast
The full-blown Spring through all her foliage shrinks,
Joyless and dead, a wide-dejected waste.
For oft, engender'd by the hazy North,
Myriads on myriads, insect armies warp   120
Keen in the poison'd breeze; and wasteful eat,
Through buds and bark, into the blacken'd core,
Their eager way. A feeble race! yet oft
The sacred sons of vengeance; on whose course
Corrosive famine waits, and kills the year.
To check this plague, the skilful farmer chaff
And blazing straw, before his orchard, burns;
Till, all involved in smoke, the latent foe
From every cranny suffocated falls;
Or scatters o'er the blooms the pungent dust   130
Of pepper, fatal to the frosty tribe;
Or, when th' envenom'd leaf begins to curl,
With sprinkled water drowns them in their nest;
Nor, while they pick them up with busy bill,
The little trooping birds unwisely scares.
    Be patient, swains! these cruel-seeming winds

Blow not in vain. Far hence they keep repress'd
Those deep'ning clouds on clouds, surcharged with rain,
That o'er the vast Atlantic hither borne,
In endless train, would quench the summer-blaze,   140
And, cheerless, drown the crude unripen'd year.
The North-east spends his rage: he now shut up
Within his iron cave, th' effusive South
Warms the wide air, and o'er the void of heaven
Breathes the big clouds with vernal showers distent.
At first a dusky wreath they seem to rise,
Scarce staining ether; but by swift degrees,
In heaps on heaps, the doubling vapour sails
Along the loaded sky, and, mingling deep,
Sits on th' horizon round, a settled gloom: 150
Not such as wintry storms on mortals shed,
Oppressing life; but lovely, gentle, kind,
And full of every hope and every joy,
The wish of Nature. Gradual sinks the breeze
Into a perfect calm; that not a breath
Is heard to quiver through the closing woods,
Or rustling turn the many-twinkling leaves
Of aspen tall. The uncurling floods, diffused
In glassy breadth, seem through delusive lapse
Forgetful of their course. 'Tis silence all,   160
And pleasing expectation. Herds and flocks
Drop the dry sprig, and mute-imploring eye
The falling verdure. Hush'd in short suspense,
The plumy people streak their wings with oil,
To throw the lucid moisture trickling off;
And wait th' approaching sign, to strike at once
Into the general choir. Ev'n mountains, vales,
And forests seem, impatient, to demand
The promised sweetness. Man superior walks
Amid the glad creation, musing praise,   170
And looking lively gratitude. At last,
The clouds consign their treasures to the fields;
And softly shaking on the dimpled pool
Prelusive drops, let all their moisture flow,

In large effusion, o'er the freshen'd world.
The stealing shower is scarce to patter heard,
By such as wander through the forest walks,
Beneath th' umbrageous multitude of leaves.
But who can hold the shade, while Heaven descends
In universal bounty, shedding herbs,   180
And fruits, and flowers, on Nature's ample lap!
Swift fancy fired anticipates their growth;
And while the milky nutriment distils,
Beholds the kindling country colour round.
    Thus all day long the full-distended clouds
Indulge their genial stores, and well-shower'd earth
Is deep enrich'd with vegetable life;
Till, in the western sky, the downward sun
Looks out, effulgent, from amid the flush
Of broken clouds, gay-shifting to his beam.   190
The rapid radiance instantaneous strikes
Th' illumined mountain, through the forest streams,
Shakes on the floods, and in a yellow mist,
Far smoking o'er the interminable plain,
In twinkling myriads lights the dewy gems.
    Moist, bright, and green, the landscape laughs around;
Full swell the woods; their every music wakes,
Mix'd in wild concert, with the warbling brooks
Increased, the distant bleatings of the hills,
And hollow lows responsive from the vales,   200
Whence blending all the sweeten'd zephyr springs.
Meantime, refracted from yon eastern cloud,
Bestriding earth, the grand ethereal bow
Shoots up immense; and every hue unfolds,
In fair proportion, running from the red,
To where the violet fades into the sky.
    Here, awful Newton! the dissolving clouds
Form, fronting on the sun, thy showery prism;
And to the sage-instructed eye unfold
The various twine of light, by thee disclosed   210
From the white mingling maze. Not so the boy;
He wondering views the bright enchantment bend,

Delightful, o'er the radiant fields, and runs
To catch the falling glory; but amazed
Beholds th' amusive arch before him fly,
Then vanish quite away. Still night succeeds;
A soften'd shade, and saturated earth
Awaits the morning-beam, to give to light,
Raised through ten thousand different plastic tubes,
The balmy treasures of the former day.   220
   Then spring the living herbs, profusely wild,
O'er all the deep-green earth, beyond the power
Of botanist to number up their tribes:
Whether he steals along the lonely dale,
In silent search; or through the forest, rank
With what the dull incurious weeds account,
Bursts his blind way; or climbs the mountain rock,
Fired by the nodding verdure of its brow.
With such a liberal hand has Nature flung
Their seeds abroad, blown them about in winds,   230
Innumerous mix'd them with the nursing mould,
The moistening current, and prolific rain.
   But who their virtues can declare? who pierce,
With vision pure, into these sacred stores
Of health, and life, and joy? the food of Man,
While yet he lived in innocence, and told
A length of golden years; unflesh'd in blood,
A stranger to the savage arts of life,
Death, rapine, carnage, surfeit, and disease;
The lord, and not the tyrant, of the world.   240
   The first fresh dawn then waked the gladden'd race
Of uncorrupted Man, nor blush'd to see
The sluggard sleep beneath its sacred beam:
For their light slumbers gently fumed away;
And up they rose as vigorous as the sun,
Or to the culture of the willing glebe,
Or to the cheerful tendance of the flock.
Meantime the song went round; and dance and sport,
Wisdom and friendly talk, successive, stole
Their hours away: while, in the rosy vale,   250

Love breathed his infant sighs, from anguish free,
And full replete with bliss; save the sweet pain,
That, inly thrilling, but exalts it more.
Nor yet injurious act, nor surly deed,
Was known among those happy sons of Heaven;
For reason and benevolence were law:
Harmonious Nature too look'd smiling on;
Clear shone the skies, cool'd with eternal gales,
And balmy spirit all: the youthful sun
Shot his best rays, and still the gracious clouds   260
Dropp'd fatness down; as o'er the swelling mead,
The herds and flocks, commixing, play'd secure.
This when, emergent from the gloomy wood,
The glaring lion saw, his horrid heart
Was meeken'd, and he join'd his sullen joy;
For music held the whole in perfect peace:
Soft sigh'd the flute; the tender voice was heard,
Warbling the varied heart; the woodlands round
Applied their quire; and winds and waters flow'd
In consonance.   Such were those prime of days.   270
    But now those white unblemish'd manners, whence
The fabling poets took their golden age,
Are found no more amid these iron times,
These dregs of life.   Now the distemper'd mind
Has lost that concord of harmonious powers,
Which forms the soul of happiness, and all
Is off the poise within: the passions all
Have burst their bounds; and reason half extinct,
Or impotent, or else approving, sees
The foul disorder.   Senseless, and deform'd,   280
Convulsive anger storms at large; or, pale
And silent, settles into fell revenge.
Base envy withers at another's joy,
And hates that excellence it cannot reach.
Desponding fear, of feeble fancies full,
Weak and unmanly, loosens every power.
    Even love itself is bitterness of soul,
A pensive anguish pining at the heart;

Or, sunk to sordid interest, feels no more
That noble wish, that never cloy'd desire,   290
Which, selfish joy disdaining, seeks alone
To bless the dearer object of its flame.
Hope sickens with extravagance; and grief,
Of life impatient, into madness swells,
Or in dead silence wastes the weeping hours.
These, and a thousand mix'd emotions more,
From ever-changing views of good and ill,
Form'd infinitely various, vex the mind
With endless storm: whence, deeply rankling, grows
The partial thought, a listless unconcern,   300
Cold, and averting from our neighbour's good;
Then dark disgust, and hatred, winding wiles,
Coward deceit, and ruffian violence:
At last, extinct each social feeling, fell
And joyless inhumanity pervades
And petrifies the heart.   Nature disturb'd
Is deem'd, vindictive, to have changed her course.
   Hence, in old dusky time, a deluge came;
When the deep-cleft disparting orb, that arch'd
The central waters round, impetuous rush'd,   310
With universal burst, into the gulf,
And o'er the high-piled hills of fractured earth
Wide dash'd the waves, in undulation vast;
Till, from the centre to the streaming clouds,
A shoreless ocean tumbled round the globe.
   The seasons since have, with severer sway,
Oppress'd a broken world: the Winter keen
Shook forth his waste of snows; and Summer shot
His pestilential heats.   Great Spring, before,
Green'd all the year; and fruits and blossoms blush'd,   320
In social sweetness, on the self-same bough:
Pure was the temperate air; an even calm
Perpetual reign'd, save what the zephyrs bland
Breathed o'er the blue expanse; for then nor storms
Were taught to blow, nor hurricanes to rage;
Sound slept the waters; no sulphureous glooms

Swell'd in the sky, and sent the lightning forth;
While sickly damps, and cold autumnal fogs,
Hung not, relaxing, on the springs of life.
But now, of turbid elements the sport,   330
From clear to cloudy tost, from hot to cold,
And dry to moist, with inward-eating change,
Our drooping days are dwindled down to nought,
Their period finish'd ere 'tis well begun.
And yet the wholesome herb neglected dies;
Though with the pure exhilarating soul
Of nutriment and health, and vital powers,
Beyond the search of art, 'tis copious blest.
For, with hot ravine fired, ensanguined Man
Is now become the lion of the plain,   340
And worse.   The wolf, who from the mighty fold
Fierce drags the bleating prey, ne'er drank her milk,
Nor wore her warming fleece: nor has the steer,
At whose strong chest the deadly tiger hangs,
E'er plough'd for him.   They too are temper'd high,
With hunger stung and wild necessity;
Nor lodges pity in their shaggy breast.
But Man, whom Nature form'd of milder clay,
With every kind emotion in his heart,
And taught alone to weep: while from her lap   350
She pours ten thousand delicacies, herbs,
And fruits, as numerous as the drops of rain,
Or beams that gave them birth: shall he, fair form !
Who wears sweet smiles, and looks erect on Heaven,
E'er stoop to mingle with the prowling herd,
And dip his tongue in gore ?   The beast of prey,
Blood-stain'd, deserves to bleed: but you, ye flocks,
What have you done ? ye peaceful people, what,
To merit death ? you, who have given us milk
In luscious streams, and lent us your own coat   360
Against the winter's cold ?   And the plain ox,
That harmless, honest, guileless animal,
In what has he offended ? he, whose toil,
Patient and ever ready, clothes the land

SPRING

SPRING

Shrill voice and note and the ... season of the ...

With all the pomp of harvest: shall he bleed,
And struggling groan beneath the cruel hands
Even of the clown he feeds? and that, perhaps,
To swell the riot of th' autumnal feast,
Won by his labour? Thus the feeling heart
Would tenderly suggest: but 'tis enough, 370
In this late age, advent'rous, to have touch'd
Light on the numbers of the Samian sage.
High Heaven forbids the bold presumptuous strain,
Whose wisest will has fix'd us in a state
That must not yet to pure perfection rise.
Now, when the first foul torrent of the brooks,
Swell'd with the vernal rains, is ebb'd away;
And, whitening, down their mossy-tinctured stream
Descends the billowy foam: now is the time,
While yet the dark-brown water aids the guile, 380
To tempt the trout. The well-dissembled fly,
The rod fine-tapering with elastic spring,
Snatch'd from the hoary steed the floating line,
And all thy slender wat'ry stores prepare.
But let not on thy hook the tortured worm,
Convulsive, twist in agonising folds;
Which, by rapacious hunger swallow'd deep,
Gives, as you tear it from the bleeding breast
Of the weak, helpless, uncomplaining wretch,
Harsh pain and horror to the tender hand. 390
    When with his lively ray the potent sun
Has pierced the streams, and roused the finny race,
Then, issuing cheerful, to thy sport repair;
Chief should the western breezes curling play,
And light o'er ether bear the shadowy clouds.
High to their fount, this day, amid their hills,
And woodlands warbling round, trace up the brooks;
The next, pursue their rocky-channell'd maze,
Down to the river, in whose ample wave
Their little Naiads love to sport at large. 400
    Just in the dubious point, where with the pool
Is mix'd the trembling stream, or where it boils
C

Around the stone, or, from the hollow'd bank
Reverted, plays in undulating flow,
There throw, nice-judging, the delusive fly;
And as you lead it round in artful curve,
With eye attentive mark the springing game.
Strait as above the surface of the flood
They wanton rise, or urged by hunger leap,
Then fix, with gentle twitch, the barbed hook: 410
Some lightly tossing to the grassy bank,
And to the shelving shore slow-dragging some,
With various hand proportion'd to their force.
If yet too young, and easily deceived,
A worthless prey scarce bends your pliant rod;
Him, piteous of his youth and the short space
He has enjoy'd the vital light of heaven,
Soft disengage, and back into the stream
The speckled captive throw.   But should you lure
From his dark haunt, beneath the tangled roots   420
Of pendant trees, the monarch of the brook,
Behoves you then to ply your finest art.
Long time he, following cautious, scans the fly;
And oft attempts to seize it, but as oft
The dimpled water speaks his jealous fear.
At last, while haply o'er the shaded sun
Passes a cloud, he desperate takes the death,
With sullen plunge.   At once he darts along,
Deep struck, and runs out all the lengthen'd line;
Then seeks the furthest ooze, the sheltering weed,   430
The cavern'd bank, his old secure abode;
And flies aloft, and flounces round the pool,
Indignant of the guile.   With yielding hand,
That feels him still, yet to his furious course
Gives way, you, now retiring, following now
Across the stream, exhaust his idle rage:
Till floating broad upon his breathless side,
And to his fate abandon'd, to the shore
You gaily drag your unresisting prize.
    Thus pass the temperate hours; but when the sun   440

Shakes from his noonday throne the scattering clouds,
Even shooting listless languor through the deeps;
Then seek the bank where flowering elders crowd,
Where scatter'd wild the lily of the vale
Its balmy essence breathes, where cowslips hang
The dewy head, where purple violets lurk,
With all the lowly children of the shade;
Or lie reclined beneath yon spreading ash,
Hung o'er the steep; whence, borne in liquid wing,
The sounding culver shoots; or where the hawk,   450
High in the beetling cliff, his eyrie builds.
There let the classic page thy fancy lead
Through rural scenes; such as the Mantuan swain
Paints in the matchless harmony of song.
Or catch thyself the landscape, gliding swift
Athwart imagination's vivid eye:
Or by the vocal woods and waters lull'd,
And lost in lonely musing, in the dream,
Confused, of careless solitude, where mix
Ten thousand wandering images of things,   460
Soothe every gust of passion into peace;
All but the swellings of the soften'd heart,
That waken, not disturb, the tranquil mind.

   Behold! yon breathing prospect bids the muse
Throw all her beauty forth. But who can paint
Like Nature? Can imagination boast,
Amid its gay creation, hues like hers?
Or can it mix them with that matchless skill,
And lose them in each other, as appears
In every bud that blows? If fancy then,   470
Unequal, fails beneath the pleasing task,
Ah! what shall language do? ah! where find words
Tinged with so many colours; and whose power,
To life approaching, may perfume my lays
With that fine oil, those aromatic gales,
That inexhaustive flow continual round?

   Yet, though successless, will the toil delight.
Come then, ye virgins and ye youths, whose hearts

Have felt the raptures of refining love!
And thou, Amanda, come, pride of my song!   480
Form'd by the Graces, loveliness itself!
Come with those downcast eyes, sedate and sweet,
Those looks demure, that deeply pierce the soul,
Where, with the light of thoughtful reason mix'd,
Shines lively fancy and the feeling heart:
Oh come! and while the rosy-footed May
Steals blushing on, together let us tread
The morning-dews, and gather in their prime
Fresh-blooming flowers, to grace thy braided hair,
And thy loved bosom that improves their sweets.   490
    See, where the winding vale its lavish stores,
Irriguous, spreads.   See, how the lily drinks
The latent rill, scarce oozing through the grass,
Of growth luxuriant; or the humid bank
In fair profusion decks.   Long let us walk
Where the breeze blows from yon extended field
Of blossom'd beans.   Arabia cannot boast
A fuller gale of joy, than, liberal, thence
Breathes through the sense, and takes the ravish'd soul.
Nor is the mead unworthy of thy foot,   500
Full of fresh verdure, and unnumber'd flowers,
The negligence of Nature, wide and wild;
Where, undisguised by mimic Art, she spreads
Unbounded beauty to the roving eye.
Here their delicious task the fervent bees,
In swarming millions, tend: around, athwart,
Through the soft air, the busy nations fly,
Cling to the bud, and, with inserted tube,
Suck its pure essence, its ethereal soul;
And oft, with bolder wing, they soaring dare   510
The purple heath, or where the wild thyme grows,
And yellow load them with the luscious spoil.
    At length the finish'd garden to the view
Its vistas opens, and its alleys green.
Snatch'd through the verdant maze, the hurried eye
Distracted wanders; now the bowery walk

Of covert close, where scarce a speck of day
Falls on the lengthen'd gloom, protracted sweeps;
Now meets the bending sky; the river now
Dimpling along, the breezy-ruffled lake,   520
The forest darkening round, the glittering spire,
Th' ethereal mountain, and the distant main.
 But why so far excursive? when at hand,
Along these blushing borders, bright with dew,
And in yon mingled wilderness of flowers,
Fair-handed Spring unbosoms every grace;
Throws out the snow-drop and the crocus first;
The daisy, primrose, violet darkly blue,
And polyanthus of unnumber'd dies;
The yellow wall-flower, stain'd with iron brown;   530
And lavish stock that scents the garden round;
From the soft wing of vernal breezes shed,
Anemonies; auriculas, enrich'd
With shining meal o'er all their velvet leaves;
And full ranunculas, of glowing red.
Then comes the tulip-race, where beauty plays
Her idle freaks; from family diffused
To family, as flies the father-dust,
The varied colours run; and while they break
On the charm'd eye, th' exulting florist marks,   540
With secret pride, the wonders of his hand.
No gradual bloom is wanting; from the bud,
First-born of Spring, to Summer's musky tribes:
Nor hyacinths, of purest virgin white,
Low-bent, and blushing inward; nor jonquils,
Of potent fragrance; nor Narcissus fair,
As o'er the fabled fountain hanging still;
Nor broad carnations, nor gay-spotted pinks;
Nor, shower'd from every bush, the damask-rose;
Infinite numbers, delicacies, smells,   550
With hues on hues expression cannot paint,
The breath of Nature, and her endless bloom.
 Hail, Source of Being! Universal Soul
Of heaven and earth! Essential Presence, hail!

To Thee I bend the knee; to Thee my thoughts,
Continual, climb; who, with a master-hand,
Hast the great whole into perfection touch'd.
By Thee the various vegetative tribes,
Wrapt in a filmy net, and clad with leaves,
Draw the live ether, and imbibe the dew.   560
By Thee disposed into congenial soils,
Stands each attractive plant, and sucks, and swells
The juicy tide; a twining mass of tubes.
At Thy command the vernal sun awakes
The torpid sap, detruded to the root
By wintry winds; that now in fluent dance,
And lively fermentation, mounting, spreads
All this innumerous-colour'd scene of things.
   As rising from the vegetable world
My theme ascends, with equal wing ascend,   570
My panting muse! and hark, how loud the woods
Invite you forth in all your gayest trim!
Lend me your song, ye nightingales! oh pour
The mazy-running soul of melody
Into my varied verse! while I deduce,
From the first note the hollow cuckoo sings,
The symphony of Spring, and touch a theme
Unknown to fame, the passion of the groves.
   When first the soul of love is sent abroad,
Warm through the vital air, and on the heart   580
Harmonious seizes, the gay troops begin,
In gallant thought, to plume the painted wing;
And try again the long-forgotten strain,
At first faint warbled. But no sooner grows
The soft infusion prevalent, and wide,
Than, all alive, at once their joy o'erflows
In music unconfined. Up-springs the lark,
Shrill-voiced and loud, the messenger of morn:
Ere yet the shadows fly, he mounted sings
Amid the dawning clouds, and from their haunts   590
Calls up the tuneful nations. Every copse
Deep-tangled, tree irregular, and bush   .

SPRING

Bending with dewy moisture o'er the heads
Of the coy quiristers that lodge within,
Are prodigal of harmony. The thrush
And wood-lark, o'er the kind-contending throng
Superior heard, run through the sweetest length
Of notes; when listening Philomela deigns
To let them joy, and purposes, in thought
Elate, to make her night excel their day. 600
The blackbird whistles from the thorny brake;
The mellow bullfinch answers from the grove;
Nor are the linnets, o'er the flowering furze
Pour'd out profusely, silent. Join'd to these,
Innumerous songsters, in the freshening shade
Of new-sprung leaves, their modulation mix
Mellifluous. The jay, the rook, the daw,
And each harsh pipe, discordant heard alone,
Aid the full concert: while the stock-dove breathes
A melancholy murmur through the whole. 610
'Tis love creates their melody, and all
This waste of music is the voice of love;
That even to birds, and beasts, the tender arts
Of pleasing teaches. Hence the glossy kind
Try every winning way inventive love
Can dictate, and in courtship to their mates
Pour forth their little souls. First, wide around,
With distant awe, in airy rings they rove,
Endeavouring by a thousand tricks to catch
The cunning, conscious, half-averted glance 620
Of their regardless charmer. Should she seem,
Softening, the least approvance to bestow,
Their colours burnish, and, by hope inspired,
They brisk advance; then, on a sudden struck,
Retire disorder'd; then again approach;
In fond rotation spread the spotted wing,
And shiver every feather with desire.
    Connubial leagues agreed, to the deep woods
They haste away, all as their fancy leads,
Pleasure, or food, or secret safety prompts; 630

That Nature's great command may be obey'd,
Nor all the sweet sensations they perceive
Indulged in vain. Some to the holly-hedge
Nestling repair, and to the thicket some;
Some to the rude protection of the thorn
Commit their feeble offspring: the cleft tree
Offers its kind concealment to a few;
Their food its insects, and its moss their nests.
Others apart, far in the grassy dale
Or roughening waste, their humble texture weave.   640
But most in woodland solitudes delight,
In unfrequented glooms, or shaggy banks,
Steep, and divided by a babbling brook,
Whose murmurs soothe them all the livelong day,
When by kind duty fix'd. Among the roots
Of hazel, pendant o'er the plaintive stream,
They frame the first foundation of their domes;
Dry sprigs of trees, in artful fabric laid,
And bound with clay together. Now 'tis nought
But restless hurry through the busy air,   650
Beat by unnumber'd wings. The swallow sweeps
The slimy pool, to build his hanging house
Intent. And often, from the careless back
Of herds and flocks, a thousand tugging bills
Pluck hair and wool; and oft, when unobserved,
Steal from the barn a straw: till soft and warm,
Clean and complete, their habitation grows.
    As thus the patient dam assiduous sits,
Not to be tempted from her tender task,
Or by sharp hunger, or by smooth delight,   660
Though the whole loosen'd Spring around her blows,
Her sympathising lover takes his stand
High on th' opponent bank, and ceaseless sings
The tedious time away; or else supplies
Her place a moment, while she sudden flits
To pick the scanty meal. Th' appointed time
With pious toil fulfill'd, the callow young,
Warm'd and expanded into perfect life,

Their brittle bondage break, and come to light,
A helpless family, demanding food   670
With constant clamour: Oh what passions then,
What melting sentiments of kindly care,
On the new parents seize! away they fly
Affectionate, and undesiring bear
The most delicious morsel to their young;
Which equally distributed, again
The search begins.   Even so a gentle pair,
By fortune sunk, but form'd of generous mould,
And charm'd with cares beyond the vulgar breast,
In some lone cot amid the distant woods,   680
Sustain'd alone by providential Heaven,
Oft as they weeping eye their infant train,
Check their own appetites, and give them all.
    Nor toil alone they scorn: exalting love,
By the great Father of the Spring inspired,
Gives instant courage to the fearful race,
And to the simple, art.   With stealthy wing,
Should some rude foot their woody haunts molest,
Amid a neighbouring bush they silent drop,
And whirring thence, as if alarm'd, deceive   690
Th' unfeeling schoolboy.   Hence, around the head
Of wandering swain, the white-wing'd plover wheels
Her sounding flight, and then directly on
In long excursion skims the level lawn,
To tempt him from her nest.   The wild-duck, hence,
O'er the rough moss, and o'er the trackless waste
The heath-hen flutters, pious fraud! to lead
The hot-pursuing spaniel far astray.
    Be not the Muse ashamed, here to bemoan
Her brothers of the grove, by tyrant Man   700
Inhuman caught, and in the narrow cage
From liberty confined, and boundless air.
Dull are the pretty slaves, their plumage dull,
Ragged, and all its brightening lustre lost;
Nor is that sprightly wildness in their notes,
Which, clear and vigorous, warbles from the beech.

Oh then, ye friends of love and love-taught song,
Spare the soft tribes, this barbarous art forbear;
If on your bosoms innocence can win,
Music engage, or piety persuade.   710
  But let not chief the nightingale lament
Her ruin'd care, too delicately framed ·
To brook the harsh confinement of the cage.
Oft when, returning with her loaded bill,
Th' astonish'd mother finds a vacant nest,
By the hard hand of unrelenting clowns
Robb'd, to the ground the vain provision falls;
Her pinions ruffle, and, low-drooping, scarce
Can bear the mourner to the poplar shade;
Where, all-abandon'd to despair, she sings   720
Her sorrows through the night; and, on the bough,
Sole-sitting, still at every dying fall
Takes up again her lamentable strain
Of winding wo; till, wide around, the woods
Sigh to her song, and with her wail resound.
  But now the feather'd youth their former bounds,
Ardent, disdain; and weighing oft their wings,
Demand the free possession of the sky:
This one glad office more, and then dissolves
Parental love at once, now needless grown.   730
Unlavish Wisdom never works in vain.
'Tis on some evening, sunny, grateful, mild,
When nought but balm is breathing through the woods,
With yellow lustre bright, that the new tribes
Visit the spacious heavens, and look abroad
On Nature's common, far as they can see,
Or wing, their range and pasture.   O'er the boughs
Dancing about, still at the giddy verge
Their resolution fails; their pinions still,
In loose libration stretch'd, to trust the void   740
Trembling refuse; till down before them fly
The parent-guides, and chide, exhort, command,
Or push them off.   The surging air receives
Its plumy burden; and their self-taught wing

Winnow the waving element. On ground
Alighted, bolder up again they lead,
Farther and farther on, the lengthening flight;
Till vanish'd every fear, and every power
Roused into life and action, light in air
Th' acquitted parents see their soaring race,   750
And, once rejoicing, never know them more.
   High from the summit of a craggy cliff,
Hung o'er the deep, such as amazing frowns
On utmost Kilda's shore, whose lonely race
Resign the setting sun to Indian worlds,
The royal eagle draws his vigorous young,
Strong-pounced, and ardent with paternal fire;
Now fit to raise a kingdom of their own,
He drives them from his fort, the towering seat,
For ages, of his empire; which, in peace,   760
Unstain'd he holds, while many a league to sea
He wings his course, and preys in distant isles.
   Should I my steps turn to the rural seat,
Whose lofty elms, and venerable oaks,
Invite the rook, who high amid the boughs,
In early Spring, his airy city builds,
And ceaseless caws amusive; there, well-pleased,
I might the various polity survey
Of the mix'd household kind. The careful hen
Calls all her chirping family around,   770
Fed and defended by the fearless cock;
Whose breast with ardour flames, as on he walks
Graceful, and crows defiance. In the pond,
The finely chequer'd duck before her train
Rows garrulous. The stately sailing swan
Gives out his snowy plumage to the gale;
And, arching proud his neck, with oary feet
Bears forward fierce, and guards his osier-isle,
Protective of his young. The turkey nigh,
Loud-threatening, reddens; while the peacock spreads   78)
His every-colour'd glory to the sun,
And swims in radiant majesty along.

O'er the whole homely scene, the cooing dove
Flies thick in amorous chase, and wanton rolls
The glancing eye, and turns the changeful neck.
   While thus the gentle tenants of the shade
Indulge their purer loves, the rougher world
Of brutes, below, rush furious into flame
And fierce desire.   Through all his lusty veins
The bull, deep-scorch'd, the raging passion feels.   790
Of pasture sick, and negligent of food,
Scarce seen, he wades among the yellow broom,
While o'er his ample sides the rambling sprays
Luxuriant shoot; or through the mazy wood
Dejected wanders, nor th' enticing bud
Crops, though it presses on his careless sense:
And oft, in jealous madd'ning fancy wrapt,
He seeks the fight; and, idly-butting, feigns
His rival gored in every knotty trunk.
Him should he meet, the bellowing war begins;   800
Their eyes flash fury; to the hollow'd earth,
Whence the sand flies, they mutter bloody deeds,
And, groaning deep, th' impetuous battle mix:
While the fair heifer, balmy-breathing, near,
Stands kindling up their rage.   The trembling steed,
With this hot impulse seized in every nerve,
Nor heeds the reign, nor hears the sounding thong;
Blows are not felt; but tossing high his head,
And by the well-known joy to distant plains
Attracted strong, all wild he bursts away;   810
O'er rocks, and woods, and craggy mountains flies;
And, neighing, on the aerial summit takes
Th' exciting gale; then, steep-descending, cleaves
The headlong torrents foaming down the hills,
Even where the madness of the straiten'd stream
Turns in black eddies round; such is the force
With which his frantic heart and sinews swell.
   Nor undelighted by the boundless Spring
Are the broad monsters of the foaming deep:
From the deep ooze and gelid cavern roused,   820

They flounce and tumble in unwieldy joy.
Dire were the strain, and dissonant, to sing
The cruel raptures of the savage kind:
How by this flame their native wrath sublimed,
They roam, amid the fury of their heart,
The far-resounding waste in fiercer bands,
And growl their horrid loves. But this the theme
I sing, enraptured, to the British Fair,
Forbids, and leads me to the mountain-brow,
Where sits the shepherd on the grassy turf,   830
Inhaling, healthful, the descending sun.
Around him feeds his many-bleating flock,
Of various cadence; and his sportive lambs,
This way and that convolved, in friskful glee,
Their frolics play. And now the sprightly race
Invites them forth; when swift, the signal given,
They start away, and sweep the massy mound
That runs around the hill; the rampart once
Of iron war, in ancient barbarous times,
When disunited Britain ever bled,   840
Lost in eternal broil: ere yet she grew
To this deep-laid indissoluble state,
Where Wealth and Commerce lift their golden heads;
And o'er our labours, Liberty and Law,
Impartial, watch; the wonder of a world!
    What is this mighty Breath, ye sages! say,
That, in a powerful language, felt, not heard,
Instructs the fowls of Heaven; and through their breast
These arts of love diffuses? What, but God?
Inspiring God! who, boundless Spirit all,   850
And unremitting Energy, pervades,
Adjusts, sustains, and agitates the whole.
He ceaseless works alone; and yet alone
Seems not to work: with such perfection framed
Is this complex stupendous scheme of things.
    But, though conceal'd, to every purer eye
Th' informing Author in his works appears:.
Chief, lovely Spring! in thee, and thy soft scenes,

The Smiling God is seen; while water, earth,
And air attest his bounty; which exalts   860
The brute-creation to this finer thought,
And annual melts their undesigning hearts
Profusely thus in tenderness and joy.
   Still let my song a nobler note assume,
And sing th' infusive force of Spring on Man;
When heaven and earth, as if contending, vie
To raise his being, and serene his soul.
Can he forbear to join the general smile
Of Nature? Can fierce passions vex his breast,
While every gale is peace, and every grove   870
Is melody? Hence! from the bounteous walks
Of flowing Spring, ye sordid sons of earth,
Hard, and unfeeling of another's wo;
Or only lavish to yourselves; away!
But come, ye generous minds! in whose wide thought
Of all his works, Creative Bounty burns
With warmest beam; and on your open front
And liberal eye, sits, from his dark retreat
Inviting modest Want. Nor, till invoked,
Can restless goodness wait; your active search   880
Leaves no cold wintry corner unexplored;
Like silent-working Heaven, surprising oft
The lonely heart with unexpected good.
   For you, the roving spirit of the wind
Blows Spring abroad; for you, the teeming clouds
Descend in gladsome plenty o'er the world;
And the sun sheds his kindest rays for you,
Ye flower of human race! in these green days,
Reviving Sickness lifts her languid head;   .
Life flows afresh; and young-eyed Health exalts   890
The whole creation round. Contentment walks
The sunny glade, and feels an inward bliss
Spring o'er his mind, beyond the power of kings
To purchase. Pure serenity apace
Induces thought, and contemplation still.
By swift degrees the love of Nature works,

And warms the bosom; till at last sublimed
To rapture, and enthusiastic heat,
We feel the present Deity, and taste
The joy of God to see a happy world!   900
    These are the sacred feelings of thy heart,
Thy heart inform'd by reason's purer ray,
O Lyttelton, the friend! thy passions thus
And meditation vary, as at large,
Courting the muse, through Hagley Park thou stray'st;
Thy British Tempe! There along the dale,
With woods o'erhung, and shagg'd with mossy rocks,
Whence on each hand the gushing waters play,
And down the rough cascade white-dashing fall,
Or gleam in lengthen'd vista through the trees,   910
You silent steal; or sit beneath the shade
Of solemn oaks, that tuft the swelling mounts
Thrown graceful round by Nature's careless hand,
And pensive listen to the various voice
Of rural peace: the herds, the flocks, the birds,
The hollow-whispering breeze, the plaint of rills,
That, purling down amid the twisted roots
Which creep around, their dewy murmurs shake
On the soothed ear. From these abstracted, oft
You wander through the philosophic world;   920
Where, in bright train, continual wonders rise,
Or to the curious or the pious eye.
And oft, conducted by historic truth,
You tread the long extent of backward time;
Planning, with warm benevolence of mind,
And honest zeal unwarp'd by party-rage,
Britannia's weal; how from the venal gulf
To raise her virtue, and her arts revive.
Or, turning thence thy view, these graver thoughts
The Muses charm: while, with sure taste refined,   93)
You draw th' inspiring breath of ancient song;
Till nobly rises, emulous, thy own.
    Perhaps thy loved Lucinda shares thy walk,
With soul to thine attuned. Then Nature all

Wears to the lover's eye a look of love;
And all the tumult of a guilty world,
Tost by ungenerous passions, sinks away.
The tender heart is animated peace;
And as it pours its copious treasures forth,
In varied converse, softening every theme,   940
You, frequent-pausing, turn, and from her eyes,
Where meeken'd sense, and amiable grace,
And lively sweetness dwell, enraptured, drink
That nameless spirit of ethereal joy,
Unutterable happiness! which love,
Alone, bestows, and on a favour'd few.
Meantime you gain the height, from whose fair brow
The bursting prospect spreads immense around,
And snatch'd o'er hill and dale, and wood and lawn,
And verdant field, and dark'ning heath between,   950
And villages embosom'd soft in trees,
And spiry towns by surging columns mark'd
Of household smoke, your eye excursive roams:
Wide-stretching from the Hall, in whose kind haunt
The hospitable Genius lingers still,
To where the broken landscape, by degrees,
Ascending, roughens into rigid hills;
O'er which the Cambrian mountains, like far clouds
That skirt the blue horizon, dusky rise.
    Flush'd by the spirit of the genial year,   960
Now from the virgin's cheek a fresher bloom
Shoots, less and less, the live carnation round;
Her lips blush deeper sweets; she breathes of youth;
The shining moisture swells into her eyes,
In brighter flow; her wishing bosom heaves,
With palpitations wild; kind tumults seize
Her veins, and all her yielding soul is love.
From the keen gaze her lover turns away,
Full of the dear ecstatic power, and sick
With sighing languishment. Ah then, ye fair!   970
Be greatly cautious of your sliding hearts:
Dare not th' infectious sigh; the pleading look,

Downcast, and low, in meek submission drest,
But full of guile. Let not the fervent tongue,
Prompt to deceive, with adulation smooth,
Gain on your purposed will. Nor in the bower,
Where woodbines flaunt, and roses shed a couch,
While evening draws her crimson curtains round,
Trust your soft minutes with betraying Man.
  And let th' aspiring youth beware of love,   980
Of the smooth glance beware; for 'tis too late,
When on his heart the torrent-softness pours;
Then wisdom prostrate lies, and fading fame
Dissolves in air away; while the fond soul,
Wrapt in gay visions of unreal bliss,
Still paints th' illusive form; the kindling grace;
Th' enticing smile; the modest-seeming eye,
Beneath whose beauteous beams, belying heaven,
Lurk searchless cunning, cruelty, and death:
And still, false-warbling in his cheated ear,   990
Her syren voice, enchanting, draws him on
To guileful shores, and meads of fatal joy.
  Even present, in the very lap of love
Inglorious laid; while music flows around,
Perfumes, and oils, and wine, and wanton hours;
Amid the roses fierce Repentance rears
Her snaky crest: a quick-returning pang
Shoots through the conscious heart; where honour still,
And great design, against th' oppressive load
Of luxury, by fits, impatient heave.   1000
  But absent, what fantastic woes, aroused,
Rage in each thought, by restless musing fed,
Chill the warm cheek, and blast the bloom of life!
Neglected fortune flies; and sliding swift,
Prone into ruin, fall his scorn'd affairs.
'Tis nought but gloom around: the darken'd sun
Loses his light: the rosy-bosom'd Spring
To weeping fancy pines; and yon bright arch,
Contracted, bends into a dusky vault.
All Nature fades extinct; and she alone   1010
D

Heard, felt, and seen, possesses every thought,
Fills every sense, and pants in every vein.
  Books are but formal dulness, tedious friends;
And sad amid the social band he sits,
Lonely, and unattentive. From his tongue
Th' unfinish'd period falls: while borne away
On swelling thought, his wafted spirit flies
To the vain bosom of his distant fair;
And leaves the semblance of a lover, fix'd
In melancholy site, with head declined   1020
And love-dejected eyes. Sudden he starts,
Shook from his tender trance, and restless runs
To glimmering shades, and sympathetic glooms,
Where the dun umbrage o'er the falling stream,
Romantic, hangs; there through the pensive dusk
Strays, in heart-thrilling meditation lost,
Indulging all to love: or on the bank
Thrown, amid drooping lilies, swells the breeze
With sighs unceasing, and the brook with tears.
  Thus in soft anguish he consumes the day,   1030
Nor quits his deep retirement, till the Moon
Peeps through the chambers of the fleecy East,
Enlighten'd by degrees, and in her train
Leads on the gentle hours; then forth he walks,
Beneath the trembling languish of her beam,
With soften'd soul, and woos the bird of eve
To mingle woes with his: or, while the world,
And all the sons of Care lie hush'd in sleep,
Associates with the midnight shadows drear;
And, sighing to the lonely taper, pours   1040
His idly-tortured heart into the page,
Meant for the moving messenger of love;
Where rapture burns on rapture, every line
With rising frenzy fired. But if on bed
Delirious flung, sleep from his pillow flies;
All night he tosses, nor the balmy power   ·
In any posture finds; till the grey morn
Lifts her pale lustre on the paler wretch,

Exanimate by love: and then perhaps
Exhausted nature sinks a while to rest, 1050
Still interrupted by distracted dreams,
That o'er the sick imagination rise,
And in black colours paint the mimic scene.
  Oft with th' enchantress of his soul he talks;
Sometimes in crowds distress'd; or if retired
To secret winding flower-enwoven bowers,
Far from the dull impertinence of Man,
Just as he, credulous, his endless cares
Begins to lose in blind, oblivious love,
Snatch'd from her yielded hand, he knows not how. 1060
Through forests huge, and long untravell'd heaths,
With desolation brown, he wanders waste,
In night and tempest wrapt; or shrinks aghast,
Back, from the bending precipice; or wades—
The turbid stream below, and strives to reach
The farther shore; where, succourless and sad,
She with extended arms his aid implores;
But strives in vain; borne by th' outrageous flood
To distance down, he rides the ridgy wave,
Or whelm'd beneath the boiling eddy sinks. 1070
  These are the charming agonies of love,
Whose misery delights. But through the heart
Should jealousy its venom once diffuse,
'Tis then delightful misery no more;
But agony unmix'd, incessant gall,
Corroding every thought, and blasting all
Love's paradise. Ye fairy prospects, then,
Ye beds of roses, and ye bowers of joy,
Farewell! Ye gleamings of departed peace,
Shine out your last! The yellow-tinging plague 1080
Internal vision taints, and in a night
Of livid gloom imagination wraps.
Ah then, instead of love-enliven'd cheeks,
Of sunny features, and of ardent eyes
With flowing rapture bright, dark looks succeed,
Suffused and glaring with untender fire;

A clouded aspect, and a burning cheek,
Where the whole poison'd soul, malignant, sits,
And frightens love away. Ten thousand fears
Invented wild, ten thousand frantic views   1090
Of horrid rivals, hanging on the charms
For which he melts in fondness, eat him up
With fervent anguish, and consuming rage.
In vain reproaches lend their idle aid,
Deceitful pride, and resolution frail,
Giving false peace a moment. Fancy pours,
Afresh, her beauties on his busy thought,
Her first endearments twining round the soul,
With all the witchcraft of ensnaring love.
Straight the fierce storm involves his mind anew,   1100
Flames through the nerves, and boils along the veins;
While anxious doubt distracts the tortured heart:
For even the sad assurance of his fears
Were ease to what he feels. Thus the warm youth,
Whom Love deludes into his thorny wilds,
Through flowery-tempting paths, or leads a life
Of fever'd rapture, or of cruel care;
His brightest flames extinguish'd all, and all
His lively moments running down to waste.
    But happy they ! the happiest of their kind !   1110
Whom gentle stars unite, and in one fate
Their hearts, their fortunes, and their beings blend.
'Tis not the coarser tie of human laws,
Unnatural oft, and foreign to the mind,
That binds their peace; but harmony itself,
Attuning all their passions into love;
Where friendship full-exerts her softest power,
Perfect esteem enliven'd by desire
Ineffable, and sympathy of soul;
Thought meeting thought, and will preventing will, 1120
With boundless confidence: for nought but love
Can answer love, and render bliss secure.
    Let him, ungenerous, who alone intent
To bless himself, from sordid parents buys

The loathing virgin, in eternal care,
Well-merited, consume his nights and days;
Let barbarous nations, whose inhuman love
Is wild desire, fierce as the suns they feel;
Let Eastern tyrants, from the light of Heaven
Seclude their bosom-slaves, meanly possess'd   1130
Of a mere lifeless, violated form;
While those whom love cements in holy faith,
And equal transport, free as Nature live,
Disdaining fear. What is the world to them,
Its pomp, its pleasure, and its nonsense all?
Who in each other clasp whatever fair
High fancy forms, and lavish hearts can wish;
Something than beauty dearer, should they look
Or on the mind, or mind-illumined face;
Truth, goodness, honour, harmony, and love,   1140
The richest bounty of indulgent Heaven.
Meantime a smiling offspring rises round,
And mingles both their graces. By degrees,
The human blossom blows; and every day,
Soft as it rolls along, shows some new charm,
The father's lustre, and the mother's bloom.
Then infant reason grows apace, and calls
For the kind hand of an assiduous care.
    Delightful task! to rear the tender thought,
To teach the young idea how to shoot,   1150
To pour the fresh instruction o'er the mind,
To breathe th' enlivening spirit, and to fix
The generous purpose in the glowing breast.
Oh speak the joy! ye, whom the sudden tear
Surprises often, while ye look around,
And nothing strikes your eye but sights of bliss,
All various nature pressing on the heart;
An elegant sufficiency, content,
Retirement, rural quiet, friendship, books,
Ease and alternate labour, useful life,   1160
Progressive virtue, and approving Heaven.
    These are the matchless joys of virtuous love;

And thus their moments fly. The Seasons thus,
As ceaseless round a jarring world they roll,
Still find them happy; and consenting Spring
Sheds her own rosy garland on their heads:
Till evening comes at last, serene and mild;
When, after the long vernal day of life,
Enamour'd more, as more remembrance swells
With many a proof of recollected love,   1170
Together down they sink in social sleep;
Together freed, their gentle spirits fly
To scenes where love and bliss immortal reign.

SUMMER.

FROM brightening fields of ether fair disclosed,
Child of the Sun, refulgent Summer comes,
In pride of youth, and felt through Nature's depth:
He comes, attended by the sultry hours,
And ever-fanning breezes, on his way;
While, from his ardent look, the turning Spring
Averts her blushful face: and earth, and skies,
All-smiling, to his hot dominion leaves.
    Hence, let me haste into the mid-wood shade,
Where scarce a sunbeam wanders through the gloom: 10
And on the dark-green grass, beside the brink
Of haunted stream, that, by the roots of oak
Rolls o'er the rocky channel, lie at large,
And sing the glories of the circling year.
    Come, Inspiration! from thy hermit-seat,

By mortal seldom found: may fancy dare,
From thy fix'd, serious eye, and raptured glance
Shot on surrounding Heaven, to steal one look
Creative of the Poet, every power
Exalting to an ecstacy of soul.   20
    And thou, my youthful Muse's early friend,
In whom the human graces all unite:
Pure light of mind, and tenderness of heart:
Genius, and wisdom; the gay social sense,
By decency chastised; goodness and wit,
In seldom-meeting harmony combined;
Unblemish'd honour, and an active zeal
For Britain's glory, Liberty, and Man:
O Dodington! attend my rural song,
Stoop to my theme, inspirit every line,   30
And teach me to deserve thy just applause.
    With what an awful world-revolving power
Were first th' unwieldy planets launch'd along
Th' illimitable void!   Thus to remain,
Amid the flux of many thousand years,
That oft has swept the toiling race of Men
And all their labour'd monuments away,
Firm, unremitting, matchless, in their course;
To the kind-temper'd change of night and day,
And of the Seasons ever stealing round,   40
Minutely faithful: Such th' all-perfect Hand!
That poised, impels, and rules the steady whole.
    When now no more th' alternate Twins are fired,
And Cancer reddens with the solar blaze,
Short is the doubtful empire of the night;
And soon, observant of approaching day,
The meek-eyed Morn appears, mother of dews,
At first faint-gleaming in the dappled East:
Till far o'er ether spreads the widening glow;
And, from before the lustre of her face,   50
White break the clouds away.   With quicken'd step,
Brown Night retires: young Day pours in apace,
And opens all the lawny prospect wide.

SUMMER

'tis now summer mild,
. . the dew breath warm, and . . . . .
H. . k. . . . . majesty . . .
. . . .

The dripping rock, the mountain's misty top,
Swell on the sight, and brighten with the dawn;
Blue, through the dusk, the smoking currents shine;
And from the bladed field the fearful hare
Limps, awkward: while along the forest glade
The wild deer trip, and often turning, gaze
At early passenger. Music awakes   60
The native voice of undissembled joy;
And thick around the woodland hymns arise.
Roused by the cock, the soon-clad shepherd leaves
His mossy cottage, where with peace he dwells;
And from the crowded fold, in order, drives
His flock, to taste the verdure of the morn.
    Falsely luxurious, will not man awake;
And, springing from the bed of sloth, enjoy
The cool, the fragrant, and the silent hour,
To meditation due and sacred song?   70
For is there aught in sleep can charm the wise?
To lie in dead oblivion, losing half
The fleeting moments of too short a life;
Total extinction of th' enlighten'd soul!
Or else to feverish vanity alive,
Wilder'd, and tossing through distemper'd dreams?
Who would in such a gloomy state remain
Longer than Nature craves: when every Muse
And every blooming pleasure wait without,
To bless the wildly-devious morning-walk?   80
    But yonder comes the powerful King of Day,
Rejoicing in the East. The lessening cloud,
The kindling azure, and the mountain's brow
Illumed with fluid gold, his near approach
Betoken glad. Lo! now, apparent all,
Aslant the dew-bright earth, and colour'd air,
He looks in boundless majesty abroad;
And sheds the shining day, that burnish'd plays
On rocks, and hills, and towers, and wand'ring streams,
High-gleaming from afar. Prime cheerer Light!   90
Of all material beings first, and best!

Efflux divine! Nature's resplendent robe!
Without whose vesting beauty all were wrapt
In unessential gloom; and thou, O Sun!
Soul of surrounding worlds! in whom best seen
Shines out thy Maker! may I sing of thee?
  'Tis by thy secret, strong attractive force,
As with a chain indissoluble bound,
Thy System rolls entire: from the far bourne
Of utmost Saturn, wheeling wide his round   100
Of thirty years; to Mercury, whose disk
Can scarce be caught by philosophic eye,
Lost in the near effulgence of thy blaze.
  Informer of the planetary train!
Without whose quickening glance their cumbrous orbs
Were brute unlovely mass, inert and dead,
And not, as now, the green abodes of life!
How many forms of being wait on thee,
Inhaling spirit! from th' unfetter'd mind,
By thee sublimed, down to the daily race,   110
The mixing myriads of thy setting beam.
  The vegetable world is also thine,
Parent of Seasons! who the pomp precede
That waits thy throne; as through thy vast domain,
Annual, along the bright ecliptic road,
In world-rejoicing state, it moves sublime.
Meantime, th' expecting nations, circled gay,
With all the various tribes of foodful earth,
Implore thy bounty, or send grateful up
A common hymn: while, round thy beaming car,   120
High-seen, the Seasons lead, in sprightly dance
Harmonious knit, the rosy-finger'd Hours;
The Zephyrs floating loose; the timely Rains;
Of bloom ethereal the light-footed Dews;
And soften'd into joy the surly Storms.
These, in successive turn, with lavish hand,
Shower every beauty, every fragrance shower,
Herbs, flowers, and fruits; till, kindling at thy touch,
From land to land is flush'd the vernal year.

Nor to the surface of enliven'd earth,   130
Graceful with hills and dales, and leafy woods,
Her liberal tresses, is thy force confined:
But, to the bowell'd cavern darting deep,
The mineral kinds confess thy mighty power.
Effulgent, hence, the veiny marble shines;
Hence Labour draws his tools; hence burnished War
Gleams on the day; the nobler works of Peace
Hence bless mankind, and generous Commerce binds
The round of nations in a golden chain.
    Th' unfruitful rock itself, impregn'd by thee,   140
In dark retirement forms the lucid stone.
The lively Diamond drinks thy purest rays,
Collected light, compact; that, polish'd bright,
And all its native lustre let abroad,
Dares, as it sparkles on the fair-one's breast,
With vain ambition emulate her eyes.
At thee the Ruby lights its deepening glow,
And with a waving radiance inward flames.
From thee the Sapphire, solid ether, takes
Its hue cerulean; and of evening tinct,   150
The purple-streaming Amethyst is thine.
With thy own smile the yellow Topaz burns.
Nor deeper verdure dies the robe of Spring,
When first she gives it to the southern gale,
Than the green Emerald shows. But, all combined,
Thick through the whitening Opal play thy beams;
Or, flying several from its surface, form
A trembling variance of revolving hues,
As the site varies in the gazer's hand.
    The very dead creation, from thy touch,   160
Assumes a mimic life. By thee refined,
In brighter mazes the relucent stream
Plays o'er the mead. The precipice abrupt,
Projecting horror on the blacken'd flood,
Softens at thy return. The desert joys
Wildly, through all his melancholy bounds.

Rude ruins glitter; and the briny deep,
Seen from some pointed promontory's top,
Far to the blue horizon's utmost verge,
Restless, reflects a floating gleam.   But this,   170
And all the much-transported Muse can sing,
Are to thy beauty, dignity, and use,
Unequal far; great delegated source
Of light, and life, and grace, and joy below!
  How shall I then attempt to sing of Him!
Who, Light Himself, in uncreated light
Invested deep, dwells awfully retired
From mortal eye, or angel's purer ken;
Whose single smile has, from the first of time,
Fill'd, overflowing, all those lamps of Heaven,   180
That beam for ever through the boundless sky:
But, should he hide his face, th' astonish'd sun,
And all the extinguish'd stars, would loosening reel
Wide from their spheres, and Chaos come again.
  And yet, was every faltering tongue of Man,
Almighty Father! silent in thy praise,
Thy works themselves would raise a general voice,
Even in the depth of solitary woods
By human foot untrod; proclaim thy power,
And to the quire celestial Thee resound,   190
Th' eternal cause, support, and end of all!
  To me be Nature's volume broad-display'd;
And to peruse its all-instructing page,
Or, haply catching inspiration thence,
Some easy passage, raptured, to translate,
My sole delight; as through the falling glooms
Pensive I stray, or with the rising dawn
On Fancy's eagle-wing excursive soar.
  Now, flaming up the heavens, the potent sun
Melts into limpid air the high-raised clouds,   200
And morning fogs, that hover'd round the hills
In party-colour'd bands; till wide unveil'd
The face of Nature shines, from where earth seems,
Far-stretch'd around, to meet the bending sphere.

Half in a blush of clust'ring roses lost,
Dew-dropping Coolness to the shade retires;
There, on the verdant turf, or flowery bed,
By gelid founts and careless rills to muse;
While tyrant Heat, dispreading through the sky,
With rapid sway, his burning influence darts   210
On Man, and beast, and herb, and tepid stream.
   Who can unpitying see the flowery race,
Shed by the morn, their new-flush'd bloom resign,
Before the parching beam? So fade the fair,
When fevers revel through their azure veins.
But one, the lofty follower of the sun,
Sad when he sets, shuts up her yellow leaves,
Drooping all night; and, when he warm returns,
Points her enamour'd bosom to his ray.
   Home, from his morning task, the swain retreats;   220
His flock before him stepping to the fold;
While the full-udder'd mother lows around
The cheerful cottage, then expecting food,
The food of innocence, and health! The daw,
The rook, and magpie, to the grey-grown oaks
That the calm village in their verdant arms,
Sheltering, embrace, direct their lazy flight;
Where on the mingling boughs they sit embower'd,
All the hot noon, till cooler hours arise.
Faint, underneath, the household fowls convene;   230
And, in a corner of the buzzing shade,
The house-dog, with the vacant greyhound, lies,
Outstretch'd, and sleepy. In his slumbers one
Attacks the nightly thief, and one exults
O'er hill and dale; till, waken'd by the wasp,
They starting snap. Nor shall the Muse disdain
To let the little noisy summer-race
Live in her lay, and flutter through her song:
Not mean though simple; to the sun ally'd,
From him they draw their animating fire.   240
   Waked by his warmer ray, the reptile young
Come winged abroad; by the light air upborne,

Lighter, and full of soul.   From every chink,
And secret corner, where they slept away
The wintry storms; or rising from their tombs,
To higher life; by myriads, forth at once,
Swarming they pour; of all the varied hues
Their beauty-beaming parent can disclose.
    Ten thousand forms! ten thousand different tribes!
People the blaze.   To sunny waters some   250
By fatal instinct fly; where on the pool
They, sportive, wheel; or, sailing down the stream,
Are snatch'd immediate by the quick-eyed trout,
Or darting salmon.   Through the greenwood glade
Some love to stray; there lodged, amused, and fed,
In the fresh leaf.   Luxurious, others make
The meads their choice, and visit every flower,
And every latent herb: for the sweet task,
To propagate their kinds, and where to wrap,
In what soft beds, their young yet undisclosed,   260
Employs their tender care.   Some to the house,
The fold, and dairy, hungry, bend their flight;
Sip round the pail, or taste the curdling cheese:
Oft, inadvertent, from the milky stream
They meet their fate; or, weltering in the bowl,
With powerless wings around them wrapt, expire.
    But chief to heedless flies the window proves
A constant death; where, gloomily retired,
The villain spider lives, cunning, and fierce,
Mixture abhorr'd! Amid a mangled heap   270
Of carcasses, in eager watch he sits,
O'erlooking all his waving snares around.
Near the dire cell the dreadless wanderer oft
Passes, as oft the ruffian shows his front;
The prey at last ensnared, he dreadful darts,
With rapid glide, along the leaning line;
And, fixing in the wretch his cruel fangs,
Strikes backward grimly pleased: the fluttering wing,
And shriller sound, declare extreme distress,
And ask the helping hospitable hand.   280

Resounds the living surface of the ground:
Nor undelightful is the ceaseless hum,
To him who muses through the woods at noon;
Or drowsy shepherd, as he lies reclined,
With half-shut eyes, beneath the floating shade
Of willows grey, close-crowding o'er the brook.
  Gradual, from these what numerous kinds descend,
Evading even the microscopic eye!
Full Nature swarms with life; one wondrous mass
Of animals, or atoms organised,   290
Waiting the vital Breath, when Parent-Heaven
Shall bid his spirit blow. The hoary fen,
In putrid streams, emits the living cloud
Of pestilence. Through subterranean cells,
Where searching sunbeams scarce can find a way,
Earth animated heaves. The flowery leaf
Wants not its soft inhabitants. Secure,
Within its winding citadel, the stone
Holds multitudes. But chief the forest-boughs,
That dance unnumber'd to the playful breeze,   300
The downy orchard, and the melting pulp
Of mellow fruit, the nameless nations feed
Of evanescent insects. Where the pool
Stands mantled o'er with green, invisible,
Amid the floating verdure millions stray.
  Each liquid, too, whether it pierces, soothes,
Inflames, refreshes, or exalts the taste,
With various forms abounds. Nor is the stream
Of purest crystal, nor the lucid air,
Though one transparent vacancy it seems,   310
Void of their unseen people. These, conceal'd
By the kind art of forming Heaven, escape
The grosser eye of Man: for, if the worlds
In worlds enclosed should on his senses burst,
From cates ambrosial, and the nectar'd bowl,
He would abhorrent turn; and in dead night,
When silence sleeps o'er all, be stunn'd with noise.
  Let no presuming impious railer tax

Creative Wisdom, as if aught was form'd
In vain, or not for admirable ends.   320
Shall little haughty ignorance pronounce
His works unwise, of which the smallest part
Exceeds the narrow vision of her mind?
As if upon a full-proportion'd dome,
On swelling columns heaved, the pride of art!
A critic-fly, whose feeble ray scarce spreads
An inch around, with blind presumption bold,
Should dare to tax the structure of the whole.
And lives the Man, whose universal eye
Has swept at once th' unbounded scheme of things;   330
Mark'd their dependence so, and firm accord,
As with unfaltering accent to conclude
That this availeth nought? Has any seen
The mighty chain of beings, lessening down
From Infinite Perfection to the brink
Of dreary Nothing, desolate abyss!
From which astonish'd thought, recoiling, turns?
Till then alone let zealous praise ascend,
And hymns of holy wonder, to that Power,
Whose wisdom shines as lovely on our minds,   340
As on our smiling eyes his servant-sun.
    Thick in yon stream of light, a thousand ways,
Upward and downward, thwarting, and convolved,
The quivering nations sport; till, tempest-wing'd,
Fierce Winter sweeps them from the face of day.
Even so luxurious Men, unheeding, pass
An idle summer life in fortune's shine;
A season's glitter! Thus they flutter on
From toy to toy, from vanity to vice;
Till, blown away by death, oblivion comes   350
Behind, and strikes them from the book of life,
    Now swarms the village o'er the jovial mead:
The rustic youth, brown with meridian toil,
Healthful and strong; full as the summer-rose
Blown by prevailing suns, the ruddy maid,
Half-naked, swelling on the sight, and all

Her kindled graces burning o'er her cheek.
Even stooping age is here; and infant-hands
Trail the long rake, or, with the fragrant load
O'ercharged, amid the kind oppression roll.   360
Wide flies the tedded grain; all in a row
Advancing broad, or wheeling round the field,
They spread the breathing harvest to the sun,
That throws refreshful round a rural smell:
Or, as they rake the green-appearing ground,
And drive the dusky wave along the mead,
The russet hay-cock rises thick behind,
In order gay.   While heard from dale to dale,
Waking the breeze, resounds the blended voice
Of happy labour, love, and social glee.   370
    Or rushing thence, in one diffusive band,
They drive the troubled flocks, by many a dog
Compell'd, to where the mazy-running brook
Forms a deep pool; this bank abrupt and high,
And that fair-spreading in a pebbled shore.
Urged to the giddy brink, much is the toil,
The clamour much, of men, and boys, and dogs,
Ere the soft fearful people to the flood
Commit their woolly sides.   And oft the swain,
On some impatient seizing, hurls them in: 380
Embolden'd then, nor hesitating more,
Fast, fast they plunge amid the flashing wave,
And panting labour to the farthest shore.
Repeated this, till deep the well-wash'd fleece
Has drunk the flood, and from his lively haunt
The trout is banish'd by the sordid stream;
Heavy, and dripping, to the breezy brow
Slow move the harmless race: where, as they spread
Their swelling treasures to the sunny ray,
Inly disturb'd, and wondering what this wild   390
Outrageous tumult means, their loud complaints
The country fill; and toss'd from rock to rock,
Incessant bleatings run around the hills.
    At last, of snowy white, the gather'd flocks
E

Are in the wattled pen innumerous press'd,
Head above head; and, ranged in lusty rows
The shepherds sit, and whet the sounding shears.
The housewife waits to roll her fleecy stores,
With all her gay-drest maids attending round.
One, chief, in gracious dignity enthroned,   400
Shines o'er the rest, the past'ral queen, and rays
Her smiles, sweet-beaming, on her shepherd-king;
While the glad circle round them yield their souls
To festive mirth, and wit that knows no gall.
Meantime, their joyous task goes on apace:
Some mingling stir the melted tar, and some,
Deep on the new-shorn vagrant's heaving side,
To stamp his master's cypher ready stand:
Others th' unwilling wether drag along;
And, glorying in his might, the sturdy boy   410
Holds by the twisted horns th' indignant ram.
Behold, where bound, and of its robe bereft,
By needy Man, that all-depending lord,
How meek, how patient, the mild creature lies!
What softness in its melancholy face,
What dumb complaining innocence appears!
Fear not, ye gentle tribes, 'tis not the knife
Of horrid slaughter that is o'er you waved;
No, 'tis the tender swain's well-guided shears,
Who having now, to pay his annual care,   420
Borrow'd your fleece, to you a cumbrous load,
Will send you bounding to your hills again.
  A simple scene! yet hence BRITANNIA sees
Her solid grandeur rise: hence she commands
Th' exalted stores of every brighter clime,
The treasures of the Sun without his rage;
Hence, fervent all, with culture, toil, and arts,
Wide glows her land: her dreadful thunder hence
Rides o'er the waves sublime; and now, even now,
Impending hangs o'er Gallia's humbled coast;   430
Hence rules the circling deep, and awes the world.
  'Tis raging Noon; and, vertical, the Sun

Darts on the head direct his forceful rays.
O'er heaven and earth, far as the ranging eye
Can sweep, a dazzling deluge reigns; and all
From pole to pole is undistinguish'd blaze.
In vain the sight, dejected to the ground,
Stoops for relief; thence hot ascending steams
And keen reflection pain. Deep to the root
Of vegetation parch'd, the cleaving fields   440
And slippery lawn an arid hue disclose;
Blast Fancy's bloom, and wither even the Soul.
Echo no more returns the cheerful sound
Of sharpening scythe: the mower sinking heaps
O'er him the humid hay, with flowers perfumed;
And scarce a chirping grasshopper is heard
Through the dumb mead. Distressful Nature pants.
The very streams look languid from afar;
Or, through th' unshelter'd glade, impatient, seem
To hurl into the covert of the grove.   450
    All-conquering Heat! oh intermit thy wrath,
And on my throbbing temples potent thus
Beam not so fierce! incessant still you flow,
And still another fervent flood succeeds,
Pour'd on the head profuse. In vain I sigh,
And restless turn, and look around for Night:
Night is far off; and hotter hours approach.
Thrice happy he! who, on the sunless side
Of a romantic mountain, forest-crown'd,
Beneath the whole collected shade reclines: 460
Or in the gelid caverns, woodbine-wrought,
And fresh-bedew'd with ever-spouting streams,
Sits coolly calm; while all the world without,
Unsatisfied, and sick, tosses in noon.
Emblem instructive of the virtuous man,
Who keeps his temper'd mind serene, and pure,
And every passion aptly harmonised,
Amid a jarring world with vice inflamed.
    Welcome, ye shades! ye bowery thickets, hail!
Ye lofty pines! ye venerable oaks!   .   470

Ye ashes wild, resounding o'er the steep!
Delicious is your shelter to the soul,
As to the hunted hart the sallying spring,
Or stream full-flowing, that his swelling sides
Laves, as he floats along the herbaged brink.
Cool, through the nerves, your pleasing comfort glides;
The heart beats glad; the fresh-expanded eye
And ear resume their watch; the sinews knit;
And life shoots swift through all the lighten'd limbs.

    Around th' adjoining brook, that purls along   480
The vocal grove, now fretting o'er a rock,
Now scarcely moving through a reedy pool,
Now starting to a sudden stream, and now
Gently diffused into a limpid plain,
A various group the herds and flocks compose,
Rural confusion!   On the grassy bank
Some ruminating lie; while others stand
Half in the flood, and often bending sip
The circling surface.   In the middle droops
The strong laborious ox, of honest front,   490
Which incomposed he shakes; and from his sides
The troublous insects lashes with his tail,
Returning still.   Amid his subjects safe,
Slumbers the monarch-swain; his careless arm
Thrown round his head, on downy moss sustain'd;
Here laid his scrip, with wholesome viands fill'd;
There, listening every noise, his watchful dog.

    Light fly his slumbers, if perchance a flight
Of angry gad-flies fasten on the herd;
That startling scatters from the shallow brook,   500
In search of lavish stream.   Tossing the foam,
They scorn the keeper's voice, and scour the plain,
Through all the bright severity of noon;
While, from their labouring breasts, a hollow moan
Proceeding, runs low-bellowing round the hills.

    Oft in this season, too, the horse, provoked,
While his big sinews full of spirits swell,
Trembling with vigour, in the heat of blood,

Springs the high fence; and, o'er the field effused,
Darts on the gloomy flood, with steadfast eye,   510
And heart estranged to fear: his nervous chest,
Luxuriant, and erect, the seat of strength!
Bears down th' opposing stream: quenchless his thirst;
He takes the river at redoubled draughts;
And with wide nostrils, snorting, skims the wave.
  Still let me pierce into the midnight depth
Of yonder grove, of wildest, largest growth;
That, forming high in air a woodland quire,
Nods o'er the mount beneath. At every step,
Solemn, and slow, the shadows blacker fall,   520
And all is awful listening gloom around.
  These are the haunts of Meditation; these
The scenes where ancient bards th' inspiring breath,
Ecstatic, felt; and, from this world retired,
Conversed with angels, and immortal forms,
On gracious errands bent; to save the fall
Of virtue struggling on the brink of vice;
In waking whispers, and repeated dreams,
To hint pure thought, and warn the favour'd soul,
For future trials fated to prepare;   530
To prompt the poet, who devoted gives
His muse to better themes; to soothe the pangs
Of dying worth, and from the patriot's breast
(Backward to mingle in detested war,
But foremost when engaged) to turn the death;
And numberless such offices of love,
Daily, and nightly, zealous to perform.
  Shook sudden from the bosom of the sky,
A thousand shapes or glide athwart the dusk,
Or stalk majestic on. Deep-roused, I feel   540
A sacred terror, a severe delight,
Creep through my mortal frame; and thus, methinks,
A voice, than human more, th' abstracted ear
Of fancy strikes:—" Be not of us afraid,
Poor kindred Man! thy fellow-creatures, we
From the same Parent-Power our beings drew,

The same our Lord, and laws, and great pursuit.
Once some of us, like thee, through stormy life,
Toil'd, tempest-beaten, ere we could attain
This holy calm, this harmony of mind,　　　　550
Where purity and peace immingle charms.
Then fear not us; but with responsive song,
Amid these dim recesses, undisturb'd
By noisy folly and discordant vice,
Of Nature sing with us, and Nature's God.
Here frequent at the visionary hour,
When musing midnight reigns or silent noon,
Angelic harps are in full concert heard,
And voices chanting from the wood-crown'd hill,
The deepening dale, or inmost sylvan glade:　　　　560
A privilege bestow'd by us, alone,
On contemplation or the hallow'd ear
Of poet, swelling to seraphic strains."
　　And art thou, Stanley, of that sacred band?
Alas, for us too soon! Though raised above
The reach of human pain, above the flight
Of human joy; yet, with a mingled ray
Of sadly-pleased remembrance, must thou feel
A mother's love, a mother's tender wo:
Who seeks thee still, in many a former scene;　　　　570
Seeks thy fair form, thy lovely-beaming eyes,
Thy pleasing converse, by gay lively sense
Inspired; where moral wisdom mildly shone,
Without the toil of art; and virtue glow'd,
In all her smiles, without forbidding pride.
But, O thou best of parents! wipe thy tears;
Or rather to Parental Nature pay
The tears of grateful joy, who for a while
Lent thee this younger self, this opening bloom
Of thy enlighten'd mind and gentle worth.　　　　580
Believe the Muse: the wintry blast of death
Kills not the buds of virtue; no, they spread,
Beneath the heavenly beam of brighter suns,
Through endless ages, into higher powers.

Thus up the mount, in airy vision rapt,
I stray, regardless whither; till the sound
Of a near fall of water every sense
Wakes from the charm of thought; swift-shrinking back,
I check my steps, and view the broken scene.
    Smooth to the shelving brink a copious flood   590
Rolls fair, and placid, where collected all,
In one impetuous torrent, down the steep
It thundering shoots, and shakes the country round.
At first, an azure sheet, it rushes broad:
Then whitening by degrees, as prone it falls,
And from the loud-resounding rocks below
Dash'd in a cloud of foam, it sends aloft
A hoary mist, and forms a ceaseless shower.
Nor can the tortured wave here find repose;
But, raging still amid the shaggy rocks,   600
Now flashes o'er the scatter'd fragments, now
Aslant the hollow'd channel rapid darts;
And falling fast from gradual slope to slope,
With wild infracted course, and lessen'd roar,
It gains a safer bed, and steals, at last,
Along the mazes of the quiet vale.
    Invited from the cliff, to whose dark brow
He clings, the steep-ascending eagle soars,
With upward pinions through the flood of day;
And, giving full his bosom to the blaze,   610
Gains on the sun; while all the tuneful race,
Smit by the afflictive noon, disorder'd droop,
Deep in the thicket; or, from bower to bower
Responsive, force an interrupted strain.
The stock-dove only through the forest coos,
Mournfully hoarse; oft ceasing from his plaint:
Short interval of weary wo! again
The sad idea of his murder'd mate,
Struck from his side by savage fowler's guile,
Across his fancy comes; and then resounds   620
A louder song of sorrow through the grove.
    Beside the dewy border let me sit,

All in the freshness of the humid air;
There in that hollow'd rock, grotesque and wild,
An ample chair moss-lined, and over head
By flowering umbrage shaded: where the bee
Strays diligent, and with th' extracted balm
Of fragrant woodbine loads his little thigh.
　　Now, while I taste the sweetness of the shade,
While Nature lies around deep-lull'd in noon,
Now come, bold Fancy! spread a daring flight,
And view the wonders of the Torrid Zone:
Climes unrelenting! with whose rage compared,
Yon blaze is feeble, and yon skies are cool.
　　See, how at once the bright effulgent sun,
Rising direct, swift chases from the sky
The short-lived twilight; and with ardent blaze
Looks gaily fierce through all the dazzling air:
He mounts his throne; but kind before him sends,
Issuing from out the portals of the morn,
The general breeze, to mitigate his fire,
And breathe refreshment on a fainting world.
Great are the scenes, with dreadful beauty crown'd
And barbarous wealth, that see, each circling year,
Returning suns and double seasons pass:
Rocks rich in gems, and mountains big with mines,
That on the high equator ridgy rise,
Whence many a bursting stream auriferous plays;
Majestic woods, of every vigorous green,
Stage above stage, high-waving o'er the hills;
Or to the far horizon wide diffused,
A boundless deep immensity of shade.
　　Here lofty trees, to ancient song unknown,
The noble sons of potent heat and floods
Prone-rushing from the clouds, rear high to Heaven
Their thorny stems, and broad around them throw
Meridian gloom.　Here, in eternal prime,
Unnumber'd fruits, of keen delicious taste
And vital spirit, drink amid the cliffs,
And burning sands that bank the shrubby vales,

Redoubled day; yet in their rugged coats
A friendly juice to cool its rage contain.
 Bear me, Pomona! to thy citron groves;
To where the lemon and the piercing lime,
With the deep orange, glowing through the green,
Their lighter glories blend. Lay me reclined
Beneath the spreading tamarind that shakes,
Fann'd by the breeze, its fever-cooling fruit.
Deep in the night the massy locust sheds,
Quench my hot limbs; or lead me through the maze,   670
Embowering endless, of the Indian fig;
Or thrown at gayer ease, on some fair brow,
Let me behold, by breezy murmurs cool'd,
Broad o'er my head the verdant cedar wave,
And high palmettos lift their graceful shade.
Or, stretch'd amid these orchards of the sun,
Give me to drain the cocoa's milky bowl,
And from the palm to draw its freshening wine;
More bounteous far than all the frantic juice
Which Bacchus pours. Nor, on its slender twigs   680
Low-bending, be the full pomegranate scorn'd;
Nor, creeping through the woods, the gelid race
Of berries. Oft in humble station dwells
Unboastful worth, above fastidious pomp.
Witness, thou best Anâna! thou the pride
Of vegetable life, beyond whate'er
The poets imaged in the golden age;
Quick let me strip thee of thy tufty coat,
Spread thy ambrosial stores, and feast with Jove!
 From these the prospect varies. Plains immense   690
Lie stretch'd below, interminable meads,
And vast savannahs, where the wandering eye,
Unfix'd, is in a verdant ocean lost.
Another Flora there, of bolder hues,
And richer sweets, beyond our garden's pride,
Plays o'er the fields, and showers with sudden hand
Exuberant spring; for oft these valleys shift
Their green-embroider'd robe to fiery brown,

And swift to green again, as scorching suns,
Or streaming dews and torrent rains, prevail.   700
    Along these lonely regions, where, retired
From little scenes of art, great Nature dwells
In awful solitude; and nought is seen
But the wild herds that own no master's stall;
Prodigious rivers roll their fatt'ning seas;
On whose luxuriant herbage, half-conceal'd,
Like a fallen cedar, far-diffused his train,
Cased in green scales, the crocodile extends.
    The flood disparts: behold! in plaited mail,
Behemoth rears his head. Glanced from his side,   710
The darted steel in idle shivers flies:
He fearless walks the plain, or seeks the hills;
Where, as he crops his varied fare, the herds,
In widening circle round, forget their food,
And at the harmless stranger wondering gaze,
    Peaceful, beneath primeval trees, that cast
Their ample shade o'er Niger's yellow stream,
And where the Ganges rolls his sacred wave;
Or mid the central depth of blackening woods,
High-raised in solemn theatre around,   720
Leans the huge elephant: wisest of brutes!
O truly wise! with gentle might endow'd,
Though powerful, not destructive! Here he sees
Revolving ages sweep the changeful earth,
And empires rise and fall; regardless he
Of what the never-resting race of Men
Project: thrice happy! could he 'scape their guile,
Who mine, from cruel avarice, his steps;
Or with his tow'ry grandeur swell their state,
The pride of kings! or else his strength pervert,   730
And bid him rage amid the mortal fray,
Astonish'd at the madness of mankind.
    Wide o'er the winding umbrage of the floods,
Like vivid blossoms glowing from afar,
Thick-swarm the brighter birds. For Nature's hand,
That with a sportive vanity has deck'd

The plumy nations, there her gayest hues
Profusely pours. But, if she bids them shine,
Array'd in all the beauteous beams of day,
Yet frugal still, she humbles them in song.   740
Nor envy we the gaudy robes they lent
Proud Mountezuma's realm, whose legions cast
A boundless radiance waving on the sun,
While Philomel is ours; while in our shades,
Through the soft silence of the listening night,
The sober-suited songstress trills her lay.
　　But come, my Muse, the desert-barrier burst,
A wild expanse of lifeless sand and sky:
And, swifter than the toiling caravan,
Shoot o'er the vale of Sennar; ardent climb   750
The Nubian mountains, and the secret bounds
Of jealous Abyssinia boldly pierce.
Thou art no ruffian, who beneath the mask
Of social commerce com'st to rob their wealth;
No holy Fury thou, blaspheming Heaven,
With consecrated steel to stab their peace,
And through the land, yet red from civil wounds,
To spread the purple tyranny of Rome.
Thou, like the harmless bee, may'st freely range,
From mead to mead bright with exalted flowers,   760
From jasmine grove to grove, may'st wander gay,
Through palmy shades and aromatic woods,
That grace the plains, invest the peopled hills,
And up the more than Alpine mountains wave.
There on the breezy summit, spreading fair,
For many a league; or on stupendous rocks,
That from the sun-redoubling valley lift,
Cool to the middle air, their lawny tops;
Where palaces, and fanes, and villas rise;
And gardens smile around, and cultured fields;   770
And fountains gush; and careless herds and flocks
Securely stray; a world within itself,
Disdaining all assault: there let me draw
Ethereal soul; there drink reviving gales,

Profusely breathing from the spicy groves,
And vales of fragrance; there at distance hear
The roaring floods, and cataracts, that sweep
From disembowell'd earth the virgin gold;
And o'er the varied landscape, restless, rove,
Fervent with life of every fairer kind:　　　　　780
A land of wonders! which the sun still eyes
With ray direct, as of the lovely realm
Enamour'd, and delighting there to dwell.
　　How changed the scene! In blazing height of noon,
The sun, oppress'd, is plunged in thickest gloom.
Still Horror reigns! a dreary twilight round,
Of struggling night and day malignant mix'd!
For to the hot equator crowding fast,
Where, highly rarefy'd, the yielding air
Admits their stream, incessant vapours roll,　　　　　790
Amazing clouds on clouds continual heap'd;
Or whirl'd tempestuous by the gusty wind,
Or silent borne along, heavy and slow,
With the big stores of steaming oceans charged.
Meantime, amid these upper seas, condensed
Around the cold aerial mountain's brow,
And by conflicting winds together dash'd,
The Thunder holds his black tremendous throne;
From cloud to cloud the rending Lightnings rage
Till, in the furious elemental war　　　　　800
Dissolved, the whole precipitated mass
Unbroken floods and solid torrents pours.
　　The treasures these, hid from the bounded search
Of ancient knowledge; whence with annual pomp,
Rich king of floods! o'erflows the swelling Nile.
From his two springs, in Gojam's sunny realm,
Pure-welling out, he through the lucid lake
Of fair Dambea rolls his infant-stream.
There, by the Naiads nursed, he sports away
His playful youth, amid the fragrant isles,　　　　　810
That with unfading verdure smile around.
Ambitious, thence the manly river breaks;

And gathering many a flood, and copious fed
With all the mellowed treasures of the sky,
Winds in progressive majesty along:
Through splendid kingdoms now devolves his maze,
Now wanders wild o'er solitary tracts
Of life-deserted sand; till, glad to quit
The joyless desart, down the Nubiau rocks,
From thundering steep to steep, he pours his urn,   820
And Egypt joys beneath the spreading wave.
  His brother Niger, too, and all the floods
In which the full-form'd maids of Afric lave
Their jetty limbs; and all that from the tract
Of woody mountains stretch'd through gorgeous Ind
Fall on Cor'mandel's coast, or Malabar;
From Menam's orient stream, that nightly shines
With insect-lamps, to where Aurora sheds
On Indus' smiling banks the rosy shower:
All, at this bounteous season, ope their urns,   830
And pour untoiling harvest o'er the land.
  Nor less thy world, Columbus, drinks, refresh'd
The lavish moisture of the melting year.
Wide o'er his isles, the branching Oronoque
Rolls a brown deluge; and the native drives
To dwell aloft on life-sufficing trees,
At once his dome, his robe, his food, and arms.
  Swell'd by a thousand streams, impetuous hurl'd
From all the roaring Andes, huge descends
The mighty Orellana. Scarce the Muse   840
Dares stretch her wing o'er this enormous mass
Of rushing water; scarce she dares attempt
The sea-like Plata; to whose dread expanse,
Continuous depth, and wondrous length of course,
Our floods are rills. With unabated force,
In silent dignity they sweep along,
And traverse realms unknown, and blooming wilds,
And fruitful deserts, worlds of solitude!
Where the sun smiles and seasons teem in vain,
Unseen, and unenjoy'd. Forsaking these,   850

O'er peopled plains they fair-diffusive flow,
And many a nation feed; and circle safe,
In their soft bosom, many a happy isle,
The seat of blameless Pan, yet undisturb'd
By Christian crimes and Europe's cruel sons.
Thus pouring on, they proudly seek the deep,
Whose vanquish'd tide, recoiling from the shock,
Yields to this liquid weight of half the globe;
And Ocean trembles for his green domain.
But what avails this wondrous waste of wealth?   860
This gay profusion of luxurious bliss?
This pomp of Nature? what their balmy meads,
Their powerful herbs, and Ceres void of pain?
By vagrant birds dispersed, and wafting winds,
What their unplanted fruits?   What the cool draughts,
Th' ambrosial food, rich gums, and spicy health,
Their forests yield?   Their toiling insects what?
Their silky pride, and vegetable robes?
Ah! what avail their fatal treasures, hid
Deep in the bowels of the pitying earth,   870
Golconda's gems, and sad Potosi's mines,
Where dwelt the gentlest children of the sun?
What all that Afric's golden rivers roll,
Her od'rous woods, and shining iv'ry stores?
Ill-fated race! the softening arts of Peace;
Whate'er the humanising Muses teach;
The godlike wisdom of the temper'd breast;
Progressive truth; the patient force of thought;
Investigation calm, whose silent powers
Command the world; the light that leads to Heaven;   880
Kind equal rule, the government of laws,
And all protecting Freedom, which alone
Sustains the name and dignity of Man:
These are not theirs.   The parent-sun himself
Seems o'er this world of slaves to tyrannise;
And, with oppressive ray, the roseate bloom
Of beauty blasting, gives the gloomy hue
And feature gross: or worse, to ruthless deeds,

Mad jealousy, blind rage, and fell revenge,
Their fervid spirit fires. Love dwells not there;   890
The soft regards, the tenderness of life,
The heart-shed tear, th' ineffable delight
Of sweet humanity: these court the beam
Of milder climes; in selfish fierce desire,
And the wild fury of voluptuous sense,
There lost. The very brute-creation there
This rage partakes, and burns with horrid fire.
  Lo! the green serpent, from his dark abode,
Which even Imagination fears to tread,
At noon forth-issuing, gathers up his train   900
In orbs immense; then, darting out anew,
Seeks the refreshing fount; by which diffused,
He throws his folds: and while, with threat'ning tongue
And deathful jaws erect, the monster curls
His flaming crest, all other thirst, appall'd,
Or shivering flies, or check'd at distance stands,
Nor dares approach. But still more direful he,
The small close-lurking minister of Fate,
Whose high-concocted venom through the veins
A rapid lightning darts, arresting swift   910
The vital current. Form'd to humble Man,
This child of vengeful Nature! There, sublimed
To fearless lust of blood, the savage race
Roam, licensed by the shading hour of guilt,
And foul misdeed, when the pure day has shut
His sacred eye. The tiger darting fierce
Impetuous on the prey his glance has doom'd;
The lively-shining leopard, speckled o'er
With many a spot, the beauty of the waste;
And, scorning all the taming arts of Man,   920
The keen hyena, fellest of the fell:
These, rushing from th' inhospitable woods
Of Mauritania, or the tufted isles,
That verdant rise amid the Libyan wild,
Innumerous glare around their shaggy king,
Majestic, stalking o'er the printed sand;

And, with imperious and repeated roars,
Demand their fated food.   The fearful flocks
Crowd near the guardian swain: the nobler herds,
Where round their lordly bull, in rural ease,   930
They ruminating lie, with horror hear
The coming rage.   Th' awaken'd village starts;
And to her fluttering breast the mother strains
Her thoughtless infant.   From the pirate's den,
Or stern Morocco's tyrant fang escaped,
The wretch half-wishes for his bonds again:
While, uproar all, the wilderness resounds,
From Atlas eastward to the frighted Nile.
    Unhappy he! who from the first of joys,
Society, cut off, is left alone   940
Amid this world of death.   Day after day,
Sad on the jutting eminence he sits;
And views the main that ever toils below;
Still fondly forming in the farthest verge
Where the round ether mixes with the wave,
Ships, dim-discover'd, dropping from the clouds:
At evening, to the setting sun he turns
A mournful eye, and down his dying heart
Sinks helpless; while the wonted roar is up,
And hiss continual through the tedious night.   950
Yet here, even here, into these black abodes
Of monsters, unappall'd, from stooping Rome,
And guilty Cæsar, Liberty retired,
Her Cato following through Numidian wilds:
Disdainful of Campania's gentle plains,
And all the green delights Ausonia pours;
When for them she must bend the servile knee,
And fawning take the splendid robber's boon.
    Nor stop the terrors of these regions here.
Commission'd demons oft, angels of wrath !   960
Let loose the raging elements.   Breathed hot,
From all the boundless furnace of the sky,
And the wide glittering waste of burning sand,
A suffocating wind the pilgrim smites

With instant death. Patient of thirst and toil,
Son of the desert! even the camel feels,
Shot through his wither'd heart, the fiery blast.
Or from the black-red ether, bursting broad,
Sallies the sudden whirlwind. Strait the sands,
Commoved around, in gathering eddies play;   970
Nearer and nearer still they darkening come;
Till, with the general all-involving storm
Swept up, the whole continuous wilds arise;
And by their noonday fount dejected thrown,
Or sunk at night in sad disastrous sleep,
Beneath descending hills, the caravan
Is buried deep. In Cairo's crowded streets
Th' impatient merchant, wondering, waits in vain,
And Mecca saddens at the long delay.
     But chief at sea, whose every flexile wave   980
Obeys the blast, the aerial tumult swells.
In the dread ocean, undulating wide,
Beneath the radiant line that girts the globe,
The circling Typhon, whirl'd from point to point,
Exhausting all the rage of all the sky,
And dire Ecnephia reign. Amid the heavens,
Falsely serene, deep in a cloudy speck
Compressed, the mighty tempest brooding dwells;
Of no regard, save to the skilful eye.
Fiery and foul, the small prognostic hangs   990
Aloft, or on the promontory's brow
Musters its force. A faint deceitful calm!
A fluttering gale, the demon sends before,
To tempt the spreading sail. Then down at once,
Precipitant, descends a mingled mass,
Of roaring winds, and flame, and rushing floods.
In wild amazement fix'd the sailor stands.
Art is too slow: by rapid Fate oppress'd,
His broad-wing'd vessel drinks the whelming tide,
Hid in the bosom of the black abyss.   1000
With such mad seas the daring Gama fought,
For many a day, and many a dreadful night,

F

Incessant, lab'ring round the stormy Cape;
By bold ambition led, and bolder thirst
Of gold. For then from ancient gloom emerged
The rising world of trade; the Genius, then,
Of navigation, that, in hopeless sloth,
Had slumber'd on the vast Atlantic deep,
For idle ages, starting, heard at last
The Lusitanian Prince; who, Heav'n-inspired,   1010
To love of useful glory roused mankind,
And in unbounded Commerce mix'd the world.
  Increasing still the terrors of these storms,
His jaws horrific arm'd with threefold fate,
Here dwells the direful shark. Lured by the scent
Of steaming crowds, of rank disease, and death,
Behold! he rushing cuts the briny flood,
Swift as the gale can bear the ship along;
And, from the partners of that cruel trade,
Which spoils unhappy Guinea of her sons,   1020
Demands his share of prey; demands themselves.
The stormy Fates descend: one death involves
Tyrants and slaves; when strait, their mangled limbs
Crashing at once, he dyes the purple seas
With gore, and riots in the vengeful meal.
  When o'er this world, by equinoctial rains
Flooded immense, looks out the joyless sun,
And draws the copious stream: from swampy fens,
Where putrefaction into life ferments,
And breathes destructive myriads; or from woods,   1030
Impenetrable shades, recesses foul,
In vapours rank and blue corruption wrapt,
Whose gloomy horrors yet no desperate foot
Has ever dared to pierce; then, wasteful, forth
Walks the dire Power of pestilent disease.
A thousand hideous fiends her course attend;
Sick Nature blasting, and to heartless wo,
And feeble desolation, casting down
The towering hopes and all the pride of Man.
Such as, of late, at Carthagena quench'd   1040

The BRITISH fire. You, gallant VERNON, saw
The miserable scene; you, pitying, saw
To infant-weakness sunk the warrior's arm;
Saw the deep-racking pang, the ghastly form,
The lip pale-quiv'ring, and the beamless eye
No more with ardour bright: you heard the groans
Of agonising ships, from shore to shore;
Heard, nightly plunged amid the sullen waves,
The frequent corse; while on each other fix'd,
In sad presage, the blank assistants seem'd,   1050
Silent, to ask, whom Fate would next demand.
   What need I mention those inclement skies,
Where, frequent o'er the sickening city, Plague,
The fiercest child of NEMESIS divine,
Descends? from Ethiopia's poison'd woods,
From stifled Cairo's filth, and fetid fields
With locust-armies putrefying heap'd,
This great destroyer sprung. Her awful rage
The brutes escape: Man is her destined prey;
Intemperate Man! and, o'er his guilty domes,   1060
She draws a close incumbent cloud of death;
Uninterrupted by the living winds,
Forbid to blow a wholesome breeze; and stain'd
With many a mixture by the sun, suffused,
Of angry aspect. Princely wisdom, then,
Dejects his watchful eye; and from the hand
Of feeble justice, ineffectual, drop
The sword and balance; mute the voice of joy,
And hush'd the clamour of the busy world.
Empty the streets, with uncouth verdure clad;   1070
Into the worst of deserts sudden turn'd
The cheerful haunt of Men: unless escaped
From the doom'd house, where matchless horror reigns,
Shut up by barbarous fear, the smitten wretch,
With frenzy wild, breaks loose; and, loud to Heaven
Screaming, the dreadful policy arraigns,
Inhuman and unwise. The sullen door,
Yet uninfected, on its cautious hinge

Fearing to turn, abhors society:
Dependants, friends, relations, Love himself,   1080
Savaged by wo, forget the tender tie,
The sweet engagement of the feeling heart.
　But vain their selfish care: the circling sky,
The wide-enlivening air is full of fate;
And, struck by turns, in solitary pangs
They fall, unblest, untended, and unmourn'd.
Thus o'er the prostrate city black Despair
Extends her raven wing; while, to complete
The scene of desolation, stretch'd around,
The grim guards stand, denying all retreat,   1090
And give the flying wretch a better death.
　Much yet remains unsung: the rage intense
Of brazen-vaulted skies, of iron fields,
Where drought and famine starve the blasted year:
Fired by the torch of noon to tenfold rage,
Th' infuriate hill that shoots the pillar'd flame;
And, roused within the subterranean world,
Th' expanding earthquake, that resistless shakes
Aspiring cities from their solid base,
And buries mountains in the flaming gulf.   1100
But 'tis enough; return, my vagrant Muse:
A nearer scene of horror calls thee home.
　Behold, slow-settling o'er the lurid grove,
Unusual darkness broods; and growing gains
The full possession of the sky; surcharged
With wrathful vapour, from the secret beds,
Where sleep the mineral generations, drawn.
Thence Nitre, Sulphur, and the fiery spume
Of fat Bitumen, steaming on the day,
With various-tinctured trains of latent flame,   1110
Pollute the sky; and in yon baleful cloud,
A reddening gloom, a magazine of fate,
Ferment; till, by the touch ethereal roused,
The dash of clouds, or irritating war
Of fighting winds, while all is calm below,
They furious spring. A boding silence reigns

Dread through the dun expanse; save the dull sound
That from the mountain, previous to the storm,
Rolls o'er the muttering earth, disturbs the flood,
And shakes the forest-leaf without a breath.   1120
Prone, to the lowest vale, th' aerial tribes
Descend: the tempest-loving raven scarce
Dares wing the dubious dusk.   In rueful gaze
The cattle stand, and on the scowling heavens
Cast a deploring eye; by Man forsook,
Who to the crowded cottage hies him fast,
Or seeks the shelter of the downward cave.
    'Tis listening fear, and dumb amazement all:
When to the startled eye the sudden glance
Appears far south, eruptive through the cloud;   1130
And following slower, in explosion vast,
The Thunder raises his tremendous voice.
At first, heard solemn o'er the verge of heaven,
The tempest growls; but as it nearer comes,
And rolls its awful burden on the wind,
The lightnings flash a larger curve, and more
The noise astounds: till over head a sheet
Of livid flame discloses wide; then shuts,
And opens wider; shuts and opens still
Expansive, wrapping ether in a blaze.   1140
Follows the loosen'd aggravated roar,
Enlarging, deepening, mingling; peal on peal
Crush'd horrible, convulsing heaven and earth.
    Down comes a deluge of sonorous hail,
Or prone-descending rain.   Wide rent, the clouds
Pour a whole flood; and yet, its flame unquench'd,
The unconquerable lightning struggles through,
Ragged and fierce, or in red whirling balls,
And fires the mountains with redoubled rage.
Black from the stroke, above the smouldering pine   1150
Stands a sad shattered trunk; and, stretch'd below,
A lifeless group the blasted cattle lie:
Here the soft flocks, with that same harmless look
They wore alive, and ruminating still

In fancy's eye; and there the frowning bull
And ox half-raised. Struck on the castled cliff
The venerable tower and spiry fane
Resign their aged pride. The gloomy woods
Start at the flash, and from their deep recess,
Wide-flaming out, their trembling inmates shake.   1160
Amid Caernarvon's mountains rages loud
The repercussive roar: with mighy crush,
Into the flashing deep, from the rude rocks
Of Penmanmaur heap'd hideous to the sky,
Tumble the smitten cliffs; and Snowdon's peak,
Dissolving, instant yields his wintry load.
Far-seen, the heights of heathy Cheviot blaze,
And Thulè bellows through her utmost isles.
    Guilt hears appall'd, with deeply-troubled thought.
And yet not always on the guilty head   1170
Descends the fated flash. Young Celadon
And his Amelia were a matchless pair;
With equal virtue formed, and equal grace,
The same, distinguished by their sex alone:
Hers the mild lustre of the blooming morn,
And his the radiance of the risen day.
    They loved: but such their guileless passion was,
As in the dawn of time inform'd the heart
Of innocence and undissembling truth.
'Twas friendship heighten'd by the mutual wish;   1180
Th' enchanting hope, and sympathetic glow,
Beam'd from the mutual eye. Devoting all
To love, each was to each a dearer self:
Supremely happy in th' awaken'd power
Of giving joy. Alone, amid the shades,
Still in harmonious intercourse they lived
The rural day, and talk'd the flowing heart,
Or sigh'd and look'd unutterable things.
    So pass'd their life, a clear united stream,
By care unruffled; till, in evil hour,   1190
The tempest caught them on the tender walk,
Heedless how far, and where its mazes stray'd;

While, with each other blest, creative love
Still bade eternal Eden smile around.
Presaging instant fate, her bosom heaved
Unwonted sighs: and stealing oft a look
Of the big gloom on Celadon, her eye
Fell tearful, wetting her disorder'd cheek.
In vain assuring love, and confidence
In Heaven, repress'd her fear; it grew, and shook   1200
Her frame near dissolution. He perceived
Th' unequal conflict, and as angels look
On dying saints, his eyes compassion shed,
With love illumined high. "Fear not," he said,
"Sweet innocence! thou stranger to offence,
And inward storm! He, who yon skies involves
In frowns of darkness, ever smiles on thee
With kind regard. O'er thee the secret shaft
That wastes at midnight, or th' undreaded hour
Of noon, flies harmless: and that very voice,   1210
Which thunders terror through the guilty heart,
With tongues of seraphs whispers peace to thine.
'Tis safety to be near thee, sure, and thus
To clasp perfection!" From his void embrace,
Mysterious Heaven! that moment, to the ground,
A blacken'd corse, was struck the beauteous maid.
But who can paint the lover as he stood,
Pierced by severe amazement, hating life,
Speechless, and fix'd in all the death of wo
So, faint resemblance! on the marble tomb,   1220
The well-dissembled mourner stooping stands,
For ever silent, and for ever sad.
    As from the face of heaven the shatter'd clouds
Tumultuous rove, th' interminable sky
Sublimer swells, and o'er the world expands
A purer azure. Through the lighten'd air
A higher lustre and a clearer calm,
Diffusive, tremble; while, as if in sign
Of danger past, a glitt'ring robe of joy,
Set off abundant by the yellow ray,   1230

Invests the fields; and Nature smiles revived.
'Tis beauty all, and grateful song around,
Join'd to the low of kine, and numerous bleat
Of flocks thick-nibbling through the clover'd vale.
And shall the hymn be marr'd by thankless Man,
Most-favour'd; who with voice articulate
Should lead the chorus of this lower world?
Shall he, so soon forgetful of the Hand
That hush'd the thunder, and serenes the sky,
Extinguish'd feel that spark the tempest waked?   1240
That sense of powers exceeding far his own,
Ere yet his feeble heart has lost its fears?
Cheer'd by the milder beam, the sprightly youth
Speeds to the well-known pool, whose crystal depth
A sandy bottom shows.   A while he stands
Gazing th' inverted landscape, half afraid
To meditate the blue profound below;
Then plunges headlong down the circling flood.
His ebon tresses, and his rosy cheek,
Instant emerge; and through th' obedient wave,   1250
At each short breathing by his lip repell'd,
With arms and legs according well, he makes,
As humour leads, an easy-winding path;
While, from his polish'd sides, a dewy light
Effuses on the pleased spectators round.
    This is the purest exercise of health,
The kind refresher of the summer-heats;
Nor, when cold Winter keens the brightening flood,
Would I weak-shivering linger on the brink.
Thus life redoubles, and is oft preserved,   1260
By the bold swimmer, in the swift illapse
Of accident disastrous.   Hence the limbs
Knit into force; and the same Roman arm,
That rose victorious o'er the conquer'd earth,
First learn'd, while tender, to subdue the wave.
Even, from the body's purity, the mind
Receives a secret sympathetic aid.
    Close in the covert of a hazel copse,

Where winded into pleasing solitudes
Runs out the rambling dale, young Damon sat,   1270
Pensive, and pierced with love's delightful pangs.
There to the stream that down the distant rocks
Hoarse-murm'ring fell, and plaintive breeze that play'd
Among the bending willows, falsely he
Of Musidora's cruelty complain'd.
She felt his flame; but deep within her breast,
In bashful coyness, or in maiden pride,
The soft return conceal'd: save when it stole
In side-long glances from her downcast eye,
Or from her swelling soul in stifled sighs.   1280
Touch'd by the scene, no stranger to his vows,
He framed a melting lay, to try her heart;
And, if an infant passion struggled there,
To call that passion forth.   Thrice happy swain!
A lucky chance, that oft decides the fate
Of mighty monarchs, then decided thine.
For lo! conducted by the laughing Loves,
This cool retreat his Musidora sought:
Warm in her cheek the sultry season glow'd;
And, robed in loose array, she came to bathe   1290
Her fervent limbs in the refreshing stream.
What shall he do? In sweet confusion lost,
And dubious flutterings, he a while remain'd:
A pure ingenuous elegance of soul,
A delicate refinement, known to few,
Perplex'd his breast, and urged him to retire:
But love forbade. Ye prudes in virtue, say,
Say, ye severest, what would you have done?
    Meantime, this fairer nymph than ever blest.
Arcadian stream, with timid eye around   1300
The banks surveying, stripp'd her beauteous limbs,
To taste the lucid coolness of the flood.
Ah then! not Paris on the piny top
Of Ida panted stronger, when aside
The rival-goddesses the veil divine
Cast unconfined, and gave him all their charms,

Than, Damon, thou; as from the snowy leg,
And slender foot, th' inverted silk she drew;
As the soft touch dissolved the virgin zone;
And through the parting robe, th' alternate breast,   1310
With youth wild-throbbing, on thy lawless gaze
In full luxuriance rose. But, desperate youth,
How durst thou risk the soul-distracting view;
As from her naked limbs, of glowing white,
Harmonious swell'd by Nature's finest hand,
In folds loose-floating fell the fainter lawn:
And fair exposed she stood, shrunk from herself,
With fancy blushing, at the doubtful breeze
Alarm'd, and starting like the fearful fawn?
Then to the flood she rush'd; the parted flood   1320
Its lovely guest with closing waves received;
And every beauty softening, every grace
Flushing anew, a mellow lustre shed:
As shines the lily through the crystal mild;
Or as the rose amid the morning dew,
Fresh from Aurora's hand, more sweetly glows.
   While thus she wanton'd, now beneath the wave
But ill-conceal'd; and now with streaming locks,
That half-embraced her in a humid veil,
Rising again, the latent Damon drew   1330
Such madd'ning draughts of beauty to the soul,
As for a while o'erwhelm'd his raptured thought
With luxury too daring. Check'd, at last,
By love's respectful modesty, he deem'd
The theft profane, if aught profane to love
Can e'er be deem'd; and, struggling from the shade,
With headlong hurry fled: but first these lines,
Traced by his ready pencil, on the bank
With trembling hand he threw: "Bathe on, my fair,
Yet unbeheld save by the sacred eye   1340
Of faithful love: I go to guard thy haunt,
To keep from thy recess each vagrant foot,
And each licentious eye." With wild surprise,
As if to marble struck, devoid of sense,

A stupid moment motionless she stood:
So stands the statue that enchants the world;
So bending tries to veil the matchless boast,
The mingled beauties of exulting Greece.
　　Recovering, swift she flew to find those robes
Which blissful Eden knew not; and, array'd　　　　1350
In careless haste, th' alarming paper snatch'd.
But, when her Damon's well-known hand she saw,
Her terrors vanish'd, and a softer train
Of mix'd emotions, hard to be described,
Her sudden bosom seized; shame void of guilt,
The charming blush of innocence, esteem
And admiration of her lover's flame,
By modesty exalted; even a sense
Of self-approving beauty stole across
Her busy thought. At length, a tender calm　　　　1360
Hush'd by degrees the tumult of her soul;
And on the spreading beech, that o'er the stream
Incumbent hung, she with the sylvan pen
Of rural lovers this confession carved,
Which soon her Damon kiss'd with weeping joy:
"Dear youth! sole judge of what these verses mean;
By fortune too much favour'd, but by love,
Alas! not favour'd less, be still as now
Discreet: the time may come you need not fly."
　　The sun has lost his rage: his downward orb　　　1370
Shoots nothing now but animating warmth,
And vital lustre; that, with various ray,
Lights up the clouds, those beauteous robes of heaven,
Incessant roll'd into romantic shapes,
The dream of waking fancy! Broad below,
Cover'd with ripening fruits, and swelling fast
Into the perfect year, the pregnant Earth
And all her tribes rejoice. Now the soft hour
Of walking comes: for him who lonely loves
To seek the distant hills, and there converse　　　1380
With Nature; there to harmonise his heart,
And in pathetic song to breathe around

The harmony to others. Social friends,
Attuned to happy unison of soul;
To whose exalting eye a fairer world,
Of which the vulgar never had a glimpse,
Displays its charms; whose minds are richly fraught
With philosophic stores, superior light;
And in whose breast, enthusiastic, burns
Virtue, the sons of interest deem romance;   1390
Now call'd abroad enjoy the falling day:
Now to the verdant Portico of woods,
To Nature's vast Lyceum, forth they walk;
By that kind School where no proud master reigns,
The full free converse of the friendly heart,
Improving and improved. Now from the world,
Sacred to sweet retirement, lovers steal,
And pour their souls in transport, which the Sire
Of love approving hears, and calls it good.
    Which way, Amanda, shall we bend our course?   1400
The choice perplexes. Wherefore should we choose?
All is the same with thee. Say, shall we wind
Along the streams? or walk the smiling mead?
Or court the forest-glades? or wander wild
Among the waving harvests? or ascend,
While radiant Summer opens all its pride,
Thy hill, delightful Shene? Here let us sweep
The boundless landscape: now the raptured eye,
Exulting swift, to huge Augusta send,
Now to the Sister-Hills that skirt her plain,   1410
To lofty Harrow now, and now to where
Majestic Windsor lifts his princely brow.
    In lovely contrast to this glorious view,
Calmly magnificent, then will we turn
To where the silver Thames first rural grows.
There let the feasted eye unwearied stray:
Luxurious, there, rove through the pendant woods
That nodding hang o'er Harrington's retreat;
And, stooping thence to Ham's embowering walks,
Beneath whose shades, in spotless peace retired,   1420

With Her the pleasing partner of his heart,
The worthy Queensb'ry yet laments his Gay;
And polish'd Cornbury woos the willing Muse.
Slow let us trace the matchless Vale of Thames;
Fair-winding up to where the Muses haunt
In Twit'nam's bowers, and for their Pope implore
The healing God; to royal Hampton's pile,
To Clermont's terrass'd height, and Esher's groves;
Where, in the sweetest solitude, embraced
By the soft windings of the silent Mole,   1430
From courts and senates Pelham finds repose.
Enchanting vale! beyond whate'er the Muse
Has of Achaia or Hesperia sung!
O vale of bliss! O softly-swelling hills!
On which the Power of Cultivation lies,
And joys to see the wonders of his toil.
    Heavens! what a goodly prospect spreads around,
Of hills, and dales, and woods, and lawns, and spires,
And glittering towns, and gilded streams, till all
The stretching landscape into smoke decays!   1440
Happy Britannia! where the Queen of Arts,
Inspiring vigour, Liberty abroad
Walks unconfined, even to thy farthest cots,
And scatters plenty with unsparing hand.
    Rich is thy soil, and merciful thy clime;
Thy streams unfailing in the Summer's drought;
Unmatch'd thy guardian-oaks; thy valleys float
With golden waves; and on thy mountains flocks
Bleat numberless; while, roving round their sides,
Bellow the blackening herds in lusty droves.   1450
Beneath, thy meadows glow, and rise unquell'd
Against the mower's scythe. On every hand
Thy villas shine. Thy country teems with wealth;
And property assures it to the swain,
Pleased and unwearied in his guarded toil.
    Full are thy cities with the sons of art;
And trade and joy, in every busy street,
Mingling are heard; even Drudgery himself,

As at the car he sweats, or dusty hews
The palace-stone, looks gay. Thy crowded ports,   1460
Where rising masts an endless prospect yield,
With labour burn, and echo to the shouts
Of hurried sailor, as he hearty waves
His last adieu, and loosening every sheet,
Resigns the spreading vessel to the wind.
    Bold, firm, and graceful, are thy generous youth,
By hardship sinew'd, and by danger fired,
Scattering the nations where they go; and first
Or on the listed plain, or stormy seas.
Mild are thy glories, too, as o'er the plans   1470
Of thriving peace thy thoughtful sires preside;
In genius, and substantial learning, high;
For every virtue, every worth, renown'd;
Sincere, plain-hearted, hospitable, kind;
Yet, like the mustering thunder when provoked,
The dread of tyrants, and the sole resource
Of those that under grim oppression groan.
    Thy Sons of Glory many! Alfred thine;
In whom the splendour of heroic war,
And more heroic peace, when govern'd well,   1480
Combine; whose hallow'd name the virtues saint,
And his own Muses love; the best of kings !
With him thy Edwards and thy Henrys shine,
Names dear to Fame; the first who deep impress'd
On haughty Gaul the terror of thy arms,
That awes her genius still.   In Statesmen thou,
And Patriots, fertile.   Thine a steady More,
Who, with a generous though mistaken zeal,
Withstood a brutal tyrant's useful rage,
Like Cato firm, like Aristides just,   1490
Like rigid Cincinnatus nobly poor:
A dauntless soul erect, who smiled on death.
    Frugal, and wise, a Walsingham is thine;
A Drake, who made thee mistress of the deep,
And bore thy name in thunder round the world.
Then flamed thy spirit high: but who can speak

The numerous worthies of the Maiden Reign?
In Raleigh mark their every glory mix'd;
Raleigh, the scourge of Spain! whose breast with all
The sage, the patriot, and the hero burn'd.   1500
Nor sunk his vigour, when a coward-reign
The warrior fetter'd, and at last resign'd,
To glut the vengeance of a vanquish'd foe.
Then, active still and unrestrain'd, his mind
Explored the vast extent of ages past,
And with his prison-hours enrich'd the world;
Yet found no times, in all the long research,
So glorious or so base, as those he proved,
In which he conquer'd, and in which he bled.
   Nor can the Muse the gallant Sidney pass,   1510
The plume of war! with early laurels crown'd,
The Lover's myrtle, and the Poet's bay.
A Hampden too is thine, illustrious land!
Wise, strenuous, firm, of unsubmitting soul,
Who stemm'd the torrent of a downward age
To slavery prone, and bade thee rise again,
In all thy native pomp of freedom bold.
Bright, at his call, thy Age of Men effulged,
Of Men on whom late time a kindling eye
Shall turn, and tyrants tremble while they read.   1520
Bring every sweetest flower, and let me strew
The grave where Russel lies; whose temper'd
   blood,
With calmest cheerfulness for thee resign'd,
Stain'd the sad annals of a giddy reign,
Aiming at lawless power, though meanly sunk
In loose inglorious luxury. With him
His friend, the British Cassius, fearless bled,
Of high determined spirit, roughly brave,
By ancient learning to th' enlighten'd love
Of ancient freedom warm'd. Fair thy renown   1530
In awful Sages and in noble Bards,
Soon as the light of dawning Science spread
Her orient ray, and waked the Muses' song.

Thine is a Bacon; hapless in his choice,
Unfit to stand the civil storm of state,
And through the smooth barbarity of courts,
With firm but pliant virtue, forward still
To urge his course: him for the studious shade
Kind Nature form'd, deep, comprehensive. clear,
Exact, and elegant; in one rich soul,　　　　　　1540
Plato, the Stagyrite, and Tully join'd.
The great deliverer he! who from the gloom
Of cloister'd monks, and jargon-teaching schools,
Led forth the true Philosophy, there long
Held in the magic chain of words and forms,
And definitions void: he led her forth,
Daughter of Heaven! that slow-ascending still,
Investigating sure the chain of things,
With radiant finger points to Heaven again.
　The generous Ashley thine, the friend of Man,　1550
Who scann'd his Nature with a brother's eye,
His weakness prompt to shade, to raise his aim,
To touch the finer movements of the mind,
And with the moral beauty charm the heart.
Why need I name thy Boyle, whose pious search
Amid the dark recesses of his works,
The great Creator sought? And why thy Locke,
Who made the whole internal world his own?
Let Newton, pure Intelligence! whom God
To mortals lent, to trace his boundless works　　1560
From laws sublimely simple, speak thy fame
In all philosophy. For lofty sense,
Creative fancy, and inspection keen
Through the deep windings of the human heart,
Is not wild Shakspere thine and Nature's boast?
Is not each great, each amiable Muse
Of classic ages in thy Milton met?
A genius universal as his theme;
Astonishing as Chaos; as the bloom
Of blowing Eden fair; as Heaven sublime.　　　1570
　Nor shall my verse that elder bard forget,

The gentle Spenser, Fancy's pleasing son;
Who like a copious river pour'd his song
O'er all the mazes of enchanted ground:
Nor thee his ancient master, laughing sage,
Chaucer, whose native manners-painting verse,
Well-moralised, shines through the Gothic cloud
Of time and language o'er thy genius thrown.
    May my song soften as thy daughters I,
Britannia, hail! for beauty is their own,   1580
The feeling heart, simplicity of life,
And elegance, and taste: the faultless form,
Shaped by the hand of harmony; the cheek,
Where the live crimson, through the native white
Soft-shooting, o'er the face diffuses bloom,
And every nameless grace; the parted lip,
Like the red rosebud moist with morning-dew,
Breathing delight; and, under flowing jet,
Or sunny ringlets, or of circling brown,
The neck slight-shaded, and the swelling breast;   1590
The look resistless, piercing to the soul,
And by the soul inform'd, when drest in love
She sits high-smiling in the conscious eye.
    Island of bliss! amid the subject seas,
That thunder round thy rocky coasts, set up,
At once the wonder, terror, and delight,
Of distant nations; whose remotest shores
Can soon be shaken by thy naval arm;
Not to be shook thyself; but all assaults
Baffling, as thy hoar cliffs the loud sea-wave.   1600
    O Thou! by whose almighty nod the scale
Of empire rises, or alternate falls,
Send forth the saving Virtues round the land,
In bright patrol: while Peace, and social Love;
The tender-looking Charity, intent
On gentle deeds, and shedding tears through smiles;
Undaunted Truth, and Dignity of mind;
Courage composed, and keen; sound Temperance,
Healthful in heart and look; clear Chastity,
G

With blushes reddening as she moves along,   1610
Disorder'd at the deep regard she draws;
Rough Industry; Activity untired,
With copious life inform'd and all awake;
While in the radiant front, superior shines
That first paternal virtue, Public Zeal;
Who throws o'er all an equal wide survey;
And, ever musing on the common weal,
Still labours glorious with some great design.
Low walks the sun, and broadens by degrees,
Just o'er the verge of day. The shifting clouds   1620
Assembled gay, a richly-gorgeous train,
In all their pomp attend his setting throne.
Air, earth, and ocean smile immense. And now,
As if his weary chariot sought the bowers
Of Amphitrite, and her tending nymphs
(So Grecian fable sung), he dips his orb;
Now half-immersed; and now a golden curve
Gives one bright glance, then total disappears.
    For ever running an enchanted round,
Passes the day, deceitful, vain, and void;   1630
As fleets the vision o'er the formful brain,
This moment hurrying wild th' impassion'd soul,
The next in nothing lost. 'Tis so to him,
The dreamer of this earth, an idle blank:
A sight of horror to the cruel wretch,
Who all day-long in sordid pleasure roll'd,
Himself an useless load, has squander'd vile,
Upon his scoundrel train, what might have cheer'd
A drooping family of modest worth.
But to the generous still-improving mind,   1640
That gives the hopeless heart to sing for joy,
Diffusing kind beneficence around,
Boastless, as now descends the silent dew;
To him the long review of order'd life
Is inward rapture, only to be felt.
    Confess'd from yonder slow-extinguish'd clouds,
All ether softening, sober Evening takes

Her wonted station in the middle air;
A thousand shadows at her beck.   First this
She sends on earth; then that of deeper dye   1650
Steals soft behind; and then a deeper still,
In circle following circle, gathers round,
To close the face of things.   A fresher gale
Begins to wave the wood, and stir the stream,
Sweeping with shadowy gust the fields of corn;
While the quail clamours for his running mate.
Wide o'er the thistly lawn, as swells the breeze,
A whitening shower of vegetable down
Amusive floats.   The kind impartial care
Of Nature nought disdains: thoughtful to feed   1660
Her lowest sons, and clothe the coming year,
From field to field the feather'd seeds she wings.
    His folded flock secure, the shepherd home
Hies, merry-hearted: and by turns relieves
The ruddy milk-maid of her brimming pail;
The beauty whom perhaps his witless heart,
Unknowing what the joy-mixt anguish means,
Sincerely loves, by that best language shown
Of cordial glances, and obliging deeds.
Onward they pass, o'er many a panting height,   1670
And valley sunk, and unfrequented; where
At fall of eve the fairy people throng,
In various game and revelry, to pass
The summer-night, as village-stories tell.
But far about they wander from the grave
Of him, whom his ungentle fortune urged
Against his own sad breast to lift the hand
Of impious violence.   The lonely tower
Is also shunn'd; whose mournful chambers hold
(So night-struck Fancy dreams) the yelling ghost.   1680
Among the crooked lanes, on every hedge,
The glow-worm lights his gem; and through the dark
A moving radiance twinkles.   Evening yields
The world to Night; not in her winter-robe
Of massy Stygian woof, but loose-array'd

In mantle dun. A faint erroneous ray,
Glanced from th' imperfect surfaces of things,
Flings half an image on the straining eye;
While wavering woods, and villages, and streams,
And rocks, and mountain tops, that long retain'd   1690
Th' ascending gleam, are all one swimming scene,
Uncertain if beheld. Sudden to heaven
Thence weary vision turns: where, leading soft
The silent hours of love, with purest ray
Sweet Venus shines; and from her genial rise,
When daylight sickens till it springs afresh,
Unrivall'd reigns, the fairest lamp of night.
   As thus th' effulgence tremulous I drink,
With cherish'd gaze, the lambent lightnings shoot
Across the sky; or horizontal dart   1700
In wondrous shapes; by fearful murmuring crowds
Portentous deem'd. Amid the radiant orbs,
That more than deck, that animate the sky,
The life-infusing suns of other worlds;
Lo! from the dread immensity of space
Returning, with accelerated course,
The rushing comet to the sun descends;
And as he sinks below the shading earth,
With awful train projected o'er the heavens,
The guilty nations tremble. But, above   1710
Those superstitious horrors that enslave
The fond sequacious herd, to mystic faith
And blind amazement prone, th' enlighten'd few,
Whose godlike minds philosophy exalts,
The glorious stranger hail. They feel a joy
Divinely great; they in their powers exult,
That wondrous force of thought, which mounting
    spurns
This dusky spot, and measures all the sky;
While, from his far excursion through the wilds
Of barren ether, faithful to his time,   1720
They see the blazing wonder rise anew,
In seeming terror clad, but kindly bent

To work the will of all-sustaining Love;
From his huge vapoury train perhaps to shake
Reviving moisture on the numerous orbs,
Through which his long ellipsis winds; perhaps
To lend new fuel to declining suns,
To light up worlds, and feed th' eternal fire.
　With thee, serene Philosophy, with thee,
And thy bright garland, let me crown my song!　　1730
Effusive source of evidence, and truth!
A lustre shedding o'er th' ennobled mind;
Stronger than summer-noon; and pure as that,
Whose mild vibrations soothe the parted soul,
New to the dawning of celestial day.
Hence through her nourish'd powers, enlarged by
　　thee,
She springs aloft, with elevated pride,
Above the tangling mass of low desires,
That bind the fluttering crowd; and, angel-wing'd,
The heights of science and of virtue gains,　　1740
Where all is calm and clear: with nature round,
Or in the starry regions, or th' abyss,
To Reason's and to Fancy's eye display'd:
The first up-tracing, from the dreary void,
The chain of causes and effects to Him,
The world-producing Essence! who alone
Possesses being; while the last receives
The whole magnificence of heaven and earth,
And every beauty, delicate or bold,
Obvious or more remote, with livelier sense,　　1750
Diffusive painted on the rapid mind.
Tutor'd by thee, hence Poetry exalts
Her voice to ages; and informs the page
With music, image, sentiment, and thought,
Never to die! the treasure of mankind!
Their highest honour, and their truest joy!
　Without thee, what were unenlighten'd Man?
A savage roaming through the woods and wilds,
In quest of prey; and with th' unfashion'd fur

Rough clad; devoid of every finer art,
And elegance of life.   Nor happiness
Domestic, mix'd of tenderness and care,
Nor moral excellence, nor social bliss,
Nor guardian law were his; nor various skill
To turn the furrow, or to guide the tool
Mechanic; nor the heaven-conducted prow
Of navigation bold, that fearless braves
The burning line, or dares the wintry pole;
Mother severe of infinite delights!
Nothing, save rapine, indolence, and guile,   1770
And woes on woes, a still revolving train!
Whose horrid circle had made human life
Than non-existence worse: but taught by thee,
Ours are the plans of policy, and peace;
To live like brothers, and conjunctive all
Embellish life.   While thus laborious crowds
Ply the tough oar, Philosophy directs
The ruling helm; or like the liberal breath
Of potent Heaven, invisible, the sail
Swells out, and bears th' inferior world along.   1780
   Nor to this evanescent speck of earth
Poorly confined, the radiant tracks on high
Are her exalted range; intent to gaze
Creation through; and, from that full complex
Of never-ending wonders, to conceive
Of the Sole Being right, who spoke the word,
And Nature moved complete.   With inward view,
Thence on th' ideal kingdom swift she turns
Her eye: and instant, at her powerful glance,
Th' obedient phantoms vanish or appear;   1790
Compound, divide, and into order shift,
Each to his rank, from plain perception up
To the fair forms of Fancy's fleeting train:
To reason then, deducing truth from truth:
And notion quite abstract; where first begins
The world of spirits, action all, and life
Unfetter'd, and unmix'd.   But here the cloud,

So wills Eternal Providence, sits deep.
Enough for us to know that this dark state,
In wayward passions lost, and vain pursuits,   1800
This Infancy of Being, cannot prove
The final issue of the works of God,
By boundless Love, and perfect Wisdom form'd,
And ever rising with the rising mind.

AUTUMN.

CROWN'D with the sickle and the wheaten sheaf,
While Autumn, nodding o'er the yellow plain,
Comes jovial on, the Doric reed once more,
Well pleased, I tune.   Whate'er the Wintry frost
Nitrous prepared; the various-blossom'd Spring
Put in white promise forth; and Summer-suns
Concocted strong, rush boundless now to view,
Full, perfect all, and swell my glorious theme.
  Onslow! the Muse, ambitious of thy name,
To grace, inspire, and dignify her song,   10
Would from the Public Voice thy gentle ear
A while engage.   Thy noble cares she knows,
The patriot virtues that distend thy thought,
Spread on thy front, and in thy bosom glow:
While listening senates hang upon thy tongue,

Devolving through the maze of eloquence
A roll of periods, sweeter than her song.
But she too pants for public virtue; she,
Though weak of power, yet strong in ardent will,
Whence'er her country rushes on her heart,   20
Assumes a bolder note, and fondly tries.
To mix the patriot's with the poet's flame.
  When the bright Virgin gives the beauteous days,
And Libra weighs in equal scales the year;
From heaven's high cope the fierce effulgence shook
Of parting Summer, a serener blue,
With golden light enliven'd, wide invests
The happy world.   Attemper'd suns arise,
Sweet-beam'd, and shedding oft through lucid clouds
A pleasing calm; while broad, and brown, below   30
Extensive harvests hang the heavy head.
Rich, silent, deep, they stand; for not a gale
Rolls its light billows o'er the bending plain:
A calm of plenty! till the ruffled air
Falls from its poise, and gives the breeze to blow.
Rent is the fleecy mantle of the sky;
The clouds fly different: and the sudden sun
By fits effulgent gilds th' illumined field,
And black by fits the shadows sweep along.
A gaily-chequer'd heart-expanding view,   40
Far as the circling eye can shoot around,
Unbounded tossing in a flood of corn.
  These are thy blessings, Industry! rough power!
Whom labour still attends, and sweat, and pain;
Yet the kind source of every gentle art,
And all the soft civility of life:
Raiser of human kind! by Nature cast,
Naked, and helpless, out amid the woods
And wilds, to rude inclement elements;
With various seeds of art deep in the mind   50
Implanted, and profusely pour'd around
Materials infinite: but idle all.
Still unexerted, in th' unconscious breast,

Slept the lethargic powers; corruption still,
Voracious, swallow'd what the liberal hand
Of bounty scatter'd o'er the savage year;
And still the sad barbarian, roving, mix'd
With beasts of prey; or for his acorn-meal
Fought the fierce tusky boar; a shiv'ring wretch!
Aghast, and comfortless, when the bleak north,   60
With Winter charged, let the mix'd tempest fly,
Hail, rain, and snow, and bitter-breathing frost:
Then to the shelter of the hut he fled;
And the wild season, sordid, pined away,
For home he had not; home is the resort
Of love, of joy, of peace and plenty, where,
Supporting and supported, polish'd friends
And dear relations mingle into bliss.
But this the rugged savage never felt,
Even desolate in crowds; and thus his days   70
Roll'd heavy, dark, and unenjoy'd along:
A waste of time! till Industry approach'd,
And roused him from his miserable sloth:
His faculties unfolded; pointed out,
Where lavish Nature the directing hand
Of Art demanded: show'd him how to raise
His feeble force by the mechanic powers;
To dig the mineral from the vaulted earth;
On what to turn the piercing rage of fire;
On what the torrent, and the gather'd blast;   80
Gave the tall ancient forest to his axe;
Taught him to chip the wood, and hew the stone,
Till by degrees the finish'd fabric rose;
Tore from his limbs the blood-polluted fur,
And wrapt them in the woolly vestment warm,
Or bright in glossy silk, and flowing lawn;
With wholesome viands fill'd his table; pour'd
The generous glass around, inspired to wake
The life-refining soul of decent wit:
Nor stopp'd at barren bare necessity; ✗   90
But still advancing bolder, led him on

To pomp, to pleasure, elegance, and grace:
And, breathing high ambition through his soul,
Set science, wisdom, glory, in his view,
And bade him be the Lord of all below.
   Then gath'ring men their nat'ral powers combined,
And form'd a Public; to the general good
Submitting, aiming and conducting all.
For this the Patriot-Council met, the full,
The free, and fairly represented Whole;   100
For this they plann'd the holy guardian laws,
Distinguish'd orders, animated arts,
And with joint force Oppression chaining, set
Imperial Justice at the helm; yet still
To them accountable: nor slavish dream'd
That toiling millions must resign their weal,
And all the honey of their search, to such
As for themselves alone themselves have raised.
   Hence every form of cultivated life
In order set, protected, and inspired,   110
Into perfection wrought. Uniting all,
Society grew numerous, high, polite,
And happy. Nurse of art! the city rear'd
In beauteous pride her tower-encircled head;
And, stretching street on street, by thousands drew
From twining woody haunts, or the tough yew
To bows strong straining, her aspiring sons.
Then Commerce brought into the public walk
The busy merchant; the big warehouse built;
Raised the strong crane; choked up the loaded street   120
With foreign plenty; and thy stream, O Thames,
Large, gentle, deep, majestic, king of floods!
Chose for his grand resort. On either hand,
Like a long wintry forest, groves of masts
Shot up their spires; the bellying sheet between
Possess'd the breezy void; the sooty hulk
Steer'd sluggish on; the splendid barge along
Row'd, regular, to harmony; around,
The boat light-skimming, stretch'd its oary wing

While deep the various voice of fervent toil   130
From bank to bank increased; whence ribb'd with oak,
To bear the British Thunder, black, and bold,
The roaring vessel rush'd into the main.
    Then too the pillar'd dome, magnific, heaved
Its ample roof; and Luxury within
Pour'd out her glittering stores: the canvas smooth,
With glowing life protuberant, to the view
Embodied rose; the statue seem'd to breathe,
And soften into flesh, beneath the touch
Of forming art, imagination-flush'd.   140
    All is the gift of Industry; whate'er
Exalts, embellishes, and renders life
Delightful. Pensive Winter cheer'd by him
Sits at the social fire, and happy hears
Th' excluded tempest idly rave along;
His harden'd fingers deck the gaudy Spring;
Without him Summer were an arid waste;
Nor to th' Autumnal months could thus transmit
Those full, mature, immeasurable stores,
That, waving round, recall my wandering song.   150
    Soon as the morning trembles o'er the sky,
And, unperceived, unfolds the spreading day;
Before the ripen'd field the reapers stand,
In fair arrray; each by the lass he loves,
To bear the rougher part, and mitigate
By nameless gentle offices her toil.
At once they stoop, and swell the lusty sheaves;
While through their cheerful band, the rural talk,
The rural scandal, and the rural jest,
Fly harmless, to deceive the tedious time,   160
And steal unfelt the sultry hours away.
Behind the master walks, builds up the shocks;
And, conscious, glancing oft on every side
His sated eye, feels his heart heave with joy.
The gleaners spread around, and here and there,
Spike after spike, their scanty harvest pick.
Be not too narrow, husbandmen; but fling

From the full sheaf, with charitable stealth,
The lib'ral handful. Think, oh grateful think!
How good the God of Harvest is to you;   170
Who pours abundance o'er your flowing fields;
While these unhappy partners of your kind
Wide-hover round you, like the fowls of heaven,
And ask their humble dole. The various turns
Of fortune ponder; that your sons may want
What now, with hard reluctance, faint, ye give.
    The lovely young Lavinia once had friends,
And Fortune smiled, deceitful, on her birth;
For, in her helpless years deprived of all,
Of every stay, save innocence and Heaven,   180
She, with her widow'd mother, feeble, old,
And poor, lived in a cottage, far retired
Among the windings of a woody vale;
By solitude and deep-surrounding shades,
But more by bashful modesty conceal'd.
Together thus they shunn'd the cruel scorn
Which virtue, sunk to poverty, would meet
From giddy passion and low-minded pride:
Almost on Nature's common bounty fed;
Like the gay birds that sung them to repose,   190
Content, and careless of to-morrow's fare.
    Her form was fresher than the morning rose,
When the dew wets its leaves; unstain'd and pure,
As is the lily, or the mountain snow.
The modest virtues mingled in her eyes,
Still on the ground dejected, darting all
Their humid beams into the blooming flowers:
Or when the mournful tale her mother told,
Of what her faithless fortune promised once,
Thrill'd in her thought, they, like the dewy star   200
Of evening, shone in tears. A native grace
Sat fair-proportion'd on her polish'd limbs,
Veil'd in a simple robe, their best attire,
Beyond the pomp of dress; for loveliness
Needs not the foreign aid of ornament,

But is, when unadorn'd, adorn'd the most.
Thoughtless of beauty, she was beauty's self,
Recluse amid the close-embowering woods.
As in the hollow breast of Apennine,
Beneath the shelter of encircling hills,   210
A myrtle rises, far from human eye,
And breathes its balmy fragrance o'er the wild;
So flourish'd, blooming, and unseen by all,
The sweet Lavinia; till, at length, compell'd
By strong Necessity's supreme command,
With smiling patience in her looks, she went
To glean Palemon's fields.   The pride of swains
Palemon was, the gen'rous and the rich;
Who led the rural life in all its joy
And elegance, such as Arcadian song   220
Transmits from ancient, uncorrupted times;
When tyrant custom had not shackled Man, ✗
But free to follow Nature was the mode.
He then, his fancy with autumnal scenes
Amusing, chanced beside his reaper-train
To walk, when poor Lavinia drew his eye;
Unconscious of her power, and turning quick
With unaffected blushes from his gaze:
He saw her charming, but he saw not half
The charms her downcast modesty conceal'd.   230
That very moment love and chaste desire
Sprung in his bosom, to himself unknown,
For still the world prevail'd, and its dread laugh,
Which scarce the firm philosopher can scorn,
Should his heart own a gleaner in the field;
And thus in secret to his soul he sigh'd:—
   "What pity! that so delicate a form,
By beauty kindled, where enlivening sense
And more than vulgar goodness seem to dwell,
Should be devoted to the rude embrace   240
Of some indecent clown! She looks, methinks,
Of old Acasto's line; and to my mind
Recalls that patron of my happy life,

From whom my lib'ral fortune took its rise;
Now to the dust gone down; his houses, lands,
And once fair-spreading family, dissolved.
'Tis said that in some lone obscure retreat,
Urged by remembrance sad, and decent pride,
Far from those scenes which knew their better days,
His aged widow and his daughter live,   250
Whom yet my fruitless search could never find,
Romantic wish! would this the daughter were!'
    When, strict inquiring, from herself he found
She was the same, the daughter of his friend,
Of bountiful Acasto, who can speak
The mingled passions that surprised his heart,
And through his nerves in shiv'ring transport ran?
Then blazed his smother'd flame, avow'd and bold;
And as he view'd her, ardent, o'er and o'er,
Love, gratitude, and pity wept at once.   260
Confused, and frighten'd at his sudden tears,
Her rising beauties flush'd a higher bloom,
As thus Palemon, passionate and just,
Pour'd out the pious rapture of his soul:—
    "And art thou then Acasto's dear remains?
She whom my restless gratitude has sought
So long in vain?   O heavens! the very same,
The soften'd image of my noble friend,
Alive his every look, his every feature,
More elegantly touch'd. Sweeter than Spring!   270
Thou sole-surviving blossom from the root
That nourish'd up my fortune! say, ah where,
In what sequester'd desert, hast thou drawn
The kindest aspect of delighted Heaven?
Into such beauty spread, and blown so fair;
Though poverty's cold wind, and crushing rain,   .
Beat keen, and heavy, on thy tender years?
O let me now, into a richer soil,
Transplant thee safe! where vernal suns and show'rs
Difluse their warmest, largest influence;   280
And of my garden be the pride and joy!

Ill it befits thee, oh, it ill befits
Acasto's daughter, his whose open stores,
Though vast, were little to his ampler heart,
The father of a country, thus to pick
The very refuse of those harvest-fields,
Which from his bounteous friendship I enjoy;
Then throw that shameful pittance from thy hand,
But ill applied to such a rugged task;
The fields, the master, all, my fair, are thine;   290
If to the various blessings which thy house
Has on me lavish'd, thou wilt add that bliss,
That dearest bliss, the power of blessing thee!"
   Here ceased the youth: yet still his speaking eye
Express'd the sacred triumph of his soul,
With conscious virtue, gratitude, and love,
Above the vulgar joy divinely raised.
Nor waited he reply.   Won by the charm
Of goodness irresistible, and all
In sweet disorder lost, she blush'd consent.   300
The news immediate to her mother brought,
While, pierced with anxious thought, she pined away
The lonely moments for Lavinia's fate;
Amazed, and scarce believing what she heard,
Joy seized her wither'd veins, and one bright gleam
Of setting life shone on her evening hours:
Not less enraptured than the happy pair;
Who flourish'd long in tender bliss, and rear'd
A numerous offspring, lovely like themselves,
And good, the grace of all the country round.   310
   Defeating oft the labours of the year,
The sultry South collects a potent blast.
At first the groves are scarcely seen to stir
Their trembling tops; and a still murmur runs
Along the soft-inclining fields of corn.
But as th' aerial tempest fuller swells,
And in one mighty stream, invisible,
Immense, the whole excited atmosphere
Impetuous rushes o'er the sounding world;
H

Strain'd to the root, the stooping forest pours   320
A rustling shower of yet untimely leaves.
High-beat, the circling mountains eddy in,
From the bare wild, the dissipated storm,
And send it in a torrent down the vale.
Exposed, and naked, to its utmost rage,
Through all the sea of harvest rolling round,
The billowy plain floats wide; nor can evade,
Though pliant to the blast, its seizing force:
Or whirl'd in air, or into vacant chaff
Shook waste. And sometimes, too, a burst of rain,   330
Swept from the black horizon, broad, descends
In one continuous flood.   Still over head
The mingling tempest weaves its gloom, and still
The deluge deepens; till the fields around
Lie sunk, and flatted, in the sordid wave.
Sudden, the ditches swell; the meadows swim.
Red, from the hills, innumerable streams
Tumultuous roar; and high above its banks
The river lift; before whose rushing tide,
Herds, flocks, and harvests, cottages, and swains,   340
Roll mingled down; all that the winds had spared
In one wild moment ruin'd; the big hopes
And well-earn'd treasures of the painful year.
    Fled to some eminence, the husbandman
Helpless beholds the miserable wreck
Driving along: his drowning ox at once
Descending, with his labours scatter'd round,
He sees; and instant o'er his shivering thought
Comes Winter unprovided, and a train
Of clamant children dear.   Ye masters, then,   350
Be mindful of the rough laborious hand,
That sinks you soft in elegance and ease;
Be mindful of those limbs in russet clad,
Whose toil to yours is warmth, and graceful pride;
And oh! be mindful of that sparing board
Which covers yours with luxury profuse,
Makes your glass sparkle, and your sense rejoice;

Nor cruelly demand what the deep rains
And all-involving winds have swept away.
   Here the rude clamour of the sportsman's joy,   360
The gun fast-thundering, and the winded horn,
Would tempt the Muse to sing the rural game:
How, in his mid-career, the spaniel struck,
Stiff, by the tainted gale, with open nose,
Outstretch'd, and finely sensible, draws full,
Fearful, and cautious, on the latent prey;
As in the sun the circling covey bask
Their varied plumes, and, watchful every way,
Through the rough stubble turn the secret eye.
Caught in the meshy snare, in vain they beat   370
Their idle wings, entangled more and more:
Nor on the surges of the boundless air,
Though borne triumphant, are they safe; the gun
Glanced just, and sudden, from the fowler's eye,
O'ertakes their sounding pinions; and again,
Immediate, brings them from the tow'ring wing,
Dead to the ground; or drives them wide-dispersed,
Wounded, and wheeling various, down the wind.
   These are not subjects for the peaceful Muse,
Nor will she stain with such her spotless song;   380
Then most delighted, when she social sees
The whole mix'd animal-creation round
Alive, and happy. 'Tis not joy to her,
This falsely-cheerful, barbarous game of death;
This rage of pleasure, which the restless youth
Awakes, impatient, with the gleaming morn;
When beasts of prey retire, that all night long,
Urged by necessity, had ranged the dark,
As if their conscious ravage shunn'd the light,
Ashamed.   Not so the steady tyrant man,   390
Who, with the thoughtless insolence of power
Inflamed, beyond the most infuriate wrath
Of the worst monster that e'er roam'd the waste,
For sport alone pursues the cruel chase,
Amid the beamings of the gentle days.

Upbraid, ye ravening tribes, our wanton rage,
For hunger kindles you, and lawless want;
But lavish fed, in Nature's bounty roll'd,
To joy at anguish, and delight in blood,
Is what your horrid bosoms never knew.   400
　　Poor is the triumph o'er the timid hare,
Scared from the corn, and now to some lone seat
Retired: the rushy fen; the ragged furze,
Stretch'd o'er the stony heath: the stubble chapt;
The thistly lawn; the thick-entangled broom;
Of the same friendly hue, the wither'd fern;
The fallow ground laid open to the sun,
Concoctive; and the nodding sandy bank,
Hung o'er the mazes of the mountain brook.
Vain is her best precaution; though she sits   410
Conceal'd, with folded ears; unsleeping eyes,
By Nature raised to take th' horizon in;
And head couch'd close betwixt her hairy feet,
In act to spring away.　The scented dew
Betrays her early labyrinth; and deep,
In scatter'd sullen openings, far behind,
With every breeze she hears the coming storm.
But nearer, and more frequent, as it loads
The sighing gale, she springs amazed, and all
The savage soul of game is up at once: 420
The pack full-opening, various; the shrill horn
Resounded from the hills; the neighing steed,
Wild for the chase; and the loud hunter's shout;
O'er a weak, harmless, flying creature, all
Mix'd in mad tumult, and discordant joy.
　　The stag, too, singled from the herd, where long
He ranged, the branching monarch of the shades,
Before the tempest drives.　At first, in speed,
He, sprightly, puts his faith; and roused by fear,
Gives all his swift aerial soul to flight;   430
Against the breeze he darts, that way the more
To leave the lessening murderous cry behind:
Deception short! though fleeter than the winds

Blown o'er the keen-air'd mountain by the north,
He bursts the thickets, glances through the glades,
And plunges deep into the wildest wood;
If slow, yet sure, adhesive to the track
Hot-steaming, up behind him come again
Th' inhuman rout, and from the shady depth
Expel him, circling through his every shift.   440
He sweeps the forest oft; and, sobbing, sees
The glades, mild opening to the golden day;
Where in kind contest with his butting friends
He wont to struggle, or his loves enjoy.
Oft in the full-descending flood he tries
To lose the scent, and lave his burning sides:
Oft seeks the herd; the watchful herd, alarm'd,
With selfish care avoid a brother's wo.
What shall he do? His once so vivid nerves,
So full of buoyant spirit, now no more   450
Inspire the course; but fainting breathless toil,
Sick, seizes on his heart: he stands at bay;
And puts his last weak refuge in despair.
The big round tears run down his dappled face;
He groans in anguish; while the growling pack,
Blood-happy, hang at his fair jutting chest,
And mark his beauteous chequer'd sides with gore.
    Of this enough. But if the sylvan youth,
Whose fervent blood boils into violence,
Must have the chase, behold, despising flight,   460
The roused-up lion, resolute and slow,
Advancing full on the protended spear,
And coward-band, that circling wheel aloof.
Slunk from the cavern, and the troubled wood,
See the grim wolf; on him his shaggy foe
Vindictive fix, and let the ruffian die:
Or, growling horrid, as the brindled boar
Grins fell destruction, to the monster's heart
Let the dart lighten from the nervous arm.
    These Britain knows not; give, ye Britons, then   470
Your sportive fury, pitiless, to pour

Loose on the nightly robber of the fold:
Him, from his craggy winding haunts unearth'd,
Let all the thunder of the chase pursue.
Throw the broad ditch behind you; o'er the hedge
High-bound, resistless; nor the deep morass
Refuse, but through the shaking wilderness
Pick your nice way; into the perilous flood
Bear fearless, of the raging instinct full;
And as you ride the torrent, to the banks   480
Your triumph sound sonorous, running round,
From rock to rock, in circling echoes tost;
Then scale the mountains to their woody tops;
Rush down the dangerous steep; and o'er the lawn,
In fancy swallowing up the space between,
Pour all your speed into the rapid game.
For happy he, who tops the wheeling chase;
Has every maze evolved, and every guile
Disclosed; who knows the merits of the pack;
. Who saw the villain seized, and dying hard,   490
Without complaint, though by a hundred mouths
Relentless torn: O glorious he, beyond
His daring peers! when the retreating horn
Calls them to ghostly halls of grey renown,
With woodland honours graced; the fox's fur,
Depending decent from the roof; and spread
Round the drear walls, with antic figures fierce,
The stag's large front: he then is loudest heard,
When the night staggers with severer toils,
With feats Thessalian Centaurs never knew,   500
And their repeated wonders shake the dome.
    But first the fuel'd chimney blazes wide;
The tankards foam; and the strong table groans
Beneath the smoking sirloin, stretch'd immense
From side to side; in which, with desperate knife,
They deep incision make, and talk the while
Of England's glory, ne'er to be defaced,
While hence they borrow vigour: or amain
Into the pasty plunged, at intervals,

If stomach keen can intervals allow,   510
Relating all the glories of the chase.
Then sated Hunger bids his brother Thirst
Produce the mighty bowl; the mighty bowl,
Swell'd high with fiery juice, steams liberal round,
A potent gale, delicious, as the breath
Of Maia to the love-sick shepherdess,
On violets diffused, while soft she hears
Her panting shepherd stealing to her arms.
Nor wanting is the brown October, drawn,
Mature and perfect, from his dark retreat   520
Of thirty years; and now his honest front
Flames in the light refulgent, not afraid
Even with the vineyard's best produce to vie.
To cheat the thirsty moments, Whist awhile
Walks his dull round, beneath a cloud of smoke,
Wreath'd, fragrant, from the pipe: or the quick dice,
In thunder leaping from the box, awake
The sounding gammon: while romp-loving miss
Is haul'd about, in gallantry robust.
    At last these puling idlenesses laid   530
Aside, frequent and full, the dry divan
Close in firm circle; and set, ardent, in
For serious drinking.   Nor evasion sly,
Nor sober shift, is to the puking wretch
Indulged apart; but earnest, brimming bowls
Lave every soul, the table floating round,
And pavement, faithless to the fuddled foot.
Thus as they swim in mutual swill, the talk,
Vociferous at once from twenty tongues,
Reels fast from theme to theme; from horses, hounds, 540
To church or mistress, politics or ghost,
In endless mazes, intricate, perplex'd.
    Meantime, with sudden interruption, loud,
Th' impatient catch bursts from the joyous heart;
That moment touch'd is every kindred soul;
And, opening in a full-mouth'd cry of joy,
The laugh the slap, the jocund curse go round;

While, from their slumbers shook, the kennel'd hounds
Mix in the music of the day again.
As when the tempest, that has vex'd the deep   550
The dark night long, with fainter murmurs falls:
So gradual sinks their mirth. Their feeble tongues,
Unable to take up the cumbrous word,
Lie quite dissolved. Before their maudlin eyes,
Seen dim, and blue, the double tapers dance,
Like the sun wading through the misty sky.
Then, sliding soft, they drop. Confused above,
Glasses and bottles, pipes and gazetteers,
As if the table even itself was drunk,
Lie a wet broken scene; and wide, below,   560
Is heap'd the social slaughter: where astride
The lubber Power in filthy triumph sits,
Slumb'rous, inclining still from side to side,
And steeps them drench'd in potent sleep till morn.
Perhaps some doctor, of tremendous paunch,
Awful and deep, a black abyss of drink,
Outlives them all; and from his buried flock
Retiring, full of rumination sad,
Laments the weakness of these latter times.
    But if the rougher sex by this fierce sport   ·570
Is hurried wild, let not such horrid joy
E'er stain the bosom of the British Fair.
Far be the spirit of the chase from them!
Uncomely courage, unbeseeming skill;
To spring the fence, to rein the prancing steed;
The cap, the whip, the masculine attire,
In which they roughen to the sense, and all
The winning softness of their sex is lost.
In them 'tis graceful to dissolve at wo;
With every motion, every word, to wave   580
Quick o'er the kindling cheek the ready blush;
And from the smallest violence to shrink
Unequal, then the loveliest in their fears;
And by this silent adulation, soft,
To their protection more engaging Man.

O may their eyes no miserable sight,
Save weeping lovers, see! a nobler game,
Through Love's enchanting wiles pursued, yet fled,
In chase ambiguous.   May their tender limbs
Float in the loose simplicity of dress!   590
And, fashion'd all to harmony, alone
Know they to seize the captivated soul,
In rapture warbled from love-breathing lips;
To teach the lute to languish; with smooth step,
Disclosing motion in its every charm,
To swim along, and swell the mazy dance;
To train the foliage o'er the snowy lawn;
To guide the pencil, turn the tuneful page;
To lend new flavour to the fruitful year,
And heighten Nature's dainties; in their race   600
To rear their graces into second life;
To give society its highest taste;
Well-order'd Home, Man's best delight to make;
And by submissive wisdom, modest skill
With every gentle care-eluding art,
To raise the virtues, animate the bliss,
And sweeten all the toils of human life:
This be the female dignity, and praise.
     Ye swains, now hasten to the hazel-bank;
Where, down yon dale, the wildly-winding brook   610
Falls hoarse from steep to steep.   In close array,
Fit for the thickets and the tangling shrub,
Ye virgins, come.   For you their latest song
The woodlands raise; the clustering nuts for you
The lover finds amid the secret shade;
And where they burnish on the topmost bough,
With active vigour crushes down the tree;
Or shakes them ripe from the resigning husk,
A glossy shower, and of an ardent brown,
As are the ringlets of Melinda's hair: 620
Melinda! form'd with every grace complete,
Yet these neglecting, above beauty wise,
And far transcending such a vulgar praise.

Hence from the busy, joy-resounding fields,
In cheerful error, let us tread the maze
Of Autumn, unconfined; and taste, revived,
The breath of orchard big with bending fruit.
Obedient to the breeze and beating ray,
From the deep-loaded bough a mellow shower
Incessant melts away. The juicy pear   630
Lies, in a soft profusion, scatter'd round.
A various sweetness swells the gentle race:
By Nature's all-refining hand prepared,
Of temper'd sun, and water, earth, and air,
In ever-changing composition mixt.   .
Such, falling frequent through the chiller night,
The fragrant stores, the wide-projected heaps
Of apples, which the lusty-handed year,
Innumerous, o'er the blushing orchard shakes.
A various spirit, fresh, delicious, keen,   640
Dwells in their gelid pores; and, active, points
The piercing cider for the thirsty tongue:
Thy native theme, and boon inspirer too,
Philips, Pomona's bard, the second thou
Who nobly durst, in rhyme-unfetter'd verse,
With British freedom sing the British song:
How, from Silurian vats, high sparkling wines
Foam in transparent floods; some strong, to cheer
The wintry revels of the labouring hind;
And tasteful some, to cool the summer hours.   650
    In this glad season, while his sweetest beams
The sun sheds equal o'er the meeken'd day;
Oh, lose me in the green delightful walks
Of Dodington, thy seat, serene and plain;
Where simple Nature reigns: and every view
Diffusive, spreads the pure Dorsetian downs,
In boundless prospect; yonder shagg'd with wood,
Here rich with harvest, and there white with flocks!
Meantime, the grandeur of thy lofty dome,
Far-splendid, seizes on the ravish'd eye.   660
New beauties rise with each revolving day;

New columns swell; and still the fresh Spring finds
New plants to quicken, and new groves to green.
Full of thy genius all! the Muses' seat:
Where, in the secret bower and winding walk,
For virtuous Young and thee they twine the bay.
Here wandering oft, fired with the restless thirst
Of thy applause, I solitary court
Th' inspiring breeze: and meditate the book
Of Nature ever open; aiming thence,   670
Warm from the heart, to learn the moral song.
Here, as I steal along the sunny wall,
Where Autumn basks, with fruit empurpled deep,
My pleasing theme continual prompts my thought;
Presents the downy peach; the shining plum;
The ruddy, fragrant nectarine; and dark,
Beneath his ample leaf, the luscious fig.
The vine too here her curling tendrils shoots;
Hangs out her clusters, glowing to the south;
And scarcely wishes for a warmer sky.   680
    Turn we a moment Fancy's rapid flight
To vigorous soils, and climes of fair extent;
Where, by the potent sun elated high,
The vineyard swells refulgent on the day;
Spreads o'er the vale; or up the mountain climbs,
Profuse; and drinks amid the sunny rocks,
From cliff to cliff increased, the heighten'd blaze.
Low bend the weighty boughs. The clusters clear,
Half through the foliage seen, or ardent flame,
Or shine transparent; while perfection breathes   690
White o'er the turgent film the living dew.
As thus they brighten with exalted juice,
Touch'd into flavour by the mingling ray,
The rural youth and virgins o'er the field,
Each fond for each to cull th' autumnal prime,
Exulting rove, and speak the vintage nigh.
Then comes the crushing swain; the country floats,
And foams unbounded with the mashy flood;
That by degrees fermented, and refined,

Round the raised nations pours the cup of joy: 700
The claret smooth, red as the lip we press
In sparkling fancy, while we drain the bowl;
The mellow-tasted burgundy; and quick,
As is the wit it gives, the gay champaign.
   Now, by the cool declining year condensed,
Descend the copious exhalations, check'd
As up the middle sky unseen they stole,
And roll the doubling fogs around the hill.
No more the mountain, horrid, vast, sublime,
Who pours a sweep of rivers from his sides,   710
And high between contending kingdoms rears
The rocky long division, fills the view
With great variety; but in a night
Of gathering vapour, from the baffled sense
Sinks dark and dreary. Thence expanding far,
The huge dusk, gradual, swallows up the plain:
Vanish the woods; the dim-seen river seems
Sullen, and slow, to roll the misty wave.
Even in the height of noon opprest, the sun
Sheds weak, and blunt, his wide-refracted ray;   720
Whence glaring oft, with many a broaden'd orb,
He frights the nations. Indistinct on earth,
Seen through the turbid air, beyond the life
Objects appear; and, wilder'd, o'er the waste
The shepherd stalks gigantic. Till at last
Wreath'd dun around, in deeper circles still,
Successive closing, sits the general fog
Unbounded o'er the world; and, mingling thick,
A formless grey confusion covers all:
As when of old (so sung the Hebrew Bard)   730
Light, uncollected, through the chaos urgea
Its infant way; nor Order yet had drawn
His lovely train from out the dubious gloom.
   These roving mists, that constant now begin
To smoke along the hilly country, these,
With weighty rains, and melted Alpine snows,
The mountain-cisterns fill, those ample stores

Of water, scoop'd among the hollow rocks;
Whence gush the streams, the ceaseless fountains play,
And their unfailing wealth the rivers draw.   740
Some sages say, that where the numerous wave
For ever lashes the resounding shore,
Drill'd through the sandy stratum, every way,
The waters with the sandy stratum rise;
Amid whose angles infinitely strain'd,
They joyful leave their jaggy salts behind,
And clear and sweeten, as they soak along.
Nor stops the restless fluid, mounting still,
Though oft amidst th' irriguous vale it springs;
But to the mountain courted by the sand,   750
That leads it darkling on in faithful maze,
Far from the parent-main, it boils again
Fresh into day; and all the glittering hill
Is bright with spouting rills.   But hence this vain
Amusive dream! why should the waters love
To take so far a journey to the hills,
When the sweet valleys offer to their toil
Inviting quiet, and a nearer bed?
Or if, by blind ambition led astray,
They must aspire; why should they sudden stop   760
Among the broken mountain's rushy dells,
And, ere they gain its highest peak, desert
Th' attractive sand that charm'd their course so long?
Besides, the hard agglomerating salts,
The spoils of ages, would impervious choke
Their secret channels; or, by slow degrees,
High as the hills protrude the swelling vales.
Old Ocean too, suck'd through the porous globe,
Had long ere now forsook his horrid bed,
And brought Deucalion's wat'ry times again.   770
    Say then, where lurk the vast eternal springs,
That, like creating Nature, lie conceal'd
From mortal eye, yet with their lavish stores
Refresh the globe, and all its joyous tribes?
O thou pervading Genius, given to Man,

To trace the secrets of the dark abyss,
O lay the mountains bare! and wide display
Their hidden structure to th' astonish'd view!
Strip from the branching Alps their piny load;
The huge incumbrance of horrific woods   780
From Asian Taurus, from Imaus stretch'd
Athwart the roving Tartar's sullen bounds!
Give opening Hemus to my searching eye,
And high Olympus pouring many a stream!
O from the sounding summits of the north,
The Dofrine Hills, through Scandinavia roll'd
To farthest Lapland and the frozen main;
From lofty Caucasus, far seen by those
Who in the Caspian and black Euxine toil;
From cold Riphean Rocks, which the wild Russ   790
Believes the stony girdle of the world;
And all the dreadful mountains wrapt in storm,
Whence wide Siberia draws her lonely floods:
O sweep th' eternal snows, hung o'er the deep,
That ever works beneath his sounding base!
Bid Atlas, propping heaven, as poets feign,
His subterranean wonders spread! unveil
The miny caverns, blazing on the day,
Of Abyssinia's cloud-compelling cliffs,
And of the bending Mountains of the Moon!   800
O'ertopping all these giant-sons of earth,
Let the dire Andes, from the radiant Line
Stretch'd to the stormy seas that thunder round
The southern pole, their hideous deeps unfold!
    Amazing scene!   Behold! the glooms disclose;
I see the rivers in their infant beds!
Deep, deep I hear them lab'ring to get free;
I see the leaning strata, artful ranged;
The gaping fissures to receive the rains,
The melting snows, and ever-dripping fogs.   810
Strow'd bibulous above I see the sands,
The pebbly gravel next, the layers then
Of mingled moulds, of more retentive earths,

The gutter'd rocks and mazy-running clefts;
That, while the stealing moisture they transmit,
Retard its motion, and forbid its waste.
Beneath th' incessant weeping of these drains
I see the rocky siphons stretch'd immense;
The mighty reservoirs of harden'd chalk,
Or stiff compacted clay, capacious form'd.   820
O'erflowing thence, the congregated stores,
The crystal treasures of the liquid world,
Through the stirr'd sands a bubbling passage burst;
And welling out, around the middle steep,
Or from the bottoms of the bosom'd hills,
In pure effusion flow. United, thus,
Th' exhaling sun, the vapour-burden'd air,
The gelid mountains, that to rain condensed,
These vapours in continual current draw,
And send them, o'er the fair-divided earth,   830
In bounteous rivers to the deep again,
A social commerce hold, and firm support
The full-adjusted harmony of things.
    When Autumn scatters his departing gleams,
Warn'd of approaching Winter, gather'd, play
The swallow-people; and toss'd wide around,
O'er the calm sky, in convolution swift,
The feather'd eddy floats; rejoicing once,
Ere to their wintry slumbers they retire;
In clusters clung, beneath the mould'ring bank,   840
And where, unpierced by frost, the cavern sweats.
Or rather into warmer climes convey'd,
With other kindred birds of season, there
They twitter cheerful, till the vernal months
Invite them welcome back: for, thronging, now
Innumerous wings are in commotion all.
    Where the Rhine loses his majestic force
In Belgian plains, won from the raging deep,
By diligence amazing, and the strong
Unconquerable hand of Liberty,   850
The stork-assembly meets; for many a day,

Consulting deep, and various, ere they take
Their arduous voyage through the liquid sky
And now their route design'd, their leaders chose,
Their tribes adjusted, clean'd their vigorous wings;
And many a circle, many a short essay,
Wheel'd round and round, in congregation full,
The figured flight ascends; and, riding high
Th' aerial billows, mixes with the clouds.
    Or, where the Northern Ocean, in vast whirls,   860
Boils round the naked melancholy isles
Of farthest Thule, and th' Atlantic surge
Pours in among the stormy Hebrides;
Who can recount what transmigrations there
Are annual made? what nations come and go?
And how the living clouds on clouds arise?
Infinite wings! till all the plume-dark air,
And rude-resounding shore, are one wild cry.
    Here the plain harmless native, his small flock,
And herd diminutive of many hues,   870
Tends on the little island's verdant swell,
The shepherd's sea-girt reign; or, to the rocks
Dire-clinging, gathers his ovarious food;
Or sweeps the fishy shore; or treasures up
The plumage, rising full, to form the bed
Of luxury. And here awhile the Muse,
High-hovering o'er the broad cerulean scene,
Sees Caledonia, in romantic view;
Her airy mountains, from the waving main,
Invested with a keen diffusive sky,   880
Breathing the soul acute; her forests huge,
Incult, robust, and tall, by Nature's hand
Planted of old; her azure lakes between,
Pour'd out extensive, and of wat'ry wealth
Full; winding deep, and green, her fertile vales;
With many a cool, translucent, brimming flood
Wash'd lovely, from the Tweed (pure parent stream,
Whose pastoral banks first heard my Doric reed,
With, sylvan Jed, thy tributary brook),

To where the north-inflated tempest foams   890
O'er Orca's or Betubium's highest peak:
Nurse of a people, in misfortune's school
Train'd up to hardy deeds; soon visited
By learning, when before the Gothic rage
She took her western flight.   A manly race,
Of unsubmitting spirit, wise and brave;
Who still through bleeding ages struggled hard
(As well unhappy Wallace can attest,
Great patriot-hero! ill requited chief!)
To hold a generous undiminish'd state;   900
Too much in vain!   Hence of unequal bounds
Impatient, and by tempting glory borne
O'er every land; for every land their life
Has flow'd profuse, their piercing genius plann'd,
And swell'd the pomp of peace their faithful toil:
As from their own clear north, in radiant streams,
Bright over Europe bursts the Boreal Morn.
    Oh! is there not some patriot, in whose power
That best, that godlike Luxury is placed,
Of blessing thousands, thousands yet unborn,   910
Through late posterity? some, large of soul,
To cheer dejected industry? to give
A double harvest to the pining swain?
And teach the lab'ring hand the sweets of toil?
How, by the finest art, the native robe
To weave; how white as hyperborean snow
To form the lucid lawn; with vent'rous oar
How to dash wide the billow; nor look on,
Shamefully passive, while Batavian fleets
Defraud us of the glittering finny swarms,   920
That heave our friths, and crowd upon our shores?
How all-enlivening trade to rouse, and wing
The prosperous sail, from every growing port
Uninjured, round the sea-encircled globe;
And thus, in soul united as in name,
Bid Britain reign the mistress of the deep?
    Yes, there are such.   And full on thee, Argyle,
    I

Her hope, her stay, her darling, and her boast,
From her first patriots and her heroes sprung,
Thy fond imploring Country turns her eye: 930
In thee, with all a mother's triumph, sees
Her every virtue, every grace combined;
Her genius, wisdom, her engaging turn,   .
Her pride of honour, and her courage tried,
Calm, and intrepid, in the very throat
Of sulph'rous war, on Tenier's dreadful field.
Nor less the palm of peace inwreaths thy brow:
For, powerful as thy sword, from thy rich tongue
Persuasion flows, and wins the high debate;
While mix'd in thee combine the charm of youth,   940
The force of manhood, and the depth of age.
Thee, Forbes, too, whom every worth attends,
As truth sincere, as weeping friendship kind;
Thee, truly generous, and in silence great,
Thy country feels through her reviving arts,
Plann'd by thy wisdom, by thy soul inform'd;
And seldom has she known a friend like thee.
     But see the fading many-colour'd woods,
Shade deepening over shade, the country round
Imbrown; a crowded umbrage, dusk, and dun,   .   95
Of every hue, from wan declining green
To sooty dark.   These now the lonesome Muse,
Low-whispering, lead into their leaf-strown walks,
And give the season in its latest view.
     Meantime, light-shadowing all, a sober calm
Fleeces unbounded ether; whose least wave
Stands tremulous, uncertain where to turn
The gentle current; while illumined wide,
The dewy-skirted clouds imbibe the sun,
And through their lucid veil his soften'd force   960
Shed o'er the peaceful world.   Then is the time,
For those whom wisdom and whom Nature charm,
To steal themselves from the degenerate crowd,
And soar above this little scene of things;
To tread low-thoughted vice beneath their feet;

To soothe the throbbing passions into peace,
And woo lone Quiet in her silent walks.
Thus solitary, and in pensive guise,
Oft let me wander o'er the russet mead,
And through the sadden'd grove, where scarce is heard 970
One dying strain, to cheer the woodman's toil.
Haply some widow'd songster pours his plaint,
Far, in faint warblings, through the tawny copse;
While congregated thrushes, linnets, larks,
And each wild throat, whose artless strains so late
Swell'd all the music of the swarming shades,
Robb'd of their tuneful souls, now shivering sit
On the dead tree, a dull despondent flock;
With not a brightness waving o'er their plumes,
And nought save chattering discord in their note.   980
O let not, aim'd from some inhuman eye,
The gun the music of the coming year
Destroy; and harmless, unsuspecting harm,
Lay the weak tribes, a miserable prey,
In mingled murder, fluttering on the ground!
The pale descending year, yet pleasing still
A gentler mood inspires; for now the leaf
Incessant rustles from the mournful grove;
Oft startling such as, studious, walk below,
And slowly circles through the waving air.   990
But should a quicker breeze amid the boughs
Sob, o'er the sky the leafy deluge streams;
Till choked, and matted with the dreary shower
The forest-walks, at every rising gale,
Roll wide the wither'd waste, and whistle bleak.
Fled is the blasted verdure of the fields;
And, shrunk into their beds, the flowery race
Their sunny robes resign.   Even what remain'd
Of stronger fruits falls from the naked tree:
And woods, fields, gardens, orchards, all around   1000
The desolated prospect thrills the soul.
He comes! he comes! in every breeze the Power
Of Philosophic Melancholy comes!

His near approach the sudden-starting tear,
The glowing cheek, the mild dejected air,
The soften'd feature, and the beating heart,
Pierced deep with many a virtuous pang, declare.
O'er all the soul his sacred influence breathes,
Inflames imagination; through the breast
Infuses every tenderness; and far   1010
Beyond dim earth exalts the swelling thought.
Ten thousand thousand fleet ideas, such
As never mingled with the vulgar dream,
Crowd fast into the Mind's creative eye.
As fast the correspondent passions rise,
As varied, and as high: devotion raised
To rapture, and divine astonishment;
The love of Nature unconfined, and, chief,
Of human race; the large ambitious wish
To make them blest; the sigh for suffering worth   1020
Lost in obscurity; the noble scorn
Of tyrant-pride; the fearless great resolve;
The wonder which the dying patriot draws,
Inspiring glory through remotest time;
Th' awaken'd throb for virtue, and for fame;
The sympathies of love, and friendship dear;
With all the social offspring of the heart.
  Oh bear me then to vast embowering shades,
To twilight groves, and visionary vales;
To weeping grottoes, and prophetic glooms;   1030
Where angel-forms athwart the solemn dusk
Tremendous sweep, or seem to sweep along:
And voices more than human, through the void
Deep-sounding, seize th' enthusiastic ear.
  Or is this gloom too much? Then lead, ye Powers,
That o'er the garden and the rural seat
Preside, which shining through the cheerful land
In countless numbers blest Britannia sees;
O lead me to the wide-extended walks,
The fair majestic paradise of Stowe!   1040
Not Persian Cyrus on Ionia's shore

E'er saw such sylvan scenes; such various art
By genius fired, such ardent genius tamed
By cool judicious art; that, in the strife,
All-beauteous Nature fears to be outdone.
And there, O Pitt! thy country's early boast,
There let me sit beneath the shelter'd slopes,
Or in that Temple where, in future times,
Thou well shalt merit a distinguish'd name;
And, with thy converse blest, catch the last smiles   1050
Of Autumn beaming o'er the yellow woods,
While there with thee th' enchanted round I walk,
The regulated wild; gay Fancy then
Will tread in thought the groves of Attic Land;
Will from thy standard taste refine her own,
Correct her pencil to the purest truth
Of Nature, or, the unimpassion'd shades
Forsaking, raise it to the human mind,
Or if hereafter she, with juster hand,
Shall draw the tragic scene, instruct her thou   1060
To mark the varied movements of the heart,
What every decent character requires,
And every passion speaks: O through her strain
Breathe thy pathetic eloquence! that moulds
Th' attentive senate, charms, persuades, exalts;
Of honest zeal th' indignant lightning throws,
And shakes corruption on her venal throne.
   While thus we talk, and through Elysian Vales
Delighted rove, perhaps a sigh escapes:
What pity, Cobham, thou thy verdant files   1070
Of order'd trees shouldst here inglorious range,
Instead of squadrons flaming o'er the field,
And long embattled hosts; when the proud foe,
The faithless vain disturber of mankind,
Insulting Gaul, has roused the world to war;
When keen, once more, within their bounds to press
Those polish'd robbers, those ambitious slaves,
The British youth would hail thy wise command,
Thy temper'd ardour and thy vet'ran skill.

The western sun withdraws the shorten'd day;   1080
And humid Evening, gliding o'er the sky,
In her chill progress, to the ground condensed
The vapours throws.   Where creeping waters ooze,
Where marshes stagnate, and where rivers wind,
Cluster the rolling fogs, and swim along
The dusky-mantled lawn.   Meanwhile the moon,
Full-orb'd and breaking through the scatter'd clouds,
Shows her broad visage in the crimson'd east;
Turn'd to the sun direct, her spotted disk,
Where mountains rise, umbrageous dales descend,   1090
And caverns deep, as optic tube descries,
A smaller earth, gives us his blaze again
Void of its flame, and sheds a softer day.
Now through the passing cloud she seems to stoop,
Now up the pure cerulean rides sublime.
Wide the pale deluge floats, and streaming mild
O'er the sky'd mountain to the shadowy vale,
While rocks and floods reflect the quiv'ring gleam,
The whole air whitens with a boundless tide
Of silver radiance, trembling round the world.   1100
But when half-blotted from the sky her light,
Fainting, permits the starry fires to burn
With keener lustre through the depth of heaven;
Or near extinct her deaden'd orb appears,
And scarce appears, of sickly beamless white;
Oft in this season, silent from the north
A blaze of meteors shoots: ensweeping first
The lower skies, they all at once converge
High to the crown of heaven, and all at once
Relapsing quick, as quickly re-ascend,   1110
And mix, and thwart, extinguish, and renew,
All ether coursing in a maze of light.
From look to look, contagious through the crowd,
The panic runs, and into wondrous shapes
Th'appearance throws: armies in meet array,
Throng'd with aerial spears and steeds of fire;
Till the long lines of full-extended war

In bleeding fight commixt, the sanguine flood
Rolls a broad slaughter o'er the plains of heaven.
As thus they scan the visionary scene,   1120
On all sides swells the superstitious din,
Incontinent; and busy frenzy talks
Of blood and battle; cities overturn'd;
And late at night in swallowing earthquake sunk,
Or hideous wrapt in fierce ascending flame
Of sallow famine, inundation, storm;
Of pestilence, and every great distress;
Empires subversed, when ruling fate has struck
Th' unalterable hour: even Nature's self
Is deem'd to totter on the brink of time.   1130
Not so the Man of philosophic eye,
And inspect sage; the waving brightness he
Curious surveys, inquisitive to know
The causes, and materials, yet unfix'd,
Of this appearance beautiful and new.
    Now black, and deep, the night begins to fall,
A shade immense! Sunk in the quenching gloom,
Magnificent and vast, are heaven and earth.
Order confounded lies; all beauty void;
Distinction lost; and gay variety   1140
One universal blot: such the fair power
Of light, to kindle and create the whole.
Drear is the state of the benighted wretch,
Who then, bewilder'd, wanders through the dark,
Full of pale fancies, and chimeras huge;
Nor visited by one directive ray,
From cottage streaming, or from airy hall.
Perhaps impatient as he stumbles on,
Struck from the root of slimy rushes, blue,
The wild-fire scatters round, or gather'd trails   1150
A length of flame deceitful o'er the moss:
Whither decoy'd by the fantastic blaze,
Now lost and now renew'd, he sinks absorpt
Rider and horse, amid the miry gulf;
While still, from day to day, his pining wife,

And plaintive children, his return await,
In wild conjecture lost.   At other times,
Sent by the better Genius of the night,
Innoxious, gleaming on the horse's mane,
The meteor sits; and shows the narrow path,   1160
That winding leads through pits of death, or else
Instructs him how to take the dangerous ford.

 The lengthen'd night elapsed, the morning shines,
Serene, in all her dewy beauty bright,
Unfolding fair the last autumnal day.
And now the mounting sun dispels the fog;
The rigid hoar-frost melts before his beam;
And hung on every spray, on every blade
Of grass, the myriad dew-drops twinkle round.

 Ah see where robb'd, and murder'd, in that pit   1170
Lies the still heaving hive! at evening snatch'd,
Beneath the cloud of guilt-concealing night,
And fix'd o'er sulphur: while, not dreaming ill,
The happy people in their waxen cells
Sat tending public cares, and planning schemes
Of temperance, for Winter poor; rejoiced
To mark, full flowing round, their copious stores.
Sudden the dark oppressive steam ascends;
And, used to milder scents, the tender race,
By thousands, tumble from their honey'd domes,   1180
Convolved, and agonising in the dust.
And was it then for this you roam'd the Spring,
Intent from flower to flower? for this you toil'd,
Ceaseless, the burning Summer-heats away?
For this in Autumn search'd the blooming waste,
Nor lost one sunny gleam, for this sad fate?
O Man! tyrannic lord! how long, how long
Shall prostrate Nature groan beneath your rage,
Awaiting renovation?   When obliged,
Must you destroy?   Of their ambrosial food   1190
Can you not borrow; and, in just return,
Afford them shelter from the wintry winds?
Or, as the sharp year pinches, with their own

Again regale them on some smiling day?
See where the stony bottom of their town
Looks desolate, and wild; with here and there
A helpless number, who the ruin'd state
Survive, lamenting weak, cast out to death.
Thus a proud city, populous and rich,
Full of the works of peace, and high in joy,   1200
At theatre or feast, or sunk in sleep
(As late, Palermo, was thy fate), is seized
By some dread earthquake, and convulsive hurl'd
Sheer from the black foundation, stench-involved,
Into a gulf of blue sulphureous flame.
    Hence every harsher sight! for now the day,
O'er heaven and earth diffused, grows warm, and high;
Infinite splendour! wide investing all.
How still the breeze! save what the filmy thread
Of dew evaporate brushes from the plain.   1210
How clear the cloudless sky! how deeply tinged
With a peculiar blue! th' ethereal arch
How swelled immense! amid whose azure throned,
The radiant sun how gay! how calm below
The gilded earth! the harvest treasures all
Now gather'd in, beyond the rage of storms,
Sure to the swain; the circling fence shut up;
And instant Winter's utmost rage defied.
While, loose to festive joy, the country round
Laughs with the loud sincerity of mirth,   1220
Shook to the wind their cares. The toil-strung youth,
By the quick sense of music taught alone,
Leaps wildly graceful in the lively dance.
Her every charm abroad, the village toast,
Young, buxom, warm, in native beauty rich,
Darts not unmeaning looks; and where her eye
Points an approving smile, with double force
The cudgel rattles, and the wrestler twines.
Age too shines out; and, garrulous, recounts
The feats of youth. Thus they rejoice; nor think   1230
That, with to-morrow's sun, their annual toil

Begins again the never-ceasing round.
  Oh knew he but his happiness, of Men
The happiest he! who far from public rage,
Deep in the vale, with a choice Few retired,
Drinks the pure pleasures of the Rural Life.
What though the dome be wanting, whose proud gate,
Each morning vomits out the sneaking crowd
Of flatterers false, and in their turn abused?
Vile intercourse! What though the glittering robe,   1240
Of every hue reflected light can give.
Or floating loose, or stiff with mazy gold
(The pride and gaze of fools!), oppress him not?
What though, from utmost land and sea purvey'd,
For him each rarer tributary life
Bleeds not, and his insatiate table heaps
With luxury and death? What though his bowl
Flames not with costly juice; nor sunk in beds,
Oft of gay care, he tosses out the night,
Or melts the thoughtless hours in idle state?   1250
What though he knows not those fantastic joys,
That still amuse the wanton, still deceive;
A face of pleasure, but a heart of pain;
Their hollow moments undelighted all?
Sure peace is his; a solid life, estranged
To disappointment, and fallacious hope:
Rich in content, in Nature's bounty rich,
In herbs and fruits; whatever greens the Spring,
When heaven descends in showers; or bends the bough
When Summer reddens, and when Autumn beams;   1260
Or in the wintry glebe whatever lies
Conceal'd, and fattens with the richest sap:
These are not wanting; nor the milky drove,
Luxuriant, spread o'er all the lowing vale;
Nor bleating mountains; nor the chide of streams,
And hum of bees, inviting sleep sincere
Into the guiltless breast, beneath the shade,
Or thrown at large amid the fragrant hay;
Nor aught besides of prospect, grove, or song,

Dim grottoes, gleaming lakes, and fountain clear.   1270
Here too dwells simple truth; plain innocence;
Unsullied beauty; sound unbroken youth,
Patient of labour, with a little pleased;
Health ever blooming; unambitious toil;
Calm contemplation, and poetic ease.
   Let others brave the flood in quest of gain,
And beat, for joyless months, the gloomy wave:
Let such as deem it glory to destroy,
Rush into blood, the sack of cities seek:
Unpierced, exulting in the widow's wail,   1280
The virgin's shriek, and infant's trembling cry:
Let some, far-distant from their native soil,
Urged or by want or harden'd avarice,
Find other lands beneath another sun:
Let this through cities work his eager way,
By legal outrage and establish'd guile,
The social sense extinct; and that ferment
Mad into tumult the seditious herd,
Or melt them down to slavery: let these
Ensnare the wretched in the toils of law,   1290
Fomenting discord, and perplexing right,
An iron race! and those of fairer front,
But equal inhumanity, in courts,
Delusive pomp, and dark cabals, delight,
Wreath the deep bow, diffuse the lying smile,
And tread the weary labyrinth of state:
While he, from all the stormy passions free
That restless Men involve, hears, and but hears,
At distance safe, the human tempest roar,
Wrapt close in conscious peace.   The fall of kings,   1300
The rage of nations, and the crush of states,
Move not the Man, who, from the world escaped,
In still retreats, and flowery solitudes,
To Nature's voice attends, from month to month,
And day to day, through the revolving year;
Admiring, sees her in her every shape;
Feels all her sweet emotions at his heart;

Takes what she liberal gives, nor thinks of more.
He, when young Spring protrudes the bursting gems,
Marks the first bud, and sucks the healthful gale   1310
Into his freshen'd soul; her genial hours
He full enjoys; and not a beauty blows,
And not an opening blossom breathes in vain.
In Summer he, beneath the living shade,
Such as o'er frigid Tempe wont to wave,
Or Hemus cool, reads what the Muse, of these
Perhaps, has in immortal numbers sung;
Or what she dictates, writes: and, oft an eye
Shot round, rejoices in the vigorous year.
    When Autumn's yellow lustre gilds the world,   1320
And tempts the sickled swain into the field,
Seized by the general joy, his heart distends
With gentle throes; and through the tepid gleams
Deep musing, then he best exerts his song.
Even Winter wild to him is full of bliss.
The mighty tempest, and the hoary waste,
Abrupt, and deep, stretch'd o'er the buried earth,
Awake to solemn thought.   At night the skies,
Disclosed and kindled by refining frost,
Pour every lustre on th' exalted eye.   1330
A friend, a book, the stealing hours secure,
And mark them down for wisdom.   With swift wing,
O'er land and sea imagination roams;
Or truth divinely breaking on his mind,
Elates his being, and unfolds his powers;
Or in his breast heroic virtue burns.
The touch of kindred, too, and love he feels;
The modest eye, whose beams on his alone
Ecstatic shine; the little strong embrace
Of prattling children, twined around his neck,   1340
And emulous to please him, calling forth
The fond parental soul.   Nor purpose gay,
Amusement, dance, or song, he sternly scorns;
For happiness and true philosophy
Are of the social still, and smiling kind.

This is the life which those who fret in guilt,
And guilty cities, never knew; the life,
Led by primeval ages, uncorrupt,
When angels dwelt, and God himself, with Man!
  Oh Nature! all-sufficient! over all!   1350
Enrich me with the knowledge of thy works!
Snatch me to heaven; thy rolling wonders there,
World beyond world, in infinite extent,
Profusely scatter'd o'er the blue immense,
Show me; their motions, periods, and their laws,
Give me to scan; through the disclosing deep
Light my blind way: the mineral strata there;
Thrust, blooming, thence the vegetable world;
O'er that the rising system, more complex,
Of animals; and higher still, the mind,   1360
The varied scene of quick-compounded thought,
And where the mixing passions endless shift;
These ever open to my ravish'd eye;
A search, the flight of time can ne'er exhaust!
  But if to that unequal; if the blood,
In sluggish streams, about my heart, forbid
That best ambition; under closing shades,
Inglorious, lay me by the lowly brook,
And whisper to my dreams. From Thee begin,
Dwell all on Thee, with Thee conclude my song;   1370
And let me never—never stray from Thee!

WINTER.

SEE Winter comes, to rule the varied year,
Sullen and sad, with all his rising train,
Vapours, and Clouds, and Storms.   Be these my theme;
These! that exalt the soul to solemn thought,
And heavenly musing.   Welcome, kindred glooms!
Congenial horrors, hail! with frequent foot,
Pleased have I, in my cheerful morn of life,
When nursed by careless solitude I lived,
And sung of Nature with unceasing joy—
Pleased have I wander'd through your rough domain;   10
Trod the pure virgin-snows, myself as pure;
Heard the winds roar, and the big torrent burst;
Or seen the deep fermenting tempest brew'd,
In the grim evening sky.   Thus pass'd the time,
Till through the lucid chambers of the South
Look'd out the joyous Spring, look'd out, and smiled.
    To thee, the patron of her first essay,
The Muse, O Wilmington! renews her song.
Since, has she rounded the revolving year;

Skimm'd the gay Spring; on eagle-pinions borne,
Attempted through the Summer-blaze to rise;
Then swept o'er Autumn with the shadowy gale;
And now among the wintry clouds again,
Roll'd in the doubling storm, she tries to soar;
To swell her note with all the rushing winds;
To suit her sounding cadence to the floods;
As is her theme, her numbers wildly great:
Thrice happy! could she fill thy judging ear
With bold description, and with manly thought.
 Nor art thou skill'd in awful schemes alone,
And how to make a mighty people thrive:
But equal goodness, sound integrity,
A firm, unshaken, uncorrupted soul
Amid a sliding age, and burning strong,
Nor vainly blazing for thy country's weal,
A steady spirit, regularly free;
These, each exalting each, the statesman light
Into the patriot; these, the public hope
And eye to thee converting, bid the Muse
Record what envy dares not flattery call.
 Now, when the cheerless empire of the sky
To Capricorn the Centaur Archer yields,
And fierce Aquarius stains th' inverted year;
Hung o'er the farthest verge of heaven, the sun
Scarce spreads through ether the dejected day.
Faint are his gleams, and ineffectual shoot
His struggling rays, in horizontal lines,
Through the thick air; as clothed in cloudy storm,
Weak, wan, and broad, he skirts the southern sky;
And, soon-descending, to the long dark night,
Wide-shading all, the prostrate world resigns.
Nor is the night unwish'd; while vital heat,
Light, life, and joy, the dubious day forsake.
Meantime, in sable cincture, shadows vast,
Deep-tinged and damp, and congregated clouds,
And all the vapoury turbulence of heaven,
Involve the face of things.   Thus Winter falls,

A heavy gloom oppressive o'er the world,
Through Nature shedding influence malign,
And rouses up the seeds of dark disease.   60
    The soul of Man dies in him, loathing life,
And black with more than melancholy views.
The cattle droop; and o'er the furrow'd land,
Fresh from the plough, the dun-discolour'd flocks,
Untended, spreading, crop the wholesome root.
Along the woods, along the moorish fens,
Sighs the sad Genius of the coming storm:
And up among the loose-disjointed cliffs,
And fractured mountains wild, the brawling brook,
And cave, presageful, send a hollow moan,   70
Resounding long in listening Fancy's ear.
    Then comes the father of the tempest forth,
Wrapt in black glooms.   First joyless rains obscure
Drive through the mingling skies with vapour foul;
Dash on the mountain's brow, and shake the woods,
That grumbling wave below.   Th' unsightly plain
Lies a brown deluge; as the low-bent clouds
Pour flood on flood, yet unexhausted still
Combine, and, deepening into night, shut up
The day's fair face.   The wanderers of heaven,   80
Each to his home retire; save those that love
To take their pastime in the troubled air,
Or skimming flutter round the dimply pool.
The cattle from th' untasted fields return,
And ask, with meaning low, their wonted stalls,
Or ruminate in the contiguous shade.
Thither the household feathery people crowd,
The crested cock, with all his female train,
Pensive, and dripping; while the cottage-hind
Hangs o'er th' enlivening blaze, and taleful there   90
Recounts his simple frolic: much he talks,
And much he laughs; nor recks the storm that blows
Without, and rattles on his humble roof.
    Wide o'er the brim, with many a torrent swell'd,
And the mix'd ruin of its banks o'erspread.
K

At last the roused-up river pours along:
Resistless, roaring, dreadful, down it comes,
From the rude mountain, and the mossy wild,
Tumbling through rocks abrupt, and sounding far;
Then o'er the sanded valley floating spreads,   100
Calm, sluggish, silent; till again, constrain'd
Between two meeting hills, it bursts away,
Where rocks and woods o'erhang the turbid stream;
There gathering triple force, rapid, and deep,
It boils, and wheels, and foams, and thunders through.
    Nature, great parent! whose unceasing hand
Rolls round the Seasons of the changeful year,
How mighty, how majestic, are thy works!
With what a pleasing dread they swell the soul,
That sees astonish'd, and astonish'd sings!   110
Ye, too, ye winds! that now begin to blow,
With boisterous sweep, I raise my voice to you.
Where are your stores, ye powerful beings! say,
Where your aerial magazines reserved,
To swell the brooding terrors of the storm?
In what far distant region of the sky,
Hush'd in deep silence, sleep ye when 'tis calm?
    When from the pallid sky the sun descends,
With many a spot, that o'er his glaring orb
Uncertain wanders, stain'd, red fiery streaks   120
Begin to flush around.   The reeling clouds
Stagger with dizzy poise, as doubting yet
Which master to obey: while rising slow,
Blank, in the leaden-colour'd east, the moon
Wears a wan circle round her blunted horns.
Seen through the turbid, fluctuating air,
The stars, obtuse, emit a shiver'd ray;
Or frequent seem to shoot athwart the gloom,
And long behind them trail the whitening blaze.
Snatch'd in short eddies, plays the wither'd leaf;   130
And on the flood the dancing feather floats.
With broaden'd nostrils to the sky upturn'd,
The conscious heifer snuffs the stormy gale.

Even as the matron, at her nightly task,
With pensive labour draws the flaxen thread,
The wasted taper and the crackling flame
Foretell the blast.   But chief the plumy race,
The tenants of the sky, its changes speak.
　Retiring from the downs, where all day long
They pick'd their scanty fare, a blackening train　　·　140
Of clamorous rooks thick-urge their weary flight,
And seek the closing shelter of the grove.
Assiduous, in his bower, the wailing owl
Plies his sad song.   The cormorant on high
Wheels from the deep, and screams along the land.
Loud shrieks the soaring heron: and with wild wing,
The circling sea-fowl cleave the flaky clouds.
Ocean, unequal press'd, with broken tide
And blind commotion heaves; while from the shore,
Eat into caverns by the restless wave,　　　　　　150
And forest-rustling mountain, comes a voice,
That, solemn sounding, bids the world prepare.
Then issues forth the storm with sudden burst,
And hurls the whole precipitated air
Down in a torrent.   On the passive main
Descends th' ethereal force, and with strong gust
Turns from its bottom the discolour'd deep.
Through the black night, that sits immense around,
Lash'd into foam, the fierce, conflicting brine
Seems o'er a thousand raging waves to burn:　　　160
Meantime the mountain-billows, to the clouds
In dreadful tumult swell'd, surge above surge,
Burst into chaos with tremendous roar.
And anchor'd navies from their stations drive,
Wild as the winds across the howling waste
Of mighty waters: now th' inflated wave
Straining they scale, and now impetuous shoot
Into the secret chambers of the deep,
The wintry Baltic thundering o'er their head.
Emerging thence again, before the breath　　　　170
Of full-exerted heaven they wing their course,

And dart on distant coasts; if some sharp rock,
Or shoal insidious, break not their career,
And in loose fragments fling them floating round.
　　Nor less at land the loosen'd tempest reigns.
The mountain thunders, and its sturdy sons
Stoop to the bottom of the rocks they shade.
Lone on the midnight steep, and all aghast,
The dark wayfaring stranger breathless toils,
And, often falling, climbs against the blast.　　　　180
Low waves the rooted forest, vex'd, and sheds
What of its tarnish'd honours yet remain;
Dash'd down, and scatter'd, by the tearing wind's
Assiduous fury, its gigantic limbs.
Thus struggling through the dissipated grove,
The whirling tempest raves along the plain;
And on the cottage thatch'd, or lordly roof,
Keen-fastening, shakes them to the solid base.
Sleep frighted flies; and round the rocking dome,
For entrance eager, howls the savage blast.　　　　190
Then, too, they say, through all the burden'd air,
Long groans are heard, shrill sounds, and distant sighs,
That, uttered by the Demon of the night,
Warn the devoted wretch of wo and death.
　　Huge uproar lords it wide.　The clouds commix'd
With stars swift-gliding sweep along the sky.
All Nature reels.　Till Nature's King, who oft
Amid tempestuous darkness dwells alone,
And on the wings of the careering wind
Walks dreadfully serene, commands a calm;　　　　200
Then straight air, sea, and earth, are hush'd at once.
　　As yet 'tis midnight deep.　The weary clouds,
Slow-meeting, mingle into solid gloom.
Now, while the drowsy world lies lost in sleep,
Let me associate with the serious Night,
And Contemplation, her sedate compeer;
Let me shake off th' intrusive cares of day,
And lay the meddling senses all aside.
　　Where now, ye lying vanities of life!

Ye ever-tempting, ever-cheating train! 210
Where are ye now? and what is your amount?
Vexation, disappointment, and remorse.
Sad, sickening thought! and yet deluded Man,
A scene of crude disjointed visions past,
And broken slumbers, rises still resolved,
With new-flush'd hopes, to run the giddy round.
　Father of light and life, thou Good supreme!
O teach me what is good! teach me Thyself!
Save me from folly, vanity, and vice;
From every low pursuit! and feed my soul 220
With knowledge, conscious peace, and virtue pure;
Sacred, substantial, never-fading bliss!
　The keener tempests rise: and fuming dun
From all the livid east, or piercing north,
Thick clouds ascend; in whose capacious womb
A vapoury deluge lies, to snow congeal'd.
Heavy they roll their fleecy world along,
And the sky saddens with the gather'd storm.
Through the hush'd air the whitening shower descends,
At first thin wavering; till at last the flakes 230
Fall broad, and wide, and fast, dimming the day
With a continual flow. The cherish'd fields
Put on their winter robe of purest white.
'Tis brightness all, save where the new snow melts
Along the mazy current. Low, the woods
Bow their hoar head; and ere the languid sun
Faint from the west emits his evening ray,
Earth's universal face, deep hid, and chill,
Is one wild dazzling waste, that buries wide
The works of Man. Drooping, the labourer-ox 240
Stands cover'd o'er with snow, and then demands
The fruit of all his toil. The fowls of heaven,
Tamed by the cruel season, crowd around
The winnowing store, and claim the little boon
Which Providence assigns them. One alone,
The redbreast, sacred to the household gods,
Wisely regardful of th' embroiling sky,

In joyless fields and thorny thickets leaves
His shivering mates, and pays to trusted Man
His annual visit.   Half-afraid, he first   250
Against the window beats; then, brisk, alights
On the warm hearth; then, hopping o'er the floor,
Eyes all the smiling family askance,
And pecks, and starts, and wonders where he is:
Till more familiar grown, the table crumbs
Attract his slender feet.   The foodless wilds
Pour forth their brown inhabitants.   The hare,
Though timorous of heart, and hard beset
By death in various forms, dark snares, and dogs,
And more unpitying Men, the garden seeks,   260
Urged on by fearless want.   The bleating kind
Eye the bleak heaven, and next the glistening earth,
With looks of dumb despair; then, sad dispersed,
Dig for the wither'd herb through heaps of snow.
    Now shepherds to your helpless charge be kind,
Baffle the raging year, and fill their pens
With food at will; lodge them below the storm,
And watch them strict; for from the bellowing east,
In this dire season, oft the whirlwind's wing
Sweeps up the burden of whole wintry plains   270
At one wide waft, and o'er the hapless flocks,
Hid in the hollow of two neigbouring hills,
The billowy tempest whelms; till, upward urged,
The valley to a shining mountain swells,
Tipt with a wreath high-curling in the sky.
    As thus the snows arise; and foul and fierce,
All Winter drives along the darken'd air;
In his own loose-revolving fields, the swain
Disaster'd stands; sees other hills ascend,
Of unknown joyless brow; and other scenes.   280
Of horrid prospect, shag the trackless plain:
Nor finds the river, nor the forest, hid
Beneath the formless wild; but wanders on
From hill to dale, still more and more astray;
Impatient flouncing through the drifted heaps,

Stung with the thoughts of home; the thoughts of home
Rush on his nerves, and call their vigour forth
In many a vain attempt.   How sinks his soul!
What black despair, what horror fills his heart!
When for the dusky spot, which fancy feign'd   290
His tufted cottage rising through the snow,
He meets the roughness of the middle waste,
Far from the track, and blest abode of Man;
While round him night resistless closes fast,
And every tempest, howling o'er his head,
Renders the savage wilderness more wild.
Then throng the busy shapes into his mind,
Of cover'd pits, unfathomably deep,
A dire descent! beyond the power of frost;
Of faithless bogs; of precipices huge,   300
Smooth'd up with snow; and, what is land unknown,
What water, of the still unfrozen spring,
In the loose marsh or solitary lake,
Where the fresh fountain from the bottom boils.
These check his fearful steps: and down he sinks
Beneath the shelter of the shapeless drift,
Thinking o'er all the bitterness of death;
Mix'd with the tender anguish Nature shoots
Through the wrung bosom of the dying Man,
His wife, his children, and his friends unseen.   310
In vain for him th' officious wife prepares
The fire fair-blazing, and the vestment warm;
In vain his little children, peeping out
Into the mingling storm, demand their sire,
With tears of artless innocence.   Alas!
Nor wife, nor children, more shall he behold,
Nor friends, nor sacred home.   On every nerve
The deadly winter seizes; shuts up sense;
And, o'er his inmost vitals creeping cold,
Lays him along the snows, a stiffen'd corse,   320
Stretch'd out, and bleaching in the northern blast.
   Ah! little think the gay licentious proud,
Whom pleasure, power and affluence surround:

They, who their thoughtless hours in giddy mirth,
And wanton, often cruel, riot waste:
Ah! little think they, while they dance along,
How many feel, this very moment, death,
And all the sad variety of pain!
How many sink in the devouring flood,
Or more devouring flame! How many bleed,   330
By shameful variance betwixt Man and Man!
How many pine in want, and dungeon-glooms;
Shut from the common air, and common use
Of their own limbs! How many drink the cup
Of baleful grief, or eat the bitter bread
Of misery! Sore pierced by wintry winds,
How many shrink into the sordid hut
Of cheerless poverty! How many shake
With all the fiercer tortures of the mind,
Unbounded passion, madness, guilt, remorse;   340
Whence tumbled headlong from the height of life,
They furnish matter for the tragic Muse!
Even in the vale, where wisdom loves to dwell,
With friendship, peace, and contemplation join'd,
How many, rack'd with honest passions, droop,
In deep retired distress! How many stand
Around the death-bed of their dearest friends,
And point the parting anguish! Thought fond Man
Of these, and all the thousand nameless ills,
That one incessant struggle render life,   350
One scene of toil, of suffering, and of fate,
Vice in his high career would stand appall'd,
And heedless rambling Impulse learn to think;
The conscious heart of Charity would warm,
And her wide-wish Benevolence dilate;
The social tear would rise, the social sigh;
And into clear perfection, gradual bliss,
Refining still, the social passions work.
    And here can I forget the generous band,
Who, touch'd with human wo, redressive search'd   360
Into the horrors of the gloomy jail?

Unpitied, and unheard, where misery moans;
Where sickness pines; where thirst and hunger burn,
And poor misfortune feels the lash of vice.
While in the land of liberty, the land
Whose every street and public meeting glow
With open freedom, little tyrants raged;
Snatch'd the lean morsel from the starving mouth;
Tore from cold wintry limbs the tatter'd weed;
Even robb'd them of the last of comforts, sleep;   370
The free-born Briton to the dungeon chain'd,
Or, as the lust of cruelty prevail'd,
At pleasure mark'd him with inglorious stripes;
And crush'd out lives, by secret barbarous ways,
That for their country would have toil'd, or bled.
O great design! if executed well,
With patient care, and wisdom-temper'd zeal.
Ye sons of mercy! yet resume the search;
Drag forth the legal monsters into light,
Wrench from their hands oppression's iron rod,   380
And bid the cruel feel the pains they give.
    Much still untouch'd remains; in this rank age,
Much is the patriot's weeding hand required.
The toils of law (what dark insidious Men
Have cumbrous added to perplex the truth,
And lengthen simple justice into trade),
How glorious were the day that saw these broke,
And every Man within the reach of right!
    By wintry famine roused, from all the tract
Of horrid mountains which the shining Alps,   390
And wavy Apennines, and Pyrenees,
Branch out stupendous into distant lands;
Cruel as death, and hungry as the grave!
Burning for blood! bony, and gaunt, and grim!
Assembling wolves in raging troops descend;
And, pouring o'er the country, bear along,
Keen as the north wind sweeps the glossy snow.
All is their prize.   They fasten on the steed,
Press him to earth, and pierce his mighty heart.

Nor can the bull his awful front defend,   400
Or shake the murdering savages away.
Rapacious at the mother's throat they fly,
And tear the screaming infant from her breast.
The godlike face of Man avails him nought.
Even beauty, force divine! at whose bright glance
The generous lion stands in soften'd gaze,
Here bleeds, a hapless undistinguish'd prey.
But if, apprised of the severe attack,
The country be shut up, lured by the scent,
On churchyards drear (inhuman to relate!)   410
The disappointed prowlers fall, and dig
The shrouded body from the grave; o'er which,
Mix'd with foul shades and frighted ghosts, they howl.
    Among those hilly regions, where embraced
In peaceful vales the happy Grisons dwell;
Oft, rushing sudden from the loaded cliffs,
Mountains of snow their gathering terrors roll.
From steep to steep, loud-thundering down they come,
A wintry waste in dire commotion all;
And herds, and flocks, and travellers, and swains,   420
And sometimes whole brigades of marching troops,
Or hamlets sleeping in the dead of night,
Are deep beneath the smothering ruin whelm'd.
    Now, all amid the rigours of the year,   .
In the wild depth of Winter, while without
The ceaseless winds blow ice, be my retreat,
Between the groaning forest and the shore,
Beat by the boundless multitude of waves,
A rural, shelter'd, solitary scene;
Where ruddy fire and beaming tapers join,   430
To cheer the gloom. There studious let me sit,
And hold high converse with the Mighty Dead,
Sages of ancient time, as gods revered;
As gods beneficent, who blest mankind
With arts, with arms, and humanised a world.
Roused at th' inspiring thought, I throw aside
The long-lived volume; and, deep-musing, hail

The sacred shades, that, slowly-rising, pass
Before my wondering eyes.   First Socrates,
Who, firmly good in a corrupted state,   440
Against the rage of tyrants single stood,
Invincible! calm Reason's holy law,
That Voice of God within th' attentive mind,
Obeying, fearless, or in life, or death.
Great moral teacher! wisest of Mankind!
Solon the next, who built his common-weal
On equity's wide base: by tender laws
A lively people curbing, yet undamp'd,
Preserving still that quick peculiar fire,
Whence in the laurell'd field of finer arts,   450
And of bold freedom, they unequall'd shone,
The pride of smiling Greece, and human-kind.
Lycurgus then, who bow'd beneath the force
Of strictest discipline, severely wise,
All human passions.   Following him, I see,
As at Thermopylæ he glorious fell,
The firm Devoted Chief, who proved by deeds
The hardest lesson which the other taught.
Then Aristides lifts his honest front;
Spotless of heart, to whom th' unflattering voice   460
Of freedom gave the noblest name of Just;
In pure majestic poverty revered;
Who, even his glory to his country's weal
Submitting, swell'd a haughty Rival's fame.
Rear'd by his care, of softer ray appears
Cimon, sweet soul'd; whose genius rising strong
Shook off the load of young debauch; abroad
The scourge of Persian pride, at home the friend
Of every worth and every splendid art;
Modest, and simple, in the pomp of wealth.   470
Then the last worthies of declining Greece,
Late call'd to glory, in unequal times,
Pensive, appear.   The fair Corinthian boast,
Timoleon, happy temper! mild and firm,
Who wept the Brother, while the Tyrant bled.

And, equal to the best, the Theban Pair,
Whose virtues, in heroic concord join'd,
Their country raised to freedom, empire, fame.
He too, with whom Athenian honour sunk,
And left a mass of sordid lees behind,
Phocion the good; in public life severe;
To virtue still inexorably firm;
But when, beneath his low illustrious roof,
Sweet peace and happy wisdom smooth'd his brow,
Not friendship softer was, nor love more kind.
And he, the last of old Lycurgus' sons,
The generous victim to that vain attempt,
To save a rotten state, Agis, who saw
Even Sparta's self to servile avarice sunk.
The two Achaian heroes close the train:
Aratus, who a while relumed the soul
Of fondly-lingering liberty in Greece:
And he, her darling as her latest hope,
The gallant Philopoemen; who to arms
Turn'd the luxurious pomp he could not cure;
Or toiling in his farm, a simple swain,
Or, bold and skilful, thundering in the field.
    Of rougher front, a mighty people come!
A race of heroes! in those virtuous times
Which knew no stain, save that with partial flame
Their dearest country they too fondly loved:
Her better founder first, the light of Rome,
Numa, who soften'd her rapacious sons:
Servius the King, who laid the solid base
On which o'er earth the vast republic spread.
Then the great Consuls venerable rise.
The Public Father who the Private quell'd,
As on the dread tribunal sternly sad.
He, whom his thankless country could not lose,
Camillus, only vengeful to her foes.
Fabricius, scorner of all-conquering gold;
And Cincinnatus, awful from the plough.
Thy Willing Victim, Carthage, bursting loose

From all that pleading Nature could oppose,
From a whole city's tears, by rigid faith
Imperious call'd, and honour's dire command.
Scipio, the gentle chief, humanely brave,
Who soon the race of spotless glory ran,
And, warm in youth, to the Poetic shade
With Friendship and Philosophy retired.   520
Tully, whose powerful eloquence awhile
Restrain'd the rapid fate of rushing Rome.
Unconquer'd Cato, virtuous in extreme.
And thou, unhappy Brutus, kind of heart,
Whose steady arm, by awful virtue urged,
Lifted the Roman steel against thy Friend.
Thousands besides, the tribute of a verse
Demand; but who can count the stars of heaven?
Who sing their influence on this lower world?
    Behold, who yonder comes! in sober state,   530
Fair, mild, and strong, as is a vernal sun?
'Tis Phœbus' self, or else the Mantuan Swain!
Great Homer too appears, of daring wing,
Parent of song! and equal by his side,
The British Muse: join'd hand in hand they walk,
Darkling, full up the middle steep to fame.
Nor absent are those shades, whose skilful touch
Pathetic drew th' impassion'd heart, and charm'd
Transported Athens with the Moral Scene:
Nor those who, tuneful, waked th' enchanting Lyre.   540
    First of your kind, society divine!
Still visit thus my nights, for you reserved,
And mount my soaring soul to thoughts like yours.
Silence, thou lonely power! the door be thine;
See on the hallow'd hour that none intrude,
Save a few chosen friends, who sometimes deign
To bless my humble roof, with sense refined,
Learning digested well, exalted faith,
Unstudied wit, and humour ever gay,
Or from the Muses' hill will Pope descend,   550
To raise the sacred hour, to bid it smile,

And with the social spirit warm the heart!
For though not sweeter his own Homer sings,
Yet is his life the more endearing song.
    Where art thou, Hammond? thou the darling pride,
The friend and lover of the tuneful throng!
Ah why, dear youth, in all the blooming prime
Of vernal genius, where disclosing fast
Each active worth, each manly virtue lay,
Why wert thou ravish'd from our hope so soon?   560
What now avails that noble thirst of fame
Which stung thy fervent breast? that treasured store
Of knowledge, early gain'd? that eager zeal
To serve thy country, glowing in the band
Of youthful patriots, who sustain her name?
What now, alas! that life-diffusing charm
Of sprightly wit? that rapture for the Muse,
That heart of friendship, and that soul of joy,
Which bade with softest light thy virtues smile?
Ah! only show'd, to check our fond pursuits,   570
And teach our humbled hopes that life is vain!
   Thus in some deep retirement would I pass
The winter-glooms, with friends of pliant soul,
Or blithe, or solemn, as the theme inspired:
With them would search, if Nature's boundless frame
Was call'd, late-rising from the void of night,
Or sprung eternal from th' Eternal Mind;
Its life, its laws, its progress, and its end.
Hence larger prospects of the beauteous whole
Would, gradual, open on our opening minds,   580
And each diffusive harmony unite
In full perfection, to th' astonish'd eye.
Then would we try to scan the moral world,
Which, though to us it seems embroil'd, moves on
In higher order; fitted, and impell'd,
By Wisdom's finest hand, and issuing all
In general Good. The sage historic Muse
Should next conduct us through the deeps of time:
Show us how empire grew, declined, and fell,

In scatter'd states; what makes the nations smile, 590
Improves their soil, and gives them double suns;
And why they pine beneath the brightest skies,
In Nature's richest lap. As thus we talk'd,
Our hearts would burn within us, would inhale
That portion of divinity, that ray
Of purest heaven, which lights the public soul
Of patriots and of heroes. But if doom'd,
In powerless humble fortune, to repress
These ardent risings of the kindling soul,
Then, even superior to ambition, we 600
Would learn the private virtues; how to glide
Through shades and plains, along the smoothest stream
Of rural life: or snatch'd away by hope,
Through the dim spaces of futurity,
With earnest eye anticipate those scenes
Of happiness and wonder; where the mind,
In endless growth and infinite ascent,
Rises from state to state, and world to world.
But when with these the serious thought is foil'd,
We, shifting for relief, would play the shapes 610
Of frolic fancy; and incessant form
Those rapid pictures, that assembled train
Of fleet ideas, never join'd before;
Whence lively Wit excites to gay surprise,
Or folly-painting Humour, grave himself,
Calls Laughter forth, deep-shaking every nerve.
    Meantime the village rouses up the fire
While well attested, and as well believed,
Heard solemn, goes the goblin-story round
Till superstitious horror creeps o'er all. 620
Or frequent in the sounding hall, thay wake
The rural gambol. Rustic mirth goes round:
The simple joke that takes the shepherd's heart,
Easily pleased; the long loud laugh, sincere;
The kiss, snatch'd hasty from the side-long maid,
On purpose guardless, or pretending sleep:
The leap, the slap, the haul; and, shook to notes

Of native music, the respondent dance.
Thus jocund fleets with them the winter night.
   The city swarms intense.   The public haunt,   630
Full of each theme, and warm with mix'd discourse,
Hums indistinct.   The sons of riot flow
Down the loose stream of false enchanted joy,
To swift destruction.   On the rankled soul
The gaming fury falls; and in one gulf
Of total ruin, honour, virtue, peace,
Friends, families, and fortune, headlong sink.
Up springs the dance along the lighted dome,
Mix'd, and evolved; a thousand sprightly ways.
The glittering court effuses every pomp;   640
The circle deepens: beam'd from gaudy robes,
Tapers, and sparkling gems, and radiant eyes,
A soft effulgence o'er the palace waves:
While, a gay insect in his summer-shine,
The fop, light-fluttering, spreads his mealy wings.
   Dread o'er the scene, the ghost of Hamlet stalks;
Othello rages; poor Monimia mourns;
And Belvidera pours her soul in love.
Terror alarms the breast; the comely tear
Steals o'er the cheek: or else the Comic Muse   650
Holds to the world a picture of itself,
And raises sly the fair impartial laugh.
Sometimes she lifts her strain, and paints the scenes
Of beauteous life; whate'er can deck mankind,
Or charm the heart, in generous Bevil show'd.
   O thou, whose wisdom, solid yet refined,
Whose patriot virtues, and consummate skill
To touch the finer springs that move the world,
Join'd to whate'er the Graces can bestow,
And all Apollo's animating fire,   660
Give thee, with pleasing dignity, to shine
At once the guardian, ornament, and joy,
Of polish'd life; permit the Rural Muse,
O Chesterfield! to grace with thee her song.
Ere to the shades again she humbly flies!

Indulge her fond ambition, in thy train
(For every Muse has in thy train a place),
To mark thy various full-accomplish'd mind:
To mark that spirit, which, with British scorn,
Rejects th' allurements of corrupted power;   670
That elegant politeness, which excels,
Even in the judgment of presumptuous France,
The boasted manners of her shining court;
That wit, the vivid energy of sense,
The truth of Nature, which, with Attic point,
And kind, well-temper'd satire, smoothly keen,
Steals through the soul, and without pain corrects.
Or, rising thence with yet a brighter flame,
O let me hail thee on some glorious day,
When to the listening senate, ardent, crowd   680
Britannia's sons, to hear her pleaded cause.
Then drest by thee, more amiably fair,
Truth the soft robe of mild persuasion wears:
Thou to assenting reason giv'st again
Her own enlighten'd thoughts: call'd from the heart,
Th' obedient passions on thy voice attend;
And even reluctant party feels awhile
Thy gracious power: as through the varied maze
Of eloquence, now smooth, now quick, now strong,
Profound and clear, you roll the copious flood.   690

   To thy loved haunt return, my happy Muse:
For now, behold, the joyous winter-days,
Frosty, succeed; and through the blue serene,
For sight too fine, th' ethereal nitre flies,
Killing infectious damps, and the spent air
Storing afresh with elemental life.
Close crowds the shining atmosphere; and binds
Our strengthen'd bodies in its cold embrace,
Constringent; feeds, and animates our blood;
Refines our spirits, through the new-strung nerves,   700
In swifter sallies darting to the brain;
Where sits the soul, intense, collected, cool,
Bright as the skies, and as the season keen.

L

    All Nature feels the renovating force
Of Winter, only to the thoughtless eye
In ruin seen.   The frost-concocted glebe
Draws in abundant vegetable soul,
And gathers vigour for the coming year.
A stronger glow sits on the lively cheek
Of ruddy fire; and luculent along   710
The purer rivers flow; their sullen deeps,
Transparent, open to the shepherd's gaze,
And murmur hoarser at the fixing frost.
    What art thou, Frost? and whence are thy keen stores
Derived, thou secret all-invading power,
Whom even th' illusive fluid cannot fly?
Is not thy potent energy unseen,
Myriads of little salts, or hook'd, or shaped
Like double wedges, and diffused immense
Through water, earth, and ether?   Hence at eve,   720
Steam'd eager from the red horizon round,
With the fierce rage of Winter deep suffused,
An icy gale, oft-shifting, o'er the pool
Breathes a blue film, and in its mid career
Arrests the bickering stream.   The loosen'd ice,
Let down the flood, and half-dissolved by day,
Rustles no more; but to the sedgy bank
Fast grows, or gathers round the pointed stone,
A crystal pavement, by the breath of heaven
Cemented firm; till, seized from shore to shore,   730
The whole imprison'd river growls below.
Loud rings the frozen earth, and hard reflects
A double noise; while, at his evening watch,
The village dog deters the nightly thief;
The heifer lows; the distant waterfall
Swells in the breeze; and, with the hasty tread
Of traveller, the hollow-sounding plain
Shakes from afar.   The full ethereal round,
Infinite worlds disclosing to the view,
Shines out intensely keen; and, all one cope   740
Of starry glitter, glows from pole to pole.

From pole to pole the rigid influence falls,
Through the still night, incessant, heavy, strong,
And seizes Nature fast. It freezes on,
Till Morn, late-rising o'er the drooping world,
Lifts her pale eye unjoyous. Then appears
The various labour of the silent night:
Prone from the dripping eave, and dumb cascade,
Whose idle torrents only seem to roar,
The pendant icicle; the frostwork fair,   750
Where transient hues, and fancied figures rise;
Wide-spouted o'er the hill, the frozen brook,
A livid tract, cold-gleaming on the morn;
The forest bent beneath the plumy wave;
And by the frost refined the whiter snow,
Incrusted hard, and sounding to the tread
Of early shepherd, as he pensive seeks
His pining flock, or from the mountain-top,
Pleased with the slippery surface, swift descends.

On blithesome frolics bent, the youthful swains,   760
While every work of Man is laid at rest,
Fond o'er the river crowd, in various sport
And revelry dissolved; where mixing glad,
Happiest of all the train! the raptured boy
Lashes the whirling top. Or, where the Rhine
Branch'd out in many a long canal extends,
From every province swarming, void of care,
Batavia rushes forth; and as they sweep,
On sounding skates, a thousand different ways,
In circling poise, swift as the winds along,   770
The then gay land is madden'd all to joy.
Nor less the northern courts, wide o'er the snow,
Pour a new pomp. Eager, on rapid sleds,
Their vigorous youth in bold contention wheel
The long-resounding course. Meantime, to raise
The manly strife, with highly-blooming charms,
Flush'd by the season, Scandinavia's dames,
Or Russia's buxom daughters, glow around.

Pure, quick, and sportful, is the wholesome day:

But soon elapsed. The horizontal sun,
Broad o'er the south, hangs at his utmost noon,
And, ineffectual, strikes the gelid cliff:
His azure gloss the mountain still maintains,
Nor feels the feeble touch.   Perhaps the vale
Relents awhile to the reflected ray:
Or from the forest falls the cluster'd snow,
Myriads of gems, that in the waving gleam
Gay twinkle as they scatter.   Thick around,
Thunders the sport of those, who with the gun,
And dog impatient bounding at the shot,
Worse than the season, desolate the fields;
And, adding to the ruins of the year,
Distress the footed or the feather'd game.
   But what is this?   Our infant Winter sinks,
Divested of his grandeur, should our eye
Astonish'd shoot into the Frigid Zone;
Where, for relentless months, continual Night
Holds o'er the glittering waste her starry reign.
   There, through the prison of unbounded wilds,
Barr'd by the hand of Nature from escape,
Wide-roams the Russian exile.   Nought around
Strikes his sad eye, but deserts lost in snow;
And heavy-loaded groves; and solid floods,
That stretch, athwart the solitary waste,
Their icy horrors to the frozen main;
And cheerless towns, far-distant, never bless'd,
Save when its annual course the caravan
Bends to the golden coast of rich Cathay;
With news of human-kind.   Yet there life glows;
Yet cherish'd there, beneath the shining waste,
The furry nations harbour; tipt with jet,
Fair ermines, spotless as the snows they press;
Sables, of glossy black; and dark embrown'd,
Or beauteous freak'd with many a mingled hue,
Thousands besides, the costly pride of courts.
There, warm together press'd, the trooping deer
Sleep on the new-fallen snows; and, scarce his head

Raised o'er the heapy wreath, the branching elk
Lies slumbering sullen in the white abyss.
The ruthless hunter wants nor dogs nor toils; 820
Nor with the dread of sounding bows he drives
The fearful flying race; with ponderous clubs,
As weak against the mountain-heaps they push
Their beating breast in vain, and piteous bray,
He lays them quivering on th' ensanguined snows,
And with loud shouts rejoicing bears them home.
There through the piny forest half-absorpt,
Rough tenant of these shades, the shapeless bear,
With dangling ice all horrid, stalks forlorn,
Slow-paced, and sourer as the storms increase; 830
He makes his bed beneath th' inclement drift,
And, with stern patience, scorning weak complaint,
Hardens his heart against assailing want.
    Wide o'er the spacious regions of the north,
That see Boötes urge his tardy wain,
A boisterous race, by frosty Caurus pierced,
Who little pleasure know, and fear no pain,
Prolific swarm. They once relumed the flame
Of lost mankind in polish'd slavery sunk;
Drove martial horde on horde, with dreadful sweep, 840
Resistless rushing o'er th' enfeebled south,
And gave the vanquish'd world another form.
    Not such the sons of Lapland: wisely they
Despise th' insensate barbarous trade of war:
They ask no more than simple Nature gives;
They love their mountains, and enjoy their storms;
No false desires, no pride-created wants,
Disturb the peaceful current of their time,
And through the restless ever-tortured maze
Of pleasure, or ambition, bid it rage. 850
Their reindeer form their riches. These, their tents,
Their robes, their beds, and all their homely wealth,
Supply their wholesome fare, and cheerful cups.
Obsequious at their call, the docile tribe
Yield to the sled their necks, and whirl them swift

O'er hill and dale, heap'd into one expanse
Of marbled snow, as far as eye can sweep,
With a blue crust of ice unbounded glazed.
By dancing meteors then, that ceaseless shake
A waving blaze refracted o'er the heavens,   860
And vivid moons, and stars that keener play
With double lustre from the glossy waste;
Even in the depth of Polar Night, they find
A wondrous day: enough to light the chase,
Or guide their daring steps to Finland fairs.
    Wish'd Spring returns; and from the hazy south,
While dim Aurora slowly moves before,
The welcome sun, just verging up at first,
By small degrees extends the swelling curve;
Till seen at last for gay rejoicing months,   870
Still round and round his spiral course he winds;
And as he nearly dips his flaming orb,
Wheels up again, and re-ascends the sky.
In that glad season, from the lakes and floods,
Where pure Niemi's fairy mountains rise,
And fringed with roses Tenglio rolls his stream,
They draw the copious fry.   With these, at eve,
They, cheerful, loaded to their tents repair;
Where, all day long in useful cares employ'd,
Their kind unblemish'd wives the fire prepare,   880
Thrice happy race! by poverty secured
From legal plunder and rapacious power:
In whom fell interest never yet has sown
The seeds of vice: whose spotless swains ne'er knew
Injurious deed; nor, blasted by the breath
Of faithless love, their blooming daughters wo.
    Still pressing on, beyond Tornea's lake,
And Hecla flaming through a waste of snow,
And farthest Greenland, to the pole itself,
Where, failing gradual, life at length goes out,   890
The Muse expands her solitary flight;
And, hovering o'er the wild stupendous scene,
Beholds new seas beneath another sky.

Throned in his palace of cerulean ice,
Here Winter holds his unrejoicing court;
And through his airy hall the loud misrule
Of driving tempest is for ever heard;
Here the grim tyrant meditates his wrath;
Here arms his winds with all-subduing frost;
Moulds his fierce hail, and treasures up his snows,   900
With which he now oppresses half the globe.
' Thence winding eastward to the Tartar's coast,
She sweeps the howling margin of the main,
Where, undissolving, from the first of time,
Snows swell on snows amazing to the sky;
And icy mountains high on mountains piled,
Seem to the shivering sailor from afar,
Shapeless and white, an atmosphere of clouds.
Projected huge and horrid, o'er the surge,
Alps frown on Alps; or rushing hideous down,   910
As if old Chaos was again return'd,
Wide-rend the deep, and shake the solid pole.
Ocean itself no longer can resist
The binding fury; but, in all its rage
Of tempest, taken by the boundless frost,
Is many a fathom to the bottom chain'd,
And bid to roar no more: a bleak expanse,
Shagg'd o'er with wavy rocks, cheerless, and void
Of every life, that from the dreary months
Flies conscious southward. Miserable they,   920
Who, here entangled in the gathering ice,
Take their last look of the descending sun;
While, full of death, and fierce with tenfold frost,
The long long night, incumbent o'er their heads,
Falls horrible. Such was the Briton's fate;
As with first prow (what have not Britons dared!)
He for the passage sought, attempted since
So much in vain, and seeming to be shut
By jealous Nature with eternal bars.
In these fell regions, in Arzina caught,   930
And to the stony deep his idle ship

Immediate seal'd, he with his hapless crew,
Each full exerted at his several task,
Froze into statues; to the cordage glued
The sailor, and the pilot to the helm.

Hard by these shores, where scarce his freezing stream
Rolls the wild Oby, live the last of Men;
And half enliven'd by the distant sun,
That rears and ripens Man, as well as plants,
Here human Nature wears its rudest form.   940
Deep from the piercing season sunk in caves,
Here by dull fires, and with unjoyous cheer,
They waste the tedious gloom.   Immersed in furs,
Doze the gross race.   Nor sprightly jest, nor song,
Nor tenderness they know; nor aught of life,
Beyond the kindred bears that stalk without,
Till morn at length, her roses drooping all,
Sheds a long twilight brightening o'er their fields,
And calls the quiver'd savage to the chase.

What cannot active government perform,   950
New-Moulding Man ?   Wide-stretching from these shores,
A people savage from remotest time,
A huge neglected empire, one vast Mind,
By Heaven inspired, from Gothic darkness call'd.
(Immortal Peter!) first of monarchs! He
His stubborn country tamed, her rocks, her fens,
Her floods, her seas, her ill-submitting sons;
And while the fierce Barbarian he subdued,
To more exalted soul he raised the Man.

Ye shades of ancient heroes! ye who toil'd   960
Through long successive ages to build up
A labouring plan of state, behold at once
The wonder done! behold the matchless prince,
Who left his native throne where reign'd till then
A mighty shadow of unreal power;
Who greatly spurn'd the slothful pomp of courts;
And roaming every land, in every port
His sceptre laid aside, with glorious hand
Unwearied plying the mechanic tool,

Gather'd the seeds of trade, of useful arts   970
Of civil wisdom, and of martial skill.
Charged with the stores of Europe home he goes!
Then cities rise amid th' illumined waste;
O'er joyless deserts smiles the rural reign:
Far-distant flood to flood is social join'd;
Th' astonish'd Euxine hears the Baltic roar;
Proud navies ride on seas that never foam'd
With daring keel before; and armies stretch
Each way their dazzling files, repressing here
The frantic Alexander of the north,   980
And awing there stern Othman's shrinking sons.
Sloth flies the land, and Ignorance, and Vice,
Of old dishonour proud: it glows around,
Taught by the Royal Hand that roused the whole,
One scene of arts, of arms, of rising trade:
For what his wisdom plann'd, and power enforced,
More potent still, his great example show'd.
   Muttering, the winds at eve, with blunted point,
Blow hollow-blustering from the south. Subdued,
The frost resolves into a trickling thaw.   990
Spotted the mountains shine: loose sleet descends,
And floods the country round. The rivers swell,
Of bonds impatient. Sudden from the hills,
O'er rocks and woods, in broad brown cataracts,
A thousand snow-fed torrents shoot at once;
And, where they rush, the wide-resounding plain
Is left one slimy waste. Those sullen seas,
That wash'd th' ungenial pole, will rest no more
Beneath the shackles of the mighty north;
But, rousing all their waves, resistless heave.   1000
And hark! the lengthening roar continuous runs
Athwart the rifted deep: at once it bursts,
And piles a thousand mountains to the clouds.
   Ill fares the bark with trembling wretches charged,
That, tost amid the floating fragments, moors
Beneath the shelter of an icy isle,
While night o'erwhelms the sea, and horror looks

More horrible.   Can human force endure
Th' assembled mischiefs that besiege them round ?
Heart-gnawing hunger, fainting weariness,   1010
The roar of winds and waves, the crush of ice,
Now ceasing, now renew'd with louder rage,
And in dire echoes bellowing round the main.
More to embroil the deep, Leviathan
And his unwieldy train, in dreadful sport,
Tempest the loosen'd brine; while through the gloom,
Far from the bleak inhospitable shore,
Loading the winds, is heard the hungry howl
Of famish'd monsters, there awaiting wrecks.
Yet Providence, that ever-waking eye!   1020
Looks down with pity on the feeble toil
Of mortals lost to hope, and lights them safe,
Through all this dreary labyrinth of fate.
   'Tis done ! dread Winter spreads his latest glooms,
And reigns tremendous o'er the conquer'd year:
How dead the vegetable kingdom lies!
How dumb the tuneful!   Horror wide extends
His desolate domain.   Behold, fond Man!
See here thy pictured life: pass some few years,
Thy flowering Spring, thy Summer's ardent strength,   1030
Thy sober Autumn fading into age,
And pale concluding Winter comes at last,
And shuts the scene.   Ah! whither now are fled
Those dreams of greatness? those unsolid hopes
Of happiness? those longings after fame?
Those restless cares? those busy bustling days?
Those gay-spent, festive nights? those veering thoughts
Lost between good and ill, that shared thy life?
All now are vanish'd! Virtue sole-survives,
Immortal, never-failing friend of Man,   1040
His guide to happiness on high.   And see !
'Tis come, the glorious morn! the second birth
Of heaven and earth! awakening Nature hears
The new-creating word, and starts to life,
In every heighten'd form, from pain and death

For ever free.   The great eternal scheme,
Involving all, and in a perfect whole
Uniting, as the prospect wider spreads,
To reason's eye refined clears up apace.
　　Ye vainly wise! ye blind presumptuous! now,   1050
Confounded in the dust, adore that Power,
And Wisdom oft arraign'd: see now the cause,
Why unassuming worth in secret lived,
And died neglected: why the good man's share
In life was gall and bitterness of soul:
Why the lone widow and her orphans pined
In starving solitude; while luxury,
In palaces, lay straining her low thought,
To form unreal wants: why heaven-born truth
And moderation fair, wore the red marks   1060
Of superstition's scourge: why licensed pain,
That cruel spoiler, that embosom'd foe,
Imbitter'd all our bliss.   Ye good distrest!
Ye noble few! who here unbending stand
Beneath life's pressure, yet bear up awhile,
And what your bounded view, which only saw
A little part, deem'd Evil is no more:
The storms of Wintry Time will quickly pass,
And one unbounded Spring encircle all.

A HYMN.

THESE, as they change, Almighty Father! these,
Are but the varied God. The rolling year
Is full of Thee. Forth in the pleasing Spring
Thy beauty walks, Thy tenderness and love.
Wide flush the fields; the softening air is balm;
Echo the mountains round; the forest smiles;
And every sense, and every heart is joy.
Then comes Thy glory in the Summer-months,
With light and heat refulgent. Then Thy sun
Shoots full perfection through the swelling year;
And oft thy voice in dreadful thunder speaks;
And oft at dawn, deep noon, or falling eve,
By brooks and groves, in hollow whispering gales.
Thy bounty shines in Autumn unconfined,
And spreads a common feast for all that lives.
In Winter awful Thou! with clouds and storms
Around Thee thrown, tempest o'er tempest roll'd,
Majestic darkness! on the whirlwind's wing,
Riding sublime, Thou bidd'st the world adore,
And humblest Nature with Thy northern blast.

Mysterious round! what skill, what force divine,
Deep felt, in these appear! a simple train,
Yet so delightful mix'd, with such kind art,
Such beauty and beneficence combined;
Shade, unperceived, so softening into shade;
And all so forming an harmonious whole;
That, as they still succeed, they ravish still.

But wandering oft, with brute unconscious gaze,
Man marks not Thee: marks not the mighty hand,
That, ever-busy, wheels the silent spheres;
Works in the secret deep; shoots, steaming, thence
The fair profusion that o'erspreads the Spring:
Flings from the sun direct the flaming day;
Feeds every creature; hurls the tempest forth;
And, as on earth this grateful change revolves,
With transport touches all the springs of life.
  Nature attend ! join every living soul,
Beneath the spacious temple of the sky,
In adoration join; and, ardent, raise
One general song !   To Him, ye vocal gales,
Breathe soft, whose Spirit in your freshness breathes;
Oh talk of Him in solitary glooms !
Where, o'er the rock, the scarcely-waving pine
Fills the brown shade with a religious awe.
And ye, whose bolder note is heard afar,
Who shake th' astonish'd world, lift high to heaven
Th' impetuous song, and say from whom you rage.
His praise, ye brooks, attune, ye trembling rills;
And let me catch it as I muse along.
Ye headlong torrents, rapid and profound;
Ye softer floods, that lead the humid maze
Along the vale; and thou, majestic main,
A secret world of wonders in thyself,
Sound His stupendous praise; whose greater voice
Or bids you roar, or bids your roarings fall.
Soft roll your incense, herbs, and fruits, and flowers,
In mingled clouds to Him; whose sun exalts,
Whose breath perfumes you, and whose pencil paints.
Ye forests bend; ye harvests wave to Him;
Breathe your still song into the reaper's heart,
As home he goes beneath the joyous moon.
Ye that keep watch in heaven, as earth asleep
Unconscious lies, effuse your mildest beams,
Ye constellations, while your angels strike,
Amid the spangled sky, the silver lyre.

Great source of day ! best image here below
Of thy Creator, ever pouring wide,
From world to world, the vital ocean round,
On Nature write with every beam His praise.
The thunder rolls; be hush'd the prostrate world;
While cloud to cloud returns the solemn hymn.
Bleat out afresh, ye hills. Ye mossy rocks,
Retain the sound: the broad responsive low,
Ye valleys, raise; for the Great Shepherd reigns,
And his unsuffering kingdom yet will come.
Ye woodlands all, awake: a boundless song
Bursts from the groves ! and when the restless day,
Expiring, lays the warbling world asleep,
Sweetest of birds ! sweet Philomela, charm
The listening shades, and teach the night His praise.
Ye chief, for whom the whole creation smiles,
At once the head, the heart, and tongue of all,
Crown the great hymn ! in swarming cities vast,
Assembled men, to the deep organ join
The long-resounding voice, oft breaking clear,
At solemn pauses, through the swelling bass;
And, as each mingling flame increases each,
In one united ardour rise to heaven.
Or, if you rather choose the rural shade,
And find a fane in every sacred grove,
There let the shepherd's flute, the virgin's lay,
The prompting seraph, and the poet's lyre,
Still sing the God of Seasons as they roll.
For me, when I forget the darling theme,
Whether the blossom blows, the Summer ray
Russets the plain, inspiring Autumn gleams,
Or Winter rises in the blackening east;
Be my tongue mute, may fancy paint no more,
And, dead to joy, forget my heart to beat !
Should fate command me to the farthest verge
Of the green earth, to distant barbarous climes,
Rivers unknown to song; where first the sun
Gilds Indian mountains, or his setting beam

Flames on th' Atlantic isles; 'tis nought to me,
Since God is ever present, ever felt,
In the void waste as in the city full;
And where He vital breathes there must be joy.
When even at last the solemn hour shall come,
And wing my mystic flight to future worlds,
I cheerful will obey; there, with new powers,
Will rising wonders sing: I cannot go
Where Universal Love not smiles around,
Sustaining all yon orbs, and all their suns;
From seeming evil still educing good,
And better thence again, and better still,
In infinite progression.   But I lose
Myself in Him, in Light ineffable !
Come, then, expressive Silence, muse His praise.

THE

CASTLE OF INDOLENCE.

CASTLE OF INDOLENCE.

CANTO I.

The Castle hight of Indolence,
And its false luxury;
Where for a little time, alas!
We lived right jollily.

I.

O MORTAL man, who livest here by toil,
Do not complain of this thy hard estate;
That like an emmet thou must ever moil,
Is a sad sentence of an ancient date;
And, certes, there is for it reason great;
For, though sometimes it makes thee weep and wail,
And curse thy star, and early drudge and late;
Withouten that would come a heavier bale,
Loose life, unruly passions, and diseases pale.

II.

In lowly dale, fast by a river's side,
With woody hill o'er hill encompass'd round,
A most enchanting wizard did abide,
Than whom a fiend more fell is nowhere found.
It was, I ween, a lovely spot of ground;
And there a season atween June and May,
Half prankt with spring, with summer half imbrown'd,
A listless climate made, where, sooth to say,
No living wight could work, ne cared even for play.

III.

Was nought around but images of rest:
Sleep-soothing groves, and quiet lawns between;
And flowery beds that slumbrous influence kest,
From poppies breathed; and beds of pleasant green,
Where never yet was creeping creature seen.
Meantime, unnumber'd glittering streamlets play'd,
And hurl'd everywhere their waters sheen;
That, as they bicker'd through the sunny glade,
Though restless still themselves, a lulling murmur made.

IV.

Join'd to the prattle of the purling rills
Were heard the lowing herds along the vale,
And flocks loud bleating from the distant hills,
And vacant shepherds piping in the dale:
And, now and then, sweet Philomel would wail,
Or stock-doves plain amid the forest deep,
That drowsy rustled to the sighing gale;
And still a coil the grasshopper did keep;
Yet all these sounds yblent inclined all to sleep.

V.

Full in the passage of the vale, above,
A sable, silent, solemn forest stood;
Where nought but shadowy forms were seen to move,
As Idless fancied in her dreaming mood:
And up the hills, on either side, a wood
Of blackening pines, aye waving to and fro,
Sent forth a sleepy horror through the blood;
And where this valley winded out, below,
The murmuring main was heard, and scarcely heard to flow.

VI.

A pleasing land of drowsy head it was,
Of dreams that wave before the half-shut eye;
And of gay castles in the clouds that pass,
For ever flushing round a summer-sky:

There eke the soft delights, that witchingly
Instil a wanton sweetness through the breast,
And the calm pleasures always hover'd nigh;
But whate'er smack'd of noyance, or unrest,
Was far far off expell'd from this delicious nest.

VII.

The landscape such, inspiring perfect ease,
Where INDOLENCE (for so the wizard hight)
Close-hid his castle 'mid emboweling trees,
That half shut out the beams of Phœbus bright,
And made a kind of chequer'd day and night;
Meanwhile, unceasing at the massy gate,
Beneath a spacious palm, the wicked wight
Was placed; and to his lute, of cruel fate
And labour harsh, complain'd, lamenting man's estate.

VIII.

Thither continua. pilgrims crowded still,
From all the roads of earth that pass there by:
For, as they chaunced to breathe on neighbouring hill,
The freshness of this valley smote their eye,
And drew them ever and anon more nigh;
Till clustering round the enchanter false they hung,
Ymolten with his syren melody;
While o'er the enfeebling lute his hand he flung,
And to the trembling chords these tempting verses sung:—

IX.

"Behold! ye pilgrims of this earth, behold!
See all, but man, with unearn'd pleasure gay:
See her bright robes the butterfly unfold,
Broke from her wintry tomb in prime of May!
What youthful bride can equal her array?
Who can with her for easy pleasure vie?
From mead to mead with gentle wing to stray,
From flower to flower on balmy gales to fly,
Is all she has to do beneath the radiant sky.

X.

"Behold the merry minstrels of the morn,
The swarming songsters of the careless grove,
Ten thousand throats! that, from the flowering thorn,
Hymn their good G..d, and carol sweet of love,
Such grateful kindly raptures them emove:
They neither plough, nor sow; ne, fit for flail,
E'er to the barn the nodden sheaves they drove:
Yet theirs each harvest dancing in the gale,
Whatever crowns the hill, or smiles along the vale.

XI.

"Outcast of nature, man! the wretched thrall
Of bitter dropping sweat, of sweltry pain,
Of cares that eat away the heart with gall,
And of the vices, an inhuman train,
That all proceed from savage thirst of gain:
For when hard-hearted interest first began
To poison earth, Astræa left the plain;
Guile, violence, and murder seized on man,
And, for soft milky streams, with blood the rivers ran.

XII.

"Come, ye who still the cumbrous load of life
Push hard up hill; but as the furthest steep
You trust to gain, and put an end to strife,
Down thunders back the stone with mighty sweep,
And hurls your labours to the valley deep,
For ever vain: come, and withouten fee,
I in oblivion will your sorrows steep,
Your cares, your toils; will steep you in a sea
Of full delight: O come, ye weary wights, to me!

XIII.

"With me, you need not rise at early dawn,
To pass the joyless day in various stounds:
Or, louting low, on upstart fortune fawn,
And sell fair honoui for some paltry pounds;

Or through the city take your dirty rounds,
To cheat, and dun, and lie, and visit pay,
Now flattering base, now giving secret wounds;
Or prowl in courts of law for human prey,
In venal senate thieve, or rob on broad highway.

XIV.

"No cocks, with me, to rustic labour call,
From village on to village sounding clear;
To tardy swain no shrill-voiced matrons squall;
No dogs, no babes, no wives, to stun your ear;
No hammers thump; no horrid blacksmith sear.
Ne noisy tradesman your sweet slumbers start,
With sounds that are a misery to hear:
But all is calm, as would delight the heart
Of Sybarite of old, all nature, and all art.

XV.

"Here nought but candour reigns, indulgent ease,
Good-natured lounging, sauntering up and down:
They who are pleased themselves must always please;
On others' ways they never squint a frown,
Nor heed what haps in hamlet or in town:
Thus, from the source of tender Indolence,
With milky blood the heart is overflown,
Is soothed and sweeten'd by the social sense;
For interest, envy, pride, and strife are banish'd hence.

XVI.

"What, what is virtue, but repose of mind,
A pure ethereal calm, that knows no storm;
Above the reach of wild ambition's wind;
Above those passions that this world deform,
And torture man, a proud malignant worm?
But here, instead, soft gales of passion play,
And gently stir the heart, thereby to form
A quicker sense of joy; as breezes stray
Aross the enliven'd skies, and make them still more gay.

XVII.

" The best of men have ever loved repose:
They hate to mingle in the filthy fray;
Where the soul sours, and gradual rancour grows,
Imbitter'd more from peevish day to day.
E'en those whom fame has lent her fairest ray,
The most renown'd of worthy wights of yore,
From a base world at last have stolen away;
So Scipio, to the soft Cumæan shore
Retiring, tasted joy he never knew before.

XVIII.

"But if a little exercise you choose,
Some zest for ease, 'tis not forbidden here:
Amid the groves you may indulge the Muse,
Or tend the blooms, and deck the vernal year;
Or softly stealing, with your watery gear,
Along the brooks, the crimson-spotted fry
You may delude; the whilst, amused, you hear
Now the hoarse stream, and now the zephyr's sigh,
Attuned to the birds, and woodland melody.

XIX.

"O grievous folly! to heap up estate,
Losing the days you see beneath the sun;
When, sudden, comes blind unrelenting fate,
And gives the untasted portion you have won
With ruthless toil, and many a wretch undone,
To those who mock you, gone to Pluto's reign,
There with sad ghosts to pine, and shadows dun:
But sure it is of vanities most vain,
To toil for what you here untoiling may obtain."

XX.

He ceased. But still their trembling ears retain'd
The deep vibrations of his witching song;
That, by a kind of magic power, constrain'd
To enter in, pell-mell, the listening throng.

Heaps pour'd on heaps, and yet they slipt along,
In silent ease; as when beneath the beam
Of summer-moons, the distant woods among,
Or by some flood all silver'd with the gleam,
The soft-embodied fays through airy portal stream:

XXI.

By the smooth demon so it order'd was,
And here his baneful bounty first began:
Though some there were who would not further pass,
And his alluring baits suspected han.
The wise distrust the too fair-spoken man.
Yet through the gate they cast a wishful eye:
Not to move on, perdie, is all they can:
For do their very best they cannot fly,
But often each way look, and often sorely sigh.

XXII.

When this the watchful wicked wizard saw,
With sudden spring he leap'd upon them straight;
And soon as touch'd by his unhallow'd paw,
They found themselves within the cursed gate;
Full hard to be repass'd, like that of fate.
Not stronger were of old the giant crew,
Who sought to pull high Jove from regal state
Though feeble wretch he seem'd, of sallow hue:
Certes, who bides his grasp, will that encounter rue.

XXIII.

For whomsoe'er the villain takes in hand,
Their joints unknit, their sinews melt apace;
As lithe they grow as any willow-wand,
And of their vanish'd force remains no trace:
So when a maiden fair, of modest grace,
In all her buxom blooming May of charms,
Is seized in some losel's hot embrace,
She waxeth very weakly as she warms,
Then sighing yields her up to love's delicious harms.

XXIV.

Waked by the crowd, slow from his bench arose
A comely, full-spread porter, swoln with sleep:
His calm, broad, thoughtless aspect breathed repose:
And in sweet torpor he was plunged deep,
Ne could himself from ceaseless yawning keep;
While o'er his eyes the drowsy liquor ran,
Through which his half-waked soul would faintly peep:
Then taking his black staff, he call'd his man,
And roused himself as much as rouse himself he can.

XXV.

The lad leap'd lightly at his master's call:
He was, to weet, a little roguish page,
Save sleep and play who minded nought at all,
Like most the untaught striplings of his age:
This boy he kept each band to disengage,
Garters and buckles, task for him unfit,
But ill becoming his grave personage,
And which his portly paunch would not permit;
So this same limber page to all performed it.

XXVI.

Meantime, the master-porter wide display'd
Great store of caps, of slippers, and of gowns;
Wherewith he those who enter'd in array'd
Loose, as the breeze that plays along the downs,
And waves the summer woods when evening frowns;
O fair undress, best dress! it checks no vein,
But every flowing limb in pleasure drowns,
And heightens ease with grace. This done, right fain,
Sir porter sat him down, and turn'd to sleep again.

XXVII.

Thus easy robed, they to the fountain sped
That in the middle of the court up-threw
A stream, high spouting from its liquid bed,
And falling back again in drizzly dew;

There each deep draughts, as deep he thirsted, drew;
It was a fountain of nepenthe rare;
Whence, as Dan Homer sings, huge pleasance grew,
And sweet oblivion of vile earthly care;
Fair gladsome waking thoughts, and joyous dreams more fair.

XXVIII.

This right perform'd, all inly pleased and still,
Withouten tromp, was proclamation made:
" Ye sons of Indolence, do what you will;
And wander where you list, through hall or glade;
Be no man's pleasure for another staid;
Let each as likes him best his hours employ,
And cursed be he who minds his neighbour's trade!
Here dwells kind ease and unreproving joy:
He little merits bliss who others can annoy."

XXIX.

Straight of these endless numbers, swarming round,
As thick as idle motes in sunny ray,
Not one eftsoons in view was to be found,
But every man stroll'd off his own glad way,
Wide o'er this ample court's blank area,
With all the lodges that thereto pertain'd,
No living creature could be seen to stray;
While solitude, and perfect silence reign'd;
So that to think you dreamt you almost was constrain'd.

XXX.

As when a shepherd of the Hebrid-Isles,*
Placed far amid the melancholy main
(Whether it be lone fancy him beguiles;
Or that aerial beings sometimes deign
To stand, embodied, to our senses plain),
Sees on the naked hill, or valley low,
The whilst in ocean Phœbus dips his wain,

---

* Those isles on the W. coast of Scotland, called the Hebrides.

A vast assembly moving to and fro:
Then all at once in air dissolves the wondrous show.

XXXI.

Ye gods of quiet, and of sleep profound!
Whose soft dominion o'er this castle sways,
And all the widely silent places round,
Forgive me, if my trembling pen displays
What never yet was sung in mortal lays.
But how shall I attempt such arduous string?
I who have spent my nights, and nightly days,
In this soul-deadening place loose-loitering:
Ah! how shall I for this uprear my moulted wing?

XXXII.

Come on, my muse, nor stoop to low despair
Thou imp of Jove, touch'd by celestial fire!
Thou yet shalt sing of war, and actions fair
Which the bold sons of Britain will inspire,
Of ancient bards thou yet shalt sweep the lyre;
Thou yet shalt tread in tragic pall the stage,
Paint love's enchanting woes, the hero's ire,
The sage's calm, the patriot's noble rage,
Dashing corruption down through every worthless age.

XXXIII.

The doors, that knew no shrill alarming bell,
Ne cursed knocker plied by villain's hand,
Self-open'd into halls, where, who can tell
What elegance and grandeur wide expand;
The pride of Turkey and of Persia land?
Soft quilts on quilts, on carpets carpets spread,
And couches stretch'd around in seemly band;
And endless pillows rise to prop the head;
So that each spacious room was one full-swelling bed;

XXXIV.

And everywhere huge cover'd tables stood,
With wines high-flavour'd and rich viands crown'd;

Whatever sprightly juice or tasteful food
On the green bosom of this earth are found,
And all old ocean 'genders in his round:
Some hand unseen these silently display'd,
Even undemanded by a sign or sound;
You need but wish, and, instantly obey'd,
Fair ranged the dishes rose, and thick the glasses play'd.

XXXV.

Here freedom reign'd, without the least alloy;
Nor gossip's tale, nor ancient maiden's gall,
Nor saintly spleen durst murmur at our joy,
And with envenom'd tongue our pleasures pall.
For why? there was but one great rule for all;
To wit, that each should work his own desire,
And eat, drink, study, sleep, as it may fall,
Or melt the time in love, or wake the lyre,
And carol what, unbid, the muses might inspire.

XXXVI.

The rooms with costly tapestry were hung,
Where was inwoven many a gentle tale;
Such as of old the rural poets sung,
Or of Arcadian or Sicilian vale:
Reclining lovers, in the lonely dale,
Pour'd forth at large the sweetly tortured heart;
Or, sighing tender passion, swell'd the gale,
And taught charm'd echo to resound their smart;
While flocks, woods, streams around, repose and peace impart.

XXXVII.

Those pleased the most, where, by a cunning hand,
Depainted was the patriarchal age;
What time Dan Abraham left the Chaldee land,
And pastured on from verdant stage to stage,
Where fields and fountains fresh could best engage.
Toil was not then: of nothing took they heed,
But with wild beasts the sylvan war to wage,

And o'er vast plains their herds and flocks to feed:
Bless'd sons of nature they ! true golden age indeed !

XXXVIII.

Sometimes the pencil, in cool airy halls,
Bade the gay bloom of vernal landscapes rise,
Or Autumn's varied shades imbrown the walls:
Now the black tempest strikes the astonish'd eyes;
Now down the steep the flashing torrent flies;
The trembling sun now plays o'er ocean blue,
And now rude mountains frown amid the skies;
Whate'er Lorraine light-touch'd with softening hue,
Or savage Rosa dash'd, or learned Poussin drew.

XXXIX.

Each sound too here to languishment inclined,
Lull'd the weak bosom, and induced ease:
Aerial music in the warbling wind,
At distance rising oft, by small degrees,
Nearer and nearer came, till o'er the trees
It hung, and breathed such soul-dissolving airs,
As did, alas! with soft perdition please:
Entangled deep in its enchanting snares,
The listening heart forgot all duties and all cares.

XL.

A certain music, never known before,
Here lull'd the pensive, melancholy mind;
Full easily obtain'd.   Behoves no more,
But sidelong, to the gently waving wind,
To lay the well tuned instrument reclined;
From which, with airy flying fingers light,
Beyond each mortal touch the most refined,
The god of winds drew sounds of deep delight:
Whence, with just cause, the harp of Æolus it hight.*

---

* The Æolian harp, here designated, has been greatly improved
in its structure by a kindred poet, the author of " The Farmer's
Boy."

XLI.

Ah me ! what hand can touch the string so fine ?
Who up the lofty diapason roll
Such sweet, such sad, such solemn airs divine,
Then let them down again into the soul:
Now rising love they fann'd; now pleasing dole
They breathed, in tender musings, through the heart;
And now a graver sacred strain they stole,
As when seraphic hands a hymn impart:
Wild warbling nature all, above the reach of art !

XLII.

Such the gay splendour, the luxurious state,
Of Caliphs old, who on the Tigris' shore,
In mighty Bagdat, populous and great,
Held their bright court, where was of ladies store;
And verse, love, music, still the garland wore:
When sleep was coy, the bard,* in waiting there,
Cheer'd the lone midnight with the muse's lore;
Composing music bade his dreams be fair,
And music lent new gladness to the morning air.

XLIII.

Near the pavilions where we slept, still ran
Soft tinkling streams, and dashing waters fell,
And sobbing breezes sigh'd, and oft began
(So work'd the wizard) wintry storms to swell,
As heaven and earth they would together mell:
At doors and windows, threatening, seem'd to call
The demons of the tempest, growling fell,
Yet the least entrance found they none at all;
Whence sweeter grew our sleep, secure in massy hall.

XLIV.

And hither Morpheus sent his kindest dreams,
Raising a world of gayer tinct and grace;

---

* The Arabian Caliphs had poets among the officers of their
court, whose office it was to do what is here described.

O'er which were shadowy cast elysian gleams,
That play'd, in waving lights, from place to place,
And shed a roseate smile on nature's face.
Not Titian's pencil e'er could so array,
So fleece with clouds the pure ethereal space;
Ne could it e'er such melting forms display,
As loose on flowery beds all languishingly lay.

XLV.

No, fair illusions! artful phantoms, no!
My Muse will not attempt your fairy land:
She has no colours that like you can glow:
To catch your vivid scenes, too gross her hand.
But sure it is, was ne'er a subtler band
Than these same guileful, angel-seeming sprights,
Who thus in dreams voluptuous, soft, and bland,
Pour'd all the Arabian heaven upon our nights,
And bless'd them oft besides with more refined delights.

XLVI.

They were, in sooth, a most enchanting train,
Even feigning virtue; skilful to unite
With evil good, and strew with pleasure pain.
But for those fiends, whom blood and broils delight;
Who hurl the wretch, as if to hell outright,
Down down black gulfs, where sullen waters sleep,
Or hold him clambering all the fearful night
On beetling cliffs, or pent in ruins deep;
They, till due time should serve, were bid far hence to keep.

XLVII.

Ye guardian spirits, to whom man is dear,
From these foul demons shield the midnight gloom:
Angels of fancy and of love, be near,
And o'er the blank of sleep diffuse a bloom:
Evoke the sacred shades of Greece and Rome,
And let them virtue with a look impart:
But chief, awhile, O! lend us from the tomb

Those long-lost friends for whom in love we smart,
And fill with pious awe and joy-mix'd wo the heart.

XLVIII.

Or are you sportive—— Bid the morn of youth
Rise to new light, and beam afresh the days
Of innocence, simplicity, and truth;
To cares estranged, and manhood's thorny ways
What transport, to retrace our boyish plays,
Our easy bliss, when each thing joy supplied;
The woods, the mountains, and the warbling maze
Of the wild brooks!—but, fondly wandering wide,
My Muse, resume the task that yet doth thee abide.

XLIX.

One great amusement of our household was,
In a huge crystal magic globe to spy,
Still as you turn'd it, all things that do pass
Upon this ant-hill earth; where constantly
Of idle busy men the restless fry
Run bustling to and fro with foolish haste,
In search of pleasures vain that from them fly,
Or which, obtain'd, the caitiffs dare not taste:—
When nothing is enjoy'd, can there be greater waste?

L.

"Of vanity the mirror," this was call'd:
Here, you a muckworm of the town might see,
At his dull desk, amid his ledgers stall'd,
Eat up with carking care and penury;
Most like to carcase parch'd on gallow-tree.
"A penny saved is a penny got:"
Firm to this scoundrel maxim keepeth he,
Ne of its rigour will he bate a jot,
Till it has quench'd his fire, and banished his pot.

LI.

Straight from the filth of this low grub, behold!
Comes fluttering forth a gaudy spendthrift heir.

N

All glossy gay, enamell'd all with gold,
The silly tenant of the summer air,
In folly lost, of nothing takes he care;
Pimps, lawyers, stewards, harlots, flatterers vile,
And thieving tradesmen, him among them share;
His father's ghost from limbo lake, the while,
Sees this, which more damnation doth upon him pile.

LII.

This globe portray'd the race of learn'd men,
Still at their books, and turning o'er the page,
Backwards and forwards: oft they snatch the pen,
As if inspired, and in a Thespian rage;
Then write, and blot, as would your ruth engage:
Why, authors, all this scrawl and scribbling sore?
To lose the present, gain the future age,
Praised to be when you can hear no more,
And much enrich'd with fame, when useless worldly store.

LIII.

Then would a splendid city rise to view,
With carts, and cars, and coaches roaring all:
Wide-pour'd abroad behold the giddy crew:
See how they dash along from wall to wall!
At every door, hark how they thundering call!
Good lord! what can this giddy rout excite?
Why, on each other with fell tooth to fall;
A neighbour's fortune, fame, or peace to blight,
And make new tiresome parties for the coming night.

LIV.

The puzzling sons of party next appear'd,
In dark cabals and nightly juntos met;
And now they whisper'd close, now shrugging rear'd
The important shoulder; then, as if to get
New light, their twinkling eyes were inward set.
No sooner Lucifer* recalls affairs,

---

* The Morning Star.

Than forth they various rush in mighty fret;
When lo! push'd up to power, and crown'd their
    cares,
In comes another set, and kicketh them down stairs.

LV.

But what most show'd the vanity of life,
Was to behold the nations all on fire,
In cruel broils engaged, and deadly strife:
Most Christian kings, inflamed by black desire,
With honourable ruffians in their hire,
Cause war to rage, and blood around to pour;
Of this sad work when each begins to tire,
Then sit them down just where they were before,
Till for new scenes of wo peace shall their force re-
    store.

LVI.

To number up the thousands dwelling here,
A useless were, and eke an endless task;
From kings, and those who at the helm appear,
To gipsies brown in summer-glades who bask.
Yea many a man, perdie, I could unmask,
Whose desk and table make a solemn show,
With tape-tied trash, and suits of fools that ask
For place or pension laid in decent row;
But these I passen by, with nameless numbers moe.

LVII.

Of all the gentle tenants of the place,
There was a man of special grave remark;
A certain tender gloom o'erspread his face.
Pensive, not sad; in thought involved, not dark;
As soot this man could sing as morning lark,
And teach the noblest morals of the heart:
But these his talents were yburied stark;
Of the fine stores he nothing would impart,
Which or boon nature gave, or nature painting art.

LVIII.

To noontide shades incontinent he ran,
Where purls the brook with sleep-inviting sound;
Or when Dan Sol to slope his wheels began,
Amid the broom he bask'd him on the ground,
Where the wild thyme and camomile are found:
There would he linger, till the latest ray
Of light sat trembling on the welkin's bound;
Then homeward through the twilight shadows stray,
Sauntering and slow.   So had he pass'd many a day.

LIX.

Yet not in thoughtless slumber were they pass'd:
For oft the heavenly fire, that lay conceal'd
Beneath the sleeping embers, mounted fast,
And all its native light anew reveal'd:
Oft as he traversed the cerulean field,
And mark'd the clouds that drove before the wind,
Ten thousand glorious systems would he build,
Ten thousand great ideas fill'd his mind;
But with the clouds they fled, and left no trace behind.

LX

With him was sometimes join'd, in silent walk
(Profoundly silent, for they never spoke),
One* shyer still, who quite detested talk:
Oft, stung by spleen, at once away he broke,
To groves of pine, and broad o'ershadowing oak;
There, inly thrill'd, he wander'd all alone,
And on himself his pensive fury wroke,
Ne ever utter'd word, save when first shone
The glittering star of eve—"Thank heaven! the day is done."

LXI.

Here lurk'd a wretch, who had not crept abroad
For forty years, ne face of mortal seen;

---

* Conjecture has applied this to Dr Armstrong, the poet.

In chamber brooding like a loathly toad:
And sure his linen was not very clean.
Through secret loopholes, that had practised been,
Near to his bed his dinner vile he took;
Unkempt, and rough, of squalid face and mien,
Our Castle's shame! whence, from his filthy nook,
We drove the villain out for fitter lair to look.

LXII.

One day there chanced into these halls to rove
A joyous youth, who took you 'at first sight;
Him the wild wave of pleasure hither drove,
Before the sprightly tempest tossing light:
Certes, he was a most engaging wight,
Of social glee, and wit humane though keen,
Turning the night to day, and day to night:
For him the merry bells had rung, I ween,
If in this nook of quiet bells had ever been.

LXIII.

But not e'en pleasure to excess is good:
What most elates, then sinks the soul as low:
When springtide joy pours in with copious flood,
The higher still the exulting billows flow,
The further back again they flagging go,
And leave us grovelling on the dreary shore:
Taught by this son of joy, we found it so;
Who, whilst he staid, he kept in gay uproar
Our madden'd castle all, the abode of sleep no more.

LXIV.

As when in prime of June a burnish'd fly,
Sprung from the meads, o'er which he sweeps along,
Cheer'd by the breathing bloom and vital sky,
Tunes up amid these airy halls his song,
Soothing at first the gay reposing throng:
And oft he sips their bowl; or nearly drown'd,
He, thence recovering, drives their beds among,

And scares their tender sleep, with trump profound;
Then out again he flies, to wing his mazy round.

LXV.

Another guest* there was, of sense refined,
Who felt each worth, for every worth he had;
Serene yet warm, humane yet firm his mind,
As little touch'd as any man's with bad;
Him through their inmost walks the Muses lad,
To him the sacred love of nature lent,
And sometimes would he make our valley glad;
Whenas we found he would not here be pent,
To him the better sort this friendly message sent:

LXVI.

" Come, dwell with us ! true son of virtue, come !
But if, alas ! we cannot thee persuade
To lie content beneath our peaceful dome,
Ne evermore to quit our quiet glade;
Yet when at last thy toils but ill apaid
Shall dead thy fire, and damp its heavenly spark,
Thou wilt be glad to seek the rural shade,
There to indulge the muse, and nature mark:
We then a lodge for thee will rear in Hagley Park."

LXVII.

Here whilom ligg'd the Esopus† of the age;
But call'd by fame, in soul ypricked deep,
A noble pride resto'ed him to the stage,
And reused him like a giant from his sleep.
Even from his slumbers we advantage reap:
With double force the enliven'd scene he wakes,
Yet quits not nature's bounds.   He knows to keep
Each due decorum: now the heart he shakes,
And now with well urged sense the enlighten'd judgmen
       takes.

---

* George, Lord Lyttelton.   † Mr Quin.

LXVIII.

A bard here dwelt, more fat than bard beseems;
Who,* void of envy, guile, and lust of gain,
On virtue still, and nature's pleasing themes,
Pour'd forth his unpremeditated strain:
The world forsaking with a calm disdain,
Here laugh'd he careless in his easy seat;
Here quaff'd, encircled with the joyous train,
Oft moralising sage: his ditty sweet
He loathed much to write, ne cared to repeat.

LXIX.

Full oft by holy feet our ground was trod,
Of clerks good plenty here you mote espy.
A little, round, fat, oily man† of God,
Was one I chiefly mark'd among the fry:
He had a roguish twinkle in his eye,
And shone all glittering with ungodly dew,
If a tight damsel chanced to trippen by;
Which, when observed, he shrunk into his mew,
And straight would recollect his piety anew.

LXX.

Nor be forgot a tribe who minded nought
(Old inmates of the place) but state-affairs:
They look'd, perdie, as if they deeply thought;
And on their brow sat every nation's cares;
The world by them is parcell'd out in shares,
When in the Hall of Smoke they congress hold,
And the sage berry, sun-burnt Mocha bears,
Has clear'd their inward eye: then, smoke-enroll'd,
Their oracles break forth mysterious as of old.

---

* The following lines of this stanza were writ by a friend of the author (since understood to have been Lord Lyttelton), and were designed to portray the character of Thomson.

† The Rev. Mr Murdoch, Thomson's friend and biographer.

LXXI.

Here languid Beauty kept her pale-faced court:
Bevies of dainty dames, of high degree,
From every quarter hither made resort;
Where, from gross mortal care and business free,
They lay, pour'd out in ease and luxury.
Or should they a vain show of work assume,
Alas! and well-a-day! what can it be ?
To knot, to twist, to range the vernal bloom;
But far is cast the distaff, spinning-wheel, and loom.

LXXII.

Their only labour was to kill the time
(And labour dire it is, and weary wo);
They sit, they loll, turn o'er some idle rhyme;
Then, rising sudden, to the glass they go,
Or saunter forth, with tottering step and slow:
This soon too rude an exercise they find;
Straight on the couch their limbs again they throw,
Where hours on hours they sighing lie reclined,
And court the vapoury god, soft breathing in the wind.*

LXXIII.

Now must I mark the villany we found,
But ah! too late, as shall eftsoons be shown.
A place here was, deep, dreary, under ground;
Where still our inmates, when unpleasing grown,

---

* After this stanza, the following one was introduced, in the
edition of 1746:—

One nymph there was, methought, in bloom of May,
On whom the idle Fiend glanced many a look,
In hopes to lead her down the slippery way
To taste of Pleasure's deep deceitful brook:
No virtues yet her gentle mind forsook:
No idle whims, no vapours fill'd her brain,
But Prudence for her youthful guide she took,
And Goodness, which no earthly vice could stain,
Dwelt in her mind; she was ne proud I ween or vain.

Diseased, and loathsome, privily were thrown:
Far from the light of heaven, they languish'd there,
Unpitied uttering many a bitter groan;
For of these wretches taken was no care:
Fierce fiends, and hags of hell, their only nurses were.

LXXIV.

Alas! the change! from scenes of joy and rest,
To this dark den, where sickness toss'd alway.
Here Lethargy, with deadly sleep oppress'd,
Stretch'd on his back, a mighty lubbard, lay,
Heaving his sides, and snored night and day;
To stir him from his traunce it was not eath,
And his half open'd eyne he shut straightway;
He led, I wot, the softest way to death,
And taught withouten pain and strife to yield the breath.

LXXV.

Of limbs enormous, but withal unsound,
Soft-swoln and pale, here lay the Hydropsy:
Unwieldy man; with belly monstrous round,
For ever fed with watery supply;
For still he drank, and yet he still was dry.
And moping here did Hypochondria sit,
Mother of spleen, in robes of various dye,
Who vexed was full oft with ugly fit;
And some her frantic deem'd, and some her deem'd a wit.

LXXVI.

A lady proud she was, of ancient blood,
Yet oft her fear her pride made crouchen low:
She felt, or fancied in her fluttering mood,   ·
All the diseases which the spittles know,
And sought all physic which the shops bestow,
And still new leeches and new drugs would try,
Her humour ever wavering to and fro;
For sometimes she would laugh, and sometimes cry,
Then sudden waxed wroth, and all she knew not why.

LXXVII.

Fast by her side a listless maiden pined,
With aching head, and squeamish heart-burnings;
Pale, bloated, cold, she seem'd to hate mankind,
Yet loved in secret all forbidden things.
And here the Tertian shakes his chilling wings;
The sleepless Gout here counts the crowing cocks,
A wolf now gnaws him, now a serpent stings;
  Whilst Apoplexy cramm'd, Intemperance knocks
Down to the ground at once, as butcher felleth ox.*

---

* The four concluding stanzas were claimed by Doctor Armstrong, and inserted in his Miscellanies.

CANTO II.

The Knight of Arts and Industry,
And his achievements fair;
That, by this Castle's overthrow,
Secured, and crowned were.

I.

ESCAPED the castle of the sire of sin,
Ah! where shall I so sweet a dwelling find?
For all around, without, and all within,
Nothing save what delightful was and kind,
Of goodness savouring and a tender mind,
E'er rose to view.   But now another strain,
Of doleful note, alas! remains behind:
I now must sing of pleasure turn'd to pain,
And of the false enchanter INDOLENCE complain.

II.

Is there no patron to protect the Muse,
And fence for her Parnassus' barren soil?
To every labour its reward accrues,
And they are sure of bread who swink and moil;
But a fell tribe the Aonian hive despoil,
As ruthless wasps oft rob the painful bee;
Thus while the laws not guard that noblest toil,
Ne for the Muses other meed decree,
They praised are alone, and starve right merrily.

III.

I care not, Fortune, what you me deny:
You cannot rob me of free Nature's grace:
You cannot shut the windows of the sky,
Through which Aurora shows her brightening face;

You cannot bar my constant feet to trace
The woods and lawns, by living stream, at eve:
Let health my nerves and finer fibres brace,
And I their toys to the great children leave:
Of fancy, reason, virtue, nought can me bereave.

IV.

Come then, my Muse, and raise a bolder song;
Come, lig no more upon the bed of sloth,
Dragging the lazy languid line along,
Fond to begin, but still to finish loath,
Thy half-writ scrolls all eaten by the moth:
Arise, and sing that generous imp of fame,
Who with the sons of softness nobly wroth,
To sweep away this human lumber came,
Or in a chosen few to rouse the slumbering flame.

V.

In Fairyland there lived a knight of old,
Of feature stern, Selvaggio well yclep'd,
A rough unpolish'd man, robust and bold,
But wondrous poor: he neither sow'd nor reap'd,
Ne stores in summer for cold winter heap'd;
In hunting all his days away he wore;
Now scorch'd by June, now in November steep'd,
Now pinch'd by biting January sore,
He still in woods pursued the libbard and the boar.

VI.

As he one morning, long before the dawn,
Prick'd through the forest to dislodge his prey,
Deep in the winding bosom of a lawn,
With wood wild fringed, he mark'd a taper's ray,
That from the beating rain and wintry fray
Did to a lonely cot his steps decoy;
There, up to earn the needments of the day,
He found dame Poverty, nor fair nor coy:
Her he compress'd, and fill'd her with a lusty boy.

VII.

Amid the greenwood shade this boy was bred,
And grew at last a knight of muchel fame,
Of active mind and vigorous lustyhed,
The Knight of Arts and Industry by name:
Earth was his bed; the boughs his roof did frame;
He knew no beverage but the flowing stream;
His tasteful, well-earn'd food the sylvan game,
Or the brown fruit with which the woodlands teem:
The same to him glad summer, or the winter breme.

VIII.

So pass'd his youthly morning, void of care,
Wild as the colts that through the commons run.
For him no tender parents troubled were,
He of the forest seem'd to be the son,
And, certes, had been utterly undone;
But that Minerva pity of him took,
With all the gods that love the rural wonne,
That teach to tame the soil and rule the crook;
Ne did the sacred Nine disdain a gentle look.

IX.

Of fertile genius him they nurtured well,
In every science, and in every art,
By which mankind the thoughtless brutes excel,
That can or use, or joy, or grace impart,
Disclosing all the powers of head and heart:
Ne were the goodly exercises spared,
That brace the nerves, or make the limbs alert.
And mix elastic force with firmness hard:
Was never knight on ground mote be with him compared.

X.

Sometimes, with early morn, he mounted gay
The hunter steed, exulting o'er the dale,
And drew the roseate breath of orient day;
Sometimes, retiring to the secret vale,

Yclad in steel, and bright with burnish'd mail,
He strain'd the bow, or toss'd the sounding spear,
Or darting on the goal, outstripp'd the gale,
Or wheel'd the chariot in its mid career,
Or strenuous wrestled hard with many a tough compeer.

XI.

At other times he pried through nature's store,
Whate'er she in the ethereal round contains,
Whate'er she hides beneath her verdant floor,
The vegetable and the mineral reigns;
Or else he scann'd the globe, those small domains,
Where restless mortals such a turmoil keep,
Its seas, its floods, its mountains, and its plains;
But more he search'd the mind, and roused from sleep
Those moral seeds whence we heroic actions reap.

XII.

Nor would he scorn to stoop from high pursuits
Of heavenly truth, and practise what she taught:
Vain is the tree of knowledge without fruits!
Sometimes in hand the spade or plough he caught,
Forth calling all with which boon earth is fraught;
Sometimes he plied the strong mechanic tool,
Or rear'd the fabric from the finest draught;
And oft he put himself to Neptune's school,
Fighting with winds and waves on the vex'd ocean pool.

XIII.

To solace then these rougher toils, he tried
To touch the kindling canvas into life;
With Nature his creating pencil vied,
With Nature joyous at the mimic strife:
Or, to such shapes as graced Pygmalion's wife,
He hew'd the marble; or, with varied fire,
He roused the trumpet, and the martial fife,
Or bade the lute sweet tenderness inspire,
Or verses framed that well might wake Apollo's lyre.

XIV.

Accomplish'd thus, he from the woods issued,
Full of great aims, and bent on bold emprise;
The work which long he in his breast had brew'd,
Now to perform he ardent did devise;
To wit, a barbarous world to civilise.
Earth was till then a boundless forest wild;
Nought to be seen but savage wood and skies;
No cities nourish'd arts, no culture smiled,
No government, no laws, no gentle manners mild.

XV.

A rugged wight, the worst of brutes, was man;
On his own wretched kind he ruthless prey'd:
The strongest still the weakest overran;
In every country mighty robbers sway'd,
And guile and ruffian force were all their trade.
Life was a scene of rapine, want, and wo;
Which this brave knight, in noble anger, made
To swear he would the rascal rout o'erthrow,
For, by the powers divine, it should no more be so!

XVI.

It would exceed the purport of my song,
To say how this best sun from orient climes
Came, beaming life and beauty all along,
Before him chasing indolence and crimes.
Still as he pass'd, the nations he sublimes,
And calls forth arts and virtues with his ray:
Then Egypt, Greece, and Rome their golden times
Successive had; but now in ruins grey
They lie, to slavish sloth and tyranny a prey.

XVII.

To crown his toils, Sir Industry then spread
The swelling sail, and made for Britain's coast.
A sylvan life till then the natives led,
In the brown shades and greenwood forest lost,

All careless rambling where it liked them most:
Their wealth the wild deer bouncing through the glade;
They lodged at large, and lived at nature's cost;
Save spear and bow, withouten other aid;
Yet not the Roman steel their naked breast dismay'd.

XVIII.

He liked the soil, he liked the clement skies,
He liked the verdant hills and flowery plains:
"Be this my great, my chosen isle," he cries,
"This, whilst my labours Liberty sustains,
This Queen of Ocean all assault disdains."
Nor liked he less the genius of the land,
To freedom apt and persevering pains,
Mild to obey, and generous to command,
Temper'd by forming Heaven with kindest, firmest hand.

XIX.

Here, by degrees, his master-work arose,
Whatever arts and industry can frame:
Whatever finish'd agriculture knows,
Fair queen of arts! from heaven itself who came,
When Eden flourish'd in unspotted fame;
And still with her sweet innocence we find,
And tender peace, and joys without a name,
That, while they ravish, tranquillise the mind:
Nature and art at once, delight and use combined.

XX.

Then towns he quicken'd by mechanic arts,
And bade the fervent city glow with toil;
Bade social commerce raise renowned marts,
Join land to land, and marry soil to soil;
Unite the poles, and without bloody spoil
Bring home of either Ind the gorgeous stores;
Or, should despotic rage the world embroil,
Bade tyrants tremble on remotest shores,
While o'er the encircling deep Britannia's thunder roars.

XXI.

The drooping Muses then he westward call'd,
From the famed city* by Propontic sea,
What time the Turk the enfeebled Grecian thrall'd;
Thence from their cloister'd walks he set them free,
And brought them to another Castalie,
Where Isis many a famous nursling breeds;
Or where old Cam soft paces o'er the lea
In pensive mood, and tunes his Doric reeds,
The whilst his flocks at large the lonely shepherd feeds.

XXII.

Yet the fine arts were what he finish'd least.
For why? They are the quintessence of all,
The growth of labouring time, and slow increased;
Unless, as seldom chances, it should fall
That mighty patrons the coy sisters call
Up to the sunshine of uncumber'd ease,
Where no rude care the mounting thought may thrall,
And where they nothing have to do but please:
Ah! gracious God! thou know'st they ask no other fees.

XXIII.

But now, alas! we live too late in time:
Our patrons now e'en grudge that little claim,
Except to such as sleek the soothing rhyme;
And yet, forsooth, they wear Mæcenas' name,
Poor sons of puft-up vanity, not fame,
Unbroken spirits, cheer! still, still remains
The eternal patron, Liberty; whose flame,
While she protects, inspires the noblest strains:
The best and sweetest far, are toil-created gains.

XXIV.

When as the knight had framed, in Britain-land,
A matchless form of glorious government,

* Constantinople.

o

In which the sovereign laws alone command, ✕
Laws establish'd by the public free consent,
Whose majesty is to the sceptre lent;
When this great plan, with each dependent art,
Was settled firm, and to his heart's content,
Then sought he from the toilsome scene to part,
And let life's vacant eve breathe quiet through the
    heart.

XXV.

For this he chose a farm in Deva's vale,
Where his long alleys peep'd upon the main:
In this calm seat he drew the healthful gale,
Here mix'd the chief, the patriot, and the swain,
The happy monarch of his sylvan train;
Here, sided by the guardians of the fold,
He walk'd his rounds, and cheer'd his blest domain:
His days, the days of unstain'd Nature, roll'd
Replete with peace and joy, like patriarchs of old.

XXVI.

Witness, ye lowing herds, who gave him milk;
Witness, ye flocks, whose woolly vestments far
Exceed soft India's cotton, or her silk;
Witness, with Autumn charged the nodding car,
That homeward came beneath sweet evening's star,
Or of September moons the radiance mild.
O hide thy head, abominable War!
Of crimes and ruffian idleness the child!
From heaven this life ysprung, from hell thy glories
    viled!

XXVII.

Nor from his deep retirement banish'd was
The amusing care of rural industry.
Still, as with grateful change the seasons pass,
New scenes arise, new landscapes strike the eye.
And all the enliven'd country beautify:

Gay plains extend where marshes slept before;
O'er recent meads the exulting streamlets fly;
Dark frowning heaths grow bright with Ceres' store,
And woods imbrown the steep, or wave along the shore.

XXVIII.

As nearer to his farm you made approach,
He polish'd Nature with a finer hand:
Yet on her beauties durst not Art encroach;
'Tis Art's alone these beauties to expand.
In graceful dance immingled, o'er the land,
Pan, Pales, Flora, and Pomona play'd:
Here, too, brisk gales the rude wild common fann'd.
A happy place; where free, and unafraid,
Amid the flowering brakes each coyer creature stray'd;

XXIX.

But in prime vigour what can last for aye?
That soul-enfeebling wizard Indolence,
I whilom sung, wrought in his works decay:
Spread far and wide was his cursed influence;
Of public virtue much he dull'd the sense,
E'en much of private; eat our spirit out,
And fed our rank luxurious vices; whence
The land was overlaid with many a lout;
Not, as old fame reports, wise, generous, bold, and
stout.

XXX.

A rage of pleasure madden'd every breast,
Down to the lowest lees the ferment ran:
To his licentious wish each must be bless'd,
With joy be fever'd; snatch it as he can.
Thus Vice the standard rear'd; her arrier-ban
Corruption call'd, and loud she gave the word,
"Mind, mind yourselves! why should the vulgar man,
The lacquey, be more virtuous than his lord?
Enjoy this span of life! 'tis all the gods afford."

XXXI.

The tidings reach'd to where, in quiet hall,
The good old knight enjoyed well-earn'd repose:
"Come, come, Sir Knight, thy children on thee call;
Come, save us yet, ere ruin round us close!
The demon Indolence thy toils o'erthrows."
On this the noble colour stain'd his cheeks,
Indignant, glowing through the whitening snows
Of venerable eld; his eye full speaks
His ardent soul, and from his couch at once he breaks.

XXXII.

"I will," he cried, "so help me, God! destroy
That villain Archimage." His page then straight
He to him call'd; a fiery-footed boy,*
Benempt Dispatch:—"My steed be at the gate;
My bard attend; quick, bring the net of fate."
This net was twisted by the sisters three;
Which, when once cast o'er harden'd wretch, too late
Repentance comes; replevy cannot be
From the strong iron grasp of vengeful destiny.

XXXIII.

He came, the bard, a little Druid wight,
Of wither'd aspect; but his eye was keen,
With sweetness mix'd. In russet brown bedight,
As is his sister* of the copses green,
He crept along, unpromising of mien.
Gross he who judges so. His soul was fair,
Bright as the children of yon azure sheen!
True comeliness, which nothing can impair,
Dwells in the mind: all else is vanity and glare.

XXXIV.

"Come," quoth the Knight, "a voice has reach'd mine ear:
The demon Indolence threats overflow

---

* The Nightingale.

To all that to mankind is good and dear:
Come, Philomelus ! let us instant go,
O'erturn his bowers, and lay his castle low.
Those men, those wretched men! who will be slaves,
Must drink a bitter wrathful cup of wo:
But some there be thy song, as from their graves,
Shall raise." Thrice happy he! who without rigour
    saves.

XXXV.

Issuing forth, the Knight bestrode his steed,
Of ardent bay, and on whose front a star
Shone blazing bright: sprung from the generous
    breed,
That whirl of active day the rapid car,
He pranced along, disdaining gate or bar.
Meantime the bard on milk-white palfrey rode;
An honest, sober beast, that did not mar
His meditations, but full softly trode:
And much they moralised as thus yfere they yode.

XXXVI.

They talk'd of virtue and of human bliss.
What else so fit for man to settle well?
And still their long researches met in this,
This Truth of Truths, which nothing can refel:
" From virtue's fount the purest joys outwell,
Sweet rills of thought that cheer the conscious soul;
While vice pours forth the troubled streams of hell,
The which, howe'er disguised, at last with dole
Will through the tortured breast their fiery torrent roll."

XXXVII.

At length it dawn'd, that fatal valley gay,
O'er which high wood-crown'd hills their summits
    rear:
On the cool height awhile our palmers stay,
And spite even of themselves their senses cheer;

Then to the vizard's wonne their steps they steer.
Like a green isle, it broad beneath them spread,
With gardens round, and wandering currents clear,
And tufted groves to shade the meadow-bed,
Sweet airs and song: and without hurry all seem'd glad.

XXXVIII.

"As God shall judge me, Knight! we must forgive,"
The half-enraptured Philomelus cried,
"The frail good man deluded here to live,
And in these groves his musing fancy hide.
Ah! nought is pure.   It cannot be denied,
That virtue still some tincture has of vice,
And vice of virtue.   What should then betide,
But that our charity be not too nice?
Come, let us those we can, to real bliss entice."

XXXIX.

"Ay, sicker," quoth the Knight, "all flesh is frail,
To pleasant sin and joyous dalliance bent;
But let not brutish vice of this avail,
And think to 'scape deserved punishment.
Justice were cruel weakly to relent;
From Mercy's self she got her sacred glaive:
Grace be to those who can, and will, repent;
But penance long, and dreary, to the slave,
Who must in floods of fire his gross foul spirit lave."

XL.

Thus holding high discourse, they came to where
The cursed carle was at his wonted trade;
Still tempting heedless men into his snare,
In witching wise as I before have said.
But when he saw, in goodly geer array'd,
The grave majestic Knight approaching nigh,
And by his side the bard so sage and staid,
His countenance fell: yet oft his anxious eye
Mark'd them, like wily fox who roosted cock doth spy.

XLI.

Nathless, with feign'd respect, he bade give back
The rabble rout, and welcomed them full kind;
Struck with the noble twain, they were not slack
His orders to obey, and fall behind.
Then he resumed his song; and unconfined,
Pour'd all his music, ran through all his strings:
With magic dust their eyne he tries to blind,
And virtue's tender airs o'er weakness flings.
What pity base his song who so divinely sings!

XLII.

Elate in thought, he counted them his own,
They listen'd so intent with fix'd delight:
But they instead, as if transmew'd to stone,
Marvell'd he could with such sweet art unite
The lights and shades of manners wrong and right.
Meantime the silly crowd the charm devour,
Wide pressing to the gate.   Swift, on the Knight
He darted fierce, to drag him to his bower,
Who backening shunn'd his touch, for well he knew its power.

XLIII.

As in throng'd amphitheatre of old,
The wary Retiarius* trapp'd his foe;
E'en so the Knight, returning on him bold,
At once involved him in the Net of Wo,
Whereof I mention made not long ago.
Enraged at first, he scorn'd so weak a jail,
And leap'd, and flew, and flounced to and fro;
But when he found that nothing could avail,
He sat him felly down, and gnaw'd his bitter nail.

XLIV.

Alarm'd, the inferior demons of the place
Raised rueful shrieks and hideous yells around;

---

* A gladiator, who made use of a net, which he threw over his
adversary.

Black stormy clouds deform'd the welkin's face,
And from beneath was heard a wailing sound,
As of infernal sprights in cavern bound;
A solemn sadness every creature strook,
And lightnings flash'd, and horror rock'd the ground:
Huge crowds on crowds outpour'd, with blemish'd
    look,
As if on Time's last verge this frame of things had
    shook.

XLV.

Soon as the short-lived tempest was yspent,
Steam'd from the jaws of vex'd Avernus' hole,
And hush'd the hubbub of the rabblement,
Sir Industry the first calm moment stole:
"There must," he cried, "amid so vast a shoal,
- Be some who are not tainted at the heart,
Not poison'd quite by this same villain's bowl!
Come then, my bard, thy heavenly fire impart;
Touch soul with soul, till forth the latent spirit start."

XLVI.

The bard obey'd; and taking from his side,
Where it in seemly sort depending hung,
His British harp, its speaking strings he tried,
The which with skilful touch he deftly strung,
Till tinkling in clear symphony they rung.
Then, as he felt the Muses come along,
Light o'er the chords his raptured hand he flung,
And play'd a prelude to his rising song:
The whilst, like midnight mute, ten thousands round him
    throng.

XLVII.

Thus, ardent, burst his strain:—" Ye hapless race,
Dire labouring here to smother reason's ray,
That lights our Maker's image in our face,
And gives us wide o'er earth unquestion'd sway;

What is the adored Supreme Perfection, say?—
What, but eternal never-resting soul,
Almighty power, and all-directing day;
By whom each atom stirs, the planets roll;
Who fills, surrounds, informs, and agitates the whole.

XLVIII.

"Come, to the beaming God your hearts unfold!
Draw from its fountain life! 'Tis thence, alone,
We can excel. Up from unfeeling mould,
To seraphs burning round the Almighty's throne,
Life rising still on life, in higher tone,
Perfection forms, and with perfection bliss.
In universal nature this clear shown,
Not needeth proof: to prove it were, I wis,
To prove the beauteous world excels the brute abyss.

XLIX.

"Is not the field, with lively culture green,
A sight more joyous than the dead morass?
Do not the skies, with active ether clean,
And fann'd by sprightly zephyrs, far surpass
The foul November fogs, and slumbrous mass
With which sad Nature veils her drooping face?
Does not the mountain stream, as clear as glass,
Gay-dancing on, the putrid pool disgrace?
The same in all holds true, but chief in human race.

L.

"It was not by vile loitering in ease,
That Greece obtain'd the brighter palm of art;
That soft yet ardent Athens learn'd to please,
To keen the wit, and to sublime the heart,
In all supreme! complete in every part!
It was not thence majestic Rome arose,
And o'er the nations shook her conquering dart:
For sluggard's brow the laurel never grows;
Renown is not the child of indolent Repose.

LI.

"Had unambitious mortals minded nought,
But in loose joy their time to wear away;
Had they alone the lap of dalliance sought,
Pleased on her pillow their dull heads to lay,
Rude Nature's state had been our state to-day;
No cities e'er their towery fronts had raised,
No arts had made us opulent and gay;
With brother brutes the human race had grazed;
None e'er had soar'd to fame, none honour'd been, none
    praised.

LII.

"Great Homer's song had never fired the breast
To thirst of glory and heroic deeds;
Sweet Maro's muse, sunk in inglorious rest,
Had silent slept amid the Mincian reeds:
The wits of modern time had told their beads,
The monkish legends been their only strains;
Our Milton's Eden had lain wrapt in weeds,
Our Shakespeare stroll'd and laugh'd with Warwick
    swains,
Ne had my master Spenser charm'd his Mulla's plains.

LIII.

"Dumb too had been the sage historic muse,
And perish'd all the sons of ancient fame;
Those starry lights of virtue, that diffuse
Through the dark depth of time their vivid flame,
Had all been lost with such as have no name.
Who then had scorn'd his ease for others' good?
Who then had toil'd rapacious men to tame?
Who in the public breach devoted stood,
And for his country's cause been prodigal of blood?

LIV.

"But should to fame your hearts unfeeling be,
If right I read, you pleasure all require:

Then hear how best may be obtain'd this fee,
How best enjoy'd this Nature's wide desire.
Toil and be glad! let Industry inspire
Into your quicken'd limbs her buoyant breath!
Who does not act is dead; absorpt entire
In miry sloth, no pride, no joy he hath:
O leaden-hearted men, to be in love with death!

LV.

"Ah! what avail the largest gifts of Heaven,
When drooping health and spirits go amiss?
How tasteless then whatever can be given!
Health is the vital principle of bliss,
And exercise of health. In proof of this,
Behold the wretch, who slugs his life away,
Soon swallow'd in disease's sad abyss;
While he whom toil has braced, or manly play,
As light as air each limb, each thought as clear as day.

LVI.

"O who can speak the vigorous joys of health!
Unclogg'd the body, unobscured the mind:
The morning rises gay, with pleasing stealth,
The temperate evening falls serene and kind.
In health the wiser brutes true gladness find:
See! how the younglings frisk along the meads,
As May comes on, and wakes the balmy wind;
Rampant with life, their joy all joy exceeds;
Yet what but high-strung health this dancing pleasaunce
    breeds?

LVII.

" But here, instead, is foster'd every ill,
Which or distemper'd minds or bodies know.
Come then, my kindred spirits! do not spill
Your talents here: this place is but a show,
Whose charms delude you to the den of wo.
Come, follow me, I will direct you right,

Where pleasure's roses, void of serpents, grow,
Sincere as sweet; come, follow this good Knight,
And you will bless the day that brought him to your
    sight.

LVIII.

"Some he will lead to courts, and some to camps;
To senates some, and public sage debates,
Where, by the solemn gleam of midnight lamps,
The world is poised, and managed mighty states;
To high discovery some, that new creates
The face of earth; some to the thriving mart;
Some to the rural reign, and softer fates;
To the sweet Muses some, who raise the heart:
All glory shall be yours, all nature, and all art!

LIX.

"There are, I see, who listen to my lay,
Who wretched sigh for virtue, but despair:
'All may be done,' methinks I hear them say,
'E'en death despised by generous actions fair;
All, but for those who to these bowers repair,
Their every power dissolved in luxury,
To quit of torpid sluggishness the lair,
And from the powerful arms of sloth get free:
'Tis rising from the dead.—Alas!—it cannot be!'

LX.

"Would you then learn to dissipate the band
Of the huge threatening difficulties dire,
That in the weak man's way like lions stand,
His soul appal, and damp his rising fire?
Resolve, resolve, and to be men aspire.
Exert that noblest privilege, alone,
Here to mankind indulged; control desire:
Let godlike reason, from her sovereign throne,
Speak the commanding word 'I will!' and it is
    done.

LXI.

"Heavens! can you then thus waste, in shameful wise,
Your few important days of trial here?
Heirs of eternity! yborn to rise
Through endless states of being, still more near
To bliss approaching, and perfection clear;
Can you renounce a fortune so sublime,
Such glorious hopes, your backward steps to steer,
And roll, with vilest brutes, through mud and slime?
No! no!—Your heaven-touch'd hearts disdain the sordid
    crime!"

LXII.

"Enough! enough!" they cried—straight, from the
    crowd,
The better sort on wings of transport fly:
As when amid the lifeless summits proud
Of Alpine cliffs, where to the gelid sky
Snows piled on snows in wintry torpor lie,
The rays divine of vernal Phœbus play;
The awaken'd heaps, in streamlets from on high,
Roused into action, lively leap away.
Glad warbling through the vales, in their new being gay.

LXIII.

Not less the life, the vivid joy serene,
That lighted up these new created men,
Than that which wings the exulting spirit clean,
When, just deliver'd from this fleshly den,
It soaring seeks its native skies agen:
How light its essence! how unclogg'd its powers,
Beyond the blazon of my mortal pen!
E'en so we glad forsook these sinful bowers,
E'en such enraptured life, such energy was ours.

LXIV.

But far the greater part, with rage inflamed,
Dire-mutter'd curses, and blasphemed high Jove:

" Ye sons of hate!" they bitterly exclaim'd,
" What brought you to this seat of peace and love?
While with kind nature, here amid the grove,
We pass'd the harmless sabbath of our time,
What to disturb it could, fell men, emove
Your barbarous hearts? Is happiness a crime?
Then do the fiends of hell rule in yon heaven sublime."

LXV.

" Ye impious wretches," quoth the knight in wrath,
" Your happiness behold!"   Then straight a wand
He waved, an anti-magic power that hath,
Truth from illusive falsehood to command.
Sudden the landscape sinks on every hand;
The pure quick streams are marshy puddles found;
On baleful heaths the groves all blacken'd stand;
And o'er the weedy foul abhorred ground,
Snakes, adders, toads, each loathsome creature crawls around.

LXVI.

And here and there, on trees by lightning scathed,
Unhappy wights who loathed life yhung;
Or, in fresh gore and recent murder bathed,
They weltering lay; or else, infuriate flung
Into the gloomy flood, while ravens sung
The funeral dirge, they down the torrent roll'd:
These, by distemper'd blood to madness stung,
Had doom'd themselves; whence oft, when night con-
  troll'd
The world, returning hither their sad spirits howl'd.

LXVII.

Meantime a moving scene was open laid;
That lazar-house, I whilom in my lay
Depainted have, its horrors deep display'd,
And gave unnumber'd wretches to the day,
Who tossing there in squalid misery lay.
Soon as of sacred light the unwonted smile

Pour'd on these living catacombs its ray,
Through the drear caverns stretching many a mile,
The sick upraised their heads, and dropp'd their woes
  awhile.

LXVIII.

"O Heaven!" they cried, "and do we once more see
Yon blessed sun, and this green earth so fair?
Are we from noisome damps of pesthouse free?
And drink our souls the sweet ethereal air?
O thou! or Knight, or God? who holdest there
That fiend, oh keep him in eternal chains!
But what for us, the children of despair,
  Brought to the brink of hell, what hope remains?
Repentance does itself but aggravate our pains."

LXIX.

The gentle Knight, who saw their rueful case,
Let fall adown his silver beard some tears.
"Certes," quoth he, "it is not e'en in grace
To undo the past, and eke your broken years:
Nathless, to nobler worlds repentance rears,
With humble hope, her eye; to her is given
A power the truly contrite heart that cheers;
  She quells the brand by which the rocks are riven;
She more than merely softens, she rejoices Heaven.

LXX.

"Then patient bear the sufferings you have earn'd,
And by these sufferings purify the mind:
Let wisdom be by past misconduct learn'd:
Or pious die, with penitence resign'd;
And to a life more happy and refined,
Doubt not, you shall, new creatures, yet arise.
Till then, you may expect in me to find
  One who will wipe your sorrow from your eyes,
One who will soothe your pangs, and wing you to the
  skies."

LXXI.

They silent heard, and pour'd their thanks in tears:
"For you," resumed the Knight with sterner tone,
"Whose hard dry hearts the obdurate demon scars,
That villain's gifts will cost you many a groan;
In dolorous mansion long you must bemoan
His fatal charms, and weep your stains away;
Till, soft and pure as infant goodness grown,
You feel a perfect change: then, who can say
What grace may yet shine forth in heaven's eternal ⟨

LXXII.

This said, his powerful wand he waved anew:
Instant, a glorious angel-train descends,
The Charities, to wit, of rosy hue;
Sweet love their looks a gentle radiance lends,
And with seraphic flame compassion blends.
At once, delighted, to their charge they fly:
When lo! a goodly hospital ascends;
In which they bade each lenient aid be nigh,
That could the sick-bed smooth of that sad company.

LXXIII.

It was a worthy edifying sight,
And gives to human-kind peculiar grace,
To see kind hands attending day and night,
With tender ministry, from place to place.
Some prop the head; some from the pallid face
Wipe off the faint cold dews weak nature sheds;
Some reach the healing draught: the whilst, to chase
The fear supreme, around their soften'd beds,
Some holy man by prayer all opening heaven dispreads.

LXXIV.

Attended by a glad acclaiming train,
Of those he rescued had from gaping hell,
Then turn'd the Knight; and, to his hall again
Soft-pacing, sought of peace the mossy cell:

Yet down his cheeks the gems of pity fell,
To see the helpless wretches that remain'd,
There left through delves and deserts dire to yell;
Amazed, their looks with pale dismay were stain'd,
And spreading wide their hands they meek repentance feign'd.

LXXV.

But ah! their scorned day of grace was past:
For (horrible to tell!) a desert wild
Before them stretch'd, bare, comfortless, and vast;
With gibbets, bones, and carcasses defiled.
There nor trim field, nor lively culture smiled;
Nor waving shade was seen, nor fountain fair;
But sands abrupt on sands lay loosely piled,
Through which they floundering toil'd with painful care,
Whilst Phœbus smote them sore, and fired the cloudless air.

LXXVI.

Then, varying to a joyless land of bogs,
The sadden'd country a grey waste appear'd;
Where nought but putrid streams and noisome fogs
For ever hung on drizzly Auster's beard;
Or else the ground, by piercing Caurus sear'd,
Was jagg'd with frost, or heap'd with glazed snow;
Through these extremes a ceaseless round they steer'd,
By cruel fiends still hurried to and fro,
Gaunt Beggary, and Scorn, with many hell-hounds moe.

LXXVII.

The first was with base dunghill rags yclad,
Tainting the gale, in which they flutter'd light;
Of morbid hue his features, sunk and sad;
His hollow eyne shook forth a sickly light;
And o'er his lank jawbone, in piteous plight,
His black rough beard was matted rank and vile;
Direful to see! a heart-appalling sight!
Meantime foul scurf and blotches him defile;
And dogs, where'er he went, still barked all the while.

P

LXXVIII.

The other was a fell despightful fiend;
Hell holds none worse in baleful bower below:
By pride, and wit, and rage, and rancour, keen'd;
Of man alike, if good or bad, the foe:
With nose upturn'd he always made a show
As if he smelt some nauseous scent; his eye
Was cold, and keen, like blast from boreal snow;
And taunts he casten forth most bitterly.
Such were the twain that off drove this ungodly fry.

LXXIX.

E'en so through Brentford town, a town of mud,
A herd of bristly swine is prick'd along;
The filthy beasts that never chew the cud,
Still grunt and squeak, and sing their troublous song,
And oft they plunge themselves the mire among:
But aye the ruthless driver goads them on,
And aye of barking dogs the bitter throng
Makes them renew their unmelodious moan;
Ne ever find they rest from their unresting fone.

BRITANNIA.

[At the time this poem was written, the Spaniards had much distressed
our merchant vessels who traded to the South American coast, and
seized the crews who had landed to cut logwood in the Bay of Cam-
peachy, which right had been conceded by treaty. The merchants
loudly complained of these outrages—remonstrances were made by the
British Ministry, but no reformation followed. Thus matters continued
till 1739, when war was formally declared.]

" Et tantas audetis tollere moles?
Quos ego—sed motos præstat componere fluctus.
Post mihi non simili pœna commissa luetis.
Maturate fugam, regique hæc dicite vestro:
Non illi imperium pelagi, sævumque tridentem,
Sed mihi sorte datum."   *Virgil.*

As on the sea-beat shore Britannia sat,
Of her degenerate sons the faded fame,
Deep in her anxious heart, revolving sad:
Bare was her throbbing bosom to the gale,
That, hoarse and hollow, from the bleak surge blew;
Loose flow'd her tresses; rent her azure robe.
Hung o'er the deep from her majestic brow
She tore the laurel, and she tore the bay.
Nor ceased the copious grief to bathe her cheek;
Nor ceased her sobs to murmur to the main.
Peace discontented, nigh departing, stretch'd
Her dove-like wings; and War, though greatly roused,
Yet mourns his fetter'd hands. While thus the queen
Of nations spoke; and what she said the muse
Recorded, faithful, in unbidden verse.

    " E'en not yon sail, that from the sky-mixt wave

Dawns on the sight, and wafts the Royal Youth,*
A freight of future glory to my shore;
E'en not the flattering view of golden days,
And rising periods yet of bright renown,
Beneath the Parents, and their endless line
Through late revolving time, can soothe my rage;
While, unchastised, the insulting Spaniard dares
Infest the trading flood, full of vain war
Despise my navies, and my merchants seize;
As, trusting to false peace, they fearless roam
The world of waters wild; made, by the toil
And liberal blood of glorious ages, mine:
Nor bursts my sleeping thunder on their head.
Whence this unwonted patience? this weak doubt?
This tame beseeching of rejected peace?
This meek forbearance? this unnative fear,
To generous Britons never known before?
And sail'd my fleets for this; on Indian tides
To float, inactive, with the veering winds?
The mockery of war! while hot disease,
And sloth distemper'd, swept off burning crowds,
For action ardent; and amid the deep,
Inglorious, sunk them in a watery grave.
There now they lie beneath the rolling flood,
Far from their friends, and country, unavenged;
And back the drooping war-ship comes again,
Dispirited and thin; her sons ashamed
Thus idly to re-view their native shore;
With not one glory sparkling in their eye,
One triumph on their tongue. A passenger,
The violated merchant comes along;
That far sought wealth, for which the noxious gale
He drew, and sweat beneath equator suns,
By lawless force detain'd; a force that soon
Would melt away, and every spoil resign,
Were once the British lion heard to roar.

---

* Frederick Prince of Wales, then lately arrived.

Whence is it that the proud Iberian thus,
In their own well-asserted element,
Dares rouse to wrath the masters of the main?
Who told him, that the big incumbent war
Would not, ere this, have roll'd his trembling ports
In smoky ruin? and his guilty stores,
Won by the ravage of a butcher'd world,
Yet unatoned, sunk in the swallowing deep,
Or led the glittering prize into the Thames?
   " There was a time (oh let my languid sons
Resume their spirit at the rousing thought!)
When all the pride of Spain, in one dread fleet,
Swell'd o'er the labouring surge; like a whole heaven
Of clouds, wide roll'd before the boundless breeze.
Gaily the splendid armament along
Exultant plough'd, reflecting a red gleam,
As sunk the sun, o'er all the flaming Vast;
Tall, gorgeous, and elate; drunk with the dream
Of easy conquest; while their bloated war,
Stretch'd out from sky to sky, the gather'd force
Of ages held in its capacious womb.
But soon, regardless of the cumbrous pomp,
My dauntless Britons came, a gloomy few,
With tempests black, the goodly scene deform'd,
And laid their glory waste. The bolts of fate
Resistless thunder'd through their yielding sides;
Fierce o'er their beauty blazed the lurid flame;
And seized in horrid grasp, or shatter'd wide,
Amid the mighty waters, deep they sunk.
Then too from every promontory chill,
Rank fen, and cavern where the wild wave works,
I swept confederate winds, and swell'd a storm.
Round the glad isle, snatch'd by the vengeful blast,
The scatter'd remnants drove; on the blind shelve,
And pointed rock, that marks the indented shore,
Relentless dash'd, where loud the northern main
Howls through the fractured Caledonian isles.
   " Such were the dawnings of my watery reign;

But since how vast it grew, how absolute, -
E'en in those troubled times, when dreadful Blake
Awed angry nations with the British name,
Let every humbled state, let Europe say,
Sustain'd, and balanced, by my naval arm.
Ah, what must those immortal spirits think
Of your poor shifts? Those, for their country's good,
Who faced the blackest danger, knew no fear,
No mean submission, but commanded peace.
Ah, how with indignation must they burn
(If aught, but joy, can touch ethereal breasts)
With shame? with grief? to see their feeble sons
Shrink from that empire o'er the conquer'd seas,
For which their wisdom plann'd, their councils glow'd,
And their veins bled through many a toiling age.
 " Oh, first of human blessings! and supreme!
Fair Peace! how lovely, how delightful thou!
By whose wide tie the kindred sons of men
Like brothers live, in amity combined
And unsuspicious faith; while honest toil
Gives every joy, and to those joys a right,
Which idle, barbarous rapine but usurps.
Pure is thy reign; when, unaccursed by blood,
Nought, save the sweetness of indulgent showers,
Trickling distils into the vernant glebe;
Instead of mangled carcasses, sad-seen,
When the blithe sheaves lie scatter'd o'er the field;
When only shining shares, the crooked knife,
And hooks imprint the vegetable wound:
When the land blushes with the rose alone,
The falling fruitage and the bleeding vine.
Oh, Peace! thou source and soul of social life;
Beneath whose calm inspiring influence,
Science his views enlarges, Art refines,
And swelling Commerce opens all her ports;
Bless'd be the man divine who gives us thee!
Who bids the trumpet hush his horrid clang,
Nor blow the giddy nations into rage;

Who sheaths the murderous blade; the deadly gun
Into the well-piled armoury returns;
And every vigour, from the work of death,
To grateful industry converting, makes
The country flourish, and the city smile.
Unviolated, him the virgin sings;
And him the smiling mother to her train.
Of him the shepherd, in the peaceful dale,
Chants; and, the treasures of his labour sure,
The husbandman of him, as at the plough,
Or team, he toils.   With him the sailor soothes,
Beneath the trembling moon, the midnight wave;
And the full city, warm, from street to street,
And shop to shop, responsive, rings of him.
   Nor joys one land alone: his praise extends
Far as the sun rolls the diffusive day;
Far as the breeze can bear the gifts of peace.
Till all the happy nations catch the song.
   "What would not, Peace! the patriot bear for thee?
What painful patience?   What incessant care?
What mix'd anxiety?   What sleepless toil?
E'en from the rash protected what reproach?
For he thy value knows; thy friendship he
To human nature; but the better thou,
The richer of delight, sometimes the more
Inevitable war; when ruffian force
Awakes the fury of an injured state.
E'en the good patient man, whom reason rules,
Roused by bold insult and injurious rage,
With sharp and sudden check the astonish'd sons
Of violence confounds; firm as his cause,
His bolder heart; in awful justice clad;
His eyes effulging a peculiar fire:
And, as he charges through the prostrate war,
His keen arm teaches faithless men no more
To dare the sacred vengeance of the just.
   "And what, my thoughtless sons, should fire you more
Than when your well-earn'd empire of the deep

The least beginning injury receives?
What better cause can call your lightning forth?
Your thunder wake? your dearest life demand?
What better cause, than when your country sees
The sly destruction at her vitals aim'd?
For oh! it much imports you, 'tis your all,
To keep your trade entire, entire the force
And honour of your fleets; o'er that to watch,
E'en with a hand severe, and jealous eye.
In intercourse be gentle, generous, just,
By wisdom polish'd, and of manners fair;
But on the sea be terrible, untamed,
Unconquerable still: let none escape,
Who shall but aim to touch your glory there.
Is there the man into the lion's den
Who dares intrude, to snatch his young away?
And is a Briton seized? and seized beneath
The slumbering terrors of a British fleet?
Then ardent rise!   Oh, great in vengeance rise!
O'erturn the proud, teach rapine to restore:
And as you ride sublimely round the world,
Make every vessel stoop, make every state
At once their welfare and their duty know
This is your glory: this your wisdom; this
The native power for which you were design'd
By fate, when fate design'd the firmest state,
That e'er was seated on the subject sea;
A state, alone, where Liberty should live, '
In these late times, this evening of mankind,
When Athens, Rome, and Carthage are no more,
The world almost in slavish sloth dissolved.
For this, these rocks around your coast were thrown;
For this, your oaks, peculiar harden'd, shoot
Strong into sturdy growth; for this, your hearts
Swell with a sullen courage, growing still
As danger grows; and strength, and toil for this
Are liberal pour'd o'er all the fervent land.
Then cherish this, this unexpensive power,

Undangerous to the public, ever prompt,
By lavish nature thrust into your hand:
And, unencumber'd with the bulk immense
Of conquest, whence huge empires rose, and fell,
Self-crush'd, extend your reign from shore to shore,
Where'er the wind your high behests can blow;
And fix it deep on this eternal base.
* For should the sliding fabric once give way,
Soon slacken'd quite, and past recovery broke,
It gathers ruin as it rolls along,
Steep rushing down to that devouring gulf,
Where many a mighty empire buried lies.
And should the big redundant flood of trade,
In which ten thousand thousand labours join
Their several currents, till the boundless tide
Rolls in a radiant deluge o'er the land;
Should this bright stream, the least inflected, point
Its course another way, o'er other lands
The various treasure would resistless pour,
Ne'er to be won again; its ancient tract
Left a vile channel, desolate, and dead,
With all around a miserable waste.
Not Egypt, were her better heaven, the Nile,
Turn'd in the pride of flow; when o'er his rocks,
And roaring cataracts, beyond the reach
Of dizzy vision piled, in one wide flash
An Ethiopian deluge foams amain
(Whence wondering fable traced him from the sky);
E'en not that prime of earth, where harvests crowd
On untill'd harvests, all the teeming year,
If of the fat o'erflowing culture robb'd,
Were then a more uncomfortable wild,
Sterile, and void; than of her trade deprived,
Britons, your boasted isle: her princes sunk;
Her high-built honour moulder'd to the dust;
Unnerved her force; her spirit vanish'd quite;
With rapid wing her riches fled away;
Her unfrequented ports alone the sign

Of what she was; her merchants scattered wide;
Her hollow shops shut up; and in her streets,
Her fields, woods, markets, villages, and roads,
The cheerful voice of labour heard no more.
"Oh, let not then waste luxury impair
That manly soul of toil which strings your nerves,
And your own proper happiness creates!
Oh, let not the soft, penetrating plague
Creep on the freeborn mind! and working there,
With the sharp tooth of many a new-form'd want,
Endless, and idle all, eat out the heart
Of liberty; the high conception blast;
The noble sentiment, the impatient scorn
Of base subjection, and the swelling wish
For general good, erasing from the mind:
While nought save narrow selfishness succeeds,
And low design, the sneaking passions all
Let loose, and reigning in the rankled breast.
Induced at last, by scarce perceived degrees,
Sapping the very frame of government,
And life, a total dissolution comes;
Sloth, ignorance, dejection, flattery, fear.
Oppression raging o'er the waste he makes;
The human being almost quite extinct;
And the whole state in broad corruption sinks.
Oh, shun that gulf: that gaping ruin shun!
And countless ages roll it far away
From you, ye heaven-beloved! May liberty,
The light of life! the sun of human-kind!
Whence heroes, bards, and patriots borrow flame,
E'en where the keen depressive north descends,
Still spread, exalt, and actuate your powers!
While slavish southern climates beam in vain.
And may a public spirit from the throne,
Where every virtue sits, go copious forth,
Live o'er the land! the finer arts inspire;
Make thoughtful Science raise his pensive head,
Blow the fresh bay, bid Industry rejoice,

And the rough sons of lowest labour smile.
As when, profuse of Spring, the loosen'd West
Lifts up the pining year, and balmy breathes
Youth, life, and love, and beauty, o'er the world.
 " But haste we from these melancholy shores,
Nor to deaf winds, and waves, our fruitless plaint
Pour weak; the country claims our active aid;
That let us roam; and where we find a spark
Of public virtue, blow it into flame.
Lo! now, my sons, the sons of freedom! meet
In awful senate; thither let us fly;
Burn in the patriot's thought, flow from his tongue
In fearless truth; myself, transform'd, preside,
And shed the spirit of Britannia round."
 This said; her fleeting form and airy train
Sunk in the gale; and nought but ragged rocks
Rush'd on the broken eye; and nought was heard
But the rough cadence of the dashing wave.

LIBERTY

PART I.

ANCIENT AND MODERN ITALY COMPARED.

The following Poem is thrown into the form of a Poetical Vision.—Its scene, the ruins of ancient Rome.—The Goddess of Liberty, who is supposed to speak through the whole, appears, characterised as British Liberty.—Gives a view of ancient Italy, and particularly of Republican Rome, in all her magnificence and glory.—This contrasted by modern Italy; its valleys, mountains, culture, cities, people: the difference appearing strongest in the capital city Rome.—The ruins of the great works of Liberty more magnificent than the borrowed pomp of Oppression; and from them revived Sculpture, Painting, and Architecture.—The old Romans apostrophised, with regard to the several melancholy changes in Italy: Horace, Tully, and Virgil, with regard to their Tibur, Tusculum, and Naples.—That once finest and most ornamented part of Italy, all along the coast of Baiæ, how changed.—This desolation of Italy applied to Britain.—Address to the Goddess of Liberty, that she would deduce from the first ages, her chief establishments, the description of which constitute the subject of the following parts of this Poem.—She assents, and commands what she says to be sung in Britain; whose happiness, arising from freedom, and a limited monarchy, she marks. —An immediate Vision attends, and paints her words.—Invocation.

O MY lamented Talbot! while with thee
The Muse gay roved the glad Hesperian round,
And drew the inspiring breath of ancient arts;
Ah! little thought she her returning verse
Should sing our darling subject to thy Shade.
And does the mystic veil, from mortal beam,
Involve those eyes where every virtue smiled,
And all thy Father's candid spirit shone?
The light of reason, pure, without a cloud;

Full of the generous heart, the mild regard;
Honour disdaining blemish, cordial faith,
And limpid truth, that looks the very soul.
But to the death of mighty nations turn
My strain: be there absorpt the private tear.
    Musing, I lay; warm from the sacred walks,
Where at each step imagination burns:
While scatter'd wide around, awful and hoar,
Lies, a vast monument, once glorious Rome,
The tomb of empire! Ruins! that efface
Whate'er, of finish'd, modern pomp can boast.
    Snatch'd by these wonders to that world where thought
Unfetter'd ranges, Fancy's magic hand
Led me anew o'er all the solemn scene,
Still in the mind's pure eye more solemn dress'd;
When straight, methought, the fair majestic Power
Of Liberty appear'd. Not, as of old,
Extended in her hand the cap, and rod,
Whose slave-enlarging touch gave double life:
But her bright temples bound with British oak,
And naval honours nodded on her brow,
Sublime of port: loose o'er her shoulder flow'd
Her sea-green robe, with constellations gay.
An island-goddess now; and her high care
The Queen of Isles, the mistress of the main.
My heart beat filial transport at the sight;
And, as she moved to speak, the awaken'd Muse
Listen'd intense. Awhile she look'd around,
With mournful eye the well-known ruins mark'd,
And then, her sighs repressing, thus began:
    " Mine are these wonders, all thou seest is mine;
But ah, how changed! the falling poor remains
Of what exalted once the Ausonian shore.
Look back through time: and, rising from the gloom,
Mark the dread scene, that paints whate'er I say.
    " The great Republic see! that glow'd, sublime,
With the mix'd freedom of a thousand states:
Raised on the thrones of kings her curule chair,

And by her fasces awed the subject world.
See busy millions quickening all the land,
With cities throng'd, and teeming culture high:
For Nature then smiled on her free-born sons,
And pour'd the plenty that belongs to men.
Behold, the country cheering, villas rise,
In lively prospect; by the secret lapse
Of brooks now lost, and streams renown'd in song;
In Umbria's closing vales, or on the brow
Of her brown hills that breathe the scented gale:
On Baiæ's viny coast; where peaceful seas,
Fann'd by kind zephyrs, ever kiss the shore,
And suns unclouded shine, through purest air:
Or in the spacious neighbourhood of Rome;
Far shining upward to the Sabine hills.
To Anio's roar, and Tibur's olive shade;
To where Prenestè lifts her airy brow;
Or downward spreading to the sunny shore,
Where Alba breathes the freshness of the main.
  " See distant mountains leave their valleys dry,
And o'er the proud Arcade their tribute pour,
To lave imperial Rome.   For ages laid,
Deep, massy, firm, diverging every way,
With tombs of heroes sacred, see her roads;
By various nations trod, and suppliant kings; ·
With legions flaming, or with triumph gay.
  " Full in the centre of these wondrous works,
The pride of earth ! Rome in her glory see !
Behold her demigods, in senate met;
All head to counsel, and all heart to act:
The commonweal inspiring every tongue
With fervent eloquence, unbribed, and bold;
Ere tame Corruption taught the servile herd
To rank obedient to a master's voice.
  " Her Forum see, warm, popular, and loud,
In trembling wonder hush'd, when the two Sires,*

---

* Lucius Junius Brutus, and Virginius.

As they the private father greatly quell'd,
Stood up the public fathers of the state.
See Justice judging there, in human shape.
Hark! how with freedom's voice it thunders high,
Or in soft murmurs sinks to Tully's tongue.

"Her tribes, her census, see; her generous troops,
Whose pay was glory, and their best reward
Free for their country and for me to die;
Ere mercenary murder grew a trade.

"Mark, as the purple triumph waves along,
The highest pomp, and lowest fall of life.

"Her festive games, the school of heroes, see;
Her Circus, ardent with contending youth:
Her streets, her temples, palaces, and baths,
Full of fair forms, of Beauty's eldest born,
And of a people cast in virtue's mould:
While sculpture lives around, and Asian hills
Lend their best stores to heave the pillar'd dome:
All that to Roman strength the softer touch
Of Grecian art can join. But language fails
To paint this sun, this centre of mankind;
Where every virtue, glory, treasure, art,
Attracted strong, in heighten'd lustre met.

"Need I the contrast mark? unjoyous view!
A land in all, in government and arts,
In virtue, genius, earth, and heaven, reversed,
Who but these far-famed ruins to behold,
Proofs of a people, whose heroic aims
Soar'd far above the little selfish sphere
Of doubting modern life; who but inflamed
With classic zeal, these consecrated scenes
Of men and deeds to trace; unhappy land,
Would trust thy wilds, and cities loose of sway?

"Are these the vales, that once exulting states
In their warm bosom fed? The mountains these,
On whose high-blooming sides my sons, of old,
I bred to glory? These dejected towns,
Where, mean and sordid, life can scarce subsist,

The scenes of ancient opulence and pomp?
  "Come! by whatever sacred name disguised,
Oppression, come! and in thy works rejoice!
See nature's richest plains to putrid fens
Turn'd by thy fury.   From their cheerful bounds,
She razed the enlivening village, farm, and seat.
First, rural toil, by thy rapacious hand
Robb'd of his poor reward, resign'd the plough:
And now he dares not turn the noxious glebe.
  'Tis thine entire.   The lonely swain himself,
Who loves at large along the grassy downs
His flocks to pasture, thy drear champaign flies.
Far as the sickening eye can sweep around,
'Tis all one desert, desolate, and grey,
Grazed by the sullen buffalo alone:
And where the rank uncultivated growth
Of rotting ages taints the passing gale.
Beneath the baleful blast the city pines,
Or sinks enfeebled, or infected burns.
Beneath it mourns the solitary road,
Roll'd in rude mazes o'er the abandon'd waste;
While ancient ways, engulf'd, are seen no more.
  "Such thy dire plains, thou self-destroyer! foe
To human-kind! thy mountains too, profuse,
Where savage nature blooms, seem their sad plaint
To raise against thy desolating rod.
There on the breezy brow, where thriving states
And famous cities, once, to the pleased sun,
Far other scenes of rising culture spread,
Pale shine thy ragged towns.   Neglected round,
Each harvest pines; the livid, lean produce
Of heartless labour; while thy hated joys,
Not proper pleasure, lift the lazy hand.
Better to sink in sloth the woes of life,
Than wake their rage with unavailing toil.
Hence, drooping art almost to nature leaves
The rude unguided year.   Thin wave the gifts
Of yellow Ceres, thin the radiant blush

Q

Of orchard reddens in the warmest ray.
To weedy wildness run, no rural wealth
(Such as dictators fed) the garden pours.
Crude the wild olive flows, and foul the vine;
Nor juice Cæcubian, nor Falernian, more,
Streams life and joy, save in the Muse's bowl.
Unseconded by art, the spinning race
Draw the bright thread in vain, and idly toil.
In vain, forlorn in wilds, the citron blows;
And flowering plants perfume the desert gale.
Through the vile thorn the tender myrtle twines:
Inglorious droops the laurel, dead to song,
And long a stranger to the hero's brow.
  "Nor half thy triumph this: cast from brute fields,
Into the haunts of men thy ruthless eye.
There buxom Plenty never turns her horn;
The grace and virtue of exterior life,
No clean convenience reigns; e'en sleep itself,
Least delicate of powers, reluctant, there,
Lays on the bed impure his heavy head.
Thy horrid walk! dead, empty, unadorn'd,
See streets whose echoes never know the voice
Of cheerful hurry, commerce many-tongued,
And art mechanic at his various task,
Fervent, employ'd. Mark the desponding race,
Of occupation void, as void of hope;
Hope, the glad ray, glanced from Eternal Good,
That life enlivens, and exalts its powers,
With views of fortune—madness all to them!
By thee relentless seized their better joys,
To the soft aid of cordial airs they fly,
Breathing a kind oblivion o'er their woes.
And love and music melt their souls away.
From feeble Justice, see how rash revenge,
Trembling, the balance snatches; and the sword,
Fearful himself, to venal ruffians gives.
See where God's altar, nursing murder, stands,
With the red touch of dark assassins stain'd.

"But chief let Rome, the mighty city! speak
The full-exerted genius of thy reign.
Behold her rise amid the lifeless waste,
Expiring nature all corrupted round:
While the lone Tiber, through the desert plain,
Winds his waste stores, and sullen sweeps along.
Patch'd from my fragments, in unsolid pomp,
Mark how the temple glares; and artful dress'd,
Amusive, draws the superstitious train.
Mark how the palace lifts a lying front,
Concealing often, in magnific jail,
Proud want; a deep unanimated gloom!
And oft adjoining to the drear abode
Of misery, whose melancholy walls
Seem its voracious grandeur to reproach.
Within the city bounds the desert see.
See the rank vine o'er subterranean roofs,
Indecent, spread; beneath whose fretted gold
It once, exulting, flow'd.   The people mark,
Matchless, while fired by me; to public good
Inexorably firm, just, generous, brave,
Afraid of nothing but unworthy life,
Elate with glory, an heroic soul
Known to the vulgar breast: behold them now
A thin despairing number, all-subdued,
The slaves of slaves, by superstition fool'd,
By vice unmann'd and a licentious rule;
In guile ingenious, and in murder brave.
Such in one land, beneath the same fair clime,
Thy sons, Oppression, are; and such were mine.
    "E'en with thy labour'd pomp, for whose vain show
Deluded thousands starve; all age-begrimed,
Torn, robb'd, and scatter'd in unnumber'd sacks,
And by the tempest of two thousand years
Continual shaken, let my ruins vie.
These roads that yet the Roman hand assert,
Beyond the weak repair of modern toil;
These fractured arches, that the chiding stream

No more delighted hear; these rich remains
Of marbles now unknown, where shines imbibed
Each parent ray; these massy columns, hew'd
From Afric's farthest shore; one granite all.
These obelisks high-towering to the sky,
Mysterious mark'd with dark Egyptian lore;
These endless wonders that this sacred* way
Illumine still, and consecrate to fame;
These fountains, vases, urns, and statues, charged
With the fine stores of art-completing Greece.
Mine is, besides, thy every later boast:
Thy Buonarotis, thy Palladios mine;
And mine the fair designs, which Raphael's† soul
O'er the live canvas, emanating, breathed.
   "What would you say, ye conquerors of earth!
Ye Romans! could you raise the laurell'd head;
Could you the country see, by seas of blood,
And the dread toil of ages won so dear;
Your pride, your triumph, your supreme delight!
For whose defence oft, in the doubtful hour,
You rush'd with rapture down the gulf of fate,
Of death ambitious! till by awful deeds,
Virtues, and courage that amaze mankind,
The queen of nations rose; possess'd of all
Which nature, art, and glory could bestow:
What would you say, deep in the last abyss
Of slavery, vice, and unambitious want,
Thus to behold her sunk? your crowded plains,
Void of her cities; unadorned your hills;
Ungraced your lakes; your ports to ships unknown;
Your lawless floods, and your abandon'd streams;
These could you know; these could you love again
Thy Tiber, Horace, could it now inspire,

---

* Via Sacra.
† Michael Angelo Buonaroti, Palladio, and Raphael d'Urbino;
the three great modern masters in sculpture, architecture, and
painting.

Content, poetic ease, and rural joy,
Soon bursting into song: while through the groves
Of headlong Anio, dashing to the vale,
In many a tortured stream, you mused along?
Yon wild retreat,* where superstition dreams,
Could, Tully, you your Tusculum believe?
And could you deem yon naked hills, that form,
Famed in old song, the ship-forsaken bay,†
Your Formian shore?   Once the delight of earth,
Where art and nature, ever smiling, join'd
On the gay land to lavish all their stores.
How changed, how vacant, Virgil, wide around,
Would now your Naples seem? disaster'd less
By Black Vesuvius thundering o'er the coast
His midnight earthquakes, and his mining fires,
Than by despotic rage:‡ that inward gnaws
A native foe; a foreign, tears without.
First from your flatter'd Cæsars this began;
Till, doom'd to tyrants an eternal prey,
Thin peopled spreads, at last, the syren plain,§
That the dire soul of Hannibal disarm'd;
And wrapt in weeds the shore‖ of Venus lies.
There Baiæ sees no more the joyous throng;
Her bank all beaming with the pride of Rome:
No generous vines now bask along the hills,
Where sport the breezes of the Tyrrhene main:
With baths and temples mix'd, no villas rise;

---

* Tusculum is reckoned to have stood at a place now called
Grotta Ferrata, a convent of monks.
   † The bay of Mola (anciently Formiæ) into which Homer
brings Ulysses and his companions. Near Formiæ Cicero had a
villa.
   ‡ Naples, then under the Austrian government.
   § Campagna Felice, adjoining to Capua.
   ‖ The coast of Baiæ, which was formerly adorned with the
works mentioned in the following lines; and where, amidst many
magnificent ruins, those of a temple erected to Venus are still to
be seen.

Nor, art-sustain'd amid reluctant waves,
Draw the cool murmurs of the breathing deep:
No spreading ports their sacred arms extend:
No mighty moles the big intrusive storm,
From the calm station roll resounding back.
An almost total desolation sits,
A dreary stillness, saddening o'er the coast;
Where,* when soft suns and tepid winters rose,
Rejoicing crowds inhaled the balm of peace;
Where citied hill to hill reflected blaze;
And where with Ceres Bacchus wont to hold
A genial strife.   Her youthful form, robust,
E'en Nature yields; by fire, and earthquake rent:
Whole stately cities in the dark abrupt
Swallow'd at once, or vile in rubbish laid,
A nest for serpents; from the red abyss
New hills, explosive, thrown; the Lucrine lake
A reedy pool: and all to Cuma's point,
The sea recovering his usurp'd domain,
And pour'd triumphant o'er the buried dome.
   " Hence, Britain, learn; my best establish'd, last,
And more than Greece, or Rome, my steady reign;
The land where, King and People equal bound
By guardian laws, my fullest blessings flow;
And where my jealous unsubmitting soul,
The dread of tyrants ! burns in every breast:
Learn hence, if such the miserable fate
Of an heroic race, the masters once
Of human-kind; what, when deprived of ME,
How grievous must be thine ? in spite of climes,
Whose sun-enliven'd ether wakes the soul
To higher powers; in spite of happy soils,
That, but by labour's slightest aid impell'd,
With treasures teem to thy cold clime unknown;
If there desponding fail the common arts,

---

* All along this coast the ancient Romans had their winter retreats; and several populous cities stood.

And sustenance of life: could life itself,
Far less a thoughtless tyrant's hollow pomp,
Subsist with thee? against depressing skies,
Join'd to full-spread oppression's cloudy brow, ·
How could thy spirits hold? where vigour find,
Forced fruits to tear from their unnative soil?
Or, storing every harvest in thy ports,
To plough the dreadful all-producing wave?"
   Here paused the Goddess.   By the cause assured,
In trembling accents thus I moved my prayer:
   " Oh first, and most benevolent of powers!
Come from eternal splendours, here on earth,
Against despotic pride, and rage, and lust,
To shield mankind: to raise them to assert
The native rights and honour of their race:
Teach me, thy lowest subject, but in zeal
Yielding to none, the progress of thy reign.
And with a strain from THEE enrich the Muse.
As thee alone she serves, her patron THOU,
And great inspirer be! then will she joy,
Though narrow life her lot, and private shade:
And when her venal voice she barters vile,
Or to thy open or thy secret foes;
May ne'er those sacred raptures touch her more,
By slavish hearts unfelt! and may her song
Sink in oblivion with the nameless crew!
Vermin of state! to thy o'erflowing light
That owe their being, yet betray thy cause."
   Then, condescending kind, the heavenly Power
Return'd:—" What here, suggested by the scene,
I slight unfold, record and sing at home,
In that bless'd isle, where (so we spirits move)
With one quick effort of my will I am.
There Truth, unlicensed, walks; and dares accost
E'en kings themselves, the monarchs of the free!
Fix'd on my rock, there, an indulgent race
O'er Britons wield the sceptre of their choice:
And there, to finish what his sires began,

A Prince behold ! for me who burns sincere,
E'en with a subject's zeal.   He my great work
Will parent-like sustain; and added give
The touch the Graces and the Muses owe.
For Britain's glory swells his panting breast;
And ancient arts he emulous revolves:
His pride to let the smiling heart abroad,
Through clouds of pomp, that but conceal the man;
To please his pleasure; bounty his delight;
And all the soul of Titus dwells in him."

    Hail, glorious theme ! but how, alas ! shall verse,
From the crude stores of mortal language drawn,
How faint and tedious, sing, what, piercing deep,
The Goddess flash'd at once upon my soul.
For, clear precision all, the tongue of gods
Is harmony itself; to every ear
Familiar known, like light to every eye.
Meantime disclosing ages, as she spoke,
In long succession pour'd their empires forth;
Scene after scene the human drama spread;
And still the embodied picture rose to sight.

    Oh THOU ! to whom the Muses owe their flame;
Who bidd'st, beneath the pole, Parnassus rise,
And Hippocrenè flow; with thy bold ease,
The striking force, the lightning of thy thought,
And thy strong phrase, that rolls profound and clear;
Oh, gracious Goddess ! reinspire my song;
While I, to nobler than poetic fame-
Aspiring, thy commands to Britons bear.

LIBERTY.

PART II.

GREECE

Liberty traced from the pastoral ages, and the first uniting of neighbouring families into civil government.—The several establishments of
Liberty, in Egypt, Persia, Phœnicia, Palestine, slightly touched upon,
down to her great establishment in Greece.—Geographical description
of Greece.—Sparta and Athens, the two principal states of Greece, described.—Influence of Liberty over all the Grecian states; with regard
to their Government, their Politeness, their Virtues, their Arts and
Sciences.—The vast superiority it gave them, in point of force and
bravery, over the Persians, exemplified by the action of Thermopylæ,
the battle of Marathon, and the retreat of the Ten Thousand.—Its full
exertion, and most beautiful effects in Athens.—Liberty the source of
free Philosophy.—The various schools which took their rise from Socrates.—Enumeration of Fine Arts: Eloquence, Poetry, Music, Sculpture,
Painting, and Architecture; the effects of Liberty in Greece, and brought
to their utmost perfection there.—Transition to the modern state of
Greece.—Why Liberty declined, and was at last entirely lost among the
Greeks.—Concluding reflection.

THUS spoke the Goddess of the fearless eye;
And at her voice, renew'd, the Vision rose:
  "First, in the dawn of time, with eastern swains,
In woods, and tents, and cottages, I lived;
While on from plain to plain they led their flocks,
In search of clearer spring, and fresher field.
These, as increasing families disclosed
The tender state, I taught an equal sway.
Few were offences, properties, and laws.
Beneath the rural portal, palm-o'erspread,
The father senate met.   There Justice dealt,

With reason then and equity the same,
Free as the common air, her prompt decree;
Nor yet had stain'd her sword with subjects' blood.
The simpler arts were all their simple wants
Had urged to light. But instant, these supplied,
Another set of fonder wants arose,
And other arts with them of finer aim;
Till, from refining want to want impell'd,
The mind by thinking push'd her latent powers
And life began to glow, and arts to shine.
  "At first, on brutes alone the rustic war
Launch'd the rude spear; swift, as he glared along,
On the grim lion, or the robber wolf.
For then young sportive life was void of toil
Demanding little, and with little pleased:
But when to manhood grown, and endless joys,
Led on by equal toils, the bosom fired;
Lewd lazy rapine broke primeval peace,
And hid in caves and idle forests drear,
From the lone pilgrim, and the wandering swain,
Seized what he durst not earn. Then brother's blood
First, horrid, smoked on the polluted skies.
Awful in justice, then the burning youth,
Led by their temper'd sires, on lawless men,
The last worst monsters of the shaggy wood,
Turn'd the keen arrow, and the sharpen'd spear.
Then war grew glorious. Heroes then arose;
Who, scorning coward self, for others lived,
Toil'd for their ease, and for their safety bled.
West, with the living day, to Greece I came:
Earth smiled beneath my beam: the Muse before
Sonorous flew, that low till then in woods
Had tuned the reed, and sigh'd the shepherd's pain;
But now, to sing heroic deeds, she swell'd
A nobler note, and bade the banquet burn.
  " For Greece my sons of Egypt I forsook;
A boastful race, that in the vain abyss
Of fabling ages loved to lose their source,

And with their river traced it from the skies.
While there my laws alone despotic reign'd,
And king, as well as people, proud obey'd;
I taught them science, virtue, wisdom, arts;
By poets, sages, legislators sought;
The school of polish'd life, and human-kind.
But when mysterious Superstition came,
And, with her Civil Sister* leagued, involved
In studied darkness the desponding mind;
Then Tyrant Power the righteous scourge unloosed:
For yielded reason speaks the soul a slave.
Instead of useful works, like Nature's, great,
Enormous, cruel wonders crush'd the land;
And round a tyrant's tomb,† who none deserved,
For one vile carcase perish'd countless lives.
Then the great Dragon‡ couch'd amid his floods,
Swell'd his fierce heart, and cried, ' This flood is mine,
'Tis I that bid it flow.' But, undeceived,
His frenzy soon the proud blasphemer felt;
Felt that, without my fertilising power,
Suns lost their force, and Niles o'erflow'd in vain.
Nought could retard me: nor the frugal state
Of rising Persia, sober in extreme,
Beyond the pitch of man, and thence reversed
Into luxurious waste: nor yet the ports
Of old Phœnicia, first for letters famed,
That paint the voice, and silent speak to sight;
Of arts prime source, and guardian ! by fair stars,
First tempted out into the lonely deep;
To whom I first disclosed mechanic arts,
The winds to conquer, to subdue the waves,
With all the peaceful power of ruling trade;
Earnest of Britain. Nor by these retain'd;
Nor by the neighbouring land, whose palmy shore
The silver Jordan laves. Before me lay

---

* Civil Tyranny.   † The Pyramids.
          ‡ The Tyrants of Egypt.

The promised Land of Arts, and urged my flight.
  "Hail, Nature's utmost boast! unrivall'd Greece!
My fairest reign! where every power benign
Conspired to blow the flower of human-kind,
And lavish'd all that genius can inspire.
Clear sunny climates, by the breezy main,
Iōnian or Ægean, temper'd kind:
Light, airy soils: a country rich, and gay;
Broke into hills with balmy odours crown'd,
And, bright with purple harvest, joyous vales;
Mountains, and streams, where verse spontaneous flow'd;
Whence deem'd by wondering men the seat of gods,
And still the mountains and the streams of song.
All that boon Nature could luxuriant pour
Of high materials, and my restless Arts
Frame into finish'd life. How many states,
And clustering towns, and monuments of fame,
And scenes of glorious deeds, in little bounds?
From the rough tract of bending mountains, beat
By Adria's here, there by Ægean waves;
To where the deep adorning Cyclade Isles
In shining prospect rise, and on the shore
Of farthest Crete resounds the Libyan main.
  "O'er all two rival cities rear'd the brow,
And balanced all. Spread on Eurotas' bank,
Amid a circle of soft rising hills,
The patient Sparta one: the sober, hard,
And man-subduing city; which no shape
Of pain could conquer, nor of pleasure charm.
Lycurgus there built, on the solid base
Of equal life, so well a temper'd state;
Where mix'd each government, in such just poise;
Each power so checking, and supporting each;
That firm for ages, and unmoved, it stood,
The fort of Greece! without one giddy hour,
One shock of faction, or of party rage.
For, drain'd the springs of wealth, Corruption there
Lay wither'd at the root. Thrice happy land!

Had not neglected art, with weedy vice
Confounded, sunk. But if Athenian arts
Loved not the soil; yet there the calm abode
Of wisdom, virtue, philosophic ease,
Of manly sense and wit, in frugal phrase
Confined, and press'd into laconic force.
There, too, by rooting thence still treacherous self,
The Public and the Private grew the same.
The children of the nursing Public all,
And at its table fed; for that they toil'd,
For that they lived entire, and even for that
The tender mother urged her son to die.
" Of softer genius, but not less intent
To seize the palm of empire, Athens rose.
Where, with bright marbles big and future pomp,
Hymettus* spread, amid the scented sky,
His thymy treasures to the labouring bee,
And to botanic hand the stores of health;
Wrapt in a soul-attenuating clime,
Between Ilissus and Cephissus† glow'd
This hive of science, shedding sweets divine,
Of active arts, and animated arms.
There, passionate for me, an easy moved,
A quick, refined, a delicate, humane,
Enlighten'd people reign'd. Oft on the brink
Of ruin, hurried by the charm of speech,
Enforcing hasty council, immature,
Totter'd the rash Democracy; unpoised,
And by the rage devour'd, that ever tears
A populace unequal: part too rich,
And part or fierce with want or abject grown.
Solon at last, their mild restorer, rose:
Allay'd the tempest; to the calm of laws
Reduced the settling whole; and, with the weight

---

* A mountain near Athens, celebrated from the earliest times
to the present day for its excellent honey.

† Two rivers, betwixt which Athens was situated.

Which the two senates* to the public lent,
As with an anchor fix'd the driving state.
    "Nor was my forming care to these confined.
For emulation through the whole I pour'd,
Noble contention! who should most excel
In government well poised, adjusted best
To public weal: in countries cultured high:
In ornamented towns, where order reigns,
Free social life, and polish'd manners fair:
In exercise, and arms; arms only drawn
For common Greece, to quell the Persian pride:
In moral science, and in graceful arts.
Hence, as for glory peacefully they strove,
The prize grew greater, and the prize of all,
By contest brighten'd, hence the radiant youth,
Pour'd every beam; by generous pride inflamed,
Felt every ardour burn: their great reward
The verdant wreath, which sounding Pisa† gave.
    "Hence flourished Greece; and hence a race of men,
As gods by conscious future times adored:
In whom each virtue wore a smiling air,
Each science shed o'er life a friendly light,
Each art was nature.   Spartan valour hence,
At the famed pass,‡ firm as an isthmus stood;
And the whole eastern ocean, waving far
As eye could dart its vision, nobly check'd.
While in extended battle, at the field
Of Marathon, my keen Athenians drove
Before their ardent band a host of slaves.
    "Hence through the continent ten thousand Greeks

---

* The Areopagus, or Supreme Court of Judicature, which
Solon reformed and improved: and the Council of Four Hundred,
by him instituted. In this council all affairs of state were deli-
berated, before they came to be voted in the assembly of the
people.

† Or Olympia, the city where the Olympic Games were celebrated.

‡ The Straits of Thermopylæ.

Urged a retreat, whose glory not the prime
Of victories can reach.   Deserts, in vain,
Opposed their course; and hostile lands, unknown:
And deep rapacious floods, dire bank'd with death;
And mountains, in whose jaws destruction grinn'd;
Hunger, and toil; Armenian snows, and storms;
And circling myriads still of barbarous foes.
Greece in their view, and glory yet untouch'd,
Their steady column pierced the scattering herds,
Which a whole empire pour'd; and held its way
Triumphant, by the sage-exalted Chief *
Fired and sustain'd.   Oh light and force of mind,
Almost almighty in severe extremes!
The sea at last from Colchian mountains seen,
Kind-hearted transport round their captains threw
The soldiers' fond embrace; o'erflow'd their eyes
With tender floods, and loosed the general voice
To cries resounding loud—'The sea! The sea!'
  "In Attic bounds hence heroes, sages, wits,
Shone thick as stars, the milky way of Greece!
And though gay wit and pleasing grace was theirs,
All the soft modes of elegance and ease;
Yet was not courage less, the patient touch
Of toiling art, and disquisition deep.
  "My spirit pours a vigour through the soul,
The unfetter'd thought with energy inspires,
Invincible in arts, in the bright field
Of nobler Science, as in that of Arms.
Athenians thus not less intrepid burst
The bonds of tyrant darkness, than they spurn'd
The Persian chains: while through the city full
Of mirthful quarrel and of witty war,
Incessant struggled taste refining taste,
And friendly free discussion, calling forth
From the fair jewel Truth its latent ray.
O'er all shone out the great Athenian Sage,†

---

* Xenophon.   † Socrates.

And Father of Philosophy: the sun,
From whose white blaze emerged, each various sect
Took various tints, but with diminish'd beam.
Tutor of Athens! he, in every street,
Dealt priceless treasure: goodness his delight,
Wisdom his wealth, and glory his reward.
Deep through the human heart, with playful art,
His simple question stole; as into truth,
And serious deeds, he smiled the laughing race;
Taught moral happy life, whate'er can bless,
Or grace mankind; and what he taught he was.
Compounded high, though plain, his doctrine broke
In different Schools: the bold poetic phrase
Of figured Plato; Xenophon's pure strain,
Like the clear brook that steals along the vale;
Dissecting truth, the Stagyrite's keen eye;
The exalted Stoic pride; the Cynic sneer;
The slow-consenting Academic doubt;
And, joining bliss to virtue, the glad ease
Of Epicurus, seldom understood.
They, ever candid, reason still opposed
To reason; and, since virtue was their aim,
Each by sure practice tried to prove his way
The best. Then stood untouch'd the solid base
Of Liberty, the liberty of mind:
For systems yet, and soul-enslaving creeds,
Slept with the monsters of succeeding times.
From priestly darkness sprung the enlightening arts
Of fire, and sword, and rage, and horrid names.
 "O Greece! thou sapient nurse of finer arts!
Which to bright science blooming fancy bore;
Be this thy praise, that thou, and thou alone,
In these hast led the way, in these excell'd,
Crown'd with the laurel of assenting Time.
 "In thy full language, speaking mighty things;
Like a clear torrent close, or else diffused
A broad majestic stream, and rolling on
Through all the winding harmony of sound

In it the power of Eloquence, at large,
Breathed the persuasive or pathetic soul;
Still'd by degrees the democratic storm,
Or bade it threatening rise, and tyrants shook,
Flush'd at the head of their victorious troops.
In it the Muse, her fury never quench'd.
By mean unyielding phrase, or jarring sound,
Her unconfined divinity display'd;
And, still harmonious, form'd it to her will:
Or soft depress'd it to the shepherd's moan,
Or raised it swelling to the tongue of gods.
  "Heroic song was thine; the Fountain Bard,*
Whence each poetic stream derives its course.
Thine the dread moral scene, thy chief delight!
Where idle Fancy durst not mix her voice,
When Reason spoke august; the fervent heart
Or plain'd, or storm'd; and in the impassion'd man,
Concealing art with art, the poet sunk.
This potent school of manners, but when left
To loose neglect, a land-corrupting plague,
Was not unworthy deem'd of public care,
And boundless cost, by thee; whose every son,
E'en last mechanic, the true taste possess'd
Of what had flavour to the nourish'd soul.
  "The sweet enforcer of the poet's strain,
Thine was the meaning music of the heart.
Not the vain trill, that, void of passion, runs
In giddy mazes, tickling idle ears;
But that deep-searching voice, and artful hand,
To which respondent shakes the varied soul.
  "Thy fair ideas, thy delightful forms,
By Love imagined, by the Graces touch'd,
The boast of well-pleased Nature! Sculpture seized,
And bade them ever smile in Parian stone.
Selecting Beauty's choice, and that again
Exalting, blending in a perfect whole,

---

* Homer.

R

Thy workmen left e'en Nature's self behind.
From those far different, whose prolific hand
Peoples a nation; they for years on years,
By the cool touches of judicious toil,
Their rapid genius curbing, pour'd it all
Through the live features of one breathing stone.
There, beaming full, it shone; expressing gods:
Jove's awful brow, Apollo's air divine,
The fierce atrocious frown of sinew'd Mars,
Or the sly graces of the Cyprian Queen.
Minutely perfect all!   Each dimple sunk,
And every muscle swell'd, as Nature taught.
In tresses, braided gay, the marble waved;
Flow'd in loose robes, or thin transparent veils;
Sprung into motion; soften'd into flesh;
Was fired to passion, or refined to soul.

   " Nor less thy pencil, with creative touch,
Shed mimic life, when all thy brightest dames,
Assembled, Zeuxis in his Helen mix'd.
And when Apelles, who peculiar knew
To give a grace that more than mortal smiled,
The soul of beauty ! call'd the Queen of Love,
Fresh from the billows, blushing orient charms.
E'en such enchantment then thy pencil pour'd,
That cruel-thoughted War the impatient torch
Dash'd to the ground; and, rather than destroy
The patriot picture,* let the city 'scape.

   " First, elder Sculpture taught her sister art
Correct design; where great ideas shone,
And in the secret trace expression spoke:
Taught her the graceful attitude; the turn,
And beauteous airs of head; the native act,
Or bold, or easy; and, cast free behind,

---

* When Demetrius besieged Rhodes, and could have reduced
the city, by setting fire to that quarter of it where stood the house
of the celebrated Protogenes, he chose rather to raise the siege,
than hazard the burning of a famous picture called Jasylus, the
masterpiece of that painter.

The swelling mantle's well-adjusted flow.
Then the bright Muse, their eldest sister, came;
And bade her follow where she led the way:
Bade earth, and sea, and air, in colours rise;
And copious action on the canvas glow:
Gave her gay Fable; spread Invention's store;
Enlarged her view; taught Composition high,
And just Arrangement, circling round one point,
That starts to sight, binds and commands the whole.
Caught from the heavenly Muse a nobler aim,
And scorning the soft trade of mere delight,
O'er all thy temples, porticoes, and schools,
Heroic deeds she traced, and warm display'd
Each moral beauty to the ravish'd eye.
There, as the imagined presence of the god
Aroused the mind, or vacant hours induced
Calm contemplation, or assembled youth
Burn'd in ambitious circle round the sage,
The living lesson stole into the heart,
With more prevailing force than dwells in words.
These rouse to glory; while, to rural life,
The softer canvas oft reposed the soul.
There gaily broke the sun-illumined cloud;
The lessening prospect, and the mountain blue,
Vanish'd in air; the precipice frown'd, dire;
White, down the rock, the rushing torrent dash'd;
The sun shone, trembling, o'er the distant main;
The tempest foam'd, immense; the driving storm
Sadden'd the skies, and, from the doubling gloom,
On the scathed oak the ragged lightning fell;
In closing shades, and where the current strays,
With Peace, and Love, and Innocence around,
Piped the lone shepherd to his feeding flock:
Round happy parents smiled their younger selves;
And friends conversed, by death divided long.
  "To public virtue thus the smiling arts,
Unblemish'd handmaids, served: the Graces they
To dress this fairest Venus.   Thus revered,

And placed beyond the reach of sordid care,
The high awarders of immortal fame,
Alone for glory thy great masters strove;
Courted by kings, and by contending states
Assumed the boasted honour of their birth.
 "In Architecture, too, thy rank supreme!
That art where most magnificent appears
The little builder man; by thee refined,
And, smiling high, to full perfection brought.
Such thy sure rules, that Goths of every age,
Who scorn'd their aid, have only loaded earth
With labour'd heavy monuments of shame.
Not those gay domes that o'er thy splendid shore
Shot, all proportion, up.   First unadorn'd,
And nobly plain, the manly Doric rose;
The Ionic then, with decent matron grace,
Her airy pillar heaved; luxuriant last,
The rich Corinthian spread her wanton wreath.
The whole so measured true, so lessen'd off
By fine proportion, that the marble pile,
Form'd to repel the still or stormy waste
Of rolling ages, light as fabrics look'd
That from the magic wand aerial rise.
 "These were the wonders that illumined Greece,
From end to end"——   Here interrupting warm,
"Where are they now?"   I cried;   "say, goddess,
          where?
And what the land, thy darling thus of old?"
"Sunk!" she resumed, "deep in the kindred gloom
Of Superstition and of Slavery sunk!
No glory now can touch their hearts, benumb'd
By loose dejected sloth and servile fear;
No science pierce the darkness of their minds;
No nobler art the quick ambitious soul
Of imitation in their breast awake.
E'en to supply the needful arts of life,
Mechanic toil denies the hopeless hand.
Scarce any trace remaining, vestige grey,

Or nodding column on the desert shore,
To point where Corinth, or where Athens stood.
A faithless land of violence, and death!
Where commerce parleys, dubious, on the shore;
And his wild impulse curious search restrains,
Afraid to trust the inhospitable clime.
Neglected nature fails; in sordid want
Sunk, and debased, their beauty beams no more.
The sun himself seems, angry, to regard,
Of light unworthy, the degenerate race;
And fires them oft with pestilential rays:
While earth, blue poison steaming on the skies,
Indignant, shakes them from her troubled sides.
But as from man to man, Fate's first decree,
Impartial Death the tide of riches rolls,
So states must die, and Liberty go round.
    "Fierce was the stand, ere Virtue, Valour, Arts,
And the soul fired by me (that often, stung·
With thoughts of better times and old renown,
From hydra-tyrants tried to clear the land),
Lay quite extinct in Greece, their works effaced,
And gross o'er all unfeeling bondage spread.
Sooner I moved my much reluctant flight,
Poised on the doubtful wing: when Greece with
        Greece
Embroil'd in foul contention fought no more
For common glory, and for common weal:
But false to Freedom, sought to quell the free;
Broke the firm band of Peace, and sacred Love,
That lent the whole irrefragable force;
And, as around the partial trophy blush'd,
Prepared the way for total overthrow.
Then to the Persian power, whose pride they scorn'd,
When Xerxes pour'd his millions o'er the land,
Sparta, by turns, and Athens, vilely sued;
Sued to be venal parricides, to spill
Their country's bravest blood, and on themselves
To turn their matchless mercenary arms.

Peaceful in Susa, then, sat the Great King,*
And by the trick of treaties, the still waste
Of sly corruption, and barbaric gold,
Effected what his steel could ne'er perform.
Profuse he gave them the luxurious draught,
Inflaming all the land: unbalanced wide
Their tottering states; their wild assemblies ruled,
As the winds turn at every blast the seas:
And by their listed orators, whose breath
Still with a factious storm infested Greece,
Roused them to civil war, or dash'd them down
To sordid peace—Peace!† that, when Sparta shook
Astonish'd Artaxerxes on his throne,
Gave up, fair-spread o'er Asia's sunny shore,
Their kindred cities to perpetual chains.
What could so base, so infamous a thought
In Spartan hearts inspire?   Jealous, they saw
Respiring Athens‡ rear again her walls:
And the pale fury fired them, once again
To crush this rival city to the dust.
For now no more the noble social soul
Of Liberty my families combined;
But by short views, and selfish passions, broke,
Dire as when friends are rankled into foes,
They mix'd severe, and waged eternal war:
Nor felt they, furious, their exhausted force;
Nor, with false glory, discord, madness blind,
Saw how the blackening storm from Thracia came.
Long years roll'd on, by many a battle stain'd,§

---

* So the Kings of Persia were called by the Greeks.

† The peace made by Antalcidas, the Lacedemonian admiral,
with the Persians; by which the Lacedemonians abandoned all
the Greeks established in the Lesser Asia to the dominion of the
King of Persia.

‡ Athens had been dismantled by the Lacedemonians, at the
end of the First Peloponnesian War, and was at this time restored
by Conon to its former splendour.

§ The Peloponnesian War.

The blush and boast of Fame! where courage, art,
And military glory shone supreme:
But let detesting ages, from the scene
Of Greece self-mangled, turn the sickening eye.
At last, when bleeding from a thousand wounds,
She felt her spirits fail; and in the dust
Her latest heroes, Nicias, Conon, lay,
Agesilaus, and the Theban friends:*
The Macedonian vulture mark'd his time,
By the dire scent of Cheronæa† lured,
And, fierce descending, seized his hapless prey.

"Thus tame submitted to the victor's yoke
Greece, once the gay, the turbulent, the bold;
For every grace, and muse, and science, born;
With arts of War, of Government elate;
To tyrants dreadful, dreadful to the best;
Whom I myself could scarcely rule: and thus
The Persian fetters, that enthrall'd the mind,
Were turn'd to formal and apparent chains.

"Unless Corruption first deject the pride
And guardian vigour of the freeborn soul,
All crude attempts of Violence are vain;
For firm within, and while at heart untouch'd,
Ne'er yet by force was Freedom overcome.
But soon as Independence stoops the head,
To Vice enslaved, and vice-created Wants;
Then to some foul corrupting hand, whose waste
These heighten'd wants with fatal bounty feeds;
From man to man the slackening ruin runs,
Till the whole state unnerved in Slavery sinks."

---

* Pelopidas and Epaminondas.
† The battle of Cheronæa, in which Philip of Macedon utterly defeated the Greeks.

LIBERTY.

PART III.

ROME.

As this part contains a description of the establishment of Liberty in Rome, it begins with a view of the Grecian Colonies settled in the southern parts of Italy, which with Sicily constituted the Great Greece of the Ancients.—With these colonies, the Spirit of Liberty, and of Republics, spreads over Italy.—Transition to Pythagoras and his philosophy, which he taught through these free states and cities.—Amidst the many small Republics in Italy, Rome the destined seat of Liberty.—Her establishment there dated from the expulsion of the Tarquins.—How differing from that in Greece.—Reference to a view of the Roman Republic given in the First Part of this Poem: to mark its Rise and Fall, the peculiar purport of this.—During its first ages, the greatest force of Liberty and Virtue exerted.—The source whence derived.—The Heroic Virtues of the Romans.—Enumeration of these Virtues.—Thence their security at home; their glory, success, and empire abroad.—Bounds of the Roman empire geographically described.—The states of Greece restored to Liberty, by Titus Quintus Flamininus, the highest instance of public generosity and beneficence.—The loss of Liberty in Rome.—Its causes, progress, and completion in the death of Brutus.—Rome under the Emperors.—From Rome the Goddess of Liberty goes among the Northern Nations; where, by infusing into them her Spirit and general principles, she lays the groundwork of her future establishments; sends them in vengeance on the Roman Empire, now totally enslaved; and then, with Arts and Sciences in her train, quits earth during the dark ages.—The celestial regions, to which Liberty retired, not proper to be opened to the view of mortals.

HERE melting mix'd with air the ideal forms
That painted still whate'er the goddess sung.
Then I, impatient.—"From extinguish'd Greece,
To what new region stream'd the Human Day?"
She softly sighing, as when Zephyr leaves,
Resign'd to Boreas, the declining year,
Resumed.—"Indignant, these last scenes I fled;*

---

* The last struggles of Liberty in Greece.

And long ere then Leucadia's cloudy cliff,
And the Ceraunian hills behind me thrown,
All Latium stood aroused.   Ages before,
Great mother of republics! Greece had pour'd,
Swarm after swarm, her ardent youth around.
On Asia, Afric, Sicily, they stoop'd,
But chief on fair Hesperia's winding shore;
Where, from Lacinium* to Etrurian vales,
They roll'd increasing colonies along,
And lent materials for my Roman reign.
With them my spirit spread; and numerous states,
And cities rose, on Grecian models form'd;
As its parental policy and arts
Each had imbibed.   Besides, to each assign'd
A guardian Genius, o'er the public weal,
Kept an unclosing eye; tried to sustain,
Or more sublime, the soul infused by me:
And strong the battle rose, with various wave,
Against the tyrant demons of the land.
Thus they their little wars and triumphs knew;
Their flows of fortune, and receding times;
But almost all below the proud regard
Of story vow'd to Rome, on deeds intent
That Truth beyond the flight of Fable bore.
 "Not so the Samian Sage;† to him belongs
The brightest witness of recording Fame.
For these free states his native isle‡ forsook,
And a vain tyrant's transitory smile,
He sought Crotona's pure salubrious air;
And through Great Greece§ his gentle wisdom taught;
Wisdom that calm'd for listening years‖ the mind,

---

* A promonotory in Calabria.

† Pythagoras.

‡ Samos, over which then reigned the tyrant Polycrates.

§ The southern parts of Italy and Sicily, so called because of the Grecian colonies there settled.

‖ His scholars were enjoined silence for five years.

Nor ever heard amid the storm of zeal.
His mental eye first launch'd into the deeps
Of boundless ether; where unnumber'd orbs,
Myriads on myriads, through the pathless sky
Unerring roll, and wind their steady way.
There he the full consenting choir beheld;
There first discern'd the secret band of love,
The kind attraction, that to central suns
Binds circling earths, and world with world unites;
Instructed thence, he great ideas form'd
Of the whole-moving, all-informing God,
The sun of beings! beaming unconfined
Light, life, and love, and ever active power:
Whom nought can image, and who best approves
The silent worship of the moral heart,
That joys in bounteous Heaven, and spreads the joy.
Nor scorn'd the soaring sage to stoop to life,
And bound his reason to the sphere of man.
He gave the four yet reigning virtues* name;
Inspired the study of the finer arts,
That civilise mankind, and laws devised
Where with enlighten'd justice mercy mix'd.
He e'en into his tender system took
Whatever shares the brotherhood of life:
He taught that life's indissoluble flame,
From brute to man, and man to brute again,
For ever shifting, runs the eternal round;
Thence tried against the blood-polluted meal,
And limbs yet quivering with some kindred soul,
To turn the human heart.   Delightful truth!
Had he beheld the living chain ascend,
And not a circling form but rising whole.
  "Amid these small republics one arose
On yellow Tiber's bank, almighty Rome,
Fated for me.   A nobler spirit warm'd
Her sons; and, roused by tyrants, nobler still

---

* The four cardinal virtues.

It burn'd in Brutus; the proud Tarquins chased,
With all their crimes; bade radiant eras rise,
And the long honours of the Consul-line.
 "Here from the fairer, not the greater, plan
Of Greece I varied; whose unmixing states,
By the keen soul of emulation pierced,
Long waged alone the bloodless war of arts,
And their best empire gain'd.   But to diffuse
O'er men an empire was my purpose now:
To let my martial majesty abroad;
Into the vortex of one state to draw
The whole mix'd force, and liberty, on earth;
To conquer tyrants, and set nations free.
 "Already have I given, with flying touch,
A broken view of this my amplest reign.
Now, while its first, last, periods you survey,
Mark how it labouring rose, and rapid fell.
 "When Rome in noontide empire grasp'd the world,
And, soon as her resistless legions shone,
The nations stoop'd around; though then appear'd
Her grandeur most; yet in her dawn of power,
By many a jealous equal people press'd,
Then was the toil, the mighty struggle then;
Then for each Roman I a hero told;
And every passing sun, and Latian scene,
Saw patriot virtues then, and awful deeds,
That or surpass the faith of modern times,
Or, if believed, with sacred horror strike.
 "For then, to prove my most exalted power,
I to the point of full perfection push'd,
To fondness and enthusiastic zeal,
The great, the reigning passion of the free;
That godlike passion! which, the bounds of self
Divinely bursting, the whole public takes
Into the heart, enlarged, and burning high
With the mix'd ardour of unnumber'd selves;
Of all who safe beneath the voted laws
Of the same parent state, fraternal, live.

From this kind sun of moral nature flow'd
Virtues, that shine the light of human-kind,
And, ray'd through story, warm remotest time.
These virtues too, reflected to their source,
Increased its flame.   The social charm went round.
The fair idea, more attractive still,
As more by virtue mark'd; till Romans, all
One band of friends, unconquerable grew.
    "Hence, when their country raised her plaintive voice,
The voice of pleading Nature was not heard;
And in their hearts the fathers throbb'd no more;
Stern to themselves, but gentle to the whole.
Hence sweeten'd Pain, the luxury of toil;
Patience, that baffled fortune's utmost rage;
High-minded Hope, which at the lowest ebb,
When Brennus conquer'd, and when Cannæ bled,
The bravest impulse felt, and scorn'd despair.
Hence Moderation a new conquest gain'd:
As on the vanquish'd, like descending heaven,
Their dewy mercy dropp'd, the bounty beam'd,
And by the labouring hand were crowns bestow'd.
Fruitful of men, hence hard laborious life,
Which no fatigue can quell, no season pierce.
Hence, Independence, with his little pleased
Serene, and self-sufficient, like a god;
In whom Corruption could not lodge one charm,
While he his honest roots to gold preferr'd;
While truly rich, and by his Sabine field,
The man maintain'd, the Roman's splendour all
Was in the public wealth and glory placed:
Or ready, a rough swain, to guide the plough;
Or else, the purple o'er his shoulder thrown,
In long majestic flow, to rule the state,
With Wisdom's purest eye; or, clad in steel,
To drive the steady battle on the foe.
Hence every passion, e'en the proudest, stoop'd
To common good. Camillus, thy revenge;
Thy glory, Fabius. All submissive hence,

Consuls, Dictators, still resign'd their rule,
The very moment that the laws ordain'd.
Though Conquest o'er them clapp'd her eagle-wings,
Her laurels wreathed, and yoked her snowy steeds
To the triumphal car; soon as expired
The latest hour of sway, taught to submit
(A harder lesson that than to command),
Into the private Roman sunk the chief:
If Rome was served, and glorious, careless they
By whom. Their country's fame they deem'd their own;
And above envy, in a rival's train,
Sung the loud Iös by themselves deserved.
Hence matchless courage. On Cremera's bank,
Hence fell the Fabii; hence the Decii died;
And Curtius plunged into the flaming gulf.
Hence Regulus the wavering fathers firm'd,
By dreadful counsel never given before;
For Roman honour sued, and his own doom.
Hence he sustain'd to dare a death prepared
By Punic rage. On earth his manly look
Relentless fix'd, he from a last embrace,
By chains polluted, put his wife aside,
His little children climbing for a kiss;
Then dumb through rows of weeping, wondering friends,
A new illustrious exile! press'd along.
Nor less impatient did he pierce the crowds
Opposing his return, than if, escaped
From long litigious suits, he glad forsook,
The noisy town awhile and city-cloud,
To breathe Venafrian, or Tarentine air.
Need I these high particulars recount?
The meanest bosom felt a thirst for fame;
Flight their worst death, and shame their only fear.
Life had no charms, nor any terrors fate,
When Rome and glory call'd. But, in one view,
Mark the rare boast of these unequall'd times.
Ages revolved unsullied by a crime:
Astrea reign'd, and scarcely needed laws

To bind a race elated with the pride
Of virtue, and disdaining to descend
To meanness, mutual violence, and wrongs.
While war around them raged, in happy Rome
All peaceful smiled, all save the passing clouds
That often hang on Freedom's jealous brow;
And fair unblemish'd centuries elapsed,
When not a Roman bled but in the field.
Their virtue such, that an unbalanced state,
Still between Noble and Plebeian tost,
As flow'd the wave of fluctuating power,
Was then kept firm, and with triumphant prow
Rode out the storms.   Oft though the native feuds,
That from the first their constitution shook
(A latent ruin, growing as it grew),
Stood on the threatening point of civil war,
Ready to rush: yet could the lenient voice
Of wisdom, soothing the tumultuous soul,
Those sons of virtue calm.   Their generous hearts
Unpetrified by self, so naked lay,
And sensible to Truth, that o'er the rage
Of giddy faction, by oppression swell'd,
Prevail'd a simple fable, and at once
To peace recover'd the divided state.
But if their often cheated hopes refused
The soothing touch; still, in the love of Rome,
The dread Dictator found a sure resource.
Was she assaulted? was her glory stain'd?
One common quarrel wide inflamed the whole.
Foes in the forum, in the field were friends,
By social danger bound; each fond for each,
And for their dearest country all, to die.
  "Thus up the hill of empire slow they toil'd:
Till, the bold summit gain'd, the thousand states
Of proud Italia blended into one;
Then o'er the nations they resistless rush'd,
And touch'd the limits of the failing world.
  " Let Fancy's eye the distant lines unite.

See that which borders wild the western main,
Where storms at large resound, and tides immense;
From Caledonia's dim cerulean coast,
And moist Hibernia, to where Atlas, lodged
Amid the restless clouds and leaning heaven,
Hangs o'er the deep that borrows thence its name.
Mark that opposed, where first the springing morn
Her roses sheds, and shakes around her dews:
From the dire deserts by the Caspian laved,
To where the Tigris and Euphrates, join'd,
Impetuous tear the Babylonian plain;
And bless'd Arabia aromatic breathes.
See that dividing far the watery north,
Parent of floods! from the majestic Rhine,
Drunk by Batavian meads, to where, seven-mouth'd,
In Euxine waves the flashing Danube roars;
To where the frozen Tanais scarcely stirs
The dead Meotic pool, or the long Rha*
In the black Scythian sea† his torrent throws.
Last, that beneath the burning zone behold:
See where it runs, from the deep-loaded plains
Of Mauritania to the Libyan sands,
Where Ammon lifts amid the torrid waste
A verdant isle, with shade and fountain fresh;
And farther to the full Egyptian shore,
To where the Nile from Ethiopian clouds,
His never drain'd ethereal urn, descends.
In this vast space what various tongues, and states!
What bounding rocks, and mountains, floods, and seas!
What purple tyrants quell'd, and nations freed!
"O'er Greece, descended chief, with stealth divine,
The Roman bounty in a flood of day:
As at her Isthmian games, a fading pomp!
Her full-assembled youth innumerous swarm'd.
On a tribunal raised, Flaminius sat:
A victor he, from the deep phalanx pierced

---

* The ancient name of the Volga.　　† The Caspian Sea.

Of iron-coated Macedon, and back
The Grecian tyrant* to his bounds repell'd.
In the high thoughtless gaiety of game,
While sport alone their unambitious hearts
Possess'd, the sudden trumpet, sounding hoarse,
Bade silence o'er the bright assembly reign.
Then thus a herald:—'To the states of Greece
The Roman people, unconfined, restore
Their countries, cities, liberties, and laws:
Taxes remit, and garrisons withdraw.'
The crowd, astonish'd half, and half inform'd,
Stared dubious round; some question'd, some exclaim'd
(Like one who, dreaming, between hope and fear,
Is lost in anxious joy), ' Be that again,
Be that again proclaim'd, distinct and loud.'
Loud, and distinct, it was again proclaim'd;
And still as midnight in the rural shade,
When the gale slumbers, they the words devour'd.
Awhile severe amazement held them mute,
Then, bursting broad, the boundless shout to Heaven
From many a thousand hearts ecstatic sprung.
On every hand rebellow'd to their joy
The swelling sea, the rocks, and vocal hills:
Through all her turrets stately Corinth† shook;
And, from the void above of shatter'd air,
The flitting bird fell breathless to the ground.
What piercing bliss, how keen a sense of fame,
Did then, Flaminius, reach thy inmost soul!
And with what deep-felt glory didst thou then
Escape the fondness of transported Greece?
Mix'd in a tempest of superior joy,
They left the sports; like Bacchanals they flew,
Each other straining in a strict embrace,
Nor strain'd a slave; and loud acclaims till night
Round the Proconsul's tent repeated rung.
Then crown'd with garlands came the festive hours;

---

* The King of Macedonia.
† The Isthmian Games were celebrated at Corinth.

And music, sparkling wine, and converse warm,
Their raptures waked anew. ' Ye gods!' they cried,
' Ye guardian gods of Greece! and are we free?
Was it not madness deem'd the very thought?
And is it true?   How did we purchase chains?
At what a dire expense of kindred blood?
And are they now dissolved?   And scarce one drop
For the fair first of blessings have we paid?
Courage, and conduct, in the doubtful field,
When rages wide the storm of mingling war,
Are rare indeed; but how to generous ends
To turn success, and conquest, rarer still:
That the great gods and Romans only know.
Lives there on earth, almost to Greece unknown.
A people so magnanimous, to quit
Their native soil, traverse the stormy deep,
And by their blood and treasure, spent for us,
Redeem our states, our liberties, and laws!
There does! there does! Oh saviour, Titus! Rome!'
Thus through the happy night they pour'd their souls,
And in my last reflected beams rejoiced.
As when the shepherd, on the mountain-brow,
Sits piping to his flocks and gamesome kids;
Meantime the sun, beneath the green earth sunk,
Slants upward o'er the scene a parting gleam:
Short is the glory that the mountain gilds,
Plays on the glittering flocks, and glads the swain;
To western worlds irrevocable roll'd,
Rapid, the source of light recalls his ray."
   Here interposing I—" Oh, Queen of men !
Beneath whose sceptre in essential rights
Equal they live; though placed for common good,
Various, or in subjection or command;
And that by common choice: alas! the scene,
With virtue, freedom, and with glory bright,
Streams into blood, and darkens into wo."
Thus she pursued:—" Near this great era, Rome
Began to feel the swift approach of fate,

S

That now her vitals gain'd: still more and more
Her deep divisions kindling into rage,
And war with pains and desolation charged.
From an unequal balance of her sons
These fierce contentions sprung: and, as increased
This hated inequality, more fierce
They flamed to tumult.   Independence fail'd;
Here by luxurious wants, by real there;
And with this virtue every virtue sunk,
As, with the sliding rock, the pile sustain'd.
A last attempt, too late, the Gracchi made,
To fix the flying scale, and poise the state.
On one side swell'd aristocratic Pride;
With Usury, the villain! whose fell gripe
Bends by degrees to baseness the free soul;
And Luxury rapacious, cruel, mean,
Mother of vice! While on the other crept
A populace in want, with pleasure fired;
Fit for proscriptions, for the darkest deeds,
As the proud feeder bade; inconstant, blind,
Deserting friends at need, and duped by foes;
Loud and seditious, when a chief inspired
Their headlong fury, but of him deprived,
Already slaves that lick'd the scourging hand.
    "This firm republic, that against the blast
Of opposition rose; that (like an oak,
Nursed on ferocious Algidum,* whose boughs
Still stronger shoot beneath the rigid axe),
By loss, by slaughter, from the steel itself
E'en force and spirit drew; smit with the calm,
The dead serene of prosperous fortune, pined.
Nought now her weighty legions could oppose;
Her† terror once, on Afric's tawny shore,
Now smoked in dust, a stabling now for wolves;
And every dreaded power received the yoke.
Besides, destructive, from the conquer'd East,

---

* A town of Latium, near Tusculum.   † Carthage.

In the soft plunder came that worst of plagues,
That pestilence of mind, a fever'd thirst
For the false joys which Luxury prepares.
Unworthy joys! that wasteful leave behind
No mark of honour, in reflecting hour,
No secret ray to glad the conscious soul;
At once involving in one ruin wealth,
And wealth-acquiring powers: while stupid self,
Of narrow gust, and hebetating sense,
Devour the nobler faculties of bliss.
Hence Roman virtue slacken'd into sloth;
Security relax'd the softening state;
And the broad eye of government lay closed.
No more the laws inviolable reign'd,
And public weal no more: but party raged;
And partial power, and license unrestrain'd,
Let Discord through the deathful city loose.
First, mild Tiberius,* on thy sacred head
The fury's vengeance fell; the first, whose blood
Had since the consuls stain'd contending Rome.
Of precedent pernicious! with thee bled
Three hundred Romans; with thy brother, next,
Three thousand more: till, into battles turn'd
Debates of peace, and forced the trembling laws,
The Forum and Comitia horrid grew,
A scene of barter'd power, or reeking gore.
When, half ashamed, Corruption's thievish arts
And ruffian force begin to sap the mounds
And majesty of laws; if not in time
Repress'd severe, for human aid too strong
The torrent turns, and overbears the whole.
"Thus Luxury, Dissension, a mix'd rage
Of boundless pleasure and of boundless wealth,
Want-wishing change, and waste-repairing war,
Rapine for ever lost to peaceful toil,
Guilt unatoned, profuse of blood Revenge,

* Tiberius Gracchus.

Corruption all avow'd, and lawless Force,
Each heightening each, alternate shook the state.
Meantime Ambition, at the dazzling head
Of hardy legions, with the laurels heap'd
And spoil of nations, in one circling blast
Combined in various storm, and from its base
The broad republic tore.　By Virtue built,
It touch'd the skies, and spread o'er shelter'd earth
An ample roof: by Virtue too sustain'd,
And balanced steady, every tempest sung
Innoxious by, or bade it firmer stand.
But when, with sudden and enormous change,
The first of mankind sunk into the last,
As once in Virtue, so in Vice extreme,
This universal fabric yielded loose,
Before Ambition still; and thundering down,
At last beneath its ruins crush'd a world.
A conquering people, to themselves a prey,
Must ever fall; when their victorious troops,
In blood and rapine savage grown, can find
No land to sack and pillage but their own.
　"By brutal Marius, and keen Sylla, first
Effused the deluge dire of civil blood,
Unceasing woes began, and this, or that,
Deep-drenching their revenge, nor virtue spared,
Nor sex, nor age, nor quality, nor name;
Till Rome, into a human shambles turn'd,
Made deserts lovely.—Oh, to well-earn'd chains,
Devoted race!—If no true Roman then,
No Scævola there was, to raise for me
A vengeful hand: was there no father, robb'd
Of blooming youth to prop his wither'd age?
No son, a witness to his hoary sire
In dust and gore defiled? no friend, forlorn?
No wretch that doubtful trembled for himself?
None brave, or wild, to pierce a monster's heart,
Who, heaping horror round, no more deserved
The sacred shelter of the laws he spurn'd?

No:—Sad o'er all profound dejection sat;
And nerveless fear. The slave's asylum theirs.
Or flight, ill-judging, that the timid back
Turns weak to slaughter; or partaken guilt.
In vain from Sylla's vanity I drew
An unexampled deed. The power resign'd,
And all unhoped the commonwealth restored,
Amazed the public, and effaced his crimes.
Through streets yet streaming from his murderous hand
Unarm'd he stray'd, unguarded, unassail'd,
And on the bed of peace his ashes laid;
A grace, which I to his demission gave.
But with him died not the despotic soul.
Ambition saw that stooping Rome could bear
A master, nor had virtue to be free.
Hence for succeeding years my troubled reign
No certain peace, no spreading prospect knew.
Destruction gather'd round. Still the black soul,
Or of a Catiline, or Rullus,* swell'd
With fell designs; and all the watchful art
Of Cicero demanded, all the force,
All the state-wielding magic of his tongue;
And all the thunder of my Cato's zeal.
With these I linger'd; till the flame anew
Burst out, in blaze immense, and wrapt the world.
The shameful contest sprung; to whom mankind
Should yield the neck: to Pompey, who conceal'd
A rage impatient of an equal name;
Or to the nobler Cæsar, on whose brow
O'er daring vice deluding virtue smiled,
And who no less a vain superior scorn'd.
Both bled, but bled in vain. New traitors rose.
The venal will be bought, the base have lords.
To these vile wars I left ambitious slaves;

---

* Publius Servilius Rullus, tribune of the people, proposed
an Agrarian Law, in appearance very advantageous for the
people, but destructive of their liberty: and which was defeated by the eloquence of Cicero, in his speech against Rullus.

And from Philippi's field, from where in dust
The last of Romans, matchless Brutus! lay,
Spread to the north untamed a rapid wing.
  "What though the first smooth Cæsars arts caress'd,
Merit, and virtue, stimulating me
Severely tender! cruelly humane!
The chain to clinch, and make it softer sit
On the new-broken still ferocious state.
From the dark Third,* succeeding, I beheld
The imperial monsters all.—A race on earth
Vindictive, sent the scourge of human-kind!
Whose blind profusion drain'd a bankrupt world;
Whose lust to forming nature seems disgrace;
And whose infernal rage bade every drop
Of ancient blood, that yet retain'd my flame,
To that of Pætus,† in the peaceful bath,
Or Rome's affrighted streets, inglorious flow.
But almost just the meanly patient death,
That waits a tyrant's unprevented stroke.
Titus indeed gave one short evening gleam;
More cordial felt, as in the midst it spread
Of storm, and horror.   The delight of men!
He who the day, when his o'erflowing hand
Had made no happy heart, concluded lost;
Trajan and he, with the mild sire‡ and son,
His son of virtue! eased awhile mankind;
And arts revived beneath their gentle beam.
Then was their last effort: what sculpture raised
To Trajan's glory, following triumphs stole;

---

* Tiberius.
  † Thrasea Pætus, put to death by Nero. Tacitus introduces
the account he gives of his death, thus:—"After having inhu-
manly slaughtered so many illustrious men, he (Nero) burned at
last with a desire of cutting off virtue itself in the person of
Thrasea," &c.
  ‡ Antoninus Pius, and his adopted son, Marcus Aurelius, afterwards called Antoninus Philosophus.

And mix'd with Gothic forms (the chisel's shame),
On that triumphal arch,* the forms of Greece.
"Meantime o'er rocky Thrace, and the deep vales
Of gelid Hæmus, I pursued my flight;
And, piercing farthest Scythia, westward swept
Sarmatia,† traversed by a thousand streams,
A sullen land of lakes, and fens immense,
Of rocks, resounding torrents, gloomy heaths,
And cruel deserts black with sounding pine;
Where nature frowns: though sometimes into smiles
She softens; and immediate, at the touch
Of southern gales, throws from the sudden glebe
Luxuriant pasture, and a waste of flowers.
But, cold-compress'd, when the whole loaded heaven
Descends in snow, lost in one white abrupt,
Lies undistinguished earth; and, seized by frost,
Lakes, headlong streams, and floods, and oceans sleep.
Yet there life glows; the furry millions there
Deep dig their dens beneath the sheltering snows:
And there a race of men prolific swarms,
To various pain, to little pleasure used;
On whom, keen-parching, beat Riphæan winds;
Hard like their soil, and like their climate fierce,
The nursery of nations!—These I roused,
Drove land on land, on people people pour'd;
Till from almost perpetual night they broke,
As if in search of day; and o'er the banks
Of yielding empire, only slave-sustain'd,
Resistless raged; in vengeance urged by me.
"Long in the barbarous heart the buried seeds
Of Freedom lay, for many a wintry age;
And though my spirit work'd, by slow degrees,
Nought but its pride and fierceness yet appear'd.

---

* Constantine's Arch, to build which, that of Trajan was destroyed, sculpture having been then almost entirely lost.

† The ancient Sarmatia contained a vast tract of country running all along the north of Europe and Asia.

Then was the night of time, that parted worlds.
I quitted earth the while. As when the tribes
Aerial, warn'd of rising winter, ride
Autumnal winds, to warmer climates borne;
So, arts and each good genius in my train,
I cut the closing gloom, and soar'd to heaven.
  " In the bright regions there of purest day,
Far other scenes, and palaces, arise,
Adorn'd profuse with other arts divine.
All beauty here below, to them compared,
Would, like a rose before the mid-day sun,
Shrink up its blossom; like a bubble break
The passing poor magnificence of kings,
For there the King of Nature, in full blaze,
Calls every splendour forth; and there his court,
Amid ethereal powers, and virtues, holds:
Angel, archangel, tutelary gods,
Of cities, nations, empires, and of worlds.
But sacred be the veil, that kindly clouds
A light too keen for mortals; wraps a view
Too softening fair, for those that here in dust
Must cheerful toil out their appointed years.
A sense of higher life would only damp
The schoolboy's task, and spoil his playful hours.
Nor could the child of Reason, feeble man,
With vigour through this infant-being drudge;
Did brighter worlds, their unimagined bliss
Disclosing, dazzle and dissolve his mind."

LIBERTY.

PART IV.

BRITAIN.

Difference betwixt the Ancients and Moderns slightly touched upon.—
Description of the dark ages.—The Goddess of Liberty, who during
these is supposed to have left earth, returns, attended with Arts and
Science.—She first descends on Italy.—Sculpture, Painting, and Architecture fix at Rome, to revive their several arts by the great models of
antiquity there, which many barbarous invasions had not been able to
destroy.—The revival of these arts marked out.—That sometimes arts
may flourish for awhile under despotic governments, though never the
natural and genuine production of them.—Learning begins to dawn.—
The Muse and Science attend Liberty, who in her progress towards Great
Britain raises several free states and cities.—These enumerated.—
Author's exclamation of joy, upon seeing the British seas and coasts rise
in the vision, which painted whatever the Goddess of Liberty said.—She
resumes her narration.—The Genius of the Deep appears, and address-
ing Liberty, associates Great Britain into his dominion.—Liberty received and congratulated by Britannia, and the native Genii or Virtues of
the island.—These described.—Animated by the presence of Liberty,
they begin their operations.—Their beneficent influence contrasted
with the works and delusions of opposing Demons.—Concludes with an
abstract of the English history, marking the several Advances of
Liberty, down to her complete establishment at the Revolution.

STRUCK with the rising scene, thus I amazed:
" Ah, Goddess, what a change? is earth the same?
Of the same kind the ruthless race she feeds?
And does the same fair sun and ether spread
Round this vile spot their all-enlivening soul?
Lo! beauty fails; lost in unlovely forms
Of little pomp, magnificence no more

Exalts the mind, and bids the public smile,
While to rapacious interest Glory leaves
Mankind, and every grace of life is gone."
　To this the Power, whose vital radiance calls
From the brute mass of man an order'd world:
　" Wait till the morning shines, and from the depth
Of Gothic darkness springs another day,
True, Genius droops; the tender ancient taste
Of Beauty, then fresh blooming in her prime,
But faintly trembles through the callous soul;
And Grandeur, or of morals, or of life,
Sinks into safe pursuits, and creeping cares.
E'en cautious Virtue seems to stoop her flight,
And aged life to deem the generous deeds
Of youth romantic. Yet in cooler thought
Well reason'd, in researches piercing deep
Through nature's works, in profitable arts,
And all that calm Experience can disclose
(Slow guide, but sure), behold the world anew
Exalted rise; with other honours crow'nd;
And, where my Spirit wakes the finer powers,
Athenian laurels still afresh shall bloom.
　" Oblivious ages pass'd; while earth, forsook
By her best Genii, lay to Demons foul,
And unchain'd Furies, an abandon'd prey.
Contention led the van; first small of size,
But soon dilating to the skies she towers:
Then, wide as air, the livid Fury spread,
And high her head above the stormy clouds,
She blazed in omens, swell'd the groaning winds
With wild surmises, battlings, sounds of war:
From land to land the maddening trumpet blew,
And pour'd her venom through the heart of man.
Shook to the pole, the North obey'd her call.
Forth rush'd the bloody power of Gothic war,
War against human-kind: Rapine, that led
Millions of raging robbers in his train:
Unlistening, barbarous Force, to whom the sword

Is reason, honour, law: the foe of arts
By monsters follow'd, hideous to behold,
That claim á their place. Outrages mix'd with these
Another species of tyrannic* rule;
Unknown before, whose cankerous shackles seized
The envenom'd soul; a wilder Fury, she
Even o'er her Elder Sister† tyrannised;
Or, if perchance agreed, inflamed her rage.
Dire was her train, and loud: the sable band,
Thundering:—'Submit, ye Laity! ye profane!
Earth is the Lord's, and therefore ours; let kings
Allow the common claim, and half be theirs;
If not, behold, the sacred lightning flies!'
Scholastic Discord, with a hundred tongues,
For science uttering jangling words obscure,
Where frighted reason never yet could dwell:
Of peremptory feature, cleric Pride,
Whose reddening cheek no contradiction bears;
And holy Slander, his associate firm,
On whom the lying Spirit still descends:
Mother of tortures! persecuting Zeal;
High flashing in her hand the ready torch,
Or poniard bathed in unbelieving blood;
Hell's fiercest fiend! of saintly brow demure,
Assuming a celestial seraph's name,
While she, beneath the blasphemous pretence
Of pleasing Parent Heaven, the Source of Love!
Has wrought more horrors, more detested deeds,
Than all the rest combined. Led on by her,
And wild of head to work her fell designs,
Came idiot Superstition; round with ears
Innumerous strow'd, ten thousand monkish forms
With legends ply'd them, and with tenets, meant
To charm or scare the simple into slaves,
And poison reason; gross, she swallows all,

---

* Church power, or ecclesiastical tyranny.
† Civil Tyranny.

The most absurd believing ever most.
Broad o'er the whole her universal night,
The gloom still doubling, Ignorance diffused.
  "Nought to be seen, but visionary monks
To councils strolling, and embroiling creeds;
Banditti Saints,* disturbing distant lands;
And unknown nations, wandering for a home.
All lay reversed: the sacred arts of rule
Turn'd to flagitious leagues against mankind,
And arts of plunder more and more avow'd;
Pure plain Devotion† to a solemn farce;
To holy dotage Virtue, even to guile,
To murder, and a mockery of oaths;
Brave ancient Freedom to the rage of slaves,‡
Proud of their state, and fighting for their chains;
Dishonour'd Courage to the bravo's trade,§
To civil broil; and Glory to romance.
Thus human life, unhinged, to ruin reel'd,
And giddy Reason totter'd on her throne.
  "At last Heaven's best inexplicable scheme,
Disclosing, bade new brightening eras smile.
The high command gone forth, Arts in my train,
And azure-mantled Science, swift we spread
A sounding pinion.   Eager pity, mix'd
With indignation, urged her downward flight.
On Latium first we stoop'd, for doubtful life
That panted, sunk beneath unnumber'd woes.
Ah, poor Italia! what a bitter cup
Of vengeance hast thou drain'd?   Goths, Vandals, Huns,
Lombards, barbarians broke from every land,
How many a ruffian form hast thou beheld?
What horrid jargons heard, where rage alone
Was all thy frighted ear could comprehend?

---

* Crusades.
† The corruptions of the Church of Rome.
‡ Vassalage, whence the attachment of clans to their chief.
§ Duelling.

How frequent by the red inhuman hand,
Yet warm with brother's, husband's, father's blood,
Hast thou thy matrons and thy virgins seen
To violation dragg'd, and mingled death?
What conflagrations, earthquakes, ravage, floods,
Have turn'd thy cities into stony wilds;
And succourless, and bare, the poor remains
Of wretches forth to Nature's common cast?
Added to these the still continued waste
Of inbred foes that on thy vitals prey,*
And, double tyrants, seize the very soul.
Where hadst thou treasures for this rapine all?
These hungry myriads, that thy bowels tore,
Heap'd sack on sack, and buried in their rage
Wonders of art; whence this grey scene, a mine
Of more than gold becomes and orient gems,
Where Egypt, Greece, and Rome united glow.
  "Here Sculpture, Painting, Architecture, bent
From ancient models to restore their arts,
Remain'd.   A little trace we how they rose.
  "Amid the hoary ruins, Sculpture first,
Deep digging, from the cavern dark and damp,
Their grave for ages, bid her marble race
Spring to new light.   Joy sparkled in her eyes,
And old remembrance thrill'd in every thought,
As she the pleasing resurrection saw.
In leaning site, respiring from his toils,
The well-known Hero,† who deliver'd Greece,
His ample chest, all tempested with force,
Unconquerable rear'd.   She saw the head,
Breathing the hero, small, of Grecian size,
Scarce more extensive than the sinewy neck:
The spreading shoulders, muscular, and broad;
The whole a mass of swelling sinews, touch'd
Into harmonious shape; she saw, and joy'd.
The yellow hunter, Meleager, raised

---

* The Hierarchy.   † The Hercules of Farnese.

His beauteous front, and through the finish'd whole
Shows what ideas smiled of old in Greece.
Of raging aspect, rush'd impetuous forth
The Gladiator:* pitiless his look,
And each keen sinew braced, the storm of war,
Ruffling, o'er all his nervous body frowns.
The dying other† from the gloom she drew:
Supported on his shorten'd arm he leans,
Prone, agonising; with incumbent fate,
Heavy declines his head; yet dark beneath
The suffering feature sullen vengeance lours,
Shame, indignation, unaccomplish'd rage,
And still the cheated eye expects his fall.
All conquest-flush'd, from prostrate Python, came
The quiver'd god.‡   In graceful act he stands,
His arm extended with the slacken'd bow:
Light flows his easy robe, and fair displays
A manly soften'd form.   The bloom of gods
Seems youthful o'er the beardless cheek to wave:
His features yet heroic ardour warms;
And sweet subsiding to a native smile,
Mix'd with the joy elating conquest gives,
A scatter'd frown exalts his matchless air.
On Flora moved; her full proportion'd limbs
Rise through the mantle fluttering in the breeze.
The Queen of Love§ arose, as from the deep
She sprung in all the melting pomp of charms.
Bashful she bends, her well taught look aside
Turns in enchanting guise, where dubious mix
Vain conscious beauty, a dissembled sense
Of modest shame, and slippery looks of love.
The gazer grows enamour'd, and the stone,
As if exulting in its conquest, smiles.
So turn'd each limb, so swell'd with softening art,
That the deluded eye the marble doubts.

---

* Fighting Gladiator.   † Dying Gladiator.
   ‡ Apollo of Belvidere.   § Venus of Medici.

At last her utmost masterpiece* she found,
That Maro fired;† the miserable sire,
Wrapt with his sons in fate's severest grasp:
The serpents, twisting round, their stringent folds
Inextricable tie.   Such passion here,
Such agonies, such bitterness of pain,
Seem so to tremble through the tortured stone,
That the touch'd heart engrosses all the view.
Almost unmark'd the best proportions pass,
That ever Greece beheld; and, seen alone,
On the rapt eye the imperious passions seize:
The father's double pangs, both for himself
And sons convulsed; to heaven his rueful look,
Imploring aid, and half accusing, cast;
His fell despair with indignation mix'd,
As the strong curling monsters from his side
His full extended fury cannot tear.
More tender touch'd, with varied art, his sons
All the soft rage of younger passions show.
In a boy's helpless fate one sinks oppress'd;
While, yet unpierced, the frighted other tries
His foot to steal out of the horrid twine.
   "She bore no more, but straight from Gothic rust
Her chisel clear'd, and dust‡ and fragments drove
Impetuous round.   Successive as it went
From son to son, with more enlivening touch,
From the brute rock it call'd the breathing form;
Till, in a legislator's awful grace
Dress'd, Buonaroti bid a Moses§ rise,
And, looking love immense, a Saviour God.§

---

* The group of Laocoon and his two sons, destroyed by two serpents.

† See Æneid II. ver. 199–227.

‡ It is reported of Michael Angelo Buonaroti, the most cele-' brated master of modern sculpture, that he wrought with a kind of inspiration, or enthusiastical fury, which produced the effect here mentioned.

§ Esteemed the two finest pieces of modern sculpture.

"Of these observant, Painting felt the fire
Burn inward.　Then ecstatic she diffused
The canvas, seized the pallet, with quick hand
The colours brew'd; and on the void expanse
Her gay creation pour'd, her mimic world.
Poor was the manner of her eldest race,
Barren, and dry; just struggling from the taste,
That had for ages scared in cloisters dim
The superstitious herd: yet glorious then
Were deem'd their works; where undeveloped lay
The future wonders that enrich'd mankind,
And a new light and grace o'er Europe cast.
Arts gradual gather streams.　Enlarging this,
To each his portion of her various gifts
The Goddess dealt, to none indulging all;
No, not to Raphael.　At kind distance still
Perfection stands, like Happiness, to tempt
The eternal chase.　In elegant design,
Improving nature: in ideas fair,
Or great, extracted from the fine antique;
In attitude, expression, airs divine;
Her sons of Rome and Florence bore the prize.
To those of Venice she the magic art
Of colours melting into colours gave.
Theirs too it was by one embracing mass
Of light and shade, that settles round the whole,
Or varies tremulous from part to part,
O'er all a binding harmony to throw,
To raise the picture, and repose the sight.
The Lombard school,* succeeding, mingled both.
　"Meantime dread fanes, and palaces, around,
Rear'd the magnific front.　Music again
Her universal language of the heart
Renew'd; and, rising from the plaintive vale,
To the full concert spread, and solemn quire.
　"E'en bigots smiled; to their protection took

---

* The school of the Caracci.

Arts not their own, and from them borrow'd pomp:
For in a tyrant's garden these awhile
May bloom, though Freedom be their parent soil.
 "And now confess'd, with gently growing gleam
The morning shone, and westward stream'd its light.
The Muse awoke. Not sooner on the wing
Is the gay bird of dawn. Artless her voice,
Untaught and wild, yet warbling through the woods
Romantic lays. But as her northern course
She, with her tutor Science in my train,
Ardent pursued, her strains more noble grew:
While Reason drew the plan, the Heart inform'd
The moral page, and Fancy lent it grace.
 "Rome and her circling deserts cast behind,
I pass'd not idle to my great sojourn.
 "On Arno's* fertile plain, where the rich vine
Luxuriant o'er Etrurian mountains roves,
Safe in the lap reposed of private bliss,
I small republics† raised. Thrice happy they !
Had social Freedom bound their peace, and arts,
Instead of ruling Power, ne'er meant for them,
Employ'd their little cares, and saved their fate.
 " Beyond the rugged Apennines, that roll
Far through Italian bounds their wavy tops,
My path, too, I with public blessings strew'd:
Free states and cities, where the Lombard plain,
In spite of culture negligent and gross,
From her deep bosom pours unbidden joys,
And green o'er all the land a garden spreads.
 "The barren rocks themselves beneath my foot,
Relenting, bloom'd on the Ligurian shore.
Thick swarming people‡ there, like emmets, seized

---

* The river Arno runs through Florence.

† The republics of Florence, Pisa, Lucca, and Sienna.

‡ The Genoese territory is reckoned very populous; but the towns and villages for the most part lie hid among the Apennine rocks and mountains.

T

Amid surrounding cliffs, the scatter'd spots,
Which Nature left in her destroying rage;*
Made their own fields, nor sigh'd for other lands.
There, in white prospect from the rocky hill
Gradual descending to the shelter'd shore,
By me proud Genoa's marble turrets rose.
And while my genuine spirit warm'd her sons,
Beneath her Dorias, not unworthy, she   .
Vied for the trident of the narrow seas,
Ere Britain yet had open'd all the main.
    "Nor be the then triumphant state forgot;†
Where,‡ push'd from plunder'd earth, a remnant still
Inspired by me, through the dark ages kept
Of my old Roman flame some sparks alive:
The seeming god-built city! which my hand
Deep in the bosom fix'd of wondering seas.
Astonish'd mortals sail'd, with pleasing awe,
Around the sea-girt walls, by Neptune fenced,
And down the briny street; where on each hand,
Amazing seen amid unstable waves,
The splendid palace shines; and rising tides,
The green steps marking, murmur at the door.
To this fair Queen of Adria's stormy gulf,
The mart of nations! long, obedient seas
Roll'd all the treasure of the radiant East.
But now no more.   Than one great tyrant worse
(Whose shared oppression lightens, as diffused),
Each subject tearing, many tyrants rose.
The least the proudest.   Join'd in dark cabal,
They jealous, watchful, silent, and severe,

---

* According to Dr Burnet's system of the Deluge.

† Venice was the most flourishing city in Europe, with regard to trade, before the passage to the East Indies by the Cape of Good Hope and America was discovered.

‡ Those who fled to some marshes in the Adriatic Gulf, from the desolation spread over Italy by an irruption of the Huns, first founded there this famous city, about the beginning of the fifth century.

Cast o'er the whole indissoluble chains:
The softer shackles of luxurious ease
They likewise added, to secure their sway.
Thus Venice fainter shines; and Commerce thus,
Of toil impatient, flags the drooping sail.
Bursting, besides, his ancient bounds, he took
A larger circle:* found another seat,†
Opening a thousand ports, and charm'd with toil,
Whom nothing can dismay, far other sons.
    "The mountains then, clad with eternal snow,
Confess'd my power.   Deep as the rampant rocks,
By Nature thrown insuperable round,
I planted there a league of friendly states,‡
And bade plain Freedom their ambition be.
There in the vale, where rural plenty fills,
From lakes, and meads, and furrow'd fields, her horn,
Chief,§ where the Leman pure emits the Rhone,
Rare to be seen! unguilty cities rise,
Cities of brothers form'd: while equal life,
Accorded gracious with revolving power,
Maintains them free; and, in their happy streets,
Nor cruel deed, nor misery, is known.
For valour, faith, and innocence of life,
Renown'd, a rough laborious people, there,
Not only give the dreadful Alps to smile,
And press their culture on retiring snows;
But, to firm order train'd and patient war,
They likewise know, beyond the nerve remiss
Of mercenary force, how to defend
The tasteful little their hard toil has earn'd,
And the proud arm of Bourbon to defy.
    "E'en, cheer'd by me, their shaggy mountains charm,
More than or Gallic or Italian plains;
And sickening Fancy oft, when absent long,

---

* The Main Ocean.   † Great Britain.   ‡ Swiss Cantons.
    § Geneva, situated on Lacus Lemanus, a small state, but noble
example of the blessings of civil and religious liberty.

Pines* to behold their Alpine views again:
The hollow-winding stream: the vale, fair spread
Amid an amphitheatre of hills;
Whence, vapour-wing'd, the sudden tempest springs.
From steep to steep ascending, the gay train
Of fogs, thick-roll'd into romantic shapes;
The flitting cloud, against the summit dash'd;
And, by the sun illumined, pouring bright
A gemmy shower; hung o'er amazing rocks,
The mountain ash, and solemn sounding pine:
The snow-fed torrent, in white mazes tost,
Down to the clear ethereal lake below:
And high o'ertopping all the broken scene,
The mountain fading into sky; where shines
On winter, winter shivering, and whose top
Licks from their cloudy magazine the snows.
   "From these descending, as I waved my course
O'er vast Germania, the ferocious nurse
Of hardy men, and hearts affronting death,
I gave some favour'd cities† there to lift
A nobler brow, and through their swarming streets,
More busy, wealthy, cheerful, and alive,
In each contented face to look my soul.
   "Thence the loud Baltic passing, black with storm,
To wintry Scandinavia's utmost bound;
There I the manly race,‡ the parent hive
Of the mix'd kingdoms, form'd into a state
More regularly free.   By keener air
Their genius purged, and temper'd hard by frost,
Tempest, and toil their nerves, the sons of those
Whose only terror was a bloodless death,
They, wise and dauntless, still sustain my cause.

---

   * The Swiss, after having been long absent from their native
country, are seized with such a violent desire of seeing it again, as
affects them with a kind of languishing indisposition called the
Swiss sickness.
   † The Hans Towns.   ‡ The Swedes.

Yet there I fix'd not.   Turning to the south,
The whispering zephyrs sigh'd at my delay."
     Here, with the shifted vision, burst my joy:—
"O the dear prospect! O majestic view!
See Britain's empire! lo! the watery vast
Wide waves, diffusing the cerulean plain.
And now, methinks, like clouds at distance seen,
Emerging white from deeps of ether, dawn
My kindred cliffs; whence wafted in the gale,
Ineffable, a secret sweetness breathes.
Goddess, forgive!—My heart, surprised, o'erflows
With filial fondness for the land you bless."
As parents to a child complacent deign
Approvance, the celestial brightness smiled;
Then thus.—"As o'er the wave resounding deep,
To my near reign, the happy isle, I steer'd
With easy wing; behold! from surge to surge,
Stalk'd the tremendous Genius of the Deep.
Around him clouds, in mingled tempest, hung;
Thick flashing meteors crown'd his starry head;
And ready thunder redden'd in his hand,
Or from it stream'd, compress'd, the gloomy cloud.
Where'er he look'd, the trembling waves recoil'd.
He needs but strike the conscious flood, and shook
From shore to shore, in agitation dire,
It works his dreadful will.   To me his voice
(Like that hoarse blast that round the cavern howls,
Mix'd with the murmurs of the falling main),
Address'd, began—'By Fate commission'd, go,
My Sister-Goddess, now, to yon blessed isle,
Henceforth the partner of my rough domain.
All my dread walks to Britons open lie.
Those that refulgent, or with rosy morn,
Or yellow evening, flame; those that, profuse,
Drunk by equator suns, severely shine;
Or those that, to the poles approaching, rise
In billows rolling into Alps of ice.
E'en, yet untouch'd by daring keel, be theirs

The vast Pacific: that on other worlds,
Their future conquest, rolls resounding tides.
Long I maintain'd inviolate my reign;
Nor Alexanders me, nor Cæsars braved.
Still, in the crook of shore, the coward sail
Till now low crept; and peddling commerce ply'd
Between near joining lands.   For Britons, chief,
It was reserved, with star-directed prow,
To dare the middle deep, and drive assured
To distant nations through the pathless main.
Chief, for their fearless hearts the glory waits,
Long months from land, while the black stormy night
Around them rages, on the groaning mast
With unshook knee to know their giddy way;
To sing, unquell'd, amid the lashing wave;
To laugh at danger.   Theirs the triumph be,
By deep Invention's keen pervading eye,
The heart of Courage, and the hand of Toil,
Each conquer'd ocean staining with their blood,
Instead of treasure robb'd by ruffian war,
Round social earth to circle fair exchange,
And bind the nations in a golden chain.
To these I honour'd stoop.   Rushing to light
A race of men behold! whose daring deeds
Will in renown exalt my nameless plains
O'er those of fabling earth, as hers to mine
In terror yield.   Nay, could my savage heart
Such glories check, their unsubmitting soul
Would all my fury brave, my tempest climb,
And might in spite of me my kingdom force.'
Here, waiting no reply, the shadowy power
Eased the dark sky, and to the deeps return'd:
While the loud thunder rattling from his hand,
Auspicious, shook opponent Gallia's shore.
   "Of this encounter glad, my way to land
I quick pursued, that from the smiling sea
Received me joyous.   Loud acclaims were heard;
And music, more than mortal, warbling, fill'd

With pleased astonishment the labouring hind,
Who for awhile the unfinish'd furrow left,
And let the listening steer forget his toil.
Unseen by grosser eye, Britannia breathed,
And her aerial train, these sounds of joy.
For of old time, since first the rushing flood,
Urged by almighty power, this favour'd isle
Turn'd flashing from the continent aside,
Indented shore to shore responsive still,
Its guardian she—the Goddess, whose staid eye
Beams the dark azure of the doubtful dawn.
Her tresses, like a flood of soften'd light
Through clouds embrown'd, in waving circles play.
Warm on her cheek sits Beauty's brightest rose,
Of high demeanour, stately, shedding grace
With every motion.   Full her rising chest;
And new ideas, from her finish'd shape,
Charm'd Sculpture taking might improve her art.
Such the fair Guardian of an isle that boasts,
Profuse as vernal blooms, the fairest dames.
High shining on the promontory's brow,
Awaiting me, she stood; with hope inflamed,
By my mix'd spirit burning in her sons,
To firm, to polish, and exalt the state.
   " The native Genii, round her, radiant smiled.
Courage, of soft deportment, aspect calm,
Unboastful, suffering long, and, till provoked,
As mild and harmless as the sporting child;
But, on just reason, once his fury roused,
No lion springs more eager to his prey:
Blood is a pastime; and his heart, elate,
Knows no depressing fear.   That Virtue known
By the relenting look, whose equal heart
For others feels, as for another self:
Of various name, as various objects wake,
Warm into action, the kind sense within:
Whether the blameless poor, the nobly maim'd,
The lost to reason, the declined in life,

The helpless young that kiss no mother's hand,
And the grey second infancy of age,
She gives in public families to live,
A sight to gladden Heaven! whither she stands
Fair beckoning at the hospitable gate,
And bids the stranger take repose and joy:
Whether, to solace honest labour, she
Rejoices those that make the land rejoice:
Or whether to Philosophy and Arts
(At once the basis and the finish'd pride
Of government and life), she spreads her hand;
Nor knows her gift profuse, nor seems to know,
Doubling her bounty, that she gives at all.
Justice to these her awful presence join'd,
The mother of the state! no low revenge,
No turbid passions in her breast ferment:
Tender, serene, compassionate of vice,
As the last wo that can afflict mankind,
She punishment awards; yet of the good
More piteous still, and of the suffering whole,
Awards it firm.   So fair her just decree,
That, in his judging peers, each on himself
Pronounces his own doom.   O happy land!
Where reigns alone this justice of the free!
'Mid the bright group Sincerity his front,
Diffusive, rear'd; his pure untroubled eye
The fount of truth.   The thoughtful Power, apart,
Now, pensive, cast on earth his fix'd regard,
Now, touch'd celestial, launch'd it on the sky.
The Genius he whence Britain shines supreme,
The land of light, and rectitude of mind.
He, too, the fire of fancy feeds intense,
With all the train of passions thence derived:
Not kindling quick, a noisy transient blaze,
But gradual, silent, lasting, and profound.
Near him Retirement, pointing to the shade,
And Independence stood: the generous pair,
That simple life, the quiet-whispering grove.

And the still raptures of the free-born soul,
To cates prefer by Virtue bought, not earn'd,
Proudly prefer them to the servile pomp,
And to the heart-embitter'd joys of slaves.
Or should the latter, to the public scene
Demanded, quit his sylvan friend awhile;
Nought can his firmness shake, nothing seduce
His zeal, still active for the commonweal;
Nor stormy tyrants, nor corruption's tools,
Foul ministers, dark-working by the force
Of secret-sapping gold. All their vile arts,
Their shameful honours, their perfidious gifts,
He greatly scorns; and, if he must betray
His plunder'd country, or his power resign,
A moment's parley were eternal shame:
Illustrious into private life again,
From dirty levees he unstain'd ascends,
And firm in senates stands the patriot's ground,
Or draws new vigour in the peaceful shade.
Aloof the bashful virtue hover'd coy,
Proving by sweet distrust distrusted worth.
Rough Labour closed the train: and in his hand,
Rude, callous, sinew-swell'd, and black with toil,
Came manly Indignation. Sour he seems,
And more than seems, by lawless pride assail'd;
Yet kind at heart, and just, and generous, there
No vengeance lurks, no pale insidious gall:
Even in the very luxury of rage,
He softening can forgive a gallant foe;
The nerve, support, and glory of the land!
Nor be Religion, rational and free,
Here pass'd in silence; whose enraptured eye
Sees Heaven with earth connected, human things
Link'd to divine: who not from servile fear,
By rights for some weak tyrant incense fit,
The God of Love adores, but from a heart
Effusing gladness, into pleasing awe
That now astonish'd swells, now in a calm

Of fearless confidence that smiles serene;
That lives devotion, one continual hymn,
And then most grateful, when Heaven's bounty most
Is right enjoy'd.   This ever cheerful Power
O'er the raised circle ray'd superior day.
    "I joy'd to join the Virtues, whence my reign
O'er Albion was to rise.   Each cheering each,
And, like the circling planets from the sun,
All borrowing beams from me, a heighten'd zeal
Impatient fired us to commence our toils,
Or pleasures rather.   Long the pungent time
Pass'd not in mutual hails; but, through the land
Darting our light, we shone the fogs away.
    "The Virtues conquer with a single look.
Such grace, such beauty, such victorious light,
Live in their presence, stream in every glance
That the soul won, enamour'd, and refined,
Grows their own image, pure ethereal flame.
Hence the foul Demons, that oppose our reign,
Would still from us deluded mortals wrap:
Or in gross shades they drown the visual ray,
Or by the fogs of prejudice, where mix,
Falsehood and truth confounded, foil the sense
With vain refracted images of bliss.
But chief around the court of flatter'd kings
They roll the dusky rampart, wall o'er wall
Of darkest pile, and with their thickest shade
Secure the throne.   No savage Alp, the den
Of wolves, and bears, and monstrous things obscene,
That vex the swain, and waste the country round,
Protected lies beneath a deeper cloud.
Yet there we sometimes send a searching ray,
As, at the sacred opening of the morn,
The prowling race retire; so, pierced severe,
Before our potent blaze these Demons fly,
And all their works dissolve——the whisper'd tale,
That, like the fabling Nile, no fountain knows.
Fair-faced Deceit, whose wily conscious eye

Ne'er looks direct. The tongue that licks the dust,
But, when it safely dares, as prompt to sting:
Smooth crocodile Destruction, whose fell tears
Ensnare. The Janus-face of courtly Pride;
One to superiors heaves submissive eyes,
On hapless worth the other scowls disdain;
Cheeks that for some weak tenderness, alone,
Some virtuous slip, can wear a blush. The laugh
Profane, when midnight bowls disclose the heart,
At starving Virtue, and at Virtue's fools.
Determined to be broke, the plighted faith;
Nay more, the godless oath, that knows no ties.
Soft-buzzing Slander; silky moths, that eat
An honest name. The harpy hand, and maw,
Of avaricious Luxury; who makes
The throne his shelter, venal laws his fort,
And, his service, who betrays his king.
  "Now turn your view, and mark from Celtic* night
To present grandeur how my Britain rose.
  "Bold were those Britons, who, the careless sons
Of Nature, roam'd the forest-bounds, at once
Their verdant city, high-embowering fane,
And the gay circle of their woodland wars:
For by the Druid† taught, that death but shifts
The vital scene, they that prime fear despised;
And, prone to rush on steel, disdain'd to spare
An ill-saved life that must again return.
Erect from Nature's hand, by tyrant force,
And still more tyrant custom, unsubdued,
Man knows no master save creating Heaven,
Or such as choice and common good ordain.
This general sense with which the nations I
Promiscuous fire, in Britons burn'd intense,
Of future times prophetic. Witness, Rome,

---

* Great Britain was peopled by the Celtæ or Gauls.
  † The Druids, among the ancient Gauls and Britons, had the care and direction of all religious matters.

Who saw'st thy Cæsar, from the naked land,
Whose only fort was British hearts, repell'd,
To seek Pharsalian wreaths. Witness, the toil,
The blood of ages, bootless to secure,
Beneath an empire's* yoke, a stubborn isle,
Disputed hard, and never quite subdued.
The North† remain'd untouch'd, where those who scorn'd
To stoop retired; and, to their keen effort
Yielding at last, recoil'd the Roman power.
In vain, unable to sustain the shock,
From sea to sea desponding legions raised
The wall immense,‡ and yet, on summer's eve,
While sport his lambkins round, the shepherd's gaze.
Continual o'er it burst the northern storm,§
As often check'd, receded; threatening hoarse
A swift return. But the devouring flood
No more endured control, when, to support
The last remains of empire,‖ was recall'd
The weary Roman, and the Briton lay
Unnerved, exhausted, spiritless, and sunk.
Great proof! how men enfeeble into slaves.
The sword¶ behind him flash'd; before him roar'd,
Deaf to his woes, the deep. Forlorn, around

---

* The Roman Empire.

† Caledonia, inhabited by the Scots and Picts; whither a great many Britons who would not submit to the Romans retired.

‡ The Wall of Severus, built upon Adrian's rampart, which ran for eighty miles quite across the country, from the mouth of the Tyne to Solway Frith.

§ Irruptions of the Scots and Picts.

‖ The Roman Empire being miserably torn by the northern nations, Britain was for ever abandoned by the Romans in the year 426 or 427.

¶ The Britons, applying to Ætius the Roman general for assistance, thus expressed their miserable condition:—" We know not which way to turn us. The Barbarians drive us to sea, and the sea forces us back to the Barbarians; between which we have only the choice of two deaths—either to be swallowed up by the waves, or butchered by the sword.

He roll'd his eye, not sparkling ardent flame,
As when Caractacus* to battle led
Silurian swains, and Boadicea† taught
Her raging troops the miseries of slaves.
  "Then (sad relief!) from the bleak coast, that hears
The German Ocean roar, deep-blooming, strong,
And yellow-hair'd, the blue-eyed Saxon came.
He came implored, but came with other aim
Than to protect: for conquest and defence
Suffices the same arm. With the fierce race
Pour'd in a fresh invigorating stream,
Blood, where unquell'd a mighty spirit glow'd.
Rash war, and perilous battle, their delight;
And immature, and red with glorious wounds,
Unpeaceful death their choice: deriving thence
A right to feast, and drain immortal bowls,
In Odin's hall;‡ whose blazing roof resounds
The genial uproar of those shades, who fall

---

  * King of the Silures, famous for his great exploits, and accounted the best general Great Britain had ever produced. The Silures were esteemed the bravest and most powerful of all the Britons: they inhabited Herefordshire, Radnorshire, Brecknockshire, Monmouthshire, and Glamorganshire.
  † Queen of the Iceni.
  ‡ It is certain that an opinion was fixed and general among them (the Goths), that death was but the entrance into another life: that all men who lived lazy and inactive lives, and died natural deaths, by sickness or by age, went into vast caves under ground, all dark and miry, full of noisome creatures usual to such places, and there for ever grovelled in endless stench and misery. On the contrary, all who gave themselves to warlike actions and enterprises, to the conquest of their neighbours and the slaughter of their enemies, and died in battle, or of violent deaths upon bold adventures or resolutions, went immediately to the vast hall or palace of Odin, their god of war, who eternally kept open house for all such guests, where they were entertained at infinite tables, in perpetual feasts and mirth, carousing in bowls made of the skulls of their enemies they had slain; according to the number of whom, every one in these mansions of pleasure was the most honoured and best entertained.—*Sir William Temple's Essay on Heroic Virtue.*

In desperate fight, or by some brave attempt;
And though more polish'd times the martial creed
Disown, yet still the fearless habit lives.
Nor were the surly gifts of war their all.
Wisdom was likewise theirs, indulgent laws,
The calm gradations of art-nursing peace,
And matchless orders, the deep basis still
On which ascends my British reign.   Untamed
To the refining subtleties of slaves,
They brought a happy government along;
Form'd by that freedom which, with secret voice,
Impartial Nature teaches all her sons,
And which of old through the whole Scythian mass
I strong inspired.   Monarchical their state,
But prudently confined, and mingled wise
Of each harmonious power: only, too much,
Imperious war into their rule infused,
Prevail'd their General-King, and Chieftain-Thanes.
   "In many a field, by civil fury stain'd,
Bled the discordant Heptarchy;* and long
(Educing good from ill) the battle groan'd;
Ere, blood-cemented, Anglo-Saxon saw
Egbert † and peace on one united throne.
   "No sooner dawn'd the fair disclosing calm
Of brighter days, when lo! the North anew,
With stormy nations black, on England pour'd
Woes the severest e'er a people felt.
The Danish Raven,‡ lured by annual prey,

---

* The seven kingdoms of the Anglo-Saxons, considered as being united into one common government, under a general-in-chief or monarch, and by the means of an assembly general, or witte-nagemot.

† Egbert, king of Wessex, who, after having reduced all the other kingdoms of the Heptarchy under his dominion, was the first King of England.

‡ A famous Danish standard was called Reafen, or Raven. The Danes imagined that, before a battle, the Raven wrought upon this standard clapped its wings or hung down its head, in token of victory or defeat.

Hung o'er the land incessant.   Fleet on fleet
Of barbarous pirates unremitting tore
The miserable coast.   Before them stalk'd,
Far seen, the Demon of devouring Flame;
Rapine, and Murder, all with blood besmear'd,
Without or ear, or eye, or feeling heart;
While close behind them march'd the sallow Power
Of desolating Famine, who delights
In grass-grown cities, and in desert fields;
And purple-spotted Pestilence, by whom
E'en Friendship scared, in sickening horror sinks
Each social sense and tenderness of life.
Fixing at last, the sanguinary race
Spread, from the Humber's loud-resounding shore,
To where the Thames devolves his gentle maze,
And with superior arm the Saxon awed.
But Superstition first, and monkish dreams,
And monk-directed cloister-seeking kings,
Had eat away his vigour, eat away
His edge of Courage, and depress'd the soul
Of conquering Freedom, which he once respired.
Thus cruel ages pass'd; and rare appear'd
White-mantled Peace, exulting o'er the vale,
As when, with Alfred,* from the wilds she came
To policed cities and protected plains.
Thus by degrees the Saxon empire sunk,
Then set entire in Hastings't bloody field.
"Compendious war! (on Britain's glory bent,
So fate ordain'd) in that decisive day,
The haughty Norman seized at once an isle,
For which, through many a century, in vain,

---

* Alfred the Great, renowned in war, and no less famous in
peace for his many excellent institutions, particularly that of
juries.

† The battle of Hastings, in which Harold II., the last of the
Saxon kings, was slain, and William the Conqueror made himself master of England.

The Roman, Saxon, Dane, had toil'd and bled.
Of Gothic nations this the final burst;
And, mix'd the genius of these people all,
Their virtues mix'd in one exalted stream,
Here the rich tide of English blood grew full.
  "Awhile my Spirit slept; the land awhile,
Affrighted, droop'd beneath despotic rage.
Instead of Edward's* equal gentle laws,
The furious victor's partial will prevail'd.
All prostrate lay; and, in the secret shade,
Deep stung but fearful Indignation gnash'd
His teeth. Of freedom, property despoil'd,
And of their bulwark, arms; with castles crush'd,
With ruffians quarter'd o'er the bridled land;
The shivering wretches, at the curfew† sound,
Dejected shrunk into their sordid beds,
And, through the mournful gloom of ancient times,
Mused sad, or dreamt of better. E'en to feed
A tyrant's idle sport, the peasant starved:
To the wild herd, the pasture of the tame,
The cheerful hamlet, spiry town, was given,
And the brown forest‡ roughen'd wide around.
  "But this so dead, so vile submission, long
Endured not. Gathering force, my gradual flame
Shook off the mountain of tyrannic sway.
Unused to bend, impatient of control,
Tyrants themselves the common tyrant check'd.
The Church, by kings intractable and fierce,

---

* Edward III., the Confessor, who reduced the West Saxon, Mercian, and Danish laws into one body; which from that time became common to all England, under the name of "The Laws of Edward."

† The Curfew-bell (from the French Couvrefeu), which was rung every night at eight of the clock, to warn the English to put out their fires and candles, under the penalty of a severe fine.

‡ The New Forest in Hampshire; to make which, the country for above thirty miles in compass was laid waste.

Denied her portion of the plunder'd state,
Or tempted, by the timorous and weak,
To gain new ground, first taught their rapine law.
The Barons next a nobler league began,
Both those of English and of Norman race,
In one fraternal nation blended now,
The nation of the Free! press'd by a band*
Of Patriots, ardent as the summer's noon
That looks delighted on, the tyrant see!
Mark! how with feign'd alacrity he bears
His strong reluctance down, his dark revenge,
And gives the Charter, by which life indeed
Becomes of price, a glory to be man.
  "Through this, and through succeeding reigns affirm'd
These long-contested rights, the wholesome winds
Of Opposition† hence began to blow,
And often since have lent the country life.
Before their breath Corruption's insect-blights,
The darkening clouds of evil counsel fly;
Or should they sounding swell, a putrid court,
A pestilential ministry, they purge,
And ventilated states renew their bloom.
  "Though with the temper'd Monarchy here mix'd
Aristocratic sway, the People still,
Flatter'd by this or that, as interest lean'd,
No full protection knew. For me reserved,
And for my Commons, was that glorious turn.
They crown'd my first attempt, in senates‡ rose
The fort of Freedom! Slow till then, alone,
Had work'd that general liberty, that soul

---

* On the 5th of June, 1215, King John, met by the Barons on Runnemede, signed the Great Charter of Liberties, or Magna Charta.

† The league formed by the Barons, during the reign of John, in the year 1213, was the first confederacy made in England in defence of the nation's interests against the king.

‡ The commons are generally thought to have been first represented in Parliament towards the end of Henry the Third's

U

Which generous nature breathes, and which, when left
By me to bondage, was corrupted Rome,
I through the northern nations wide diffused.
Hence many a people, fierce with freedom, rush'd
From the rude iron regions of the North,
To Libyan deserts swarm protruding swarm,
And pour'd new spirit through a slavish world.
Yet, o'er these Gothic states, the King and Chiefs
Retain'd the high prerogative of war,
And with enormous property engross'd
The mingled power.   But on Britannia's shore
Now present, I to raise my reign began
By raising the Democracy, the third
And broadest bulwark of the guarded state.
Then was the full, the perfect plan disclosed
Of Britain's matchless constitution, mix'd
Of mutual checking and supporting powers,
King, Lords, and Commons; nor the name of free
Deserving, while the vassal-many droop'd:
For since the moment of the whole they form,
So, as depress'd or raised, the balance they
Of public welfare and of glory cast.
Mark from this period the continual proof.
    " When Kings of narrow genius, minion-rid,
Neglecting faithful worth for fawning slaves;
Proudly regardless of their people's plaints,
And poorly passive of insulting foes;
Double, not prudent, obstinate, not firm,
Their mercy fear, necessity their faith;
Instead of generous fire, presumptuous, hot,

reign.   To a parliament called in the year 1264, each county was
ordered to send four knights, as representatives of their respective shires: and to a parliament called in the year following, each
county was ordered to send, as their representatives, two knights,
and each city and borough as many citizens and burgesses.   Till
then, history makes no mention of them; whence a very strong
argument may be drawn, to fix the original of the House of
Commons to that era.

Rash to resolve, and slothful to perform:
Tyrants at once and slaves, imperious, mean,
To want rapacious joining shameful waste;
By counsels weak and wicked, easy roused
To paltry schemes of absolute command,
To seek their splendour in their sure disgrace,
And in a broken ruin'd people wealth:
When such o'ercast the state, no bond of love,
No heart, no soul, no unity, no nerve,
Combined the loose disjointed public, lost
To fame abroad, to happiness at home.
    "But when an Edward,* and a Henry† breathed
Through the charm'd whole one all-exerting soul:
Drawn sympathetic from his dark retreat,
When wide-attracted merit round them glow'd:
Then counsels just, extensive, generous, firm,
Amid the maze of state, determined kept
Some ruling point in view: when on the stock
Of public good and glory grafted, spread
Their palms, their laurels; or if thence they stray'd,
Swift to return, and patient of restraint:
When regal state, pre-eminence of place,
They scorn'd to deem pre-eminence of ease,
To be luxurious drones, that only rob
The busy hive: as in distinction, power,
Indulgence, honour, and advantage, first;
When they too claim'd in virtue, danger, toil,
Superior rank; with equal hand, prepared
To guard the subject, and to quell the foe:
When such with me their vital influence shed,
No mutter'd grievance, hopeless sigh, was heard;
No foul distrust through wary senates ran,
Confined their bounty, and their ardour quench'd:
On aid, unquestion'd liberal aid was given:
Safe in their conduct, by their valour fired,
Fond where they led victorious armies rush'd;

---

* Edward III.   † Henry V.

And Cressy, Poitiers, Agincourt* proclaim
What kings supported by almighty Love,
And people fired with Liberty, can do.

"Be veil'd the savage reigns,† when kindred rage
The numerous once Plantagenets devour'd,
A race to vengeance vow'd! and when, oppress'd
By private feuds, almost extinguish'd lay
My quivering flame.   But, in the next, behold!
A cautious tyrant‡ lend it oil anew.

"Proud, dark, suspicious, brooding o'er his gold,
As how to fix his throne he jealous cast
His crafty views around; pierced with a ray,
Which on his timid mind I darted full,
He mark'd the Barons of excessive sway,
At pleasure making and unmaking kings;§
And hence, to crush these petty tyrants, plann'd
A law,|| that let them, by the silent waste
Of luxury, their landed wealth diffuse,
And with that wealth their implicated power.
By soft degrees a mighty change ensued,
E'en working to this day.   With streams, de luced
From these diminish'd floods, the country smiled.
As when impetuous from the snow-heap'd Alps,
To vernal suns relenting, pours the Rhine;
While, undivided, oft, with wasteful sweep,
He foams along; but through Batavian meads,
Branch'd into fair canals, indulgent flows;
Waters a thousand fields; and culture, trade,
Towns, meadows, gliding ships, and villas mix'd,
A rich, a wondrous landscape rises round.

---

* The famous battles, gained by the English over the French.

† During the civil wars betwixt the families of York and Lancaster.

‡ Henry VII.

§ The famous Earl of Warwick, during the reigns of Henry VI. and Edward IV., was called the "King Maker."

| Permitting the Barons to alienate their lands.

His furious son* the soul-enslaving chain,†
Which many a doating venerable age
Had link by link strong twisted round the land,
Shook off. No longer could be borne a power,
From Heaven pretended, to deceive, to void
Each solemn tie, to plunder without bounds,
To curb the generous soul, to fool mankind;
And, wild at last, to plunge into a sea
Of blood and horror. The returning light,
That first through Wickliff‡ streak'd the priestly gloom,
Now burst in open day. Bared to the blaze,
Forth from the haunts of Superstition§ crawl'd
Her motley sons, fantastic figures all;
And, wide dispersed, their useless fetid wealth
In graceful labour bloom'd, and fruits of peace.
"Trade, join'd to these, on every sea display'd
A daring canvas, pour'd with every tide
A golden flood. From other worlds‖ were roll'd
The guilty glittering stores, whose fatal charms,
By the plain Indian happily despised,
Yet work'd his wo; and to the blissful groves,
Where Nature lived herself among her sons,
And Innocence and Joy for ever dwelt,
Drew rage unknown to pagan climes before
The worst the zeal-inflamed barbarian drew.
Be no such horrid commerce, Britain, thine!
But want for want, with mutual aid, supply.
"The Commons thus enrich'd, and powerful grown,
Against the Barons weigh'd. Eliza then,

---

* Henry VIII.   † Of papal dominion.
‡ John Wickliff, doctor of divinity, who, towards the close of the fourteenth century, published doctrines very contrary to those of the Church of Rome, and particularly denying the papal authority. His followers grew very numerous, and were called Lollards.
§ Suppression of monasteries.
‖ The Spanish West Indies.

Amid these doubtful motions, steady, gave
The beam to fix.   She! like the secret Eye,
That never closes on a guarded world,
So sought, so mark'd, so seized the public good,
That self-supported, without one ally,
She awed her inward, quell'd her circling foes.
Inspired by me, beneath her sheltering arm,
In spite of raging universal sway,†
And raging seas repress'd, the Belgic states,
My bulwark on the Continent, arose.
Matchless in all the spirit of her days!
With confidence, unbounded, fearless love
Elate, her fervent people waited gay,
Cheerful demanded the long threaten'd fleet,*
And dash'd the pride of Spain around their isle.
Nor ceased the British thunder here to rage:
The deep, reclaim'd, obey'd its awful call;
In fire and smoke Iberian ports involved,
The trembling foe even to the centre shook
Of their new conquer'd world, and, skulking, stole
By veering winds their Indian treasure home.
Meantime, Peace, Plenty, Justice, Science, Arts,
With softer laurels crown'd her happy reign.
As yet uncircumscribed the regal power,
And wild and vague prerogative remain'd;
A wide voracious gulf, where swallow'd oft
The helpless subject lay.   This to reduce
To the just limit, was my great effort.
   "By means that evil seem to narrow man,
Superior Beings work their mystic will:
From storm and trouble thus a settled calm,
At last, effulgent, o'er Britannia smiled.
   "The gathering tempest Heaven-commission'd came,

---

† The dominion of the house of Austria.
 * The Spanish Armada.   Rapin says, that after proper measures had been taken, the enemy was expected with uncommon
alacrity.

Came in the prince,* who, drunk with flattery, dreamt
His vain pacific counsels ruled the world;
Though scorn'd abroad, bewilder'd in a maze
Of fruitless treaties; while at home enslaved,
And by a worthless crew insatiate drain'd,
He lost his people's confidence and love:
Irreparable loss ! whence crowns become
An anxious burden.   Years inglorious pass'd:
Triumphant Spain the vengeful draught enjoy'd:
Abandon'd Frederick† pined, and Raleigh bled.
But nothing that to these internal broils,
That rancour, he began ; while lawless sway
He, with his slavish Doctors, tried to rear
On metaphysic,‡ on enchanted ground,
And all the mazy quibbles of the schools:
As if for one, and sometimes for the worst,
Heaven had mankind in vengeance only made.
Vain the pretence ! not so the dire effect,
The fierce, the foolish discord§ thence derived,
That tears the country still, by party rage
And ministerial clamour kept alive.
In action weak, and for the wordy war
Best fitted, faint this prince pursued his claim:
Content to teach the subject herd, how great,
How sacred he ! how despicable they !
   "But his unyielding son‖ these doctrines drank,
With all a bigot's rage (who never damps
By reasoning his fire); and what they taught,
Warm, and tenacious, into practice push'd.

---

* James I.

† Elector Palatine, and who had been chosen King of
Bohemia, but was stripped of all his dominions and dignities by
the Emperor Ferdinand, while James the First, his father-in-
law, being amused from time to time, endeavoured to mediate a
peace.

‡ The monstrous and till then unheard-of doctrines of divine
indefeasible hereditary right, passive obedience, &c.

§ The parties of Whig and Tory.   ‖ Charles I.

Senates, in vain, their kind restraint applied:
The more they struggled to support the laws,
His justice-dreading ministers the more
Drove him beyond their bounds. Tired with the check
Of faithful Love, and with the flattery pleased
Of false designing Guilt, the fountain* he
Of Public Wisdom and of Justice shut.
Wide mourn'd the land.   Straight to the voted aid
Free, cordial, large, of never-failing source,
The illegal imposition follow'd harsh,
With execration given, or ruthless squeezed
From an insulted people, by a band
Of the worst ruffians, those of tyrant power.
Oppression walk'd at large, and pour'd abroad
Her unrelenting train: informers, spies,
Bloodhounds, that sturdy Freedom to the grove
Pursue; projectors of aggrieving schemes,
Commerce to load for unprotected seas,†
To sell the starving many to the few,‡
And drain a thousand ways the exhausted land,
E'en from that place, whence healing Peace should flow,
And Gospel truth, inhuman bigots shed
Their poison§ round; and on the venal bench,
Instead of justice, party held the scale,
And violence the sword.   Afflicted years,
Too patient, felt at last their vengeance full.
  "'Mid the low murmurs of submissive fear
And mingled rage, my Hampden raised his voice,
And to the laws appeal'd; the laws no more
In judgment sat, behoved some other ear.
When instant from the keen resentive North,
By long oppression, by religion roused,
The guardian army came.   Beneath its wing

---

  * Parliaments.   † Ship-money.   ‡ Monopolies.
  § The raging High-Church sermons of these times, inspiring a
spirit of slavish submission to the court, and of bitter persecution
against those whom they call Church and State Puritans.

Was call'd, though meant to furnish hostile aid,
The more than Roman senate. There a flame
Broke out, that clear'd, consumed, renew'd the land.
In deep emotion hurl'd, nor Greece, nor Rome,
Indignant bursting from a tyrant's chain,
While, full of me, each agitated soul
Strung every nerve and flamed in every eye,
Had e'er beheld such light and heat combined
Such heads and hearts! such dreadful zeal, led on
By calm majestic wisdom, taught its course
What nuisance to devour; such wisdom fired
With unabating zeal, and aim'd sincere
To clear the weedy state, restore the laws,
And for the future to secure their sway.
—"This then the purpose of my mildest sons.
But man is blind. A nation once inflamed
(Chief, should the breath of factious fury blow,
With the wild rage of mad enthusiast swell'd)
Not easy cools again. From breast to breast,
From eye to eye, the kindling passions mix
In heighten'd blaze; and, ever wise and just,
High Heaven to gracious ends directs the storm.
Thus in one conflagration Britain, wrapt,
And by Confusion's lawless sons despoil'd,
King, Lords, and Commons, thundering to the ground,
Successive, rush'd—Lo! from their ashes rose,
Gay beaming radiant youth, the Phœnix State.*
  "The grievous yoke of vassalage, the yoke
Of private life, lay by those flames dissolved;
And, from the wasteful, the luxurious king,†
Was purchased‡ that which taught the young to bend.
Stronger restored, the Commons tax'd the whole,
And built on that eternal rock their power.
The Crown, of its hereditary wealth
Despoil'd, on senates more dependent grew,

---

* At the Restoration.   † Charles II.   ‡ Court of Wards.

And they more frequent, more assured.   Yet lived,
And in full vigour spread that bitter root,
The passive doctrines, by their patrons first,
Opposed ferocious, when they touch themselves.
  "This wild delusive cant; the rash cabal
Of hungry courtiers, ravenous for prey;
The bigot, restless in a double chain
To bind anew the land; the constant need
Of finding faithless means, of shifting forms,
And flattering senates, to supply his waste;
These tore some moments from the careless prince,
And in his breast awaked the kindred plan.
By dangerous softness long he mined his way;
By subtle arts, dissimulation deep;
By sharing what corruption shower'd, profuse;
By breathing wide the gay licentious plague,
And pleasing manners, fitted to deceive.
  "At last subsided the delirious joy,
On whose high billow, from the saintly reign,
The nation drove too far.   A pension'd king,
Against his country bribed by Gallic gold,
The Port* pernicious sold, the Scylla since
And fell Charybdis of the British seas;
Freedom attack'd abroad,† with surer blow
To cut it off at home; the saviour league‡
Of Europe broke; the progress e'en advanced
Of universal sway,§ which to reduce,
Such seas of blood and treasure Britain cost;
The millions, by a generous people given,
Or squander'd vile, or to corrupt, disgrace,
And awe the land with forces‖ not their own
Employ'd; the darling church herself betray'd;
All these, broad glaring, oped the general eye,

---

* Dunkirk.

† The war in conjunction with France, against the Dutch.

‡ The Triple Alliance.   § Under Louis XIV.

‖ A standing army, raised without the consent of Parliament.

And waked my spirit, the resisting soul.
  " Mild was, at first, and half-ashamed the check
Of senates, shook from the fantastic dream
Of absolute submission, tenets vile!
Which slaves would blush to own, and which reduced
To practice, always honest nature shock.
Not e'en the mask removed, and the fierce front
Of tyranny disclosed; nor trampled laws;
Nor seized each badge of freedom* through the land:
Nor Sidney bleeding for the unpublish'd page;
Nor on the bench avow'd corruption placed,
And murderous rage itself, in Jefferies' form;†
Nor endless acts of arbitrary power,
Cruel and false, could raise the public arm.
Distrustful, scatter'd, of combining chiefs
Devoid, and dreading blind rapacious war,
The patient public turns not, till impell'd
To the near verge of ruin. Hence I roused
The bigot king,‡ and hurried fated on
His measures immature. But chief his zeal,
Out-flaming Rome herself, portentous scared
The troubled nation: Mary's horrid days
To fancy bleeding rose, and the dire glare
Of Smithfield lighten'd in its eyes anew.
Yet silence reign'd. Each on another scowl'd
Rueful amazement, pressing down his rage:
As, mustering vengeance, the deep thunder frowns,
Awfully still, waiting the high command
To spring. Straight from his country Europe saved,
To save Britannia, lo! my darling son,
Than hero more! the patriot of mankind!
Immortal Nassau came. I hush'd the deep,
By demons roused, and bade the listed winds,§

---

* The charters of corporations.
      † Judge Jefferies.   ‡ James II.
  § The Prince of Orange, in his passage to England, though his
fleet had been at first dispersed by a storm, was afterwards extremely favoured by several changes of wind.

Still shifting as behoved, with various breath,
Waft the deliverer to the longing shore.
See! wide alive, the foaming channel* bright
With swelling sails, and all the pride of war,
Delightful view! when Justice draws the sword:
And mark! diffusing ardent soul around,
And sweet contempt of death, My streaming flag,†
E'en adverse navies‡ bless'd the binding gale,
Kept down the glad acclaim, and silent joy'd.
Arrived, the pomp, and not the waste, of arms
His progress mark'd. The faint opposing host§
For once, in yielding their best victory found,
And by desertion proved exalted faith:
While his the bloodless conquest of the heart,
Shouts without groan, and triumph without war.
  "Then dawn'd the period destined to confine
The surge of wild prerogative, to raise
A mound restraining its imperious rage.
And bid the raving deep no farther flow.
Nor where, without that fence, the swallow'd state
Better than Belgian plains without their dykes,
Sustaining weighty seas. This, often saved
By more than human hand, the public saw,

---

* Rapin, in his " History of England," says, "On the third of November, the fleet entered the Channel, and lay by between Calais and Dover, to stay for the ships that were behind. Here the Prince called a council of war. It is easy to imagine what a glorious show the fleet made. Five or six hundred ships in so narrow a channel, and both the English and French shores covered with numberless spectators, are no common sight. For my part, who was then on board the fleet, I own it struck me extremely."

† The Prince placed himself in the main body, carrying a flag with English colours, and their highnesses' arms surrounded with this motto, "The Protestant Religion and the Liberties of England;" and underneath, the motto of the house of Nassau, "Je maintiendrai," I will maintain.—*Rapin.*

‡ The English fleet.   § The king's army.

And seized the white-wing'd moment. Pleased* to yield
Destructive power, a wise heroic prince†
E'en lent his aid—Thrice happy! did they know
Their happiness, Britannia's bounded kings.
What though not theirs the boast, in dungeon glooms,
To plunge bold freedom; or, to cheerless wilds,
To drive him from the cordial face of friend;
Or fierce to strike him at the midnight hour,
By mandate blind, not justice, that delights
To dare the keenest eye of open day.
What though no glory to control the laws,
And make injurious will their only rule,
They deem it. What though, tools of wanton power,
Pestiferous armies swarm not at their call.
What though they give not a relentless crew
Of civil furies, proud oppression's fangs!
To tear at pleasure the dejected land,
With starving labour pampering idle waste.
To clothe the naked, feed the hungry, wipe
The guiltless tear from lone affliction's eye;
To raise hid merit, set the alluring light
Of virtue high to view; to nourish arts,
Direct the thunder of an injured state,
Make a whole glorious people sing for joy,
Bless human-kind, and through the downward depth
Of future times to spread that better sun
Which lights up British soul: for deeds like these,
The dazzling fair career unbounded lies:
While (still superior bliss!) the dark abrupt
Is kindly barr'd, the precipice of ill.
O luxury divine! O poor to this,
Ye giddy glories of despotic thrones!
By this, by this indeed, is imaged Heaven,
By boundless good without the power of ill.
  "And now behold! exalted as the cope

---

* By the Bill of Rights and the Act of Succession.
† William III.

That swells immense o'er many-peopled earth,
And like it free, my fabric stands complete,
The palace of the laws.   To the four heavens
Four gates impartial thrown, unceasing crowds,
With kings themselves the hearty peasant mix'd,
Pour urgent in.   And though to different ranks
Responsive place belongs, yet equal spreads
The sheltering roof o'er all; while plenty flows,
And glad contentment echoes round the whole.
Ye floods, descend! Ye winds, confirming, blow!
Nor outward tempest, nor corrosive time,
Nought but the felon undermining hand
Of dark Corruption, can its frame dissolve,
And lay the toil of ages in the dust."

LIBERTY.

PART V.

THE PROSPECT.

The author addresses the Goddess of Liberty, marking the happiness and grandeur of Great Britain, as arising from her influence.—She resumes her discourse, and points out the chief Virtues which are necessary to maintain her establishment there.—Recommends, as its last ornament and finishing, Sciences, Fine Arts, and Public works.—The encouragement of these urged from the example of France, though under a despotic government.—The whole concludes with a prospect of future times, given by the Goddess of Liberty: this described by the author, as it passes in vision before him.

HERE interposing, as the Goddess paused:—
"O bless'd Britannia! in thy presence bless'd,
Thou guardian of mankind! whence spring, alone,
All human grandeur, happiness, and fame;
For toil, by thee protected, feels no pain;
The poor man's lot with milk and honey flows;
And, gilded with thy rays, even death looks gay.
Let other lands the potent blessings boast
Of more exalting suns. Let Asia's woods,
Untended, yield the vegetable fleece:
And let the little insect-artist form,
On higher life intent, its silken tomb.
Let wondering rocks, in radiant birth, disclose
The various tinctured children of the sun.
From the prone beam let more delicious fruits,
A flavour drink, that in one piercing taste
Bids each combine. Let Gallic vineyards burst
With floods of joy; with mild balsamic juice

The Tuscan olive.   Let Arabia breathe
Her spicy gales, her vital gums distil.
Turbid with gold, let southern rivers flow;
And orient floods draw soft, o'er pearls, their maze.
Let Afric vaunt her treasures; let Peru
Deep in her bowels her own ruin breed,
The yellow traitor that her bliss betray'd—
Unequall'd bliss——and to unequall'd rage!
Yet nor the gorgeous East, nor golden South,
Nor, in full prime, that new discover'd world,
Where flames the falling day, in wealth and praise,
Shall with Britannia vie; while, Goddess, she
Derives her praise from thee, her matchless charms.
Her hearty fruits the hand of freedom own;
And warm with culture, her thick clustering fields
Prolific teem.   Eternal verdure crowns
Her meads; her gardens smile eternal spring.
She gives the hunter-horse, unquell'd by toil,
Ardent, to rush into the rapid chase:
She, whitening o'er her downs, diffusive, pours
Unnumber'd flocks: she weaves the fleecy robe,
That wraps the nations: she, to lusty droves,
The richest pasture spreads; and, hers, deep-wave
Autumnal seas of pleasing plenty round.
These are delights: and by no baneful herb,
No darting tiger, no grim lion's glare,
No fierce-descending wolf, no serpent roll'd
In spires immense progressive o'er the land,
Disturb'd.   Enlivening these, add cities, full
Of wealth, of trade, of cheerful toiling crowds;
Add thriving towns; add villages and farms,
Innumerous sow'd along the lively vale,
Where bold unrivall'd peasants happy dwell;
Add ancient seats, with venerable oaks
Embosom'd high, while kindred floods below
Wind through the mead; and those of modern band,
More pompous, add, that splendid shine afar.
Need I her limpid lakes, her rivers name

Where swarm the finny race? Thee, chief, O Thames!
On whose each tide, glad with returning sails,
Flows in the mingled harvest of mankind!
And thee, thou Severn, whose prodigious swell,
And waves, resounding, imitate the main!
Why need I name her deep capacious ports,
That point around the world? and why her seas?
All ocean is her own, and every land
To whom her ruling thunder ocean bears.
She too the mineral feeds: the obedient lead,
The warlike iron, nor the peaceful less,
Forming of life art-civilised the bond;
And that* the Tyrian merchant sought of old,
Not dreaming then of Britain's brighter fame.
She rears to freedom an undaunted race:
Compatriot zealous, hospitable, kind,
Hers the warm Cambrian: hers the lofty Scot,
To hardship tamed, active in arts and arms,
Fired with a restless, an impatient flame,
That leads him raptured where ambition calls:
And English merit hers; where meet, combined,
Whate'er high fancy, sound judicious thought,
An ample generous heart, undrooping soul,
And firm tenacious valour can bestow.
Great nurse of fruits, of flocks, of commerce, she!
Great nurse of men! by thee, O Goddess, taught,
Her old renown I trace, disclose her source
Of wealth, of grandeur, and to Britons sing
A strain the Muses never touch'd before.
    "But how shall this thy mighty kingdom stand?
On what unyielding base? how finish'd shine?"
    At this her eye, collecting all its fire,
Beam'd more than human; and her awful voice,
Majestic thus she raised: "To Britons bear
This closing strain, and with intenser note
Loud let it sound in their awaken'd ear:

---

* Tin.

x

"On virtue can alone my kingdom stand,
On public virtue, every virtue join'd.
For, lost this social cement of mankind,
The greatest empires, by scarce-felt degrees,
Will moulder soft away; till, tottering loose,
They, prone at last, to total ruin rush.
Unbless'd by virtue, government a league
Becomes, a circling junto of the great,
To rob by law; religion mild, a yoke
To tame the stooping soul, a trick of state
To mask their rapine, and to share the prey.
What are, without it, senates; save a face
Of consultation deep and reason free,
While the determined voice and heart are sold?
What boasted freedom, save a sounding name?
And what election, but a market vile
Of slaves self-barter'd?   Virtue! without thee,
There is no ruling eye, no nerve, in states;
War has no vigour, and no safety peace:
E'en justice warps to party, laws oppress,
Wide through the land their weak protection fails,
First broke the balance, and then scorn'd the sword.
Thus nations sink, society dissolves;
Rapine, and guile, and violence break loose,
Everting life, and turning love to gall;
Man hates the face of man, and Indian woods
And Libya's hissing sands to him are tame.
  "By those three virtues be the frame sustain'd
Of British freedom: independent life;
Integrity in office; and, o'er all
Supreme, a passion for the commonweal.
  "Hail! Independence, hail!   Heaven's next best gift,
To that of life and an immortal soul!
The life of life! that to the banquet high
And sober meal gives taste; to the bow'd roof
Fair-dream'd repose, and to the cottage charms.
Of public freedom, hail, thou secret source!
Whose streams, from every quarter confluent, form

My better Nile, that nurses human life.
By rills from thee deduced, irriguous, fed,
The private field looks gay, with nature's wealth
Abundant flows, and blooms with each delight
That nature craves.   Its happy master there,
The only freeman, walks his pleasing round:
Sweet-featured peace attending; fearless truth;
Firm resolution; goodness, blessing all
That can rejoice; contentment, surest friend;
And, still fresh stores from nature's book derived,
Philosophy, companion ever new.
These cheer his rural, and sustain or fire,
When into action call'd, his busy hours.
Meantime true judging moderate desires,
Economy and taste, combined, direct
His clear affairs, and from debauching fiends
Secure his little kingdom.   Nor can those
Whom fortune heaps, without these virtues reach
That truce with pain, that animated ease,
That self-enjoyment springing from within;
That independence, active or retired,
Which make the soundest bliss of man below:
But, lost beneath the rubbish of their means,
And drain'd by wants to nature all unknown,
A wandering, tasteless, gaily wretched train,
Though rich, are beggars, and though noble, slaves.
    "Lo! damn'd to wealth, at what a gross expense
They purchase disappointment, pain, and shame.
Instead of hearty, hospitable cheer,
See! how the hall with brutal riot flows;
While in the foaming flood, fermenting, steep'd,
The country maddens into party rage.
Mark! those disgraceful piles of wood and stone;
Those parks and gardens, where, his haunts betrimm'd,
And nature by presumptuous art oppress'd,
The woodland genius mourns.   See! the full board
That steams disgust, and bowls that give no joy;
No truth invited there, to feed the mind;

Nor wit, the wine-rejoicing reason quaffs.
Hark! how the dome with insolence resounds,
With those retain'd by vanity to scare
Repose and friends. To tyrant fashion, mark!
The costly worship paid, to the broad gaze
Of fools. From still delusive day to day,
Led an eternal round of lying hope,
See! self-abandon'd, how they roam adrift,
Dash'd o'er the town, a miserable wreck!
Then to adore some warbling eunuch turn'd,
With Midas' ears they crowd; or to the buzz
Of masquerade unblushing: or, to show
Their scorn of nature, at the tragic scene
They mirthful sit, or prove the comic true.
But, chief, behold! around the rattling board,
The civil robbers ranged; and e'en the fair,
The tender fair, each sweetness laid aside,
As fierce for plunder as all-licenced troops
In some sack'd city. Thus dissolved their wealth,
Without one generous luxury dissolved,
Or quarter'd on it many a needless want,
At the throng'd levee bends the venal tribe;
With fair but faithless smiles each varnish'd o'er,
Each smooth as those that mutually deceive,
And for their falsehood each despising each;
Till shook their patron by the wintry winds,
Wide flies the wither'd shower, and leaves him bare.
O far superior Afric's sable sons,
By merchant pilfer'd, to these willing slaves!
And rich, as unsqueezed favourite, to them,
Is he who can his virtue boast alone.
  "Britons! be firm!—nor let corruption sly
Twine round your heart indissoluble chains!
The steel of Brutus burst the grosser bonds
By Cæsar cast o'er Rome; but still remain'd
The soft enchanting fetters of the mind,
And other Cæsars rose. Determined, hold
Your independence; for, that once destroy'd,

Unfounded, Freedom is a morning dream,
That flits aerial from the spreading eye.
"Forbid it, Heaven! that ever I need urge
Integrity in office on my sons!
Inculcate common honour——not to rob——
And whom?—the gracious, the confiding hand,
That lavishly rewards? the toiling poor,
Whose cup with many a bitter drop is mix'd;
The guardian public; every face they see,
And every friend; nay, in effect themselves.
As in familiar life, the villain's fate
Admits no cure; so, when a desperate age
At this arrives, I the devoted race
Indignant spurn, and hopeless soar away.
"But, ah too little known to modern times!
Be not the noblest passion past unsung;
That ray peculiar, from unbounded love
Effused, which kindles the heroic soul;
Devotion to the public. Glorious flame!
Celestial ardour! in what unknown worlds,
Profusely scatter'd through the blue immense,
Hast thou been blessing myriads, since in Rome,
Old virtuous Rome, so many deathless names
From thee their lustre drew: since, taught by thee,
Their poverty put splendour to the blush,
Pain grew luxurious, and e'en death delight?
O wilt thou ne'er, in thy long period, look,
With blaze direct, on this my last retreat?
"'Tis not enough, from self right understood
Reflected, that thy rays inflame the heart:
Though virtue not disdains appeals to self,
Dreads not the trial; all her joys are true,
Nor is there any real joy save hers.
Far less the tepid, the declaiming race,
Foes to corruption, to its wages friends,
Or those whom private passions, for awhile,
Beneath my standard list; can they suffice
To raise and fix the glory of my reign?

"An active flood of universal love
Must swell the breast. First, in effusion wide,
The restless spirit roves creation round,
And seizes every being: stronger then
It tends to life, whate'er the kindred search
Of bliss allies: then, more collected, still,
It urges human-kind; a passion grown,
At last, the central parent public calls
Its utmost effort forth, awakes each sense,
The comely, grand, and tender. Without this,
This awful pant, shook from sublimer powers
Than those of self, this heaven-infused delight,
This moral gravitation, rushing prone
To press the public good, my system soon,
Traverse, to several selfish centres drawn,
Will reel to ruin: while for ever shut
Stand the bright portals of desponding fame.
"From sordid self shoot up no shining deeds.
None of those ancient lights, that gladden earth,
Give grace to being, and arouse the brave
To just ambition, virtue's quickening fire!
Life tedious grows, an idly bustling round,
Fill'd up with actions animal and mean,
A dull gazette! The impatient reader scorns
The poor historic page; till kindly comes
Oblivion, and redeems a people's shame.
Not so the times when, emulation-stung,
Greece shone in genius, science, and in arts,
And Rome in virtues dreadful to be told!
To live was glory then! and charm'd mankind
Through the deep periods of devolving time,
Those, raptured, copy; these, astonish'd, read.
"True, a corrupted state, with every vice
And every meanness foul, this passion damps.
Who can, unshock'd, behold the cruel eye?
The pale inveigling smile! the ruffian front!
The wretch abandon'd to relentless self,
Equally vile if miser or profuse?

Powers not of God, assiduous to corrupt?
The fell deputed tyrant, who devours
The poor and weak, at distance from redress?
Delirious faction bellowing loud my name?
The false fair-seeming patriot's hollow boast?
A race resolved on bondage, fierce for chains,
My sacred rights a merchandise alone
Esteeming, and to work their feeder's will
By deeds, a horror to mankind, prepared,
As were the dregs of Romulus of old?
Who these indeed can undetesting see?—
But who unpitying? to the generous eye
Distress is virtue; and, though self-betray'd,
A people struggling with their fate must rouse
The hero's throb. Nor can a land, at once,
Be lost to virtue quite. How glorious then!
Fit luxury for gods! to save the good,
Protect the feeble, dash bold vice aside,
Depress the wicked, and restore the frail.
Posterity, besides! the young are pure,
And sons may tinge their father's cheek with shame.
  "Should then the times arrive (which Heaven avert!)
That Britons bend unnerved, not by the force
Of arms, more generous and more manly, quell'd,
But by corruption's soul-dejecting arts,
Arts impudent! and gross! by their own gold,
In part bestow'd, to bribe them to give all,
With party raging, or immersed in sloth,
Should they Britannia's well-fought laurels yield
To slily conquering Gaul; e'en from her brow
Let her own naval oak be basely torn,
By such as tremble at the stiffening gale,
And nerveless sink while others sing rejoiced:
Or (darker prospect! scarce one gleam behind
Disclosing) should the broad corruptive plague
Breathe from the city to the farthest hut,
That sits serene within the forest shade;
The fever'd people fire, inflame their wants.

And their luxurious thirst, so gathering rage,
That, were a buyer found, they stand prepared
To sell their birthright for a cooling draught.
Should shameless pens for plain corruption plead;
The hired assassins of the commonweal!
Deem'd the declaiming rant of Greece and Rome,
Should public virtue grow the public scoff,
Till private, failing, staggers through the land:
Till round the city loose mechanic want,
Dire prowling nightly, makes the cheerful haunts
Of men more hideous than Numidian wilds,
Nor from its fury sleeps the vale in peace;
And murders, horrors, perjuries abound:
Nay, till to lowest deeds the highest stoop;
The rich, like starving wretches, thirst for gold;
And those, on whom the vernal showers of Heaven
All-bounteous fall, and that prime lot bestow,
A power to live to nature and themselves,
In sick attendance wear their anxious days,
With fortune, joyless, and with honours, mean.
Meantime, perhaps, profusion flows around,
The waste of war, without the works of peace;
No mark of millions in the gulf absorpt
Of uncreating vice, none but the rage
Of roused corruption still demanding more.
That very portion, which (by faithful skill
Employ'd) might make the smiling public rear
Her ornamented head, drill'd through the hands
Of mercenary tools, serves but to nurse
A locust band within, and in the bud
Leaves starved each work of dignity and use.
    "I paint the worst.   But should these times arrive,
If any nobler passion yet remain,
Let all my sons all parties fling aside,
Despise their nonsense, and together join;
Let worth and virtue scorning low despair,
Exerted full, from every quarter shine,
Commix'd in heighten'd blaze.   Light flash'd to light,

Moral, or intellectual, more intense
By giving glows.   As on pure winter's eve,
Gradual, the stars effulge; fainter, at first,
They, straggling, rise; but when the radiant host,
In thick profusion pour'd, shine out immense,
Each casting vivid influence on each,
From pole to pole a glittering deluge plays,
And worlds above rejoice, and men below.
  "But why to Britons this superfluous strain?—
Good nature, honest truth e'en somewhat blunt,
Of crooked baseness an indignant scorn,
A zeal unyielding in their country's cause,
And ready bounty, wont to dwell with them—
Nor only wont—wide o'er the land diffused,
In many a bless'd retirement still they dwell.
  "To softer prospect turn we now the view,
To laurell'd science, arts, and public works,
That lend my finish'd fabric comely pride,
Grandeur, and grace.   Of sullen genius he!
Cursed by the Muses! by the Graces loathed!
Who deems beneath the public's high regard
These last enlivening touches of my reign.
However puff'd with power, and gorged with wealth,
A nation be; let trade enormous rise,
Let East and South their mingled treasure pour,
Till, swell'd impetuous, the corrupting flood
Burst o'er the city, and devour the land:
Yet these neglected, these recording arts,
Wealth rots, a nuisance; and, oblivious sunk,
That nation must another Carthage lie.
If not by them, on monumental brass,
On sculptured marble, on the deathless page,
Impress'd, renown had left no trace behind:
In vain, to future times, the sage had thought,
The legislator plann'd, the hero found
A beauteous death, the patriot toil'd in vain.
The awarders they of Fame's immortal wreath
They rouse ambition, they the mind exalt,

Give great ideas, lovely forms infuse,
Delight the general eye, and, dress'd by them,
The moral Venus glows with double charms.
   "Science, my close associate, still attends
Where'er I go. Sometimes, in simple guise,
She walks the furrow with the consul-swain,
Whispering unletter'd wisdom to the heart,
Direct; or, sometimes, in the pompous robe
Of fancy dress'd, she charms Athenian wits,
And a whole sapient city round her burns.
Then o'er her brow Minerva's terrors nod:
With Xenophon, sometimes in dire extremes,
She breathes deliberate soul, and makes retreat*
Unequall'd glory: with the Theban sage,
Epaminondas, first and best of men!
Sometimes she bids the deep-embattled host,
Above the vulgar reach, resistless form'd,
March to sure conquest—never gain'd before!†
Nor on the treacherous seas of giddy state
Unskilful she: when the triumphant tide
Of high-swoln empire wears one boundless smile,
And the gale tempts to new pursuits of fame,
Sometimes, with Scipio, she collects her sail,
And seeks the blissful shore of rural ease,
Where, but the Aonian maids, no syrens sing;
Or should the deep-brew'd tempest muttering rise,
While rocks and shoals perfidious lurk around,
With Tully she her wide-reviving light
To senates holds; a Catiline confounds,

---

   * The famous Retreat of the Ten Thousand was chiefly conducted by Xenophon.

   † Epaminondas, after having beat the Lacedæmonians and
their allies, in the battle of Leuctra, made an incursion, at the
head of a powerful army, into Laconia. It was now six hundred
years since the Dorians had possessed this country, and in all that
time the face of an enemy had not been seen within their terri-
tories.—*Plutarch in Agesilaus.*

And saves awhile from Cæsar sinking Rome.
Such the kind power, whose piercing eye dissolves
Each mental fetter, and sets reason free;
For me inspiring an enlighten'd zeal,
The more tenacious as the more convinced
How happy freemen, and how wretched slaves.
To Britons not unknown, to Britons full
The Goddess spreads her stores, the secret soul
That quickens trade, the breath unseen that wafts
To them the treasures of a balanced world.
But finer arts (save what the Muse has sung
In daring flight, above all modern wing)
Neglected droop the head; and public works,
Broke by corruption into private gain,
Not ornament, disgrace; not serve, destroy.
    Shall Britons, by their own joint wisdom ruled
Beneath one Royal Head, whose vital power
Connects, enlivens, and exerts the whole;
In finer arts, and public works, shall they
To Gallia yield? yield to a land that bends
Depress'd, and broke, beneath the will of one?
Of one who, should the unkingly thirst of gold,
Or tyrant passions, or ambition, prompt,
Calls locust-armies o'er the blasted land:
Drains from its thirsty bounds the springs of wealth,
His own insatiate reservoir to fill:
To the lone desert patriot-merit frowns,
Or into dungeons arts, when they their chains,
Indignant, bursting; for their nobler works
All other license scorn but truth's and mine.
Oh, shame to think! shall Britons, in the field
Unconquer'd still, the better laurel lose?
E'en in that monarch's reign,* who vainly dreamt,
By giddy power, betray'd, and flatter'd pride,
To grasp unbounded sway; while, swarming round,
His armies dared all Europe to the field;

---

* Louis XIV.

To hostile hands while treasure flow'd profuse,
And, that great source of treasure, subjects' blood,
Inhuman squander'd, sicken'd every land;
From Britain, chief, while my superior sons,
In vengeance rushing, dash'd his idle hopes,
And bade his agonising heart be low:
E'en then, as in the golden calm of peace,
What public works, at home, what arts arose!
What various science shone! what genius glow'd!
   "'Tis not for me to paint, diffusive shot
O'er fair extents of land, the shining road;
The flood-compelling arch; the long canal,*
Through mountains piercing and uniting seas:
The dome† resounding sweet with infant joy,
From famine saved, or cruel-handed shame;
And that† where valour counts his noble scars,
The land where social pleasure loves to dwell,
Of the fierce demon, Gothic duel, freed;
The robber from his farthest forest chased;
The turbid city clear'd, and, by degrees,
Into sure peace the best police refined;
Magnificence, and grace, and decent joy.
Let Gallic bards record, how honour'd arts,
And science, by despotic bounty bless'd,
At distance flourish'd from my parent-eye.
Restoring ancient taste, how Boileau rose:
How the big Roman soul shook, in Corneille,
The trembling stage. In elegant Racine,
How the more powerful, though more humble voice
Of nature-painting Greece, resistless, breathed
The whole awaken'd heart. How Moliere's scene,
Chastised and regular, with well-judged wit,
Not scatter'd wild, and native humour, graced,
Was life itself. To public honours raised,

---

* The Canal of Languedoc.
† The Hospitals for Foundlings and Invalids.

How learning in warm seminaries* spread;
And, more for glory than the small reward,
How emulation strove. How their pure tongue
Almost obtain'd what was denied their arms.
From Rome, awhile, how Painting, courted long,
With Poussin came; ancient design that lifts
A fairer front, and looks another soul.
How the kind art,† that, of unvalued price,
The famed and only picture, easy, gives,
Refined her touch, and, through the shadow'd piece,
All the live spirit of the painter pour'd.
Coyest of arts, how Sculpture northward deign'd
A look, and bade her Girardon arise.
How lavish grandeur blazed; the barren waste,
Astonish'd saw the sudden palace swell,
And fountains spout amid its arid shades.
For leagues, bright vistas opening to the view,
How forests in majestic gardens smiled.
How menial arts, by their gay sisters taught,
Wove the deep flower, the blooming foliage train'd
In joyous figures o'er the silky lawn,
The palace cheer'd, illumed the storied wall,
And with the pencil vied the glowing loom.‡
 "These laurels, Louis, by the droppings raised
Of thy profusion, its dishonour shade,
And, green through future times, shall bind thy brow;
While the vain honours of perfidious war
Wither abhorr'd, or in oblivion lost.
With what prevailing vigour had they shot,
And stole a deeper root, by the full tide
Of war-sunk millions fed?   Superior still,
How had they branch'd luxuriant to the skies,
In Britain planted, by the potent juice
Of Freedom swell'd?   Forced is the bloom of arts,

---

 * The Academies of Sciences, of the Belles Lettres, and of
Painting.

     † Engraving.   ‡ The tapestry of the Gobelins.

A false uncertain spring, when Bounty gives,
Weak without me, a transitory gleam.
Fair shine the slippery days, enticing skies
Of favour smile, and courtly breezes blow;
Till arts, betray'd, trust to the flattering air
Their tender blossom: then malignant rise
The blights of Envy, of those insect clouds,
That, blasting merit, often cover courts:
Nay, should, perchance, some kind Mæcenas aid
The doubtful beamings of his prince's soul,
His wavering ardour fix, and unconfined
Diffuse his warm beneficence around;
Yet death, at last, and wintry tyrants come,
Each sprig of genius killing at the root.
But when with me imperial Bounty joins,
Wide o'er the public blows eternal spring;
While mingled autumn every harvest pours
Of every land; whate'er Invention, Art,
Creating Toil, and Nature can produce."

 Here ceased the Goddess; and her ardent wings,
Dipt in the colours of the heavenly bow,
Stood waving radiance round, for sudden flight
Prepared, when thus, impatient, burst my prayer:—
 " O forming light of life! O better sun!
Sun of mankind! by whom the cloudy North,
Sublimed, not envies Languedocian skies,
That, unstain'd ether all, diffusive smile:
When shall we call these ancient laurels ours?
And when thy work complete?" Straight with her hand,
Celestial red, she touch'd my darken'd eyes.
As at the touch of day the shades dissolve,
So quick, methought, the misty circle clear'd,
That dims the dawn of being here below:
The future shone disclosed, and, in long view,
Bright rising eras instant rush'd to light.
 " They come! great Goddess! I the times behold!
The times our fathers, in the bloody field,
Have earn'd so dear, and, not with less renown,

In the warm struggles of the senate fight.
The times I see! whose glory to supply,
For toiling ages, Commerce round the world
Has wing'd unnumber'd sails, and from each land
Materials heap'd, that, well employ'd, with Rome
Might vie our grandeur, and with Greece our art.
   "Lo! Princes I behold! contriving still,
And still conducting firm some brave design;
Kings! that the narrow joyless circle scorn,
Burst the blockade of false designing men,
Of treacherous smiles, of adulation fell,
And of the blinding clouds around them thrown:
Their court rejoicing millions; Worth, alone,
And Virtue dear to them; their best delight,
In just proportion, to give general joy;
Their jealous care thy kingdom to maintain;
The public glory theirs; unsparing love
Their endless treasure; and their deeds their praise.
With thee they work. Nought can resist your force:
Life feels it quickening in her dark retreats:
Strong spread the blooms of Genius, Science, Art;
His bashful bounds disclosing Merit breaks;
And, big with fruits of glory, Virtue blows
Expansive o'er the land. Another race
Of generous youth, of patriot sires, I see!
Not those vain insects fluttering in the blaze
Of court, and ball, and play; those venal souls,
Corruption's veteran unrelenting bands,
That, to their vices slaves, can ne'er be free.
   "I see the fountains purged! whence life derives
A clear or turbid flow; see the young mind
Not fed impure by chance, by flattery fool'd,
Or by scholastic jargon bloated proud,
But fill'd and nourish'd by the light of Truth.
Then beam'd through fancy the refining ray,
And pouring on the heart, the passions feel
At once informing light and moving flame;
Till moral, public, graceful action crowns

The whole.   Behold! the fair contention glows,
In all that mind or body can adorn,
And form to life.   Instead of barren heads,
Barbarian pedants, wrangling sons of pride,
And truth-perplexing metaphysic wits,
Men, patriots, chiefs, and citizens are form'd.
  "Lo! Justice, like the liberal light of heaven,
Unpurchased shines on all; and from her beam,
Appalling guilt, retire the savage crew,
That prowl amid the darkness they themselves
Have thrown around the laws.   Oppression grieves;
See! how her legal furies bite the lip,
While Yorkes and Talbots their deep snares detect,
And seize swift justice through the clouds they raise
  "See! social Labour lifts his guarded head,
And men not yield to government in vain.
From the sure land is rooted ruffian force,
And the lewd nurse of villains, idle waste;
Lo! razed their haunts, down dash'd their maddening bowl,
A nation's poison! beauteous order reigns!
Manly submission, unimposing toil,
Trade without guile, civility that marks
From the foul herd of brutal slaves thy sons,
And fearless peace.   Or should affronting war
To slow but dreadful vengeance rouse the just,
Unfailing fields of freemen I behold!
That know, with their own proper arm, to guard
Their own bless'd isle against a leaguing world.
Despairing Gaul her boiling youth restrains,
Dissolved her dream of universal sway:
The winds and seas are Britain's wide domain;
And not a sail, but by permission, spreads.
  "Lo! swarming southward on rejoicing suns,
Gay colonies extend; the calm retreat
Of undeserved distress, the better home
Of those whom bigots chase from foreign lands.
Nor built on rapine, servitude, and wo,
And in their turn some petty tyrant's prey;

But, bound by social Freedom, firm they rise;
Such as, of late, an Oglethorpe has form'd,
And, crowding round, the charm'd Savannah sees.
"Horrid with want and misery, no more
Our streets the tender passenger afflict.
Nor shivering age, nor sickness without friend,
Or home, or bed to bear his burning load;
Nor agonising infant, that ne'er earn'd
Its guiltless pangs; I see! the stores, profuse,
Which British bounty has to these assign'd,
No more the sacrilegious riot swell
Of cannibal devourers! right applied,
No starving wretch the land of freedom stains:
If poor, employment finds; if old, demands,
If sick, if maim'd, his miserable due;
And will, if young, repay the fondest care.
Sweet sets the sun of stormy life; and sweet
The morning shines, in Mercy's dews array'd.
Lo! how they rise! these families of Heaven!
That! chief* (but why, ye bigots!—why so late?)
Where blooms and warbles glad a rising age;
What smiles of praise! and, while their song ascends,
The listening seraph lays his lute aside.
"Hark! the gay Muses raise a nobler strain,
With active nature, warm impassion'd truth,
Engaging fable, lucid order, notes
Of various string, and heartfelt image fill'd.
Behold! I see the dread delightful school
Of temper'd passions, and of polish'd life,
Restored: behold! the well-dissembled scene
Calls from embellish'd eyes the lovely tear,
Or lights up mirth in modest cheeks again.
Lo! vanish'd monster land. Lo! driven away
Those that Apollo's sacred walks profane:
Their wild creation scatter'd, where a world
Unknown to nature, Chaos more confused,

---

* The Foundling Hospital.

Y

O'er the brute scene its Ourang-Outangs pours;
Detested forms! that, on the mind impress'd,
Corrupt, confound, and barbarise an age,
  "Behold! all thine again the Sister-Arts,
Thy graces they, knit in harmonious dance.
Nursed by the treasure from a nation drain'd
Their works to purchase, they to nobler rouse
Their untamed genius, their unfetter'd thought;
Of pompous tyrants, and of dreaming monks,
The gaudy tools, and prisoners, no more.
  "Lo! numerous domes a Burlington confess:
For kings and senates fit, the palace see!
The temple breathing a religious awe;
E'en framed with elegance the plain retreat,
The private dwelling.   Certain in his aim,
Taste, never idly working, saves expense.
  "See! sylvan scenes, where Art alone pretends
To dress her mistress, and disclose her charms:
Such as a Pope in miniature has shown;*
A Bathurst o'er the widening forest† spreads;
And such as form a Richmond, Chiswick, Stowe.
  "August, around, what public works I see!
Lo! stately streets; lo! squares that court the breeze,
In spite of those to whom pertains the care,
Ingulfing more than founded Roman ways;
Lo! ray'd from cities o'er the brighten'd land,
Connecting sea to sea, the solid road.
Lo! the proud arch (no vile exactor's stand)
With easy sweep bestrides the chasing flood.
See! long canals, and deepen'd rivers join
Each part with each, and with the circling main
The whole enliven'd isle.   Lo! ports expand,
Free as the winds and waves, their sheltering arms.
Lo! streaming comfort o'er the troubled deep,
On every pointed coast the lighthouse towers;——

* At his Twickenham Villa.   † Okely woods, near Cirencester.

And, by the broad imperious mole repell'd,
Hark ! how the baffled storm indignant roars."
 As thick to view these varied wonders rose,
Shook all my soul with transport, unassured,
The Vision broke ; and, on my waking eye,
Rush'd the still ruins of dejected Rome.

·

POEMS.

THE HAPPY MAN.

[FIRST PRINTED 1729.]

HE's not the happy man, to whom is given
A plenteous fortune by indulgent Heaven;
Whose gilded roofs on shining columns rise,
And painted walls enchant the gazer's eyes:
Whose table flows with hospitable cheer,
And all the various bounty of the year;
Whose valleys smile, whose gardens breathe the spring,
Whose carved mountains bleat, and forests sing?
For whom the cooling shade in summer twines,
While his full cellars give their generous wines;
From whose wide fields unbounded autumn pours
A golden tide into his swelling stores:
Whose winter laughs; for whom the liberal gales
Stretch the big sheet, and toiling commerce sails;
When yielding crowds attend, and pleasure serves;
While youth, and health, and vigour string his nerves.
E'en not all these, in one rich lot combined,
Can make the happy man, without the mind:
Where judgment sits clear-sighted, and surveys
The chain of reason with unerring gaze;
Where fancy lives, and to the brightening eyes,
His fairer scenes, and bolder figures rise;
Where social love exerts her soft command,
And lays the passions with a tender hand,
Whence every virtue flows, in rival strife,
And all the moral harmony of life.

Nor canst thou, Dodington, this truth decline—
Thine is the fortune, and the mind is thine.

ON ÆOLUS'S HARP.

Ethereal race, inhabitants of air,
  Who hymn your God amid the secret grove;
Ye unseen beings, to my harp repair,
  And raise majestic strains, or melt in love.

Those tender notes, how kindly they upbraid!
  With what soft wo they thrill the lover's heart!
Sure from the hand of some unhappy maid,
  Who died for love, these sweet complainings part.

But hark! that strain was of a graver tone,
  On the deep strings his hand some hermit throws;
Or he, the sacred Bard,* who sat alone
  In the drear waste, and wept his people's woes.

Such was the song which Zion's children sung,
  When by Euphrates' stream they made their plaint;
And to such sadly solemn notes are strung
  Angelic harps, to soothe a dying saint.

Methinks I hear the full celestial choir,
  Through heaven's high dome their awful anthem raise
Now chanting clear, and now they all conspire
  To swell the lofty hymn from praise to praise.

Let me, ye wandering spirits of the wind,
  Who, as wild fancy prompts you, touch the string,
Smit with your theme, be in your chorus join'd,
  For, till you cease, my Muse forgets to sing.

HYMN ON SOLITUDE.

[FIRST PRINTED 1729.]

Hail, mildly pleasing Solitude,
Companion of the wise and good;
But from whose holy, piercing eye,
The herd of fools and villains fly.

---

* Jeremiah.

Oh! how I love with thee to walk,
And listen to thy whisper'd talk,
Which innocence and truth imparts,
And melts the most obdurate hearts.

A thousand shapes you wear with ease,
And still in every shape you please.
Now wrapt in some mysterious dream,
A lone philosopher you seem;
Now quick from hill to vale you fly,
And now you sweep the vaulted sky;
A shepherd next, you haunt the plain,
And warble forth your oaten strain.
A lover now, with all the grace
Of that sweet passion in your face;
Then, calm'd to friendship, you assume
The gentle-looking Hertford's bloom.
As, with her Musidora, she
(Her Musidora fond of thee),
Amid the long-withdrawing vale,
Awakes the rivall'd nightingale.

Thine is the balmy breath of morn,
Just as the dew-bent rose is born;
And while meridian fervours beat,
Thine is the woodland dumb retreat;
But chief, when evening scenes decay,
And the faint landscape swims away,
Thine is the doubtful soft decline,
And that best hour of musing thine.

Descending angels bless thy train,
The virtues of the sage, and swain;
Plain innocence in white array'd
Before thee lifts her fearless head;
Religion's beams around thee shine,
And cheer thy glooms with light divine:

About thee sports sweet Liberty;
And rapt Urania sings to thee.

Oh, let me pierce thy secret cell!
And in thy deep recesses dwell;
Perhaps from Norwood's oak-clad hill,
When meditation has her fill,
I just may cast my careless eyes,
Where London's spiry turrets rise,
Think of its crimes, its cares, its pain,
Then shield me in the woods again.

A PARAPHRASE

ON THE

LATTER PART OF THE SIXTH CHAPTER OF ST MATTHEW.

[FIRST PRINTED 1729.]

When my breast labours with oppressive care,
And o'er my cheek descends the falling tear;
While all my warring passions are at strife,
O, let me listen to the words of life!
Raptures deep-felt His doctrine did impart,
And thus he raised from earth the drooping heart.
   " Think not, when all your scanty stores afford—
Is spread at once upon the sparing board;
Think not, when worn the homely robe appears,
While on the roof the howling tempest bears;
What further shall this feeble life sustain,
And what shall clothe these shivering limbs again!
Say, does not life its nourishment exceed?
And the fair body its investing weed?
   " Behold! and look away your low despair—
See the light tenants of the barren air:

To them, nor stores, nor granaries belong,
Nought but the woodland and the pleasing song;
Yet your kind heavenly Father bends his eye
On the least wing that flits along the sky;
To Him they sing, when Spring renews the plain,
To him they cry, in Winter's pinching reign;
Nor is their music, nor their plaint in vain;
He hears the gay and the distressful call,
And with unsparing bounty fills them all.
  "Observe the rising lily's snowy grace,
Observe the various vegetable race;
They neither toil, nor spin, but careless grow,
Yet see how warm they blush! how bright they glow!
What regal vestments can with them compare?
What king so shining? or what queen so fair?
If ceaseless thus the fowls of heaven he feeds,
If o'er the fields such lucid robes he spreads:
Will he not care for you, ye faithless, say?
Is he unwise? or are ye less than they?

ON THE DEATH OF HIS MOTHER.

Ye fabled Muses, I your aid disclaim,
Your airy raptures, and your fancied flame:
True genuine wo my throbbing breast inspires—
Love prompts my lays, and filial duty fires;
My soul springs instant at the warm design,
And the heart dictates every flowing line.
See! where the kindest, best of mothers lies,
And Death has closed her ever watching eyes;
Has lodged at last in peace her weary breast,
And lull'd her many piercing cares to rest.
No more the orphan train around her stands,
While her full heart upbraids her needy hands!
No more the widow's lonely fate she feels,
The shock severe that modest want conceals,

The oppressor's scourge, the scorn of wealthy pride,
And poverty's unnumber'd ills beside.
For see! attended by the angelic throng,
Through yonder worlds of light she glides along,
And claims the well-earn'd raptures of the sky:
Yet fond concern recalls the mother's eye;
She seeks the helpless orphans left behind:
So hardly left! so bitterly resign'd!
Still, still! is she my soul's diurnal theme,
The waking vision, and the wailing dream:
Amid the ruddy sun's enlivening blaze
O'er my dark eyes her dewy image plays,
And in the dread dominion of the night
Shines out again the sadly pleasing sight.
Triumphant virtue all around her darts,
And more than volumes every look imparts—
Looks, soft, yet awful; melting, yet serene;
Where both the mother and the saint are seen.
But ah! that night—that torturing night remains;
May darkness dye it with the deepest stains,
May joy on it forsake her rosy bowers,
And streaming sorrow blast its baleful hours,
When on the margin of the briny flood,
Chill'd with a sad presaging damp, I stood,
Took the last look, ne'er to behold her more,
And mix'd our murmurs with the wavy roar;
Heard the last words fall from her pious tongue,
Then wild into the bulging vessel flung,
Which soon, too soon, convey'd me from her sight,
Dearer than life, and liberty, and light!
Why was I then, ye powers, reserved for this?
Nor sunk that moment in the vast abyss?
Devour'd at once by the relentless wave,
And whelm'd for ever in a watery grave?—
Down, ye wild wishes of unruly wo!—
I see her with immortal beauty glow;
The early wrinkle, care-contracted, gone,
Her tears all wiped, and all her sorrows flown;

The exalting voice of Heaven I hear her breathe,
To soothe her soul in agonies of death.
I see her through the mansions blest above,
And now she meets her dear expecting Love.
Heart-cheering sight! but yet, alas! o'erspread
By the dark gloom of Grief's uncheerful shade.
Come then, of reason the reflecting hour,
And let me trust the kind o'erruling Power,
Who from the right commands the shining day,
The poor man's portion, and the orphan's stay.

EPITAPH ON MISS STANLEY,

IN HOLYROOD CHURCH, SOUTHAMPTON.

E. S.

Once a lively image of human nature,
Such as God made it
When he pronounced every work of his to be good.
To the memory of Elizabeth Stanley,
Daughter of George and Sarah Stanley;
Who to all the beauty, modesty,
And gentleness of nature,
That ever adorned the most amiable woman,
Joined all the fortitude, elevation,
And vigour of mind,
That ever exalted the most heroical man;
Who, having lived the pride and delight of her parents,
The joy, the consolation, and pattern of her friends,
A mistress not only of the English and French,
But in a high degree of the Greek and Roman learning,
Without vanity or pedantry,
At the age of eighteen,
After a tedious, painful, desperate illness,
Which, with a Roman spirit,
And a Christian resignation,

She endured so calmly, that she seemed insensible
To all pain and suffering, except that of her friends,
    Gave up her innocent soul to her Creator,
And left to her mother, who erected this monument,
The memory of her virtues for her greatest support;
    Virtues which, in her sex and station of life,
        Were all that could be practised,
        And more than will be believed,
Except by those who know what this inscription relates.

Here, Stanley, rest! escaped this mortal strife,
Above the joys, beyond the woes of life,
Fierce pangs no more thy lively beauties stain,
And sternly try thee with a year of pain;
No more sweet patience, feigning oft relief,
Lights thy sick eye, to cheat a parent's grief:
With tender art to save her anxious groan,
No more thy bosom presses down its own:
Now well-earn'd peace is thine, and bliss sincere:
Ours be the lenient, not unpleasing tear!
  O born to bloom, then sink beneath the storm;
To show us virtue in her fairest form;
To show us artless reason's moral reign,
What boastful science arrogates in vain;
The obedient passions knowing each their part;
Calm light the head, and harmony the heart!
  Yes, we must follow soon, will glad obey;
When a few suns have roll'd their cares away,
Tired with vain life, will close the willing eye:
'Tis the great birthright of mankind to die.
Bless'd be the bark, that wafts us to the shore,
Where death-divided friends shall part no more:
To join thee there, here with thy dust repose,
Is all the hope thy hapless mother knows.

ON THE DEATH OF MR AIKMAN.

[Mr Aikman was born in Scotland, and was designed for the profession
of the law; but went to Italy, and returned a painter. He was patronised
in Scotland by the Duke of Argyle, and afterwards met with encouragement to scttle in London; but falling into a long and languishing disease,
he died at his house in Leicester Fields, June 1731, aged 50. Boyse wrote
a panegyric upon him, and Mallet an epitaph.—See "Walpole's Anec-
dotes," vol. iv. p. 41.]

Oh, could I draw, my friend, thy genuine mind,
Just as the living forms by thee design'd;
Of Raphael's figures none should fairer shine,
Nor Titian's colours longer last than mine.
A mind in wisdom old, in lenience young,
From fervent truth where every virtue sprung;
Where all was real, modest, plain, sincere;
Worth above show, and goodness unsevere:
View'd round and round, as lucid diamonds throw
Still as you turn them a revolving glow,
So did his mind reflect with secret ray,
In various virtues, Heaven's internal day;
Whether in high discourse it soar'd sublime,
And sprung impatient o'er the bounds of Time,
Or wandering nature through with raptured eye,
Adored the Hand that turn'd yon azure sky:
Whether to social life he bent his thought,
And the right poise of mingling passions sought,
Gay converse bless'd; or in the thoughtful grove
Bid the heart open every source of love:
New varying lights still set before your eyes
The just, the good, the social, or the wise.
For such a death who can, who would, refuso
The friend a tear, a verse the mournful muse?
Yet pay we just acknowledgment to Heaven,
Though snatch'd so soon, that Aikman e'er was given.
A friend, when dead, is but removed from sight,
Hid in the lustre of eternal light:

Oft with the mind he wonted converse keeps
In the lone walk, or when the body sleeps
Lets in a wandering ray, and all elate
Wings and attracts her to another state;
And, when the parting storms of life are o'er,
May yet rejoin him in a happier shore.
As those we love decay, we die in part,
String after string is sever'd from the heart;
Till loosen'd life at last—but breathing clay—
Without one pang, is glad to fall away.
Unhappy he who latest feels the blow,
Whose eyes have wept o'er every friend laid low,
Dragg'd lingering on from partial death to death;
And dying, all he can resign is breath.

ON THE REPORT THAT A WOODEN BRIDGE

WAS TO BE BUILT AT WESTMINSTER.

By Rufus' hall, where Thames polluted flows,
Provoked, the Genius of the river rose,
And thus exclaim'd: "Have I, ye British swains,
Have I for ages laved your fertile plains?
Given herds, and flocks, and villages increase,
And fed a richer than a golden fleece?
Have I, ye merchants, with each swelling tide,
Pour'd Afric's treasure in, and India's pride?
Lent you the fruit of every nation's toil?
Made every climate yours, and every soil?
Yet, pilfer'd from the poor, by gaming base,
Yet must a wooden bridge my waves disgrace?
Tell not to foreign streams the shameful tale,
And be it publish'd in no Gallic vale."
He said; and plunging to his crystal dome,
While o'er his head the circling waters foam.

THE INCOMPARABLE SOPORIFIC DOCTOR.

[FIRST PRINTED 1729.]

Sweet, sleeky Doctor! dear pacific soul!
Lay at the beef, and suck the vital bowl!
Still let the involving smoke around thee fly,
And broad-look'd dulness settle in thine eye.
Ah! soft in down these dainty limbs repose,
And in the very lap of slumber doze;
But chiefly on the lazy day of grace,
Call forth the lambent glories of thy face;
If aught the thoughts of dinner can prevail,
And sure the Sunday's dinner cannot fail.
To the thin church in sleepy pomp proceed,
And lean on the lethargic book thy head.
These eyes wipe often with the hallow'd lawn,
Profoundly nod, immeasurably yawn.
Slow let the prayers by thy meek lips be sung,
Now let thy thoughts be distanced by thy tongue;
If e'er the lingerers are within a call,
Or if on prayers thou deign'st to think at all.
Yet—only yet—the swimming head we bend;
But when serene, the pulpit you ascend,
Through every joint a gentle horror creeps,
And round you the consenting audience sleeps.
So when an ass with sluggish front appears,
The horses start, and prick their quivering ears;
But soon as e'er the sage is heard to bray,
The fields all thunder, and they bound away.

TO SERAPHINA.

The wanton's charms, however bright,
Are like the false illusive light,
Whose flattering unauspicious blaze
To precipices oft betrays:

But that sweet ray your beauties dart,
Which clears the mind, and cleans the heart,
Is like the sacred queen of night,
Who pours a lovely gentle light
Wide o'er the dark, by wanderers blest,
Conducting them to peace and rest.
A vicious love depraves the mind.
'Tis anguish, guilt, and folly join'd;
But Seraphina's eyes dispense
A mild and gracious influence;
Such as in visions angels shed
Around the heaven-illumined head.
To love thee, Seraphina, sure
Is to be tender, happy, pure;
'Tis from low passions to escape,
And woo bright virtue's fairest shape;
'Tis ecstacy with wisdom join'd;
And heaven infused into the mind.

VERSES ADDRESSED TO AMANDA.

Ah, urged too late! from beauty's bondage free,
Why did I trust my liberty with thee?
And thou, why didst thou, with inhuman heart,
If not resolved to take, seduce my heart?
Yes, yes, you said, for lovers' eyes speak true;
You must have seen how fast my passion grew:
And, when your glances chanced on me to shine,
How my fond soul ecstatic sprung to thine!
But mark me, fair one—what I now declare,
Thy deep attention claims and serious care:
It is no common passion fires my breast;
I must be wretched or I must be blest!
My woes all other remedy deny;
Or, pitying, give me hope, or bid me die!

TO THE SAME,

WITH A COPY OF "THE SEASONS."

Accept, loved Nymph, this tribute due
To tender friendship, love, and you:
But with it take what breathed the whole—
O take to thine the poet's soul.
If Fancy here her power displays,
And if a heart exalts these lays—
You, fairest, in that fancy shine,
And all that heart is fondly thine.

SONGS.

A NUPTIAL SONG.

Come, gentle Venus! and assuage
A warring world, a bleeding age.
For nature lives beneath thy ray,
The wintry tempests haste away,
A lucid calm invests the sea,
Thy native deep is full of thee:
The flowering earth where'er you fly,
Is all o'er spring, all sun the sky.
A genial spirit warms the breeze; ·
Unseen among the blooming trees,
The feather'd lovers tune their throat,
The desert growls a soften'd note,
Glad o'er the meads the cattle bound, ·
And love and harmony go round.
   But chief into the human heart
You strike the dear delicious dart;
You teach us pleasing pangs to know,
To languish in luxurious wo,
To feel the generous passions rise,
Grow good by gazing, mild by sighs;
Each happy moment to improve,
And fill the perfect year with love.
   Come, thou delight of heaven and earth!
To whom all creatures owe their birth;
Oh, come, sweet smiling! tender, come!
And yet prevent our final doom.
For long the furious god of war
Has crush'd us with his iron cai

Has raged along our ruin'd plains,
Has foil'd them with his cruel stains,
Has sunk our youth in endless sleep,
And made the widow'd virgin weep.
Now let him feel thy wonted charms,
Oh, take him to thy twining arms!
And, while thy bosom heaves on his,
While deep he prints the humid kiss,
Ah, then! his stormy heart control,
And sigh thyself into his soul.

TO AMANDA.

Unless with my Amanda bless'd,
   In vain I twine the woodbine bower;
Unless to deck her sweeter breast,
   In vain I rear the breathing flower.

Awaken'd by the genial year,
   In vain the birds around me sing;
In vain the freshening fields appear:—
   Without my love. there is no Spring.

TO FORTUNE.

For ever, Fortune, wilt thou prove
An unrelenting foe to love,
And when we meet a mutual heart,
Come in between, and bid us part:

Bid us sigh on from day to day,
And wish, and wish the soul away;
Till youth and genial years are flown,
And all the love of life is gone?

But busy, busy still art thou,
To bind the loveless, joyless vow,

The heart from pleasure to delude,
And join the gentle to the rude.

For pomp, and noise, and senseless show,
To make us Nature's joys forego,
Beneath a gay dominion groan,
And put the golden fetter on!

For once, O Fortune, hear my prayer,
And I absolve thy future care;
All other blessings I resign,
Make but the dear Amanda mine.

COME, GENTLE GOD.

Come, gentle God of soft desire,
　Come and possess my happy breast,
Not fury-like in flames and fire,
　Or frantic folly's wildness drest;

But come in friendship's angel-guise;
　Yet dearer thou than friendship art,
More tender spirit in thy eyes,
　More sweet emotions at thy heart.

O, come with goodness in thy train,
　With peace and pleasure void of storm;
And wouldst thou me for ever gain,
　Put on Amanda's winning form.

TO HER I LOVE.

Tell me, thou soul of her I love,
　Ah! tell me, whither art thou fled;
To what delightful world above,
　Appointed for the happy dead?

Or dost thou, free, at pleasure roam,
   And sometimes share thy lover's wo;
Where, void of thee, his cheerless home
   Can now, alas! no comfort know!

Oh! if thou hover'st round my walk,
   While, under every well-known tree,
I to thy fancied shadow talk,
   And every tear is full of thee:

Should then the weary eye of grief,
   Beside some sympathetic stream,
In slumber find a short relief,
   Oh, visit thou my soothing dream!

TO THE GOD OF FOND DESIRE.

One day the God of fond desire,
   On mischief bent, to Damon said,
" Why not disclose your tender fire,
   Not own it to the lovely maid!"

The shepherd mark'd his treacherous art,
   And, softly sighing, thus replied:
"'Tis true, you have subdued my heart,
   But shall not triumph o'er my pride.

The slave, in private only bears
   Your bondage, who his love conceals;
But when his passion he declares,
   You drag him at your chariot-wheels."

THE LOVER'S FATE.

Hard is the fate of him who loves,
   Yet dares not tell his trembling pain,
But to the sympathetic groves,
   But to the lonely listening plain,

. Oh! when she blesses next your shade,
   Oh! when her footsteps next are seen
In flowery tracts along the mead,
   In fresher mazes o'er the green:

Ye gentle spirits of the vale,
   To whom the tears of love are dear,
From dying lilies waft a gale,
   And sigh my sorrows in her ear.

Oh! tell her what she cannot blame,
   Though fear my tongue must ever bind;
Oh, tell her, that my virtuous flame
   Is, as her spotless soul, refined.

Not her own guardian-angel eyes
   With chaster tenderness his care,
Not purer her own wishes rise,
   Not holier her own sighs in prayer.

But if at first her virgin fear
   Should start at love's suspected name,
With that of friendship soothe her ear—
   True love and friendship are the same.

TO THE NIGHTINGALE.

O nightingale, best poet of the grove,
   That plaintive strain can ne'er belong to thee,
Bless'd in the full possession of thy love:
   O lend that strain, sweet Nightingale, to me!

'Tis mine, alas! to mourn my wretched fate:
   I love a maid who all my bosom charms,
Yet lose my days without this lovely mate;
   Inhuman fortune keeps her from my arms.

You, happy birds! by nature's simple laws
   Lead your soft lives, sustain'd by nature's fare;

You dwell wherever roving fancy draws,
　And love and song is all your pleasing care:

But we, vain slaves of interest and of pride,
　Dare not be bless'd, lest envious tongues should blame:
And hence, in vain, I languish for my bride!
　O mourn with me, sweet bird, my hapless flame.

TO MYRA.

O thou, whose tender serious eyes
　Expressive speak the mind I love;
The gentle azure of the skies,
　The pensive shadows of the grove:

O mix their beauteous beams with mine,
　And let us interchange our hearts;
Let all their sweetness on me shine;
　Pour'd through my soul be all their darts.

Ah! 'tis too much! I cannot bear
　At once so soft, so keen a ray:
In pity then, my lovely fair,
　O turn those killing eyes away!

But what avails it to conceal
　One charm, where nought but charms I see?
Their lustre then again reveal,
　And let me, Myra, die of thee!

SONGS IN THE MASQUE OF "ALFRED."*

TO PEACE.

O peace! the fairest child of Heaven,
　To whom the sylvan reign was given,

---

* The Masque of Alfred was the joint composition of Thomson and Mallet; hence the authorship of the following songs is somewhat doubtful.

The vale, the fountain, and the grove,
With every softer scene of love:
Return, sweet Peace! and cheer the weeping swain!
Return, with Ease and Pleasure in thy train.

TO ALFRED.

FIRST SPIRIT.

Hear, Alfred, father of the state,
  Thy genius Heaven's high will declare!
What proves the hero truly great,
  Is never, never to despair:
    Is never to despair.

SECOND SPIRIT.

Thy hope awake, thy heart expand,
  With all its vigour, all its fires.
Arise! and save a sinking land!
  Thy country calls, and Heaven inspires.

BOTH SPIRITS.

Earth calls, and Heaven inspires.

"SWEET VALLEY, SAY."

Sweet valley, say, where, pensive lying,
For me, our children, England, sighing,
  The best of mortals leans his head.
Ye fountains, dimpled by my sorrow,
Ye brooks that my complainings borrow,
  O lead me to his lonely bed:
      Or if my lover,
        Deep woods, you cover,
Ah whisper where your shadows o'er him spread.

'Tis not the loss of pomp and pleasure,
Of empire or of tinsel treasure,
   That drops this tear, that swells this groan:
No; from a nobler cause proceeding,
A heart with love and fondness bleeding,
   I breathe my sadly pleasing moan,
      With other anguish,
      I scorn to languish,
For love will feel no sorrows but his own.

"FROM THOSE ETERNAL REGIONS."

From those eternal regions bright,
Where suns, that never set in night,
   Diffuse the golden day:
Where Spring, unfading, pours around,
O'er all the dew-impearl'd ground,
   Her thousand colours gay:
O whether on the fountain's flowery side,
      Whence living waters glide,
      Or in the fragrant grove,
Whose shade embosoms peace and love,
New pleasures all our hours employ,
And ravish every sense with every joy!
      Great heirs of empire! yet unborn,
      Who shall this island late adorn;
   A monarch's drooping thought to cheer,
      Appear! appear! appear!

CONTENTMENT.

If those who live in shepherd's bower,
   Press not the rich and stately bed;
The new-mown hay and breathing flower
   A softer couch beneath them spread.

If those who sit at shepherd's board,
  Soothe not their taste by wanton art;
They take what Nature's gift afford,
  And take it with a cheerful heart.

If those who drain the shepherd's bowl,
  No high and sparkling wines can boast;
With wholesome cups they cheer the soul,
  And crown them with the village toast.

If those who join in shepherd's sport,
  Gay dancing on the daisied ground,
Have not the splendour of a court;
  Yet love adorns the merry round.

RULE, BRITANNIA!

WITH VARIATIONS.

When Britain first, at Heaven's command,
  Arose from out the azure main,
This was the charter of the land,
  And guardian angels sung this strain:
    "Rule, Britannia, rule the waves;
    Britons never will be slaves."

The nations not so bless'd as thee
  Must, in their turns, to tyrants fall;
While thou shalt flourish great and free,
  The dread and envy of them all.
    "Rule," &c.

Still more majestic shalt thou rise,
  More dreadful from each foreign stroke;
As the loud blast that tears the skies
  Serves but to root thy native oak.
    "Rule," &c.

Thee haughty tyrants ne'er shall tame:
  All their attempts to bend thee down

Will but arouse thy generous flame,
   But work their wo, and thy renown.
    "Rule," &c.

To thee belongs the rural reign;
   Thy cities shall with commerce shine:
All thine shall be the subject main:
   And every shore it circles thine.
    "Rule," &c.

The Muses, still with freedom found,
   Shall to thy happy coast repair:
Bless'd isle! with matchless beauty crown'd,
   And manly hearts to guard the fair:
    "Rule, Britannia, rule the waves;
    Britons never will be slaves."

PROLOGUE TO TANCRED AND SIGISMUNDA.

Bold is the man! who, in this nicer age,
Presumes to tread the chaste corrected stage.
Now, with gay tinsel arts, we can no more
Conceal the want of Nature's sterling ore.
Our spells are vanish'd, broke our magic wand,
That used to waft you over sea and land.
Before your light the fairy people fade,
The demons fly—the ghost itself is laid.
In vain of martial scenes the loud alarms,
The mighty prompter thundering out, to arms,
The playhouse posse clattering from afar,
The close-wedged battle, and the din of war.
Now, e'en the senate seldom we convene:
The yawning fathers nod behind the scene.
Your taste rejects the glittering false sublime,
To sigh in metaphor, and die in rhyme.
High rant is tumbled from his gallery throne:
Description dreams—nay, similes are gone.

What shall we then? to please you how devise,
Whose judgment sits not in your ears and eyes?
Thrice happy! could we catch great Shakspere's art,
To trace the deep recesses of the heart;
His simple plain sublime, to which is given
To strike the soul with darted flame from heaven;
Could we awake soft Otway's tender wo,
The pomp of verse and golden lines of Rowe.

We to your hearts apply; let them attend;
Before their silent candid bar we bend.
If warm'd, they listen, 'tis our noblest praise;
If cold, they wither all the Muse's bays.

EPILOGUE TO TANCRED AND SIGISMUNDA.

Cramm'd to the throat with wholesome moral stuff,
Alas! poor audience! you have had enough.
Was ever hapless heroine of a play
In such a piteous plight as ours to-day?
Was ever woman so by love betray'd?
Match'd with two husbands, and yet—die a maid.
But bless me!—hold—What sounds are these I hear!—
I see the Tragic Muse herself appear.

> [The back scene opens, and discovers a romantic sylvan land-
> scape; from which Mrs Cibber, in the character of the
> Tragic Muse, advances slowly to music, and speaks the
> following lines:—

Hence with your flippant epilogue, that tries
To wipe the virtuous tear from British eyes:
That dares my moral, tragic scene profane,
With strains—at best, unsuiting, light and vain.
Hence from the pure unsullied beams that play
In yon fair eyes where virtue shines—Away!

Britons, to you from chaste Castalian groves,
Where dwell the tender, oft unhappy loves!

Where shades of heroes roam, each mighty name,
And court my aid to rise again to fame;
To you I come, to Freedom's noblest seat,
And in Britannia fix my last retreat.
    In Greece and Rome, I watch'd the public weal,
The purple tyrant trembled at my steel:
Nor did I less o'er private sorrows reign,
And mend the melting heart with softer pain.
On France and you then rose my brightening star,
With social ray—The arts are ne'er at war.
O, as your fire and genius stronger blaze,
As yours are generous Freedom's bolder lays,
Let not the Gallic taste leave yours behind,
In decent manners and in life refined;
Banish the motley mode to tag low verse,
The laughing ballad to the mournful hearse.
When through five acts your hearts have learnt to glow,
Touch'd with the sacred force of honest wo;
O keep the dear impression on your breast,
Nor idly lose it for a wretched jest.

EPILOGUE TO AGAMEMNON.

Our bard, to modern epilogue a foe,
Thinks such mean mirth but deadens generous wo;
Dispels in idle air the moral sigh,
And wipes the tender tear from Pity's eye:
No more with social warmth the bosom burns;
But all the unfeeling selfish man returns.
    Thus he began:—And you approved the strain;
Till the next couplet sunk to light and vain.
You check'd him there.—To you, to reason just,
He owns he triumph'd in your kind disgust.
Charm'd by your frown, by your displeasure graced,
He hails the rising virtue of your taste

Wide will its influence spread as soon as known:
Truth, to be loved, needs only to be shown:
Confirm it, once, the fashion to be good
(Since fashion leads the fool, and awes the rude):
No petulance shall wound the public ear;
No hand applaud what honour shuns to hear;
No painful blush the modest cheek shall stain;
The worthy breast shall heave with no disdain.
Chastised to decency, the British stage
Shall oft invite the fair, invite the sage:
Both shall attend well pleased, well pleased depart;
Or, if they doom the verse, absolve the heart.

PROLOGUE TO MALLET'S MUSTAPHA.

Since Athens first began to draw mankind,
To picture life, and show the impassion'd mind,
The truly wise have ever deem'd the stage
The moral school of each enlighten'd age.
There, in full pomp, the Tragic Muse appears,
Queen of soft sorrows, and of useful fears.
Faint is the lesson reason's rules impart:
She pours it strong, and instant through the heart.
If virtue is her theme, we sudden glow
With generous flame; and what we feel, we grow.
If vice she paints, indignant passions rise;
The villain sees himself with loathing eyes.
His soul starts, conscious, at another's groan,
And the pale tyrant trembles on his throne.
    To-night, our meaning scene attempts to show
What fell events from dark suspicion flow;
Chief when it taints a lawless monarch's mind,
To the false herd of flattering slaves confined,
The soul sinks gradual to so dire a state;
E'en excellence but serves to feed its hate;

To hate remorseless cruelty succeeds,
And every worth, and every virtue bleeds.
Behold, our author at your bar appears,
His modest hopes depress'd by conscious fears.
Faults he has many—but to balance those,
His verse with heartfelt love of virtue glows:
All slighter errors let indulgence spare,
And be his equal trial full and fair.
For this best British privilege we call,
Then, as he merits, let him stand or fall.

TO THE REVEREND PATRICK MURDOCK,

RECTOR OF STRADISHALL, IN SUFFOLK.   1738.

Thus safely low, my friend, thou canst not fall:
Here reigns a deep tranquillity o'er all:
No noise, no care, no vanity, no strife;
Men, woods, and fields, all breathe untroubled life.
Then keep each passion down, however dear;
Trust me, the tender are the most severe.
Guard, while 'tis thine, thy philosophic ease,
And ask no joy but that of virtuous peace;
That bids defiance to the storms of fate·
High bliss is only for a higher state!

TO

HIS ROYAL HIGHNESS THE PRINCE OF WALES.

While secret-leaguing nations frown around,
　　Ready to pour the long-expected storm;
While she, who wont the restless Gaul to bound,
　　Britannia, drooping, grows an empty form;
While on our vitals selfish parties prey,
And deep corruption eats our soul away:

Yet in the Goddess of the main appears
  A gleam of joy, gay-flushing every grace,
As she the cordial voice of millions hears,
  Rejoicing, zealous, o'er thy rising race:
Straight her rekindling eyes resume their fire,
The Virtues smile, the Muses tune the lyre.

But more enchanting than the Muses' song,
  United Britons thy dear offspring hail:
The city triumphs through her glowing throng,
  The shepherd tells his transport to the dale;
The sons of roughest toil forget their pain,
And the glad sailor cheers the midnight main.

Can aught from fair Augusta's gentle blood,
  And thine, thou friend of Liberty! be born:
Can aught save what is lovely, generous, good;
  What will at once defend us, and adorn?
From thence prophetic joy new Edwards eyes,
New Henries, Annas, and Elizas rise.

May fate my fond devoted days extend,
  To sing the promised glories of thy reign!
What though, by years depress'd, my Muse might bend;
  My heart will teach her still a nobler strain:
How, with recover'd Britain, will she soar,
When France insults, and Spain shall rob no more.

MEMORY OF THE RIGHT HON. LORD TALBOT,

LATE CHANCELLOR OF GREAT BRITAIN,

Addressed to his Son.

[FIRST PRINTED IN 1737.]

While with the public, you, my lord, lament
A friend and father lost, permit the Muse—

The Muse assign'd of old a double theme—
To praise dead worth and humble living pride,
Whose generous task begins where interest ends;
Permit her on a Talbot's tomb to lay
This cordial verse sincere, by truth inspired,
Which means not to bestow but borrow fame.
Yes, she may sing his matchless virtues now—
Unhappy that she may.—But where begin?
How from the diamond single out each ray,
Where all, though trembling with ten thousand hues,
Effuse one dazzling undivided light?

Let the low-minded of these narrow days
No more presume to deem the lofty tale
Of ancient times, in pity to their own,
Romance. In Talbot we united saw
The piercing eye, the quick enlighten'd soul,
The graceful ease, the flowing tongue of Greece,
Join'd to the virtues and the force of Rome.

Eternal Wisdom, that all-quickening sun,
Whence every life, in just proportion, draws
Directing life and actuating flame,
Ne'er with a larger portion of its beams
Awaken'd mortal clay. Hence steady, calm,
Diffusive, deep, and clear, his reason saw,
With instantaneous view, the truth of things;
Chief what to human life and human bliss
Pertains, that noblest science, fit for man:
And hence, responsive to his knowledge, glow'd
His ardent virtue. Ignorance and vice,
In consort foul, agree; each heightening each;
While virtue draws from knowledge brighter fire.

What grand, what comely, or what tender sense,
What talent, or what virtue was not his?
What that can render man or great, or good,
Give useful worth, or amiable grace?
Nor could he brook in studious shade to lie,
In soft retirement, indolently pleased
With selfish peace. The Syren of the wise

2 A

(Who steals the Aonian song, and, in the shape
Of Virtue, woos them from a worthless world),
Though deep he felt her charms, could never melt
His strenuous spirit, recollected, calm,
As silent night, yet active as the day.
The more the bold, the bustling, and the bad,
Press to usurp the reins of power, the more
Behoves it virtue, with indignant zeal,
To check their combination. Shall low views
Of sneaking interest or luxurious vice,
The villain's passions quicken more to toil,
And dart a livelier vigour through the soul,
Than those that mingled with our truest good,
With present honour and immortal fame,
Involve the good of all?   An empty form
Is the weak Virtue, that amid the shade
Lamenting lies, with future schemes amused,
While Wickedness and Folly, kindred powers,
Confound the world.   A Talbot's, different far.
Sprung ardent into action: action, that disdain'd
To lose in death-like sloth one pulse of life
That might be saved; disdain'd for coward ease,
And her insipid pleasures, to resign
The prize of glory, the keen sweets of toil,
And those high joys that teach the truly great
To live for others, and for others die.
    Early, behold! he breaks benign on life.
Not breathing more beneficence, the spring
Leads in her swelling train the gentle airs:
While gay, behind her, smiles the kindling waste
Of ruffian storms and Winter's lawless rage.
In him Astrea, to this dim abode
Of ever wandering men, return'd again:
To bless them his delight, to bring them back
From thorny error, from unjoyous wrong,
Into the paths of kind primeval faith,
Of happiness and justice.   All his parts,
His virtues all, collected, sought the good

Of human-kind.   For that he, fervent, felt
The throb of patriots, when they model states:
Anxious for that, nor needful sleep could hold
His still-awaken'd soul; nor friends had charms
To steal, with pleasing guile, one useful hour;
Toil knew no languor, no attraction joy.
Thus with unwearied steps, by Virtue led,
He gain'd the summit of that sacred hill,
Where, raised above black Envy's darkening clouds,
Her spotless temple lifts its radiant front.
Be named, victorious ravagers, no more!
Vanish, ye human comets! shrink your blaze!
Ye that your glory to your terrors owe,
As, o'er the gazing desolated earth,
You scatter famine, pestilence, and war;
Vanish! before this vernal sun of fame;
Effulgent sweetness! beaming life and joy.
    How the heart listen'd while he, pleading, spoke!
While on the enlighten'd mind, with winning art,
His gentle reason so persuasive stole,
That the charm'd hearer thought it was his own.
Ah! when, ye studious of the laws, again
Shall such enchanting,lessons bless your ear!
When shall again the darkest truths, perplex'd,
Be set in ample day! when shall the harsh
And arduous open into smiling ease?
The solid mix with elegant delight?
His was the talent with the purest light
At once to pour conviction on the soul,
And warm with lawful flame the impassion'd heart.
That dangerous gift with him was safely lodged
By Heaven—He, sacred to his country's cause,
To trampled want and worth, to suffering right,
To the lone widow's and her orphan's woes,
Reserved the mighty charm.   With equal brow,
Despising then the smiles or frowns of power,
He all that noblest eloquence effused,
Which generous passion, taught by reason, breathes:

Then spoke the man; and over barren art,
Prevail'd abundant nature.   Freedom then
His client was, humanity and truth.

    Placed on the seat of justice, there he reign'd,
In a superior sphere of cloudless day,
A pure intelligence.   No tumult there,
No dark emotion, no intemperate heat,
No passion ere disturb'd the clear serene
That round him spread.   A zeal for right alone,
The love of justice, like the steady sun,
Its equal ardour lent; and sometimes raised
Against the sons of violence, of pride,
And bold deceit, his indignation gleam'd,
Yet still by sober dignity restrain'd
As intuition quick, he snatch'd the truth,
Yet with progressive patience, step by step,
Self-diffident, or to the slower kind,
He through the maze of falsehood traced it on,
Till, at the last, evolved, it full appeared,
And e'en the loser own'd the just decree.

    But when, in senates, he, to freedom firm,
Enlighten'd Freedom, plann'd salubrious laws,
His various learning, his wide knowledge, then,
His insight deep into Britannia's weal,
Spontaneous seem'd from simple sense to flow,
And the plain patriot smoothed the brow of law.
To specious swell, no frothy pomp of words
Fell on the cheated ear; no studied maze
Of declamation, to perplex the right,
He darkening threw around: safe in itself,
In its own force, all-powerful Reason spoke;
While on the great, the ruling point, at once,
He stream'd decisive day, and show'd it vain
To lengthen further out the clear debate.
Conviction breathes conviction; to the heart,
Pour'd ardent forth in eloquence unbid,
The heart attends: for let the venal try
Their every hardening stupifying art

Truth must prevail, zeal will enkindle zeal,
And Nature, skilful touch'd, is honest still.
  Behold him in the councils of his prince.
What faithful light he lends!   How rare, in courts,
Such wisdom! such abilities! and join'd
To virtue so determined, public zeal,
And honour of such adamantine proof,
As e'en corruption, hopeless, and o'erawed,
Durst not have tempted! yet of manners mild,
And winning every heart, he knew to please,
Nobly to please; while equally he scorn'd
Or adulation to receive, or give.
Happy the state, where wakes a ruling eye
Of such inspection keen, and general care!
Beneath a guard so vigilant, so pure,
Toil may resign his careless head to rest,
And ever jealous freedom sleep in peace.
Ah! lost untimely! lost in downward days!
And many a patriot council with him lost!
Counsels, that might have humbled Britain's foe,
Her native foe, from eldest time by fate
Appointed, as did once a Talbot's arms.
  Let learning, arts, let universal worth,
Lament a patron lost, a friend and judge,
Unlike the sons of vanity, that veil'd
Beneath the patron's prostituted name,
Dare sacrifice a worthy man to pride,
And flush confusion o'er an honest cheek.
When he conferr'd a grace, it seem'd a debt
Which he to merit, to the public, paid,
And to the great all-bounteous Source of good!
His sympathising heart itself received
The generous obligation he bestow'd.
This, this indeed, is patronising worth.
Their kind protector him the Muses own,
But scorn with noble pride the boasted aid
Of tasteless vanity's insulting hand.
The gracious stream, that cheers the letter'd world,

Is not the noisy gift of summer's noon,
Whose sudden current, from the naked root,
Washes the little soil which yet remain'd,
And only more dejects the blushing flowers:
No, 'tis the soft-descending dews at eve,
The silent treasures of the vernal year,
Indulging deep their stores, the still night long;
Till, with returning morn, the freshen'd world,
Is fragrance all, all beauty, joy, and song.

Still let me view him in the pleasing light
Of private life, where pomp forgets to glare,
And where the plain unguarded soul is seen.
There, with that truest greatness he appear'd,
Which thinks not of appearing; kindly veil'd
In the soft graces of the friendly scene,
Inspiring social confidence and ease.
As free the converse of the wise and good,
As joyous, disentangling every power,
And breathing mix'd improvement with delight,
As when amid the various-blossom'd spring,
Or gentle beaming autumn's pensive shade,
The philosophic mind with nature talks.
Say ye, his sons, his dear remains, with whom
The father laid superfluous state aside,
Yet raised your filial duty thence the more,
With friendship raised it, with esteem, with love,
Beyond the ties of love, oh! speak the joy,
The pure serene, the cheerful wisdom mild,
The virtuous spirit, which his vacant hours,
In semblance of amusement, through the breast
Infused.   And thou, O Rundle!* lend thy strain,
Thou darling friend! thou brother of his soul!
In whom the head and heart their stores unite:
Whatever fancy paints, invention pours,
Judgment digests, the well-tuned bosom feels,
Truth natural, moral, or divine, has taught,

---

* Dr Rundle, bishop of Derry in Ireland.

The Virtues dictate, or the Muses sing.
Lend me the plaint, which to the lonely main,
With memory conversing, you will pour,
As on the pebbled shore you, pensive, stray,
Where Derry's mountains a bleak crescent form,
And 'mid their ample round receive the waves,
That from the frozen pole, resounding, rush,
Impetuous.   Though from native sunshine driven,
Driven from your friends, the sunshine of the soul,
By slanderous zeal, and politics infirm,
Jealous of worth; yet will you bless your lot,
Yet will you triumph in your glorious fate,
Whence Talbot's friendship glows to future times,
Intrepid, warm; of kindred tempers born;
Nursed, by experience, into slow esteem,
Calm confidence unbounded, love not blind,
And the sweet light from mingled minds disclosed,
From mingled chymic oils as bursts the fire.
    I too remember well that cheerful bowl,
Which round his table flow'd.   The serious there
Mix'd with the sportive, with the learn'd the plain;
Mirth soften'd wisdom, candour temper'd mirth;
And wit its honey lent, without the sting.
Not simple nature's unaffected sons,
The blameless Indians, round their forest-cheer,
In sunny lawn or shady covert set,
Hold more unspotted converse; nor, of old,
Rome's awful consuls, her dictator swains,
As on the product of their Sabine farms
They fared, with stricter virtue fed the soul;
Nor yet in Athens, at an Attic meal,
Where Socrates presided, fairer truth,
More elegant humanity, more grace,
Wit more refined, or deeper science reign'd.
    But far beyond the little vulgar bounds
Of family, or friends, or native land,
By just degrees, and with proportion'd flame,
Extended his benevolence: a friend

To human-kind, to parent nature's works.
Of free access, and of engaging grace,
Such as a brother to a brother owes,
He kept an open judging ear for all,
And spread an open countenance, where smiled
The fair effulgence of an open heart;
While on the rich, the poor, the high, the low,
With equal ray, his ready goodness shone:
For nothing human foreign was to him.

Thus to a dread inheritance, my lord,
And hard to be supported, you succeed:
But, kept by virtue, as by virtue gain'd,
It will, through latest time, enrich your race,
When grosser wealth shall moulder into dust,
And with their authors in oblivion sunk
Vain titles lie, the servile badges oft
Of mean submission, not the meed of worth.
True genuine honour its large patent holds
Of all mankind, through every land and age,
Of universal reason's various sons,
And e'en of God himself, sole perfect Judge!
Yet know these noblest honours of the mind
On rigid terms descend: the high-placed heir,
Scann'd by the public eye, that, with keen gaze,
Malignant seeks out faults, cannot through life,
Amid the nameless insects of a court,
Unheeded steal: but, with his sire compared,
He must be glorious, or he must be scorn'd.
This truth to you, who merit well to bear
A name to Britons dear, the officious Muse
May safely sing, and sing without reserve.

Vain were the plaint, and ignorant the tear,
That should a Talbot mourn. Ourselves, indeed,
Our country robb'd of her delight and strength,
We may lament. Yet let us, grateful, joy
That we such virtues knew, such virtues felt,
And feel them still, teaching our views to rise
Through ever brightening scenes of future worlds.

Be dumb, ye worst of zealots! ye that, prone
To thoughtless dust, renounce that generous hope,
Whence every joy below its spirit draws,
And every pain its balm: a Talbot's light,
A Talbot's virtues claim another source
Than the blind maze of undesigning blood;
Nor when that vital fountain plays no more,
Can they be quench'd amid the gelid stream.
  Methinks I see his mounting spirit, freed
From tangling earth, regain the realms of day,
Its native country: whence to bless mankind,
Eternal Goodness on this darksome spot
Had ray'd it down awhile. Behold! approved
By the tremendous Judge of heaven and earth,
And to the Almighty Father's presence join'd,
He takes his rank, in glory, and in bliss,
Amid the human worthies. Glad around
Crowd his compatriot shades, and point him out,
With joyful pride, Britannia's blameless boast.
Ah! who is he, that with a fonder eye
Meets thine enraptured?—'Tis the best of sons!
The best of friends!—— Too soon is realised
That hope, which once forbade thy tears to flow!
Meanwhile the kindred souls of every land
(Howe'er divided in the fretful days
Of prejudice and error), mingled now,
In one selected never-jarring state,
Where God himself their only monarch reigns,
Partake the joy; yet, such the sense that still
Remains of earthly woes, for us below,
And for our loss, they drop a pitying tear.
But cease, presumptuous Muse, nor vainly strive
To quit this cloudy sphere, that binds thee down:
'Tis not for mortal hand to trace these scenes—
Scenes, that our gross ideas grovelling cast
Behind, and strike our boldest language dumb.
  Forgive, immortal shade! if aught from earth,
From dust low warbled, to those groves can rise,

Where flows celestial harmony, forgive
This fond superfluous verse.   With deep-felt voice,
On every heart impress'd, thy deeds themselves
Attest thy praise.   Thy praise the widow's sighs,
And orphan's tears embalm.   The good, the bad,
The sons of justice and the sons of strife,
All who or freedom or who interest prize,
A deep-divided nation's parties all,
Conspire to swell thy spotless praise to Heaven.
Glad Heaven receives it, and seraphic lyres
With songs of triumph thy arrival hail.
How vain this tribute then! this lowly lay!
Yet nought is vain that gratitude inspires.
The Muse, besides, her duty thus approves
To virtue, to her country, to mankind,
To ruling nature, that, in glorious charge,
As to her priestess, gives it her to hymn
Whatever good and excellent she forms.

TO THE

MEMORY OF SIR ISAAC NEWTON.

INSCRIBED TO THE RIGHT HON. SIR ROBERT WALPOLE.

[FIRST PRINTED 1727.]

Shall the great soul of Newton quit this earth,
To mingle with his stars; and every Muse,
Astonish'd into silence, shun the weight
Of honours due to his illustrious name?
But what can man?   E'en now the sons of light,
In strains high warbled to seraphic lyre,
Hail his arrival on the coast of bliss.
Yet am not I deterr'd, though high the theme,

And sung to harps of angels, for with you,
Ethereal flames! ambitious, I aspire
In Nature's general symphony to join.
   And what new wonders can ye show your guest?
Who, while on this dim spot, where mortals toil
Clouded in dust, from Motion's simple laws,
Could trace the secret hand of Providence,
Wide working through this universal frame.
   Have ye not listen'd while he bound the suns
And planets to their spheres! the unequal task
Of human-kind till then. Oft had they roll'd
O'er erring man the year, and oft disgraced
The pride of schools, before their course was known
Full in its causes and effects to him,
All-piercing sage! Who sat not down and dream'd
Romantic schemes, defended by the din
Of specious words, and tyranny of names;
But, bidding his amazing mind attend,
And with heroic patience years on years
Deep-searching, saw at last the system dawn,
And shine, of all his race, on him alone.
   What were his raptures then! how pure! how strong!
And what the triumphs of old Greece and Rome,
By his diminish'd, but the pride of boys
In some small fray victorious! when, instead
Of shatter'd parcels of this earth usurp'd
By violence unmanly, and sore deeds
Of cruelty and blood, Nature herself
Stood all-subdued by him, and open laid
Her every latent glory to his view.
   All intellectual eye, our solar round
First gazing through, he, by the blended power
Of gravitation and projection, saw
The whole in silent harmony revolve.
From unassisted vision hid, the moons,
To cheer remoter planets numerous form'd,
By him in all their mingled tracts were seen.
He also fix'd our wandering Queen of Night,

Whether she wanes into a scanty orb,
Or, waxing broad, with her pale shadowy light,
In a soft deluge overflows the sky.
Her every motion clear-discerning, he
Adjusted to the mutual main, and taught
Why now the mighty mass of waters swells
Resistless, heaving on the broken rocks,
And the full river turning: till again
The tide revertive, unattracted, leaves
A yellow waste of idle sands behind.
  Then breaking hence, he took his ardent flight
Through the blue infinite: and every star,
Which the clear concave of a winter's night
Pours on the eye, or astronomic tube,
Far stretching, snatches from the dark abyss;
Or such as further in successive skies
To fancy shine alone, at his approach
Blazed into suns, the living centre each
Of an harmonious system: all combined,
And ruled unerring by that single power,
Which draws the stone projected to the ground.
  O unprofuse magnificence divine!
O wisdom truly perfect! thus to call
From a few causes such a scheme of things,
Effects so various, beautiful, and great,
A universe complete! And O, beloved
Of Heaven! whose well-purged penetrating eye
The mystic veil transpiercing, inly scann'd
The rising, moving, wide-establish'd frame.
  He, first of men, with awful wing pursued
The Comet through the long elliptic curve,
As round innumerous worlds he wound his way;
Till, to the forehead of our evening sky
Return'd, the blazing wonder glares anew,
And o'er the trembling nations shakes dismay.
  The heavens are all his own; from the wide rule
Of whirling vortices, and circling spheres,
To their first great simplicity restored.

The schools astonish'd stood; but found it vain
To combat still with demonstration strong,
And unawaken'd dream beneath the blaze
Of truth.   At once their pleasing visions fled,
With the gay shadows of the morning mix'd,
When Newton rose, our philosophic sun!
    The aerial flow of Sound was known to him,
From whence it first in wavy circles breaks,
Till the touch'd organ takes the message in.
Nor could the darting beam of speed immense
Escape his swift pursuit, and measuring eye.
E'en light itself, which everything displays,
Shone undiscover'd, till his brighter mind
Untwisted all the shining robe of day;
And from the whitening undistinguish'd blaze,
Collecting every ray into his kind,
To the charm'd eye educed the gorgeous train
Of parent colours.   First the flaming red
Sprung vivid forth; the tawny orange next;
And next delicious yellow; by whose side
Fell the kind beams of all-refreshing green.
Then the pure blue, that swells autumnal skies,
Ethereal play'd; and then, of sadder hue,
Emerged the deepen'd indigo, as when
The heavy-skirted evening droops with frost.
While the last gleamings of refracted light
Died in the fainting violet away.
These, when the clouds distil the rosy shower,
Shine out distinct adown the watery bow;
While o'er our heads the dewy vision bends
Delightful, melting on the fields beneath.
Myriads of mingling dyes from these result,
And myriads still remain; infinite source
Of beauty, ever blushing, ever new.
    Did ever poet image aught so fair,
Dreaming in whispering groves, by the hoarse brook?
Or prophet, to whose rapture heaven descends?
E'en now the setting sun and shifting clouds,

Seen, Greenwich, from thy lovely heights, declare
How just, how beauteous the refractive law.
   The noiseless tide of Time, all bearing down
To vast eternity's unbounded sea,
Where the green islands of the happy shine,
He stemm'd alone; and to the source (involved
Deep in primeval gloom) ascending, raised
His lights at equal distances, to guide
Historian, wilder'd on his darksome way.
   But who can number up his labours? who
His high discoveries sing? but when a few
Of the deep-studying race can stretch their minds
To what he knew: in fancy's lighter thought,
How shall the Muse then grasp the mighty theme?
   What wonder thence that his devotion swell'd
Responsive to his knowledge? For could he,
Whose piercing mental eye diffusive saw
The finish'd university of things,
In all its order, magnitude, and parts,
Forbear incessant to adore that Power
Who fills, sustains, and actuates the whole?
   Say ye, who best can tell, ye happy few,
Who saw him in the softest lights of life,
All unwithheld, indulging to his friends
The vast unborrow'd treasures of his mind,
Oh, speak the wondrous man! how mild, how calm,
How greatly humble, how divinely good;
How firmly stablish'd on eternal truth;
Fervent in doing well, with every nerve
Still pressing on, forgetful of the past,
And panting for perfection: far above
Those little cares, and visionary joys,
That so perplex the fond impassion'd heart
Of ever-cheated, ever-trusting man.
   And you, ye hopeless, gloomy-minded tribe,
You who, unconscious of those nobler flights
That reach impatient at immortal life,
Against the prime endearing privilege

Of being dare contend—say, can a soul
Of such extensive, deep, tremendous powers,
Enlarging still, be but a finer breath
Of spirits dancing through their tubes awhile,
And then for ever lost in vacant air?
 But hark! methinks I hear a warning voice,
Solemn as when some awful change is come,
Sound through the world—"'Tis done!—The measure's full;
And I resign my charge."—Ye mouldering stones,
That build the towering pyramid, the proud
Triumphal arch, the monument effaced
By ruthless ruin, and whate'er supports
The worshipp'd name of hoar antiquity,
Down to the dust! what grandeur can ye boast,
While Newton lifts his column to the skies,
Beyond the waste of time? Let no weak drop
Be shed for him. The virgin in her bloom
Cut off, the joyous youth, and darling child,
These are the tombs that claim the tender tear,
And elegiac song. But Newton calls
For other notes of gratulation high;
That now he wanders through those endless worlds
He here so well descried, and wondering talks,
And hymns their Author with his glad compeers.
O Britain's boast! whether with angels thou
Sittest in dread discourse, or fellow-bless'd,
Who joy to see the honour of their kind;
Or whether, mounted on cherubic wing,
Thy swift career is with the whirling orbs,
Comparing things with things, in rapture lost,
And grateful adoration, for that light
So plenteous ray'd into thy mind below,
From light himself; oh, look with pity down
On human-kind, a frail erroneous race!
Exalt the spirit of a downward world!
O'er thy dejected Country chief preside,
And be her Genius call'd! her studies raise,
Correct her manners, and inspire her youth.

For, though depraved and sunk, she brought thee forth,
And glories in thy name: she points thee out
To all her sons, and bids them eye thy star:
While in expectance of the second life,
When time shall be no more, thy sacred dust
Sleeps with her kings, and dignifies the scene.

THE

POETICAL WORKS

OF

THOMAS GRAY.

CONTENTS.

ELEGY.

WRITTEN IN A COUNTRY CHURCHYARD.

THE curfew tolls the knell of parting day,
 The lowing herd winds slowly o'er the lea,
The ploughman homeward plods his weary way,
 And leaves the world to darkness and to me.

Now shades the glimmering landscape on the sight,
 And all the air a solemn stillness holds,
Save where the beetle wheels his droning flight,
 And drowsy tinklings lull the distant folds;

Save that from yonder ivy-mantled tower,
 The moping owl does to the moon complain
Of such as, wand'ring near her secret bower,
 Molest her ancient solitary reign.

Beneath those rugged elms, that yew-tree's shade,
 Where heaves the turf in many a mould'ring heap,
Each in his narrow cell for ever laid,
 The rude forefathers of the hamlet sleep.

The breezy call of incense-breathing Morn,
 The swallow twitt'ring from the straw-built shed,
The cock's shrill clarion, or the echoing horn,
 No more shall rouse them from their lowly bed.

For them no more the blazing hearth shall burn,
 Or busy housewife ply her evening care;
No children run to lisp their sire's return,
 Or climb his knees, the envied kiss to share.

Oft did the harvest to their sickle yield,
　　Their furrow oft the stubborn glebe has broke;
How jocund did they drive their team afield!
　　How bow'd the woods beneath their sturdy stroke!

Let not ambition mock their useful toil,
　　Their homely joys, and destiny obscure;
Nor grandeur hear, with a disdainful smile,
　　The short and simple annals of the poor:

The boast of heraldry, the pomp of power,
　　And all that beauty, all that wealth ere gave,
Await alike the inevitable hour—
　　The paths of glory lead but to the grave.

Nor you, ye proud, impute to these the fault,
　　If memory o'er the tomb no trophies raise,
Where through the long-drawn aisle and fretted vault,
　　The pealing anthem swells the note of praise.

Can storied urn or animated bust
　　Back to its mansion call the fleeting breath?
Can honour's voice provoke the silent dust,
　　Or flatt'ry soothe the dull cold ear of Death?

Perhaps in this neglected spot is laid
　　Some heart once pregnant with celestial fire,
Hands that the rod of empire might have sway'd,
　　Or waked to ecstacy the living lyre.

But knowledge to their eyes her ample page,
　　Rich with the spoils of time, did ne'er unroll;
Chill penury repress'd their noble rage,
　　And froze the genial current of the soul.

Full many a gem of purest ray serene,
　　The dark unfathom'd caves of ocean bear;
Full many a flower is born to blush unseen,
　　And waste its sweetness on the desert air.

Some village-Hampden, that with dauntless breast
　　The little tyrant of his fields withstood,

Some mute inglorious Milton here may rest,
  Some Cromwell guiltless of his country's blood.

Th' applause of list'ning senates to command,
  The threats of pain and ruin to despise,
To scatter plenty o'er a smiling land,
  And read their history in a nation's eyes—

Their lot forbade, nor circumscribed alone
  Their growing virtues, but their crimes confined;
Forbade to wade through slaughter to a throne,
  And shut the gates of mercy on mankind,

The struggling pangs of conscious truth to hide,
  To quench the blushes of ingenuous shame,
Or heap the shrine of luxury and pride
  With incense kindled at the Muse's flame.

* Far from the madding crowd's ignoble strife,
  Their sober wishes never learn'd to stray;
Along the cool sequester'd vale of life
  They kept the noiseless tenor of their way.

Yet ev'n these bones from insult to protect
  Some frail memorial still erected nigh,
With uncouth rhymes and shapeless sculpture deck'd,
  Implores the passing tribute of a sigh.

---

* Between this and the preceding stanza, in the first MS. of
the poem, were the four following:—
  The thoughtless world to majesty may bow,
    Exalt the brave, and idolise success;
  But more to innocence their safety owe,
    Than pow'r or genius e'er conspired to bless.

  And thou who, mindful of the unhonour'd Dead,
    Dost in these notes their artless tales relate,
  By night and lonely contemplation led
    To wander in the gloomy walks of fate:

  Hark! how the sacred calm, that breathes around,
    Bids every fierce tumultuous passion cease;
  In still small accents whispering from the ground,
    A grateful earnest of eternal peace.

Their name, their years, spelt by th' unletter'd Muse,
  The place of fame and elegy supply;
And many a holy text around she strews,
  That teach the rustic moralist to die.

For who to dumb forgetfulness a prey
  This pleasing anxious being e'er resign'd,
Left the warm precincts of the cheerful day,
  Nor cast one longing, ling'ring look behind?

On some fond breast the parting soul relies,
  Some pious drops the closing eye requires;
Ev'n from the tomb the voice of nature cries,
  Ev'n in our ashes live their wonted fires.

For thee, who, mindful of the unhonour'd Dead,
  Dost in these lines their artless tale relate,
If chance, by lonely contemplation led,
  Some kindred spirit shall inquire thy fate,

Haply some hoary-headed swain may say—
  "Oft have we seen him at the peep of dawn,
Brushing with hasty step the dews away,
  To meet the sun upon the upland lawn.*

There, at the foot of yonder nodding beech,
  That wreaths its old fantastic roots so high,

  No more, with reason and thyself at strife,
    Give anxious cares and endless wishes room;
  But through the cool sequester'd vale of life
    Pursue the silent tenor of thy doom.

And here the poem was originally intended to conclude, before
the happy idea of the hoary-headed swain, &c., suggested itself
to him.

  * Variation:—"On the high brow of yonder hanging lawn."
After which, in the first manuscript, followed this stanza:—

    Him have we seen the greenwood side along,
      While o'er the heath we hied, our labour done,
    Oft as the woodlark piped her farewell song,
      With wistful eyes pursue the setting sun.

His listless length at noontide would he stretch,
    And pore upon the brook that babbles by.

Hard by yon wood, now smiling as in scorn,
    Muttering his wayward fancies, he would rove:
Now drooping, woful wan, like one forlorn,
    Or crazed with care, or cross'd in hopeless love.

One morn I miss'd him on the 'custom'd hill,
    Along the heath, and near his fav'rite tree:
Another came; nor yet beside the rill,
    Nor up the lawn, nor at the wood was he.

The next, with dirges due, in sad array,
    Slow through the church-way path we saw him borne—
Approach and read (for thou canst read) the lay,
    Graved on the stone beneath yon aged thorn."

THE EPITAPH.*

Here rests his head upon the lap of earth
    A youth to fortune and to fame unknown;
Fair science frown'd not on his humble birth,
    And melancholy mark'd him for her own.

Large was his bounty, and his soul sincere,
    Heav'n did a recompense as largely send:
He gave to misery all he had—a tear;
    He gain'd from Heaven ('twas all he wish'd)—a friend.

No farther seek his merits to disclose,
    Or draw his frailties from their dread abode;
There they alike in trembling hope repose,
    The bosom of his Father and his God.

---

* Before the epitaph, was originally inserted a very beautiful stanza, which was printed in some of the first editions, but
afterwards omitted, because he thought that it was too long a pa-
renthesis in this place. The lines, however, are in themselves
exquisitely fine, and demand preservation:—
    There scatter'd oft, the earliest of the year,
        By hands unseen, are showers of violets found;
    The redbreast loves to build and warble there,
        And little footsteps lightly print the ground.

ODES.

ON THE SPRING.

Lo! where the rosy-bosom'd hours,
   Fair Venus' train, appear,
Disclose the long-expecting flowers,
   And wake the purple year;
The Attic warbler pours her throat,
Responsive to the cuckoo's note,
   The untaught harmony of spring;
While, whisp'ring pleasure as they fly,
Cool zephyrs through the clear blue sky
   Their gather'd fragrance fling.

Where'er the oak's thick branches stretch
   A broader, browner shade,
Where'er the rude and moss-grown beech
   O'er-canopies the glade,
Beside some water's rushy brink
With me the Muse shall sit, and think
   (At ease reclined in rustic state)
How vain the ardour of the crowd!
How low, how little, are the proud!
   How indigent the great!

Still is the toiling hand of care,
   The panting herds repose—
Yet hark! how through the peopled air
   The busy murmur glows!
The insect youth are on the wing,
Eager to taste the honied spring,
   And float amid the liquid noon;
Some lightly o'er the current skim,
Some show their gaily-gilded trim,
   Quick-glancing to the sun.

To contemplation's sober eye
　　Such is the race of man:
And they that creep, and they that fly,
　　Shall end where they began.
Alike the busy and the gay
But flutter through life's little day,
　　In fortune's varying colours drest:
Brush'd by the hand of rough mischance,
Or chill'd by age, their airy dance
　　They leave, in dust to rest.

Methinks I hear, in accents low,
　　The sportive kind reply:
Poor moralist! and what art thou?
　　A solitary fly!
Thy joys no glitt'ring female meets,
No hive hast thou of hoarded sweets,
　　No painted plumage to display;
On hasty wings thy youth is flown,
Thy sun is set, thy spring is gone—
　　We frolic while 'tis May.

ON THE DEATH OF A FAVOURITE CAT,

DROWNED IN A TUB OF GOLD FISHES.

'Twas on a lofty vase's side,
Where China's gayest art had dyed
　　The azure flowers that blow—
Demurest of the tabby kind,
The pensive Selima reclined,
　　Gazed on the lake below.

Her conscious tail her joy declared;
The fair round face, the snowy beard,
　　The velvet of her paws,

Her coat, that with the tortoise vies,
Her ears of jet, and emerald eyes,
　　She saw; and purr'd applause.

Still had she gazed; but 'midst the tide
Two angel forms were seen to glide,
　　The genii of the stream:
Their scaly armour's Tyrian hue
Through richest purple to the view
　　Betray'd a golden gleam.

The hapless nymph with wonder saw:
A whisker first, and then a claw,
　　With many an ardent wish,
She stretch'd in vain to reach the prize.
What female heart can gold despise?
　　What cat's averse to fish?

Presumptuous maid! with looks intent
Again she stretch'd, again she bent,
　　Nor knew the gulf between
(Malignant fate sat by, and smiled):
The slipp'ry verge her feet beguiled—
　　She tumbled headlong in.

Eight times emerging from the flood,
She mew'd to every watery god
　　Some speedy aid to send:
No Dolphin came, no Nereid stirr'd;
Nor cruel *Tom*, nor *Susan* heard—
　　A fav'rite has no friend!

From hence, ye beauties undeceived,
Know, one false step is ne'er retrieved,
　　And be with caution bold.
Not all that tempts your wandering eyes
And heedless hearts, is lawful prize;
　　Nor all that glisters gold.

ON A DISTANT PROSPECT OF ETON COLLEGE.

Ἄνθρωπος· ἱκανὴ πρόφασις εἰς τὸ δυσυχεῖν.—MENANDER.

Ye distant spires, ye antique towers,
   That crown the watery glade,
Where grateful science still adores
   Her Henry's* holy shade;
And ye, that from the stately brow
Of Windsor's heights th' expanse below
   Of grove, of lawn, of mead survey,
Whose turf, whose shade, whose flowers among,
Wanders the hoary Thames along
   His silver-winding way!

Ah, happy hills! ah, pleasing shade!
   Ah, fields beloved in vain,
Where once my careless childhood stray'd,
   A stranger yet to pain!
I feel the gales that from ye blow,
A momentary bliss bestow,
   As waving fresh their gladsome wing,
My weary soul they seem to soothe,
And, redolent of joy and youth,
   To breathe a second spring.

Say, Father Thames—for thou hast seen
   Full many a sprightly race,
Disporting on thy margin green,
   The paths of pleasure trace—
Who foremost now delight to cleave
With pliant arm thy glassy wave?
   The captive linnet which inthral?
What idle progeny succeed
To chase the rolling circle's speed,
   Or urge the flying ball?

---

* King Henry VI., founder of the college.

While some, on earnest business bent,
　　Their murm'ring labours ply
'Gainst graver hours, that bring constraint
　　To sweeten liberty;
Some bold adventurers disdain
The limits of their little reign,
　　And unknown regions dare descry:
Still as they run they look behind,
They hear a voice in every wind,
　　And snatch a fearful joy.

Gay hope is theirs by fancy fed,
　　Less pleasing when possest;
The tear forgot as soon as shed,
　　The sunshine of the breast:
Theirs buxom health of rosy hue,
Wild wit, invention ever new,
　　And lively cheer of vigour born;
The thoughtless day, the easy night,
The spirits pure, the slumbers light,
　　That fly the approach of morn.

Alas! regardless of their doom,
　　The little victims play:
No sense have they of ills to come,
　　Nor care beyond to-day.
Yet see how all around them wait
The ministers of human fate,
　　And black misfortune's baleful train!
Ah, show them where in ambush stand
To seize their prey the murd'rous band!
　　Ah, tell them they are men!

These shall the fury passions tear,
　　The vultures of the mind,
Disdainful anger, pallid fear,
　　And shame that skulks behind;
Or pining love shall waste their youth,
Or jealousy with rankling tooth,
　　That inly gnaws the secret heart,

And envy wan, and faded care,
Grim-visaged comfortless despair,
  And sorrow's piercing dart.

Ambition this shall tempt to rise,
  Then whirl the wretch from high,
To bitter scorn a sacrifice,
  And grinning infamy.
The stings of falsehood those shall try,
And hard unkindness' alter'd eye,
  That mocks the tear it forced to flow;
And keen remorse with blood defiled,
And moody madness laughing wild
  Amid severest wo.

Lo! in the vale of years beneath
  A grizzly troop are seen,
The painful family of Death,
  More hideous than their queen:
This racks the joints, this fires the veins,
That every labouring sinew strains,
  Those in the deeper vitals rage:
Lo! poverty, to fill the band,
That numbs the soul with icy hand,
  And slow-consuming age.

To each his suff'rings: all are men
  Condemn'd alike to groan—
The tender for another's pain,
  Th' unfeeling for his own.
Yet, ah! why should they know their fate?
Since sorrow never comes too late,
  And happiness too swiftly flies,
Thought would destroy their paradise.
No more; where ignorance is bliss,
  'Tis folly to be wise.

TO ADVERSITY.

———Ζῆνα
Τον φρονειν Βροτους ὁδω-
σαντα, τῳ παθει μαθων
Θεντα κυριως εχειν.
ÆSCHYLUS, *in "Agamemnon."*

Daughter of Jove, relentless power,
　　Thou tamer of the human breast,
Whose iron scourge and torturing hour.
　　The bad affright, afflict the best!
Bound in thy adamantine chain,
The proud are taught to taste of pain,
　　And purple tyrants vainly groan
With pangs unfelt before, unpitied and alone.

When first thy sire to send on earth
　　Virtue, his darling child, design'd,
To thee he gave the heav'nly birth,
　　And bade to form her infant mind.
Stern rugged nurse! thy rigid lore,
With patience many a year she bore:
　　What sorrow was, thou bad'st her know,
And from her own she learn'd to melt at others' wo.

Scared at thy frown terrific, fly
　　Self-pleasing folly's idle brood—
Wild laughter, noise, and thoughtless joy—
　　And leave us leisure to be good.
Light they disperse, and with them go
The summer friend, the flatt'ring foe:
　　By vain prosperity received,
To her they vow their truth, and are again believed.

Wisdom, in sable garb array'd,
　　Immersed in rapturous thought profound,
And Melancholy, silent maid
　　With leaden eye, that loves the ground,

Still on thy solemn steps attend,—
Warm Charity, the general friend,
　　With Justice to herself severe,
And Pity, dropping soft the sadly-pleasing tear

Oh, gently on thy suppliant's head,
　　Dread goddess, lay thy chast'ning hand!
Not in thy Gorgon terrors clad,
　　Nor circled with the vengeful band
(As by the impious thou art seen),
With thund'ring voice, and threat'ning mien,
　　With screaming horror's funeral cry,
Despair, and fell Disease, and ghastly Poverty.

Thy form benign, oh goddess, wear—
　　Thy milder influence impart—
Thy philosophic train be there
　　To soften, not to wound my heart.
The generous spark extinct revive—
Teach me to love and to forgive—
　　Exact my own defects to scan—
What others are to feel, and know myself a man.

THE PROGRESS OF POESY.

PINDARIC.

Φωνᾶντα συνετοῖσιν' ἐς
Δὲ τὸ πᾶν ἑρμηνέων χατίζει.

PINDAR, *Olymp.* 2.

Awake, Æolian lyre, awake,
And give to rapture all thy trembling strings!
From Helicon's harmonious springs*
A thousand rills their mazy progress take:

---

* The subject and simile, as usual with Pindar, are united.
The various sources of poetry, which give life and lustre to all
its touches, are here described; its quiet majestic progress enrich-
2 c

The laughing flowers that round them blow,
Drink life and fragrance as they flow.
Now the rich stream of music winds along
Deep, majestic, smooth, and strong,
Through verdant vales, and Ceres' golden reign;
Now rolling down the steep amain,
Headlong, impetuous, see it pour:
The rocks and nodding groves, re-bellow to the roar.

Oh! sovereign of the willing soul,*
Parent of sweet and solemn-breathing airs,
Enchanting shell! the sullen cares,   -
And frantic passions hear thy soft crontrol.
On Thracia's hills the Lord of War
Has curb'd the fury of his car,
And dropp'd his thirsty lance at thy command.
Perching on the sceptred hand
Of Jove, thy magic lulls the feather'd king
With ruffled plumes, and flagging wing:
Quench'd in dark clouds of slumber lie
The terror of his beak, and light'nings of his eye.

Thee the voice, the dance obey,†
Temper'd to thy warbled lay.
O'er Idalia's velvet-green
The rosy-crowned loves are seen
On Cytherea's day
With antic sport, and blue-eyed pleasures,
Frisking light in frolic measures;
Now pursuing, now retreating,
Now in circling troops they meet;

---

ing every subject (otherwise dry and barren) with a pomp of
diction and luxuriant harmony of numbers; and its more rapid
and irresistible course, when swollen and hurried away by the
conflict of tumultuous passions.

* Power of harmony to calm the turbulent sallies of the soul.
The thoughts are borrowed from the first Pythian of Pindar.

† Power of harmony to produce all the graces of motion in the
body.

To brisk notes in cadence beating
Glance their many-twinkling feet.
Slow melting strains their queen's approach declare:
Where'er she turns the Graces homage pay.
With arms sublime, that float upon the air,
In gliding state she wins her easy way:
O'er her warm cheek and rising bosom move
The bloom of young desire and purple light of love.

Man's feeble race what ills await—*
Labour, and penury, the racks of pain,
Disease, and sorrow's weeping train,
And death, sad refuge from the storms of fate!
The fond complaint, my song, disprove,
And justify the laws of Jove.
Say, has he given in vain the heav'nly Muse?
Night, and all her sickly dews,
Her spectres wan, and birds of boding cry,
He gives to range the dreary sky;
Till down the eastern cliffs afar
Hyperion's march they spy, and glitt'ring shafts of war.

In climes beyond the solar road,†
Where shaggy forms o'er ice-built mountains roam,
The Muse has broke the twilight gloom,
To cheer the shiv'ring native's dull abode.
And oft, beneath the odorous shade
Of Chili's boundless forests laid,
She deigns to hear the savage youth repeat,
In loose numbers wildly sweet,
Their feather-cinctured chiefs, and dusky loves.
Her track, where'er the goddess roves,

---

* To compensate the real and imaginary ills of life, the Muse
was given to mankind by the same Providence that sends the
day by its cheerful presence to dispel the gloom and terrors of
the night.

† Extensive influence of poetic genius over the remotest and
most uncivilised nations: its connection with liberty, and the
virtues that naturally attend on it.

Glory pursue, and generous Shame,
Th' unconquerable Mind, and Freedom's holy flame.

Woods, that wave o'er Delphi's steep,*
Isles, that crown th' Ægean deep,
Fields, that cool Ilissus laves,
Or where Mæander's amber waves
In lingering lab'rinths creep—
How do your tuneful echoes languish,
Mute, but to the voice of anguish?
Where each old poetic mountain
Inspiration breathed around,
Ev'ry shade and hallow'd fountain
Murmur'd deep a solemn sound;
Till the sad Nine in Greece's evil hour
Left their Parnassus for the Latian plains.
Alike they scorn the pomp of tyrant Power,
And coward Vice, that revels in her chains.
When Latium had her lofty spirit lost,
They sought, oh Albion! next thy sea-encircled coast

Far from the sun and summer-gale,
In thy green lap was nature's darling† laid,
What time, where lucid Avon stray'd,
To him the mighty mother did unveil
Her awful face: the dauntless child
Stretch'd forth his little arms and smiled.
This pencil take (she said) whose colours clear
Richly paint the vernal year:
Thine, too, these golden keys, immortal boy!
This can unlock the gates of joy,

---

* Progress of poetry from Greece to Italy, and from Italy to
England. Chaucer was not unacquainted with the writings of
Dante or of Petrarch. The Earl of Surrey and Sir Thomas
Wyatt had travelled in Italy, and formed their taste there;
Spenser imitated the Italian writers; Milton improved on them:
but this school expired soon after the Restoration, and a new one
arose on the French model, which subsisted almost to our own time.

† Shakspere.

Of horror that, and thrilling fears,
Or ope the sacred source of sympathetic tears.

Nor second he,* that rode sublime
Upon the seraph-wings of ecstacy,
The secrets of the abyss to spy.
He pass'd the flaming bounds of Place and Time:
The living throne, the sapphire blaze,
Where angels tremble while they gaze,
IIe saw; but, blasted with excess of light,
Closed his eyes in endless night.
Behold where Dryden's less presumptuous car,
Wide o'er the fields of glory bear
Two coursers of ethereal race,
With necks in thunder clothed, and long-resounding
    pace.

Hark, his hands the lyre explore!
Bright-eyed fancy, hovering o'er,
Scatters from her pictured urn
Thoughts that breathe, and words that burn.
But ah! 'tis heard no more———
Oh! lyre divine, what daring spirit
Wakes thee now? though he inherit
Nor the pride nor ample pinion,
That the Theban Eaglet† bear,
Sailing with supreme dominion,
Through the azure deep of air:
Yet oft before his infant eyes would run
Such forms, as glitter in the Muse's ray,
With orient hues, unborrow'd of the sun:
Yet shall he mount, and keep his distant way
Beyond the limits of a vulgar fate,
Beneath the good how far—but far above the great.

---

* Milton.   † Pindar.

THE BARD.

PINDARIC.*

" Ruin seize thee, ruthless king!
Confusion on thy banners wait,
Though, fann'd by conquest's crimson wing,
They mock the air with idle state!
Helm, nor hauberk's twisted mail,
Nor e'en thy virtues, tyrant, shall avail
To save thy secret soul from nightly fears,
From Cambria's curse, from Cambria's tears!"
Such were the sounds, that o'er the crested pride
Of the first Edward scatter'd wild dismay,
As down the steep of Snowdon's shaggy side
He wound with toilsome march his long array.
Stout Glo'ster† stood aghast in speechless trance:
To arms! cried Mortimer,‡ and couch'd his quiv'ring lance.

On a rock, whose haughty brow
Frowns o'er old Conway's foaming flood,
Robed in the sable garb of wo,
With haggard eyes the poet stood
(Loose his beard, and hoary hair
Stream'd, like a meteor, to the troubled air),
And with a master's hand, and prophet's fire,
Struck the deep sorrows of his lyre.
" Hark, how each giant oak, and desert cave,
Sighs to the torrent's awful voice beneath!

---

* This ode is founded on a tradition current in Wales, that
Edward the First, when he completed the conquest of that country, ordered all the Bards that fell into his hands to be put to
death.

† Gilbert de Clare, surnamed the Red, Earl of Gloucester and
Hertford, son-in-law to King Edward.

‡ Edmond de Mortimer, lord of Wigmore. Both of these
were *Lords-Marchers*, whose lands lay on the borders of Wales,
and who both probably accompanied the king in this expedition.

O'er thee, O king! their hundred arms they wave,
Revenge on thee in hoarser murmurs breathe;
Vocal no more, since Cambria's fatal day,
To high-born Hoel's harp, or soft Llewellyn's lay.

"Cold is Cadwallo's tongue,
That hush'd the stormy main:
Brave Urien sleeps upon his craggy bed:
Mountains, ye mourn in vain
Modred, whose magic song
Made huge Plinlimmon bow his cloud-topp'd head.
On dreary Arvon's shore* they lie,
Smear'd with gore, and ghastly pale:
Far, far aloof th' affrighted ravens sail;
The famish'd eagle screams, and passes by.
Dear lost companions of my tuneful art,
Dear, as the light that visits these sad eyes,
Dear, as the ruddy drops that warm my heart,
Ye died amidst your dying country's cries!
No more I weep. They do not sleep:
On yonder cliffs, a grizzly band,
I see them sit, they linger yet,
Avengers of their native land:
With me in dreadful harmony they join,
And† weave with bloody hands the tissue of thy line.

" Weave the warp, and weave the woof,
The winding-sheet of Edward's race:
Give ample room, and verge enough
The characters of hell to trace.
Mark the year, and mark the night,
When Severn shall re-echo with affright
The shrieks of death through Berkley's roofs that ring,
Shrieks of an agonising king!‡

---

* The shores of Caernarvonshire opposite to the Isle of Anglesea.
† See the Norwegian ode, that follows.
‡ Edward the Second.

She-wolf of France,* with unrelenting fangs
That tear'st the bowels of thy mangled mate,
From thee be born,† who o'er thy country hangs
The scourge of Heav'n!　What terrors round him wait!
Amażement in his van, with flight combined,
And sorrow's faded form, and solitude behind.

　　" Mighty victor, mighty lord,
Low on his funeral couch‡ he lies!
No pitying heart, no eye, afford
A tear to grace his obsequies.
Is the sable Warrior§ fled?
Thy son is gone: he rests among the dead.
The swarm, that in thy noontide beam were born?
Gone to salute the rising morn.
Fair laughs the morn,‖ and soft the zephyr blows,
While proudly riding o'er the azure realm
In gallant trim the gilded vessel goes—
Youth on the prow, and pleasure at the helm—
Regardless of the sweeping whirlwind's sway,
That, hush'd in grim repose, expects his evening prey.

　　" Fill high the sparkling bowl,¶
The rich repast prepare,
Reft of a crown, he yet may share the feast!
Close by the regal chair

---

* Isabel of France, Edward the Second's adulterous Queen.

† Triumphs of Edward the Third of France.

‡ Death of Edward III., abandoned by his children, and even robbed in his last moments by his courtiers and his mistress.

§ Edward the Black Prince, dead some time before his father.

‖ Magnificence of Richard the Second's reign. See Froissart, and other contemporary writers.

¶ Richard the Second (as we are told by Archbishop Scroop and the confederate Lords in their manifesto, by Thomas of Walsingham, and all the older writers) was starved to death. The story of his assassination by Sir Piers of Exon is of much later date.

Fell Thirst and Famine scowl
A baleful smile upon their baffled guest.
Heard ye the din of battle bray*
Lance to lance, and horse to horse?
Long years of havoc urge their destined course,
And through the kindred squadrons mow their way.
Ye towers of Julius,† London's lasting shame,
With many a foul and midnight murder fed,
Revere his consort's‡ faith, his father's§ fame,
And spare the meek usurper's‖ holy head!
Above, below, the rose of snow,
Twined with her blushing foe, we spread:
The bristled Boar¶ in infant gore
Wallows beneath the thorny shade.
Now, brothers, bending o'er th' accursed loom,
Stamp we our vengeance deep, and ratify his doom.

"Edward, lo! to sudden fate
(Weave the woof: the thread is spun!)
Half of thy heart we consecrate:**
(The web is wove: the work is done!)
Stay, O stay! nor thus forlorn,
Leave me unbless'd, unpitied, here to mourn:
In yon bright track, that fires the western skies,
They melt, they vanish from my eyes.
But oh! what solemn scenes on Snowdon's height,
Descending slow their glittering skirts unroll?

---

* Ruinous civil wars of York and Lancaster.

† The oldest part of the Tower of London is vulgarly attributed to Julius Cæsar.

‡ Margaret of Anjou. § Henry the Fifth.

‖ Henry the Sixth was very near being canonised.

¶ The silver Boar was the badge of Richard the Third, whence he was usually known in his own time by the name of *the Boar*.

** Eleanor of Castile died a few years after the conquest of Wales. The heroic proof she gave of her affection for her husband is well known. The monuments of his regret, and sorrow for the loss of her, are still to be seen at Northampton, Geddington, Waltham, and other places.

Visions of glory, spare my aching sight;
Ye unborn ages, crowd not on my soul!
No more our long-lost Arthur* we bewail:
All hail, ye genuine kings,† Britannia's issue, hail.

"Girt with many a baron bold,
Sublime their starry fronts they rear;
And gorgeous dames, and statesmen old
In bearded majesty, appear.
In the midst a form divine—
Her eye proclaims her of the Briton-line;
Her lion-port,‡ her awe-commanding face,
Attemper'd sweet to virgin grace.
What strings symphonious tremble in the air!
What strains of vocal transport round her play!
Hear from the grave, great Taliessin,§ hear;
They breathe a soul to animate thy clay.
Bright Rapture calls, and soaring, as she sings,
Waves in the eye of heav'n her many-colour'd wings.

"The verse adorn again,
Fierce war, and faithful love,
And truth severe, by fairy fiction dress'd!
In buskin'd measures move,‖

---

* It was the common belief of the Welsh, that King Arthur was still alive in Fairyland, and should return again to reign over Britain.

† Both Merlin and Taliessin had prophesied, that the Welsh should regain their sovereignity over this island, which seemed to be accomplished in the house of Tudor.

‡ Speed, relating an audience given by Queen Elizabeth to Paul Dzialinski, Ambassador of Poland, says, "And thus she, lion-like rising, daunted the malapert orator no less with her stately port and majestical deporture, than with the tartnesse of her princelie cheekes."

§ Taliessin, Chief of the Bards, flourished in the sixth century. His works are still preserved, and his memory held in high veneration, among his countrymen.

‖ Shakspere.

Pale Grief, and pleasing Pain,
With Horror, tyrant of the throbbing breast!
A voice as of the cherub-choir*
Gales from blooming Eden bear;
And distant warblings lessen on my ear,†
That lost in long futurity expire.
Fond impious Man, think'st thou yon sanguine cloud,
Raised by thy breath, has quench'd the orb of day?
To-morrow he repairs the golden flood,
And warms the nations with redoubled ray.
Enough for me: With joy I see
The different doom our fates assign:
Be thine despair, and sceptred care,
To triumph, and to die, are mine."
He spoke, and headlong from the mountain's height
Deep in the roaring tide he plunged to endless night.

THE FATAL SISTERS.

FROM THE NORSE TONGUE.‡

Now the storm begins to lower
(Haste, the loom of hell prepare),

---

* Milton.

† The succession of poets after Milton's time,

‡ To be found in the "Orcades of Thormodus Torfæus; Hafniæ," 1697, folio; and also in "Bartholinus."

In the eleventh century, Sigurd, Earl of Orkney, went with a fleet of ships, and a considerable body of troops, into Ireland, to the assistance of Sictryg of the Silken Beard, who was then making war on his father-in-law, Brian, King of Dublin. The earl and all his forces were cut to pieces, and Sictryg was in danger of a total defeat; but the enemy had a greater loss by the death of Brian, their king, who fell in the action. On Christmas-day (the day of battle), a native of Caithness, in Scotland, saw, at a distance, a number of persons on horseback, riding full speed

Iron sleet of arrow shower*
  Hurtles in the darken'd air.†

Glitt'ring lances are the loom,
  Where the dusky warp we strain;
Weaving many a soldier's doom,
  Orkney's wo, and Randver's bane.

See the grizzly texture grow
  ('Tis of human entrails made),
And the weights, that play below,
  Each a gasping warrior's head.

Shafts for shuttles, dipp'd in gore,
  Shoot the trembling cords along.
Sword, that once a monarch bore,
  Keep the tissue close and strong!

Mista black, terrific maid,
  Sangrida, and Hilda see,
Join the wayward work to aid:
  'Tis the woof of victory.

---

towards a hill, and seeming to enter into it. Curiosity led him
to follow them, till, looking through an opening in the rocks, he
saw twelve gigantic figures resembling women: they were all employed about a loom; and as they wove, they sung the following
dreadful song; which, when they had finished, they tore the web
into twelve pieces, and (each taking her portion) galloped six to
the north, and as many to the south. These were the Valkyriur,
female divinities, servants of Odin (or Woden) in the Gothic
mythology. Their name signifies *Choosers of the slain.* They
were mounted on swift horses, with drawn swords in their hands;
and in the throng of battle selected such as were destined to
slaughter, and conducted them to Valhalla, the hall of Odin, or
paradise of the brave; where they attended the banquet, and
served the departed heroes with horns of mead and ale.

* " How quick they wheel'd, and flying, behind them shot
  Sharp sleet of arrowy show'r."—*Paradise Regained.*

† " The noise of battle hurtled in the air."
                      SHAKSPERE'S *Julius Cæsar.*

Ere the ruddy sun be set,
  Pikes must shiver, javelins sing,
Blade with clattering buckler meet,
  Hauberk crash, and helmet ring.

(Weave the crimson web of war)
  Let us go, and let us fly,
Where our friends the conflict share,
  Where they triumph, where they die.

As the paths of fate we tread,
  Wading through th' ensanguined field;
Gondula, and Geira, spread
  O'er the youthful king your shield.

We the reins to slaughter give,
  Ours to kill, and ours to spare:
Spite of danger he shall live.
  (Weave the crimson web of war.)

They, whom once the desert-beach
  Pent within its bleak domain,
Soon their ample sway shall stretch
  O'er the plenty of the plain.

Low the dauntless earl is laid,
  Gored with many a gaping wound:
Fate demands a nobler head;
  Soon a king shall bite the ground.

Long his loss shall Erin weep,
  Ne'er again his likeness see;
Long her strains in sorrow steep,
  Strains of immortality!

Horror covers all the heath,
  Clouds of carnage blot the sun.
Sisters, weave the web of death;
  Sisters, cease, the work is done!

Hail the task, and hail the hands!
  Songs of joy and triumph sing!

Joy to the victorious bands;
   Triumph to the younger king.

Mortal, thou that hear'st the tale,
   Learn the tenor of our song:
Scotland, through each winding vale
   Far and wide the notes prolong.

Sisters, hence with spurs of speed;
   Each her thundering falchion wield;
Each bestride her sable steed—
   Hurry, hurry to the field!

THE DESCENT OF ODIN.*

FROM THE NORSE TONGUE.

Uprose the king of men with speed,
And saddled straight his coal-black steed:
Down the yawning steep he rode
That leads to Hela's† drear abode.
Him the dog of darkness spied—
His shaggy throat he open'd wide,
While from his jaws, with carnage fill'd,
Foam and human gore distill'd:

Hoarse he bays with hideous din,
Eyes that glow, and fangs that grin;
And long pursues, with fruitless yell,
The father of the powerful spell.
Onward still his way he takes
(The groaning earth beneath him shakes),

---

* The original is to be found in " Bartholinus, *De causis con-temnendæ mortis;* Hafniæ," 1689, quarto.
      "Upreis Odinn allda gautr," &c.
   † Niflheimr, the hell of the Gothic nations, consisted of nine worlds, to which were devoted all such as died of sickness, old age, or by any other means than in battle: over it presided Hela, the Goddess of Death.

Till full before his fearless eyes
The portals nine of hell arise.

Right against the eastern gate,
By the moss-grown pile he sate,
Where long of yore to sleep was laid
The dust of the prophetic maid.
Facing to the northern clime,
Thrice he traced the Runic rhyme,
Thrice pronounced, in accents dread,
The thrilling verse that wakes the dead,
Till from out the hollow ground
Slowly breathed a sullen sound.

PROPHETESS.

What call unknown, what charms presume
To break the quiet of the tomb?
Who thus afflicts my troubled sprite,
And drags me from the realms of night?
Long on these mould'ring bones have beat
The winter's snow, the summer's heat,
The drenching dews, and driving rain!—
Let me, let me sleep again.
Who is he, with voice unblest,
That calls me from the bed of rest?

ODIN.

A traveller, to thee unknown,
Is he that calls, a warrior's son.
Thou the deeds of light shalt know;
Tell me what is done below,
For whom yon glitt'ring board is spread?
Drest for whom yon golden bed?

PROPHETESS.

Mantling in the goblet see
The pure bev'rage of the bee;
O'er it hangs the shield of gold—
'Tis the drink of Balder bold.
Balder's head to death is given:
Pain can reach the sons of Heaven!

Unwilling I my lips unclose:
Leave me, leave me to repose.

ODIN.

Once again my call obey!
Prophetess, arise, and say,
What dangers Odin's child await—
Who the author of his fate?

PROPHETESS.

In Hoder's hand the hero's doom:
His brother sends him to the tomb.
Now my weary lips I close:
Leave me, leave me to repose.

ODIN.

Prophetess, my spell obey—
Once again, arise, and say,
Who th' avenger of his guilt?
By whom shall Hoder's blood be spilt?

PROPHETESS.

In the caverns of the west,
By Odin's fierce embrace comprest,
A wondrous boy shall Rinda bear,
Who ne'er shall comb his raven hair,
Nor wash his visage in the stream,
Nor see the sun's departing beam,
Till he on Hoder's corse shall smile
Flaming on the fun'ral pile.
Now my weary lips I close:
Leave me, leave me to repose.

ODIN.

Yet awhile my call obey!
Prophetess, awake, and say,
What virgins these, in speechless wo,
That bend to earth their solemn brow,
That their flaxen tresses tear,
And snowy veils, that float in air?
Tell me whence their sorrows rose:
Then I leave thee to repose.

PROPHETESS.

Ha! no traveller art thou—
King of men, I know thee now,
Mightiest of a mighty line ——

ODIN.

No boding maid of skill divine
Art thou, nor prophetess of good;
But mother of the giant-brood!

PROPHETESS.

Hie thee hence, and boast at home,
That never shall inquirer come
To break my iron-sleep again
Till Lok* has burst his tenfold chain:
Never, till substantial Night
Has re-assumed her ancient right;
Till warp'd in flames, in ruin hurl'd,
Sinks the fabric of the world.

THE TRIUMPHS OF OWEN.†

FROM THE WELSH.

Owen's praise demands my song,
Owen swift, and Owen strong,
Fairest flower of Roderic's stem,
Gwyneth's‡ shield, and Britain's gem.

---

* *Lok* is the evil being, who continues in chains till the *Twilight of the Gods* approaches, when he shall break his bonds; the human race, the stars, and sun, shall disappear; the earth sink in the seas, and fire consume the skies: even Odin himself and his kindred deities shall perish.—See Mallet's "Northern Antiquities.'

† From Mr Evans' "Specimens of the Welsh Poetry, 1764." Owen succeeded his father Griffin in the principality of North Wales, A.D. 1120. This battle was fought nearly forty years afterwards.

‡ North Wales.

2 D

He nor heaps his brooded stores,
Nor on all profusely pours;
Lord of every regal art,
Liberal hand, and open heart.

Big with hosts of mighty name,
Squadrons three against him came;
This the force of Erin hiding,
Side by side as proudly riding,
On her shadow long and gay
Lochlin* ploughs the wat'ry way;
There the Norman sails afar
Catch the winds, and join the war:
Black and huge along they sweep,
Burdens of the angry deep.

Dauntless on his native sands
The Dragon-son† of Mona stands;
In glitt'ring arms and glory drest,
High he rears his ruby crest.
There the thund'ring strokes begin,
There the press, and there the din;
Talymalfra's rocky shore
Echoing to the battle's roar.
Check'd by the torrent-tide of blood
Backward Menaï rolls his flood;
While, heap'd his master's feet around,
Prostrate warriors gnaw the ground.
Where his glowing eyeballs turn,
Thousand banners round him burn:
Where he points his purple spear,
Hasty, hasty Rout is there,
Marking with indignant eye
Fear to stop, and Shame to fly.

---

* Denmark.

† The Red-Dragon is the device of Cadwallader, which all his
descendants bore on their banners.

There Confusion, Terror's child,
Conflict fierce, and Ruin wild,
Agony, that pants for breath,
Despair and honourable Death.

THE DEATH OF HOEL.

FROM THE WELSH.[*]

Had I but the torrent's might,
With headlong rage and wild affright
Upon Deïra's squadrons hurl'd,
To rush, and sweep them from the world!

Too, too secure in youthful pride
By them my friend, my Hoel, died,
Great Cian's son: of Madoc old
He ask'd no heaps of hoarded gold;
Alone in Nature's wealth array'd,
He ask'd, and had the lovely maid.

To Cattraeth's vale in glitt'ring row
Twice two hundred warriors go;
Every warrior's manly neck
Chains of regal honour deck,
Wreath'd in many a golden link:
From the golden cup they drink
Nectar, that the bees produce,
Or the grape's ecstatic juice.
Flush'd with mirth and hope they burn:
But none from Cattraeth's vale return,
Save Aëron brave, and Conan strong
(Bursting through the bloody throng),
And I, the meanest of them all,
That live to weep, and sing their fall.

---

[*] Of Aneurim, styled the Monarch of the Bards. He flourished about the time of Taliessin, A.D. 570. This ode is extracted from the Gododin (See Mr Evans' "Specimens," p. 71 and 73).

FOR MUSIC.*

IRREGULAR.

Air.

" Hence, avaunt ('tis holy ground),
Comus and his midnight crew;
And Ignorance with looks profound,
And dreaming Sloth of pallid hue,
Mad Sedition's cry profane,
Servitude that hugs her chain!
Nor in these consecrated bowers
Let painted Flatt'ry hide her serpent-train in flowers;

Chorus.

Nor Envy base, nor creeping Gain,
Dare the Muse's walk to stain,
While bright-eyed Science watches round;—
Hence, away, 'tis holy ground!"

Recitative.

From yonder realms of empyrean day
Bursts on my ear th' indignant lay:
There sit the sainted sage, the bard divine,
The few, whom genius gave to shine
Through every unborn age, and undiscover'd clime.
Rapt in celestial transport they:
Yet hither oft a glance from high
They send of tender sympathy
To bless the place, whereon their opening soul
First the genuine ardour stole.
'Twas Milton struck the deep-toned shell,
And as the choral warblings round him swell,
Meek Newton's self bends from his state sublime,
And nods his hoary head, and listens to the rhyme.

* This ode was performed in the Senate-house at Cambridge,
July 1, 1769, at the Installation of his Grace Augustus Henry
Fitzroy, Duke of Grafton Chancellor of the University.

Air.

"Ye brown o'er-arching groves,
That contemplation loves,
Where willowy Camus lingers with delight!
Oft at the blush of dawn
I trod your level lawn,
Oft woo'd the gleam of Cynthia silver bright
In cloisters dim, far from the haunts of folly,
With freedom by my side, and soft-eyed melancholy."

Recitative.

But hark! the portals sound, and pacing forth
With solemn steps and slow,
High potentates, and dames of royal birth,
And mitred fathers in long order go:
Great Edward* with the lilies on his brow
From haughty Gallia torn,
And sad Chatillon,† on her bridal morn
That wept her bleeding love, and princely Clare,‡
And Anjou's heroine,§ and the paler Rose,||
The rival of her crown, and of her woes,

---

* Edward the Third, who added the fleur de lys of France to the arms of England. He founded Trinity College.

† Mary de Valentia, Countess of Pembroke, daughter of Guy de Chatillon, Comte de St Paul in France: of whom tradition says, that her husband Audemar de Valentia, Earl of Pembroke, was slain at a tournament on the day of his nuptials. She was the foundress of Pembroke College or Hall, under the name of Aula Mariæ de Valentia.

‡ Elizabeth de Burg, Countess of Clare, was wife of John de Burg, son and heir of the Earl of Ulster, and daughter of Gilbert de Clare, Earl of Gloucester, by Joan of Acres, daughter of Edward the First. Hence the poet gives her the epithet of "princely." She founded Clare Hall.

§ Margaret of Anjou, wife of Henry the Sixth, foundress of Queen's College. The poet has celebrated her conjugal fidelity in "The Bard."

|| Elizabeth Widville, wife of Edward the Fourth (hence called the paler rose, as being the House of York). She added to the foundation of Margaret of Anjou.

And either Henry* there,
The murder'd saint, and the majestic lord,
That broke the bonds of Rome
(Their tears, their little triumphs o'er,
Their human passions now no more,
Save charity, that glows beyond the tomb).

Recitative accompanied.

All that on Granta's fruitful plain
Rich streams of regal bounty pour'd,
And bade these awful fanes and turrets rise,
To hail their Fitzroy's festal morning come;
And thus they speak in soft accord
The liquid language of the skies.

Quartetto.

" What is grandeur, what is power?
Heavier toil, superior pain:
What the bright reward we gain?
The grateful memory of the good.
Sweet is the breath of vernal shower,
The bee's collected treasures sweet,
Sweet music's melting fall, but, sweeter yet,
The still small voice of gratitude."

Recitative.

Foremost, and leaning from her golden cloud,
The venerable Marg'ret† see!
" Welcome, my noble son (she cries aloud),
To this, thy kindred train, and me:
Pleased in thy lineaments we trace
A Tudor's fire, a Beaufort's‡ grace.

---

* Henry the Sixth and Eighth, the former the founder of King's, the latter the greatest benefactor to Trinity College.

† Countess of Richmond and Derby, the mother of Henry the Seventh, foundress of St John's and Christ's Colleges.

‡ The Countess was a Beaufort, and married to a Tudor: hence the application of this line to the Duke of Grafton, who claims descent from both these families.

Air.

Thy liberal heart, thy judging eye,
The flower unheeded shall descry,
And bid it round heaven's altars shed
The fragrance of its blushing head;
Shall raise from earth the latent gem
To glitter on the diadem.

Recitative.

" Lo, Granta waits to lead her blooming band !
Not obvious, not obtrusive, she
No vulgar praise, no venal incense flings;
Nor dares, with courtly tongue refined,
Profane thy inborn royalty of mind;
She reveres herself and thee.
With modest pride to grace thy youthful brow,
The laureate wreath that Cecil* wore, she brings,
And to thy just, thy gentle hand,
Submits the fasces of her sway,
While spirits blest above and men below
Join with glad voice the loud symphonious lay.

Grand Chorus.

" Through the wild waves as they roar,
With watchful eye and dauntless mien
Thy steady course of honour keep,
Nor fear the rocks, nor seek the shore:
The star of Brunswick smiles serene,
And gilds the horrors of the deep."

---

* Lord Treasurer Burleigh was Chancellor of the University
in the reign of Queen Elizabeth.

A LONG STORY.*

In Britain's isle, no matter where,
    An ancient pile of building stands;†
The Huntingdons and Hattons there
    Employ'd the power of fairy hands

To raise the ceiling's fretted height,
    Each pannel in achievements clothing,
Rich windows that exclude the light,
    And passages that lead to nothing.

Full oft within the spacious walls,
    When he had fifty winters o'er him,
My grave Lord-keeper‡ led the brawls;
    The seal and maces danced before him.

---

* The poet has thus spoken of the origin of these verses:—
" The ' Elegy,' previous to its publication, was handed about
in MS., and had amongst other admirers the Lady Cobham,
who resided in the mansionhouse at Stoke-Pogeis. The performance inducing her to wish for the author's acquaintance, Lady
Schaub and Miss Speed, then at her house, undertook to intro-
duce her to it. These two ladies waited upon the author at his
aunt's solitary habitation, where he at that time resided, and not
finding him at home, they left a card behind them. Mr Gray,
surprised at such a compliment, returned the visit; and, as the
beginning of this intercourse bore some appearance of romance,
he gave the humorous and lively account of it which the ' Long
Story' contains."

† The mansionhouse at Stoke-Pogeis, then in the possession of
Viscountess Cobham. The house formerly belonged to the Earls
of Huntingdon and the family of Hatton.

‡ Sir Christopher Hatton, promoted by Queen Elizabeth for his
graceful person and fine dancing. Brawls were a sort of figure-
dance then in vogue, and probably deemed as elegant as our modern cotillons, or still more modern quadrilles.

His bushy beard and shoe-strings green,
    His high-crown'd hat and satin doublet,
Moved the stout heart of England's queen,
    Though Pope and Spaniard could not trouble it.

What, in the very first beginning!
    Shame of the versifying tribe!
Your history whither are you spinning?
    Can you do nothing but describe?

A house there is (and that's enough)
    From whence one fatal morning issues
A brace of warriors, not in buff,
    But rustling in their silks and tissues.

The first came cap-á-pie from France,
    Her conquering destiny fulfilling,
Whom meaner beauties eye askance,
    And vainly ape her art of killing

The other Amazon kind Heaven
    Had arm'd with spirit, wit, and satire;
But Cobham had the polish given,
    And tipp'd her arrows with good-nature.

To celebrate her eyes, her hair,
    Coarse panegyrics would but teaze her;
Melissa is her *nom de guerre;*
    Alas! who would not wish to please her?

With bonnet blue and capuchine,
    And aprons long, they hid their armour,
And veil'd their weapons bright and keen,
    In pity to the country farmer.

Fame in the shape of Mr P——t*
    (By this time all the parish know it)
Had told that thereabouts there lurk'd
    A wicked imp they call a poet,

---

* Mr Robert Purt, Fellow of King's College, Cambridge, a neighbour of Mr Gray's when the latter resided at Stoke.

Who prowl'd the country far and near,
　Bewitch'd the children of the peasants,
Dried up the cows and lamed the deer,
　And suck'd the eggs and kill'd the pheasants.

My lady heard their joint petition,
　Swore by her coronet and ermine,
She'd issue out her high commission
　To rid the manor of such vermin.

The heroines undertook the task;
　Through lanes unknown, o'er stiles, they ventured,
Rapp'd at the door, nor staid to ask,
　But bounce into the parlour enter'd.

The trembling family they daunt—
　They flirt, they sing, they laugh, they tattle,
Rummage his mother, pinch his aunt,
　And up-stairs in a whirlwind rattle.

Each hole and cupboard they explore,
　Each creek and cranny of his chamber,
Run hurry-skurry round the floor,
　And o'er the bed and tester clamber;

Into the drawers and china pry,
　Papers and books, a huge imbroglio!
Under a tea-cup he might lie,
　Or creased like dog's-ears in a folio.

On the first marching of the troops,
　The Muses, hopeless of his pardon,
Convey'd him underneath their hoops
　To a small closet in the garden;

(So rumour says; who will believe?)
　But that they left the door ajar,
Where safe, and laughing in his sleeve,
　He heard the din of distant war.

Short was his joy: he little knew
　The power of magic was no fable;

Out of the window whisk they flew,
  But left a spell upon the table.

The words too eager to unriddle,
  The poet felt a strange disorder;
Transparent bird-lime form'd the middle,
  And chains invisible the border.

So cunning was the apparatus,
  The powerful pot-hooks did so move him,
That will-he nill-he to the great house
  He went as if the devil drove him.

Yet on his way (no sign of grace,
  For folks in fear are apt to pray)
To Phœbus he preferr'd his case,
  And begg'd his aid that dreadful day.

The Godhead would have back'd his quarrel,
  But with a blush, on recollection,
Own'd that his quiver and his laurel
  'Gainst four such eyes were no protection.

The court was sat, the culprit there:
  Forth from their gloomy mansions creeping,
The Lady Janes and Joans repair,
  And from the gallery stand peeping:

Such as in silence of the night
  Come (sweep) along some winding entry
(Styack* has often seen the sight),
  Or at the chapel-door stand sentry,

In peakèd hoods and mantles tarnish'd,
  Sour visages enough to scare ye,
High dames of honour once that garnish'd
  The drawing-room of fierce Queen Mary !

The peeress comes: the audience stare,
  And doff their hats with due submission;
She curtseys as she takes her chair
  To all the people of condition.

---

* The housekeeper.

The bard with many an artful fib
　　Had in imagination fenced him,
Disproved the arguments of Squib,*
　　And all that Groom† could urge against him.

But soon his rhetoric forsook him,
　　When he the solemn hall had seen;
A sudden fit of ague shook him;
　　He stood as mute as poor Macleane.‡

Yet something he was heard to mutter—
　　"How in the park beneath an old tree
(Without design to hurt the butter,
　　Or any malice to the poultry)

He once or twice had penn'd a sonnet,
　　Yet hoped that he might save his bacon;
Numbers would give their oaths upon it,
　　He ne'er was for a conj'rer taken."

The ghostly prudes with hagged face
　　Already had condemn'd the sinner:
My lady rose, and with a grace—
　　She smiled, and bid him come to dinner.

"Jesu-Maria! Madam Bridget,
　　Why, what can the viscountess mean?"
Cried the square hoods in woful fidget,
　　"The times are alter'd quite and clean!

Decorum's turn'd to mere civility;
　　Her air and all her manners show it:
Commend me to her affability!
　　Speak to a commoner and poet!"

　　　　　[*Here* 500 *Stanzas are lost.*]
And so God save our noble king,
　　And guard us from long-winded lubbers,
That to eternity would sing,
　　And keep my lady from her rubbers.

---

* The steward.　　　　　　† Groom of the chamber.
‡ A famous highwayman, hanged the week before.

ALLIANCE OF EDUCATION AND GOVERNMENT

ESSAY I.

A FRAGMENT.

—— Ποταγ' ῷ γαθέ; τὰν γὰρ ἀοιδὰν
Οὔτι πω εἰς Ἀΐδαν γε τὸν ἐκλελαθοντα φυλαξεῖς.—THEOCRITUS.

As sickly plants betray a niggard earth,
Whose barren bosom starves her gen'rous birth,
Nor genial warmth, nor genial juice retains
Their roots to feed and fill their verdant veins;
And, as in climes where Winter holds his reign,
The soil though fertile will not teem in vain,
Forbids her gems to swell, her shades to rise,
Nor trusts her blossoms to the churlish skies;
So draw mankind in vain the vital airs,
Unform'd, unfriended, by those kindly cares
That health and vigour to the soul impart,
Spread the young thought, and warm the op'ning heart;
So fond instruction on the growing powers
Of nature idly lavishes her stores,
If equal justice with unclouded face
Smile not indulgent on the rising race,
And scatter with a free though frugal hand
Light golden showers of plenty o'er the land:
But tyranny has fix'd her empire there,
To check their tender hopes with chilling fear,
And blast the blooming promise of the year.
  This spacious animated scene survey,
From where the rolling orb that gives the day
His sable sons with nearer course surrounds,
To either pole and life's remotest bounds,
How rude soe'er th' exterior form we find,
Howe'er opinion tinge the varied mind,
Alike to all the kind impartial Heaven
The sparks of truth and happiness has given.
With sense to feel, with mem'ry to retain,
They follow pleasure and they fly from pain;

Their judgment mends the plan their fancy draws,
The event presages, and explores the cause;
The soft returns of gratitude they know,
By fraud elude, by force repel the foe;
While mutual wishes mutual woes endear,
The social smile and sympathetic tear.
  Say, then, through ages by what fate confined
To different climes seem different souls assign'd?
Here measured laws and philosophic ease
Fix and improve the polish'd arts of peace;
There industry and gain their vigils keep,
Command the winds, and tame th' unwilling deep;
Here force and hardy deeds of blood prevail,
There languid pleasure sighs in every gale.
Oft o'er the trembling nations from afar
Has Scythia breathed the living cloud of war,
And where the deluge bursts with sweepy sway,
Their arms, their kings, their gods, were roll'd away.
As oft have issued, host impelling host,
The blue-eyed myriads from the Baltic coast:
The prostrate south to the destroyer yields
Her boasted titles and her golden fields:
With grim delight the brood of Winter view
A brighter day, and heavens of azure hue,
Scent the new fragrance of the breathing rose,
And quaff the pendant vintage as it grows.
Proud of the yoke, and pliant to the rod,
Why yet does Asia dread a monarch's nod,
While European freedom still withstands
Th' encroaching tide that drowns her less'ning lands,
And sees far off, with an indignant groan,
Her native plains and empires once her own?
Can opener skies and suns of fiercer flame
O'erpower the fire that animates our frame,
As lamps that shed at eve a cheerful ray
Fade and expire beneath the eye of day?
Need we the influence of the northern star
To string our nerves, and steel our hearts to war?

And where the face of nature laughs around,
Must sick'ning Virtue fly the tainted ground
Unmanly thought! what seasons can control,
What fancied zone can circumscribe the soul,
Who conscious of the source from whence it springs
By Reason's light on Resolution's wings,
Spite of her frail companion, dauntless goes
O'er Lybia's deserts and through Zembla's snows?
She bids each slumbering energy awake,
Another touch, another temper take,
Suspends th' inferior laws that rule our day:
The stubborn elements confess her sway,
Their little wants their low desires refine,
And raise the mortal to a height divine.

   Not but the human fabric from the birth
Imbibes a flavour of its parent earth:
As various tracks enforce a various toil,
The manners speak the idiom of their soil.
An iron race the mountain-cliffs maintain,
Foes to the gentler genius of the plain;
For where unwearied sinews must be found
With sidelong plough to quell the flinty ground,
To turn the torrent's swift descending flood,
To brave the savage rushing from the wood,
What wonder if to patient valour train'd,
They guard with spirit what by strength they gain'd?
And while their rocky ramparts round they see,
The rough abode of want and liberty
(As lawless force from confidence will grow),
Insult the plenty of the vales below?
What wonder in the sultry climes that spread
Where Nile redundant o'er his summer-bed
From his broad bosom life and verdure flings,
And broods o'er Egypt with his wat'ry wings,
If with adventurous oar and ready sail
The dusky people drive before the gale,
Or on frail floats to neighbouring cities ride,
That rise and glitter o'er the ambient tide?

THE TRAGEDY OF "AGRIPPINA:" A FRAGMENT.

ACT I. SCENE I.

PERSONS.—*Agrippina, the Empress-Mother, and Aceronia,*
her confidante.

AGRIPPINA.

'Tis well, begone! your errand is perform'd:
  [*Speaks as to Anicetus entering.*
The message needs no comment.   Tell your master
His mother shall obey him.   Say you saw her
Yielding due reverence to his high command:
Alone, unguarded, and without a lictor,
As fits the daughter of Germanicus,
Say, she retired to Antium, there to tend
Her household cares, a woman's best employment.
What if you add, how she turn'd pale, and trembled;
You think you spied a tear stand in her eye,
And would have dropp'd, but that her pride restrain'd it?
(Go! you can paint it well) 'twill profit you
And please the stripling.   Yet 'twould dash his joy
To hear the spirit of Britannicus
Yet walks on earth: at least, there are who know
Without a spell to raise, and bid it fire
A thousand haughty hearts, unused to shake
When a boy frowns, nor to be lured with smiles,
To taste of hollow kindness, or partake
His hospitable board: they ate, aware
Of the unpledged bowl—they love not aconite.

ACERONIA.

He's gone; and much I hope these walls alone
And the mute air are privy to your passion.
Forgive your servant's fears, who sees the danger
Which fierce resentment cannot fail to raise
In haughty youth, and irritated power.

AGRIPPINA.

And dost thou talk to me, to me, of danger,
Of haughty youth, and irritated power?
To her that gave it being, her that arm'd
This painted Jove, and taught his novice hand
To aim the fork'd bolt, whilst he stood trembling,
Scared at the sound, and dazzled at its brightness?
'Tis like, thou hast forgot, when yet a stranger
To adoration, to the grateful steam
Of flattery's incense and obsequious vows
From voluntary realms, a puny boy,
Deck'd with no other lustre than the blood
Of Agrippina's race, he lived unknown
To fame or fortune; haply eyed at distance
Some edileship, ambitious of the power
To judge of weights and measures; scarcely dared
On Expectation's strongest wing to soar
High as the consulate, that empty shade
Of long forgotten liberty, when I
Oped his young eye to bear the blaze of greatness,
Show'd him where empire tower'd, and bade him strike
The noble quarry. Gods! then was the time
To shrink from danger; Fear might then have worn
The mask of Prudence: but a heart like mine,
A heart that glows with the pure Julian fire,
If bright Ambition from her craggy seat
Display the radiant prize, will mount undaunted,
Gain the rough heights, and grasp the dangerous honour

ACERONIA.

Through various life I have pursued your steps,
Have seen your soul, and wonder'd at its daring;
Hence rise my fears. Nor am I yet to learn
How vast the debt of gratitude which Nero
To such a mother owes: the world you gave him,
Suffices not to pay the obligation.
I well remember too (for I was present),
When in a secret and dead hour of night,

2 E

Due sacrifice perform'd with barbarous rites
Of mutter'd charms and solemn invocation,
You bade the magi call the dreadful Powers,
That read futurity, to know the fate
Impending o'er your son.   Their answer was,
If the son reign, the mother perishes.
"Perish," you cried, "the mother! reign the son!"
He reigns; the rest is Heaven's, which oft has bade,
Even when its will seem'd wrote in lines of blood,
Th' unthought event disclose a whiter meaning.
Think, too, how oft in weak and sickly minds
The sweets of kindness, lavishly indulged,
Rankle to gall; and benefits too great
To be repaid sit heavy on the soul
As unrequited wrongs.   The willing homage
Of prostrate Rome, the senate's joint applause,
The riches of the earth, the train of pleasures
That wait on youth and arbitrary sway—
These were your gift, and with them you bestow'd
The very power he has to be ungrateful.

AGRIPPINA.

   Thus ever grave and undisturbed Reflection
Pours its cool dictates in the madding ear
Of Rage, and thinks to quench the fire it feels not.
Say'st thou, I must be cautious, must be silent
And tremble at the phantom I have raised?
Carry to him thy timid counsels: he
Perchance may heed 'em.   Tell him, too, that one,
Who had such liberal power to give, may still
With equal power resume that gift and raise
A tempest that shall shake its own creation
To its original atoms.   Tell me! say,
This mighty emperor, this dreaded hero,
Has he beheld the glittering front of war?
Knows his soft ear the trumpet's thrilling voice,
And outcry of the battle?   Have his limbs
Sweat under iron harness?   Is he not

The silken son of dalliance, nursed in ease
And pleasure's flowery lap?—Rubellius lives,
And Sylla has his friends, though school'd by fear
To bow the supple knee, and court the times
With shows of fair obeisance: and a call
Like mine, might serve belike to wake pretensions
Drowsier than theirs, who boast the genuine blood
Of our imperial house.

ACERONIA.

Did I not wish to check this dangerous passion,
I might remind my mistress that her nod
Can rouse eight hardy legions, wont to stem
With stubborn nerves the tide, and face the rigour
Of bleak Germania's snows.   Four, not less brave,
.That in Armenia quell the Parthian force
Under the warlike Corbulo, by you
Mark'd for their leader—these, by ties confirm'd,
Of old respect and gratitude, are yours.
Surely the Masians too, and those of Egypt,
Have not forgot your sire: The eye of Rome,
And the prætorian camp have long revered,
With custom'd awe, the daughter, sister, wife,
And mother of their Cæsars.

AGRIPPINA.

Ha! by Juno,
It bears a noble semblance.   On this base
My great revenge shall rise; or say we sound
The trump of liberty; there will not want,
Even in the servile senate, ears to own
Her spirit-stirring voice; Soranus there,
And Cassius; Vetus too, and Thrasea,
Minds of the antique cast, rough, stubborn souls,
That struggle with the yoke.   How shall the spark
Unquenchable, that glows within their breasts,
Blaze into freedom, when the idle herd
(Slaves from the womb, created but to stare
And bellow in the circus) yet will start,

And shake 'em at the name of liberty,
Stung by a senseless word, a vain tradition,
As there were magic in it?   Wrinkled beldames
Teach it their grandchildren as somewhat rare
That anciently appear'd; but when, extends
Beyond their chronicle.   Oh! 'tis a cause
To arm the hand of childhood, and rebrace
The slacken'd sinews of time-wearied age.
Yes, we may meet, ungrateful boy, we may
Again the buried Genius of old Rome
Shall from the dust uprear his reverend head,
Roused by the shout of millions: there before
His high tribunal thou and I appear.
Let majesty sit on thy awful brow,
And lighten from thy eye: around thee call
The gilded swarm that wantons in the sunshine
Of thy full favour: Seneca be there,
In gorgeous phrase of labour'd eloquence
To dress thy plea, and Burrhus strengthen it
With his plain soldier's oath, and honest seeming.
Against thee liberty and Agrippina:
The world, the prize; and fair befall the victors.
But soft! why do I waste the fruitless hours
In threats unexecuted?   Haste thee, fly
These hated walls, that seem to mock my shame,
And cast me forth in duty to their lord!

ACERONIA.

'Tis time we go; the sun is high advanced,
And, ere mid-day, Nero will come to Baia.

AGRIPPINA.

My thought aches at him; not the basilisk
More deadly to the sight, than is to me
The cool injurious eye of frozen kindness.
I will not meet its poison.   Let him feel
Before he sees me.

ACERONIA.

Why then stays my sovereign,
Where he so soon may ——?

AGRIPPINA.

Yes, I will be gone,
But not to Antium—all shall be confess'd,
Whate'er the frivolous tongue of giddy fame
Has spread among the crowd; things that but whisper'd,
Have arch'd the hearer's brow, and riveted
His eyes in fearful ecstacy! No matter
What, so 't be strange and dreadful—sorceries,
Assassinations, poisoning—the deeper
My guilt, the blacker his ingratitude.
And you, ye manes of ambition's victims,
Enshrined Claudius, with the pitied ghosts
Of Syllani, doom'd to early death
(Ye unavailing horrors, fruitless crimes!),
If from the realms of night my voice ye hear,
In lieu of penitence and vain remorse
Accept my vengeance! Though by me ye bled,
He was the cause. My love, my fears for him,
Dried the soft springs of pity in my heart,
And froze them up with deadly cruelty.
Yet, if your injured shades demand my fate,
If murder cries for murder, blood for blood,
Let me not fall alone; but crush his pride,
And sink the traitor in his mother's ruin.

[*Exeunt.*

SCENE II.

Otho. Poppaea.

OTHO.

Thus far we're safe! Thanks to the rosy queen
Of amorous thefts: and had her wanton son
Lent us his wings, we could not have beguiled
With more elusive speed the dazzled sight
Of wakeful jealousy. Be gay securely;
Dispel, my fair, with smiles, the tim'rous cloud
That hangs on thy clear brow. So Helen look'd,
So her white neck reclined, so was she borne

By the young Trojan to his gilded bark
With fond reluctance, yielding modesty,
And oft reverted eye, as if she knew not
Whether she fear'd, or wish'd to be pursued.

  *   *   *   *   *

ON VICISSITUDE.

Now the golden morn aloft
 Waves her dew bespangled wing,
With vermeil cheek, and whisper soft,
 She woos the tardy spring;
Till April starts, and calls around
The sleeping fragrance from the ground,
And lightly o'er the living scene
Scatters his freshest, tenderest green.

New-born flocks, in rustic dance,
 Frisking ply their feeble feet;
Forgetful of their wintry trance,
 The birds his presence greet:
But chief the skylark warbles high
His trembling thrilling ecstacy,
And, lessening from the dazzled sight,
Melts into air and liquid light.

Yesterday the sullen year
 Saw the snowy whirlwind fly;
Mute was the music of the air,
 The herd stood drooping by:
Their raptures now that wildly flow,
No yesterday, nor morrow know;
'Tis man alone that joy descries
With forward and reverted eyes.

Smiles on past Misfortune's brow
 Soft Reflection's hand can trace,
And o'er the cheek of Sorrow throw
 A melancholy grace;

While Hope prolongs our happier hour,
Or deepest shades, that dimly lower
And blacken round our weary way,
Gilds with a gleam of distant day.

Still, where rosy Pleasure leads,
    See a kindred Grief pursue;
Behind the steps that Misery treads
    Approaching Comfort view:
The hues of bliss more brightly glow,
Chastised by sabler tints of wo;
And blended form, with artful strife,
The strength and harmony of life.

See the wretch, that long has tost
    On the thorny bed of pain,
At length repair his vigour lost,
    And breathe, and walk again:
The meanest flowret of the vale,
The simplest note that swells the gale,
The common sun, the air, the skies,
To him are sweetest Paradise.

Humble Quiet builds her cell
    Near the course where Pleasure flows;
She eyes the clear crystalline well,
    And tastes it as it goes.

* * * * *

AN IMITATION FROM THE GODODIN.*

Have ye seen the tusky boar,
Or the bull with sullen roar,
On surrounding foes advance ?
So Caradoc bore his lance.
Conan's name, my lay rehearse,
Build to him the lofty verse,

---

* See "The Death of Hoel," p. 497.

Sacred tribute of the bard,
Verse, the hero's sole reward !
As the flame's devouring force,
As the whirlwind in its course,
As the thunder's fiery stroke
Glancing on the shiver'd oak,
Did the sword of Conan mow
The crimson harvest of the foe.

TRANSLATION OF A PASSAGE FROM STATIUS.*

Third in the labours of the Disc came on,
With sturdy step and slow, Hippomedon ;
Artful and strong, he poised the well-known weight,
By Phlegyas warn'd, and fired by Mnestheus' fate,
That to avoid, and this to emulate.
His vigorous arm he tried before he flung,
Braced all his nerves, and every sinew strung;
Then, with a tempest's whirl, and wary eye,
Pursued his cast, and hurl'd the orb on high.
The orb on high, tenacious of its course,
True to the mighty arm that gave it force,
Far overleaps all bound, and joys to see
Its ancient lord secure of victory.
The theatre's green height and woody wall
Tremble ere it precipitates its fall;
The ponderous mass sinks in the cleaving ground,
While vales, and woods, and echoing hills rebound:
As when from Ætna's smoking summit broke,
The eyeless Cyclops heaved the craggy rock,
Where Ocean frets beneath the dashing oar,
And parting surges round the vessel roar :

---

* This was made by Mr Gray while at Cambridge, in the year
1736, and at the age of twenty. Mr Mason expressed his belief
that it was Gray's first attempt in English verse.

'Twas there he aim'd the meditated harm,
And scarce Ulysses 'scaped his giant arm.
A tiger's pride the victor bore away,
With native sports and artful labour gay:
A shining border round the margin roll'd,
And calm'd the terrors of his claws in gold.

HYMN TO IGNORANCE.*

A FRAGMENT.

Hail, horrors, hail! ye ever gloomy bowers,
Ye gothic fanes, and antiquated towers,
Where rushy Camus' slowly-winding flood
Perpetual draws his humid train of mud:
Glad I revisit thy neglected reign,
Oh, take me to thy peaceful shade again!
　　But chiefly thee, whose influence breathed from high,
Augments the native darkness of the sky;
Ah, Ignorance! soft salutary Power!
Prostrate with filial reverence I adore.
Thrice hath Hyperion roll'd his annual race,
Since weeping I forsook thy fond embrace.
Oh say, successful dost thou still oppose
Thy leaden ægis 'gainst our ancient foes?
Still stretch, tenacious of thy right divine,
The massy sceptre o'er thy slumbering line?
And dews Lethean through the land dispense,
To steep in slumbers each benighted sense?
If any spark of wit's delusive ray
Break out, and flash a momentary day,
With damp, cold touch forbid it to aspire,
And huddle up in fogs the dangerous fire.
　　Oh say—she hears me not, but, careless grown,
Lethargic nods upon her ebon throne.

---

* This is supposed to have been written about the year 1742,
the time when Mr Gray returned to Cambridge.

Goddess! awake, arise, alas my fears!
Can powers immortal feel the force of years?
Not thus of old, with ensigns wide unfurl'd,
She rode triumphant o'er the vanquish'd world;
Fierce nations own'd her unresisted might,
And all was Ignorance, and all was Night.
   Oh! sacred ages! times for ever lost!
(The Schoolman's glory, and the Churchman's boast),
For ever gone—yet still to Fancy new,
Her rapid wings the transient scene pursue,
And bring the buried ages back to view.
   High on her car, behold the Grandam ride
Like old Sesostris with barbaric pride;
* * * a team of harness'd monarchs bend
    *   *   *   *   *

SONNET

ON THE DEATH OF MR RICHARD WEST.*

In vain to me the smiling Mornings shine,
   And redd'ning Phœbus lifts his golden fire;
The birds in vain their amorous descant join,
   Or cheerful fields resume their green attire.
These ears, alas! for other notes repine,
   A different object do these eyes require:
My lonely anguish melts no heart but mine;
   And in my breast th' imperfect joys expire.
Yet Morning smiles the busy race to cheer,
   And new-born pleasures bring to happier men:
The fields to all their wonted tribute bear:
   To warm their little loves the birds complain.
I fruitless mourn to him that cannot hear,
   And weep the more, because I weep in vain.

---

* Only son of the Right Hon. Richard West, Lord Chancellor
of Ireland. He died June 1, 1742, in the 26th year of his age.

EPITAPH

ON MRS CLARKE.*

Lo! where this silent marble weeps,
A Friend, a Wife, a Mother sleeps:
A heart within whose sacred cell
The peaceful Virtues loved to dwell.
Affection warm, and Faith sincere,
And soft Humanity were there.
In agony, in death resign'd,
She felt the wound she left behind.
Her infant Image here below
Sits smiling on a father's wo:
Whom what awaits, while yet he strays
Along the lonely vale of days?
A pang, to secret sorrow dear;
A sigh; an unavailing tear;
Till Time shall every grief remove,
With life, with memory, and with love

EPITAPH

ON SIR WILLIAM PEERE WILLIAMS,

CAPTAIN IN BURGOYNE'S DRAGOONS.

Here, foremost in the dangerous paths of fame,
  Young Williams fought for England's fair renown;
His mind each Muse, each Grace adorn'd his frame,
  Nor Envy dared to view him with a frown.

At Aix, his voluntary sword he drew:†
  There first in blood his infant honour seal'd;
From fortune, pleasure, science, love, he flew,
  And scorn'd repose when Britain took the field.

---

* The wife of Dr Clarke, physician at Epsom, died April 27,
1757, and is buried in the church of Beckenham, Kent.
† In the expedition to Aix, he was on board the Magnanime,
with Lord Howe; and was deputed to receive the capitulation.

With eyes of flame, and cool undaunted breast,
    Victor he stood on Bellisle's rocky steeps—
Ah, gallant youth! this marble tells the rest,
    Where melancholy Friendship bends and weeps.

STANZAS TO MR BENTLEY.*

A FRAGMENT.

In silent gaze the tuneful choir among,
    Half pleased, half blushing, let the Muse admire,
While Bentley leads her Sister-Art along,
    And bids the pencil answer to the lyre.

See, in their course, each transitory thought
    Fix'd by his touch a lasting essence take;
Each dream, in Fancy's airy colouring wrought,
    To local symmetry and life awake!

The tardy rhymes that used to linger on,
    To censure cold, and negligent of fame,
In swifter measures animated run,
    And catch a lustre from his genuine flame.

Ah! could they catch his strength, his easy grace,
    His quick creation, his unerring line;
The energy of Pope they might efface,
    And Dryden's harmony submit to mine.

But not to one in this benighted age
    Is that diviner inspiration given
That burns in Shakspere's or in Milton's page—
    The pomp and prodigality of heaven:

As when conspiring in the diamond's blaze,
    The meaner gems, that singly charm the sight,
Together dart their intermingled rays,
    And dazzle with a luxury of light.

* Mr Bentley had made a set of designs for Mr Gray's poems.

Enough for me, if to some feeling breast
My lines a secret sympathy *impart;*
And as their pleasing influence *flows confess'd.*
A sigh of soft reflection *heave the heart* *

S O N G.†

Thyrsis, when he left me, swore
   In the spring he would return—
Ah ! what means the opening flower,
   And the bud that decks the thorn.
'Twas the nightingale that sung !
'Twas the lark that upward sprung !

Idle notes ! untimely green !
   Why such unavailing haste ?
Gentle gales and sky serene
   Prove not always winter past.
Cease, my doubts, my fears to move,
Spare the honour of my love.

A M A T O R Y   L I N E S.‡

With Beauty, with Pleasure surrounded, to languish—
To weep, without knowing the cause of my anguish—
To start from short slumbers, and wish for the morning—
To close my dull eyes when I see it returning—
Sighs sudden and frequent, looks ever dejected,
Words that steal from my tongue, by no meaning connected—
Ah, say, fellow-swains, how these symptoms befell me ?
They smile, but reply not—sure DELIA CAN TELL ME !

---

* The words in italic were supplied by Mr Mason.
  † Written, at the request of Miss Speed, to an old air of Ge-
miniani: the idea is from the French.
  ‡ This jeu d'esprit was found among the MSS. of Gray, and
printed in a note in the second volume of Warton's edition of
Pope.

TOPHET.*

AN EPIGRAM.

Thus Tophet look'd; so grinn'd the brawling fiend,
Whilst frighted prelates bow'd, and call'd him friend.
Our Mother-Church, with half-averted sight,
Blush'd as she bless'd her grizzly proselyte;
Hosannas rung through hell's tremendous borders,
And Satan's self had thoughts of taking orders.

IMPROMPTU,

*Suggested by a View, in 1766, of the Seat and Ruins of a
Deceased Nobleman, at Kingsgate, Kent.*

Old, and abandon'd by each venal friend,
  Here H——d† form'd the pious resolution
To smuggle a few years, and strive to mend
  A broken character and constitution.

On this congenial spot he fix'd his choice:
  Earl Goodwin trembled for his neighbouring sand;
Here sea-gulls scream, and cormorants rejoice,
  And mariners, though shipwreck'd, dread to land.

Here reign the blustering North and blighting East,
  No tree is heard to whisper, bird to sing;
Yet nature could not furnish out the feast,
  Art he invokes new horrors still to bring.

---

* Mr Etough, of Cambridge University, the person satirised,
was as remarkable for the eccentricities of his character, as for
his personal appearance. A Mr Tyson, of Benet College, made
an etching of his head, and presented it to Mr Gray, who at-
tached to it the above lines. Some information respecting Mr
Etough (who was rector of Therfield, Herts, and of Colm-
worth, Bedfordshire), may be found in the "Gentleman's Magazine," Vol. lvi., pp. 25, 281.

† Henry Fox, first Lord Holland.

Here mouldering fanes and battlements arise,
   Turrets and arches nodding to their fall,
Unpeopled monast'ries delude our eyes,
   And mimic desolation covers all.

"Ah !" said the sighing peer, "had B—te been true,*
   Nor M—'s, R—'s, B—'s friendship vain,
Far better scenes than these had bless'd our view,
   And realised the beauties which we feign:

Purged by the sword, and purified by fire,
   Then had we seen proud London's hated walls:
Owls would have hooted in St Peter's choir,
   And foxes stunk and litter'd in St Paul's."

---

* Lord Bute. The other names are probably those of Murray, Rigby, and Bedford.

THE END.